Target

WITHDRAWN

Target

SIMON KERNICK

BANTAM PRESS

LONDON • TORONTO • SYDNEY • AUCKLAND • JOHANNESBURG

TRANSWORLD PUBLISHERS
61–63 Uxbridge Road, London W5 5SA
A Random House Group Company
www.rbooks.co.uk

First published in Great Britain
in 2009 by Bantam Press
an imprint of Transworld Publishers

Copyright © Simon Kernick 2009

Simon Kernick has asserted his right under the Copyright, Designs
and Patents Act 1988 to be identified as the author of this work.

This book is a work of fiction and, except in the case of historical fact, any resemblance to
actual persons, living or dead, is purely coincidental.

A CIP catalogue record for this book
is available from the British Library.

ISBN 9780593060032 (cased)
9780593060049 (tbp)

Addresses for Random House Group Ltd companies outside the UK
can be found at: www.randomhouse.co.uk
The Random House Group Ltd Reg. No. 954009

The Random House Group Limited supports The Forest Stewardship
Council (FSC), the leading international forest-certification organization. All our
titles that are printed on Greenpeace-approved FSC-certified paper carry the FSC logo.
Our paper procurement policy can be found at
www.rbooks.co.uk/environment

Typeset in 11/16pt Times New Roman by
Falcon Oast Graphic Art Ltd.
Printed and bound in Great Britain by
CPI Mackays, Chatham, ME5 8TD

2 4 6 8 10 9 7 5 3 1

Mixed Sources
Product group from well-managed
forests and other controlled sources
www.fsc.org   Cert no. TT-COC-2139
© 1996 Forest Stewardship Council
FSC

For Mr Pink and Ali Karim

Prologue

Two weeks ago

Sir Henry Portman was a man who liked his vices. He drank like a professional, gambled like an amateur, and still managed a pack of cigarettes a day, the odd Cuban cigar and a good four thousand calories of the kind of rich, fatty food that makes dieticians tear their hair out, and everyone else salivate.

But his favourite vice – the one he could least do without and the one, if truth be told, that kept him at a half-reasonable thirteen and a half stone rather than the twenty he'd probably otherwise have been – was extra-marital sex. In twenty-eight years of marriage, Sir Henry had enjoyed a total of 347 sexual partners (348 if you included his wife), a figure he kept constantly updated in a small black leather notebook he'd bought for that express purpose. Even now, in his mid fifties, his appetites were showing no signs of diminishing.

What had diminished, however, were his looks, so more and more these days he had to rely on the services of prostitutes. This didn't bother him unduly. He found that paying for sex had many advantages. There were none of the complications associated with having secret lovers, nor the potential embarrassments caused by asking them to do things that might be considered unusual. Because where sex was concerned, Sir Henry's tastes were somewhat eclectic, which was why he was currently tied to a bed wearing a shiny PVC blindfold and not much else in an upscale Islington brothel, waiting for a svelte nineteen-year-old beauty called Nadia to come in and tease and torment him to the heights of sexual ecstasy.

He heard the door opening and Nadia making her soft, slow entrance. As she approached the bed, Sir Henry licked his lips and swallowed, barely able to stand the incredible sense of anticipation he always experienced in these first moments.

'You've been a bad boy,' she whispered in her heavily accented English, her fingers stroking his thigh, the touch so light and soft it sent him into paroxysms of ecstasy.

'I know,' he hissed back. 'God, I know . . .'

Nadia's fingers moved away and she made a strange mewing sound, which stopped almost as quickly as it began.

The room fell silent. Sir Henry moved about on the bed, waiting for her to touch him again.

Something warm and wet dripped heavily on to his chest and belly, moving down towards his groin. What was she pouring on him? It wasn't candle wax. That was hotter.

The dripping stopped, and he heard movement by the bed. He felt the first stirrings of concern, but it was still mixed with a sense of excitement. Was Nadia suddenly becoming more adventurous? Normally she followed a set routine.

The silence continued. Still she didn't touch him.

'Nadia? Are you there?'

Nothing.

'Nadia?' Louder now.

The PVC blindfold was ripped off him in one movement and he was left blinking hard against the brightness in the room.

Nadia stared down at him blankly. She was pale and naked and beautiful, and a narrow stiletto blade jutted out of her chest. Sir Henry saw the thin curtain of blood running down her body. There was blood on him, too. Lots of it, splattered in an angry pattern.

For several seconds he was struck dumb, registering but not understanding the terrible sight in front of him. Nadia wasn't moving. She was just standing there, her pale eyes wide open yet utterly sightless. Then, as he watched, she gradually slid down the side of the bed and disappeared from view.

A man in a snarling wolf mask that covered his whole head stood in her place. In one gloved hand he held the bloodstained knife that had just been used on Nadia. It glinted wickedly in the light from the overhead lamp. Behind the mask, the man's eyes were wide and staring.

Sir Henry opened his mouth to cry out, terror surging through him, but a gloved palm was slammed hard across it.

Then, very slowly, the bloody knife moved towards his face until the tip of the blade took up his whole field of vision.

'Do you want me to cut your eye out?' asked the man in the mask. His voice was harsh and guttural. Sir Henry recognized the accent as Northern Irish.

Sir Henry made desperate 'no' noises under the glove. He shut his eyes as the blade advanced, felt it touch the skin of his eyelid.

'I'm going to remove my hand now,' continued the man, his tone even, almost conversational. 'If you scream, I'll blind you. Do you understand?'

Sir Henry's muffled yeses seemed to convince him and he took away both the hand and the blade in one movement.

'Please don't kill me,' Sir Henry begged, hugely aware of his utter helplessness. God, he should have known that this would happen.

These people were animals . . . and somehow he'd allowed himself to get involved with them. It was like some kind of terrible nightmare.

'We hear you're getting cold feet, Sir Henry,' continued the man in the wolf mask, running the blade gently down his belly, scraping up Nadia's blood.

'No, no, I'm not. I swear.'

'Don't lie. If you lie, you lose an eye. Do you understand that?'

'Yes, yes, I understand. I do.'

'Good. I executed the girl so you'd know to take what I say seriously.'

'There was no need to do that. I would have taken you seriously.'

Sir Henry had a feeling that the man was smiling behind the mask.

'No,' he said, 'I don't think you would have done. But you do now, don't you? If I can kill a young woman, imagine what I could do to you. Or your wife. Or your daughter. What's her name? Jane, isn't it?' He twirled the tip of the blade through the mass of Sir Henry's pubic hair. 'She's a pretty thing. I saw her coming out of your house the other day. Yes, very pretty.'

At the mention of his daughter, Sir Henry felt his guts clench savagely. At that moment, incredibly, he didn't even think about the knife. 'Please. Not Jane. Hurt me instead if you have to, but leave her alone. I'm begging you.'

'There's really no point in begging, Sir Henry. If I have to, I'll slaughter your family one by one and feed you the pieces.'

'What do you want?'

'I want you to answer all of my questions truthfully. One mistake' – he paused, the blade touching the base of Sir Henry's penis – 'and I start cutting.'

'I'll tell the truth, I swear it!' And he meant it too. Once again, he was gambling. Making the snap judgement that he was better off to them alive not dead, and guessing that they knew everything anyway.

'Good. Now, you've been getting cold feet, haven't you?'

Sir Henry nodded vigorously. 'Yes, yes, I have, but I haven't spoken to anyone, I promise. I went to Kensington police station and I went inside but I came back out again five minutes later because I knew that it was too risky to say anything. It's just that I'm terrified things are going to go wrong, and I'm going to get caught—'

'There's no need to be,' said the man in the mask, his tone surprisingly sympathetic. 'I'm looking after the operation, and it won't go wrong on my watch. But you were right not to say anything. It would have cost you your family.' He removed the knife from Sir Henry's crotch and bent down, lifting up Nadia's corpse by its long auburn hair. 'And you can see that now, can't you? What happens if you attempt to fuck us? We can get you absolutely anywhere.'

'Please,' whispered Sir Henry, 'put her down. I can't bear to look at her.'

The man in the mask let the body go and it dropped to the floor with a dull thud.

Sir Henry swallowed. He felt nauseous. He'd had no great feelings for Nadia, but the thought that it could just as easily be his beautiful daughter lying there made him want to throw up the three-course meal he'd enjoyed only a few hours earlier. 'What are you going to do with her?' he asked.

'Don't worry about it. We know the owners of this establishment. She'll be made to disappear. If I were you, I'd worry about yourself.'

'I will.'

'I know you will. The lives of your family depend on it.'

With a sudden movement, the man's knife hand darted out and

the next second Sir Henry felt a sharp pain at the base of his penis, and the warm sensation of blood trickling down on to his balls. He started to cry out, afraid of what had been done to him, but the man put a gloved finger to his snarling wolf lips, stopping him instantly. He knew better than even to think about defying his tormentor.

'It's just a little taster of what might happen, Sir Henry,' he said casually. 'No permanent damage.'

He leaned over and cut the bond securing Sir Henry's right wrist to the bed, then turned and walked out of the room, leaving him there, naked, bleeding and alone, wondering whether his conscience would ever forgive him for what he was about to do.

Sunday

One

Sometimes a person's fate rests on a single, seemingly innocuous decision. For me it was the moment I agreed to go out for a quick beer that Sunday afternoon with my neighbour from down the road, a balding hipster called Ramon who taught salsa at the local community centre and who, against all the evidence, considered himself a magnet for female attention. I'd been cooped up working at home for most of the weekend, and although I didn't tend to like being seen in public with Ramon, who always wore a red or black bandanna, the idea of a relaxing afternoon drink round the corner from where we both lived in the bland but pleasant north London suburb of Colindale seemed like a decent enough idea.

But we all know what it's like. Where alcohol's concerned, things rarely turn out like you expect them to, and our relaxing drink quickly turned into four or five, followed by a cheap all-you-can-eat Chinese meal on the high street, and finally a trip into the West End, which was where I found myself at half past ten that night, wandering round a sweaty, heaving bar just off Long Acre, having lost a salsa-ing Ramon somewhere among the crowds a good twenty minutes before.

By this point, I'd had enough. At one time I'd liked this place. Back in the old days, when I was working in the City, I'd come here most weeks, and had even known most of the bar staff by name. But plenty of water had passed under the bridge since then, and now, at thirty-four, I felt old and out of place, the booze making me maudlin as it offered up memories of times when life was fun and easy and I was the same age as everyone else there. It was definitely time to go, but as I put down the half-full bottle of Becks I'd been nursing for the best part of an hour and headed for the exit, I spotted her coming the other way.

I hadn't seen Jenny in close to a year but the moment she caught my eye she grinned and came over, giving me a hug and landing a sloppy kiss on each cheek. 'Rob Fallon, long time no see,' she shouted above the noise, taking a step back and looking me up and down. 'You look good.'

I doubted if that was the case, not in my current state, but I wasn't going to argue. 'So do you,' I answered in that inane way people tend to do, except in this case I was telling the truth.

Jenny always looked good. She was tall and pretty with long blonde hair that was at least four-fifths natural, and the kind of golden skin the experts like to tell you is unhealthy for Caucasians, but which in her case looked anything but. I think she was twenty-seven or twenty-eight, but she could easily have passed for five years younger. It was her eyes that were her standout feature, though. They were very big and very brown, and when she fixed you with them it took a supreme effort to look away. Not that many men would want to.

If you're concluding from this that I was in love with this girl, then you'd be wrong. There was definitely an attraction there – from my point of view anyway – and we'd always got on extremely well. But there were two things that had always held me back. One: I was still in love with someone else, although after two years I knew my ex-wife Yvonne was never going to take me back. And two: I would never have met Jenny if it hadn't been for the fact that she'd been my best mate Dom's girlfriend. Because of this we'd only ever spent time together in situations where Dom was present, and since they were no longer an item, we'd lost touch. Until now.

It could have been a brief throwaway conversation, the kind people who don't really know each other have all the time, but I'd been feeling pretty lonely lately, and maybe it was the booze too, because the attraction that had probably always been there began to kick in again, and pretty hard too. So, as we shouted in each other's ears over the noise and I caught the soft scent of her perfume, I took the plunge and asked her if she fancied going somewhere else.

To be honest, I wouldn't normally have been so forward, but again, I think it was the booze. I wasn't expecting a yes either. The chances were she was here with friends who were more reliable than Ramon, and she wasn't going to leave them to go off with her ex-boyfriend's mate.

But she said she would.

And in that one moment, my fate was sealed.

We went round the corner to a quieter, more traditional pub where there were plenty of spare tables. I bought the drinks – sparkling water for me, a dry white wine spritzer for her – and we caught up on things.

Jenny worked for a web-based travel agency and she'd just come back from a nine-day trip to Mauritius and the Seychelles checking out hotels, which she told me, rather unconvincingly, was harder work than it sounded. That was the cue for us to talk about travelling and share the usual backpacker stories.

The thing I found about talking to Jenny was that the conversation always flowed naturally. I never felt like I had to put on a front, or be someone I wasn't. Maybe that was because as Dom's girlfriend she'd always been untouchable so there'd never been any need. But tonight we both avoided any mention of Dom, and when we finished our drinks Jenny bought another round, insisting I have something alcoholic so she didn't have the guilt of drinking alone. I plumped for a vodka Red Bull, hoping it would perk me up.

'So,' she said, returning to the table with the drinks, 'did you ever finish that book you were writing?'

A little bit of background here. In the days when Jenny was seeing Dom, I was working on a book. In fact, I'd been working on it for a grand total of three years, ever since I'd cashed in my share options and left the investment bank where I was employed to begin a new life in rural France with Yvonne and our then one-year-old daughter Chloe. It had always been my ambition to be an author, and I'd done enough writing in my spare time to think it was worth trying to make a go of it. It was going to be my retirement plan. Pen a succession of popular and critically acclaimed novels while growing organic fruit and vegetables on our idyllic patch of Burgundy countryside.

Unfortunately, it hadn't worked out quite like that. The book in question – *Conspiracy: A Thriller*, a high-octane page-turner set in the murky world of high finance (that was my tag line) – turned out to be one hell of a lot harder to write than I'd thought. I just couldn't get the plot right, and when I did, the end result was seven hundred pages long and possibly the most unthrilling thriller I've ever had to read in my life. During all this I'd become almost impossible to live with, and the idyllic Burgundy countryside, all those hundreds of square miles of it, had begun to drive me mad. Worse still, Yvonne loved it.

You can probably guess the rest. We argued like crazy as my dreams, held for so long during those long-drawn-out days in the office, steadily fell apart. I was selfish. I kept threatening to up sticks and head home. One day, Yvonne decided she'd had enough and told me I was welcome to go. We agreed to have a three-month trial separation. I returned to England, staying in Dom's spare room, hoping that the change of scenery would provide the inspiration I needed for *Conspiracy*. But it didn't. Instead, just as I was about to ask to move back in with Yvonne, having finally realized that living without her and Chloe would only make me unhappy, she announced that she'd met someone else. His name was Nigel, and he was another ex-pat. She and Chloe are still living with him, except now they've moved south, to Montpellier.

And my high-octane page-turner set in the murky world of high finance?

'No,' I told Jenny, a rueful smile on my face. 'I never did finish it.'

'That's a pity,' she said, looking disappointed. 'After all the work you put into it.'

'Sometimes you've just got to know when to quit.' I took a decent gulp of the vodka Red Bull. 'But,' I added, keen to keep her interest, 'I'm not the kind to give up. I'm writing another one now, and guess what?'

Her face brightened. 'What?'

'I've got an agent, a guy who thinks he can sell it. I sent him the first ten chapters and he took me on on the basis of them.'

'Can you tell me what it's about?' she asked, leaning forward in her seat, sounding genuinely interested.

So I told her all about Maxwell.

Maxwell was something of a legend in north London underworld circles, a former loanshark and enforcer now in his fifties who was reputed to be as strong as an ox and possessed of the highly useful loansharking talent of being able to punch open doors. In other words, not the kind of man you wanted to cross. I'd met him a few months back at a party in Hoxton hosted by one of Ramon's salsa students. Maxwell was standing around dealing coke and generally looking menacing, and somehow I'd ended up talking to him.

When I told him I was a writer (which strictly speaking was true, even though I'd never been paid a penny for it), Maxwell had suddenly become very interested. 'I've got plenty of stories to tell,' he growled, following this revelation with the immortal line 'you could turn my life into a book', which, even as a rank amateur in the literary world, I must have heard a hundred times before, usually from people whose lives would have made a bloody awful book. But in Maxwell's case, I'd seen a degree of potential.

By this time, *Conspiracy* was already pretty much down the pan, so I'd gone to the cottage in Berkshire where Maxwell had retired on his ill-gotten gains to interview him, not entirely sure what to expect. What I got was a friendly charismatic guy who was a hugely gregarious storyteller with a never-ending stream of original anecdotes, who'd clearly lived the kind of life that would make a perfect book. I envisaged it as a kind of British riposte to *Goodfellas*: a thug's journey through Britain's seedy underbelly from childhood to middle age, encompassing the crimes he'd committed along the way, and adding in a few he hadn't, including a couple of murders, just for good measure.

Maxwell hadn't taken much persuading. Since he loved talking about his exploits it stood to reason that he'd jump at the chance to make some money from them. And so, a couple of months earlier, we'd finally got down to work, and I'd produced the first ten chapters, focusing on his early life, which was the part that got me my agent. Since then I'd been ploughing slowly through the rest of it, trying to ignore the fact that what little money I had left in the world was rapidly running out. I'd even contemplated tapping Maxwell for a loan, but had quickly thought better of it. My front door was flimsy and I didn't think he'd grant me any special favours if I didn't pay him back.

When I'd finished talking, having thrown in a couple of choice Maxwell anecdotes, Jenny shook her head in amazement. 'God,' she said, draining the last of her second spritzer, 'it's incredible to think people like that exist.'

'I can promise you they do.'

'He sounds awful,' she said with a mock shudder, but I could tell from the look in her eyes that a part of her had found hearing about him exciting.

'He's like a lot of criminals,' I answered, trying to sound authoritative. 'They can be great fun right up until the minute you piss them off. Then they're not very nice people at all.'

She looked at me and smiled, and I was sure there was something suggestive in her expression. The pub was shutting and, apart from the barman who was collecting up the glasses, we were the only ones left.

I suddenly realized that I didn't want this evening to end. I hadn't been out on my own with a woman for months, and I was enjoying her company. 'Do you fancy going on somewhere?' I asked, trying to sound as casual as possible. 'I know a couple of wine bars round here where we can get a late drink.'

'I would do, but I've got work in the morning and I could do without the sore head.'

Jenny got to her feet, and I followed suit. I was disappointed, but I didn't show it. It was probably for the best: she was Dom's ex-girlfriend and it didn't feel right being too interested in her.

But as we stepped out of the pub and into the chilly night air, she surprised me by asking if I fancied popping round to hers for a nightcap. 'I'm only a five-minute taxi ride from here.'

It was difficult to tell from her tone and demeanour whether she meant the invitation as an extension to our chat or something more, but either way I forgot my earlier inhibitions, hesitating for all of a second before answering, 'Sure, that'd be great.' After all, it could do no harm. Just a drink. See what happens.

How wrong I was.

Two

Jenny lived in a flashy-looking new-build apartment block in one of the nicer parts of north Islington which, with its bright lights and reliance on tinted glass, looked more like the head office of some trendy management consultants than the kind of place anyone in their right mind would want to live. It also looked extremely pricey, and I remember thinking that I ought to become a web-based travel agent if it paid that much, but knowing at the same time that it didn't.

As the taxi pulled up outside, she reached into her handbag to pay the driver but, chivalrous to the last, I gave him my last ten-pound note, which, with London cab prices being what they are, only just managed to cover it.

'There's something I ought to tell you,' she said when we were standing on the pavement.

The last time I'd heard that line it was followed by my ex-wife dropping the bombshell that she'd fallen in love with a man called Nigel. Trying not to let that bother me, I adopted the most neutral expression I could manage and asked Jenny what it was.

She put a hand on my arm, and fixed me with those big brown

eyes. I noticed she was a little unsteady on her feet. 'You know me and Dom broke up a while back?'

'Uh-huh,' I said, conscious that I was wobbling too.

'He's been trying to get back with me recently. Phoning up. Calling round. Things like that.'

I had a sinking feeling. I'd thought the two of them were history. Dom hadn't been mentioned all evening, and now, hearing his name spoken out loud, I experienced a sudden rush of guilt.

'I know you and he are very good friends,' she continued, 'so I thought it was fair to tell you that. He's really interested in us starting up again. But I'm not.' She moved closer so our faces were only a few inches apart. 'That's why you're here.'

I wasn't sure what to say, so I plumped for saying nothing. Nor did I resist as she took me by the hand and led me up to the front entrance of the building, although I now knew this was going to be more than just an extension to our chat.

Inside, the foyer was empty, and I noticed Jenny frown as she swiped a card through the space-age-looking reader, releasing the lock on the double doors. 'There should be a doorman on duty,' she said. 'That's what we pay our maintenance for.'

I wasn't quite sure what you needed a doorman for if you had to use a key to get in the building, but I was pleased he wasn't there. I didn't want any witnesses to what I knew was going to be the betrayal of my oldest friend, especially if – God forbid – Dom and Jenny ever did get back together. Although to be fair, that wasn't sounding too likely.

As we got inside and she pressed for the lifts, I heard rapid footsteps coming from the hallway behind the front desk. It sounded like the doorman was returning, so as the lift doors opened I hurried inside and pressed myself against the wall, still worried about being seen.

Jenny followed me in, standing in the middle, and as the doors began to shut she called out, 'Hello, John, I thought you'd gone on strike.'

'Toilet break,' I heard the doorman call back, and then the doors closed, and she pressed for Floor 9.

We looked at each other for a long second and I knew immediately what was going to happen. She leaned forward. So did I.

The first kiss was hesitant, just like it always seems to be in the movies, and I felt my last twinge of guilt evaporating.

The second kiss was harder, longer, and I hardly noticed the lift doors opening again. We paused for a couple of seconds, then she took me by the hand and led me down a short corridor to her front door, kissing me once again before we manoeuvred our way inside, still attached to each other at the mouth.

Jenny's place was nice, as befitted a swanky building like this, opening directly into a spacious, neatly furnished lounge with floor-to-ceiling windows offering views across the park.

She let go of me for a moment and took a step backwards. 'I'm not always this forward, you know.'

'I know,' I said. Which I didn't, of course, but I thought this was probably what she wanted to hear.

'It's just I've always had a bit of a soft spot for you.'

'I guess I've had one for you as well,' I admitted.

'Do you want a drink of something?'

I'll never forget my next words, mainly because they were so hackneyed, and did whatever reputation I had as a romantic or a wordsmith no good at all. 'No,' I said, 'I just want you.'

Something about it must have worked, though, because the next second we were kissing again.

We remained like this for several minutes, our hands running up and down each other's bodies, exploring hungrily, before she whispered huskily that it was time to go to bed.

I wasn't arguing, and we walked sideways, crab-like, still locked together, through to a spacious bedroom with mirrors on the walls and a king-sized bed with black satin sheets which, I have to say, looked to be designed for just this kind of encounter.

She pulled my jacket off and flung it into the corner, then tugged at my belt.

Unfortunately, this was also the moment when, with impeccable timing, I experienced every man's nightmare in this situation: the nagging urge to pee. I really didn't want to say anything for fear of breaking the mood, but I also knew that, my bladder being what it was, I was going to have to, otherwise the urge would get steadily stronger, which would risk ruining everything.

I waited another thirty seconds, hoping it would go away. It didn't.

'I've just got to go to the bathroom,' I mumbled into her lips.

'It's over there,' she mumbled back, pointing at a door to my right. 'Don't be long.'

'I won't,' I said, breaking away.

The bathroom was vaguely disappointing after the opulence of the rest of the apartment. It might have been en suite but it was windowless and way too small, as if the designers had made a mistake with their measurements and run out of room, and it was quite a squeeze to stand in front of the toilet without tumbling backwards into the bathtub.

There are few things more likely to put off a first-time lover than hearing her partner peeing loudly, so I turned the sink's cold tap fully on to mask the noise. Then, once I'd finished and flushed, I washed my hands and inspected myself in the mirror, thinking that I wasn't looking too bad considering I'd been out drinking for the best part of the last eight hours. I even pulled a sexy pout, looking at myself sideways on.

Which was the moment when I heard Jenny gasp once, very loudly, and cry out.

I froze.

The cry was stifled suddenly. Someone had a hand over her mouth. And then I heard movement outside the door and the unmistakable sound of two men whispering urgently to each other.

'Hold her still,' I heard one of them hiss, his accent harsh and distinctly Northern Irish. 'I need to get the needle in.'

Jenny's muffled cries suddenly became more desperate.

'Shut the fuck up and stop wriggling!' I heard the other one snap in a rough London accent, followed by the sound of a hard slap.

I had no idea what was going on in there but I knew I had to intervene because Jenny was being attacked. But I was absolutely rooted to the spot. I'm no hard man like Maxwell. I'm just an ordinary mortal coward who reads the stories in the papers every day about the senseless killings of those individuals brave enough to help victims of crime. I'd always said that I would never ignore someone's cry for help because I'd never be able to live with myself if I did. But now that it was happening, only feet away, I found that I couldn't move as the fear and adrenalin coursed and swirled through my body.

Jenny's cries stopped. Just like that.

Do something! my inner voice roared at me. But what the hell could I do?

'Thank Christ for that,' said the Londoner with a loud sigh, his tone suddenly more relaxed. 'She's a looker though, ain't she?'

'Don't even think about it,' answered the Irishman dismissively, and this time his voice came from right outside the bathroom door. 'We haven't got time. Get her off the bed. I need a leak.'

As he spoke, the door handle began to turn.

Jesus Christ! The bastard was going to come in here, and I'd locked the door! As soon as he realized that it was locked, he'd know there was someone in the apartment, and that would be it. I was trapped. One minute preparing to make love to an attractive woman, the next praying for my life.

The handle kept turning. The guy kept talking. My heart kept hammering.

Do something!

I leaned over and flicked back the bolt, hoping his voice would muffle the sound. Then, moving quickly and trying to make as little noise as possible, I stepped into the bathtub and pulled the shower curtain across so that I was hidden.

Just in time. In the next second, the door opened and he came in, shutting it roughly behind him.

I froze again, teeth clenched, not even daring to breathe as he stood in front of the toilet and unzipped, grunting loudly, only inches away. He was medium height, with the kind of contoured leanness that suggested he worked out a lot more than me, and if I'd put out my hand, I could have tapped him on the shoulder through the curtain – he was that close.

He seemed to take for ever, and every single second I wondered if some sixth sense would alert him to my presence. But at last he finished, and as he flushed and walked back out, not bothering to wash his hands, I finally breathed again.

This time he left the door open and, though I knew that in the interests of self-preservation, if not honour, I should stay exactly where I was until they left, then call the police, I couldn't resist peeking round the edge of the curtain.

From the tight angle I had, I could see the bottom quarter of the bed and the area immediately in front of it, which was taken up with what looked like a large cleaning trolley. I could also see Jenny's bare legs from the knees downwards, now missing the jeans she'd been wearing when I'd left her just a few minutes earlier. The intruders were nowhere to be seen. I could only assume they were going to rape her, the bastards, although I knew they wouldn't have had time to undress her. She'd clearly been undressing for me and I was filled with anger at the thought of these bastards violating her.

I moved away from the curtain's edge, looking round for something to use as a weapon. Amid all the clutter round the bath there was an antique brass soap dish shaped like a giant goldfish, and I picked it up, feeling a satisfying heaviness. It wasn't a lot but it would have to do.

Gripping it in my right hand, I slowly peeked out again. Now I saw one of the intruders properly for the first time. It wasn't the one who'd taken a leak. This guy was big and well built, with a shaven head and the kind of face that didn't waste a lot of time on pity. He was dressed in a blue boiler suit and was carrying a prone, unconscious Jenny over to the cleaning trolley. She was in her bra and underwear, and she'd been gagged with a handkerchief and had her hands tied behind her back. There was something so vulnerable about her in that position that it made me shake with rage.

Yet still I didn't move. Even when he stopped and dumped her into the trolley like a sack of rubbish. Because I was so damn terrified. Because, in the end, I knew that I wouldn't have a chance fighting this man, let alone two of them, and I kept telling myself that there was no point intervening now because it wouldn't actually benefit Jenny. That it would be far better simply to wait until they went and phone the police.

I couldn't see the other one, but then I heard him speak from somewhere behind the door, his words, delivered in that hard Northern Irish accent, cutting through the room like a knife. 'Whose is this, then?'

And then, as he came into view with his back to me, my heart sank.

Because the bastard was holding my jacket, and in the last second before I slid back behind the curtain, I saw both men turn to look in my direction.

Three

Every muscle in my body tensed, and I held on to the soap dish like grim death. I was cornered, and there was absolutely no way out. My jacket's a faded brown leather, distinctly male, and a good three sizes too big for Jenny who was no more than five five and at least eight inches shorter than me. So these guys would know a man was here somewhere, and there weren't exactly a lot of places he'd have to hide in.

Or would they? There was a chance they'd assume that someone had left it here. Maybe I was going to be OK.

But if so, why did the guy pick it up?

The terror I was feeling was worse than anything I'd ever experienced. My legs felt weak and I thought I might collapse at any moment.

What should I do? Run? Stay put? Run? Stay put? I was completely and utterly torn.

The two men were silent for what felt like a long, long time. Then I heard quiet footfalls, first on the bedroom carpet, then on the tiled bathroom floor, and I saw a silhouette appear.

The shower curtain shot back and I was face to face with a man in his forties whose malicious smile was like a bloodless slash across a pale, wraith-like face stretched so tight by plastic surgery that his big saucer-shaped eyes looked like they'd long ago lost the ability to close. Thinning, wiry hair sprang from his scalp like jet-black brush wires.

This was the Irishman, and he was still holding my jacket in one gloved hand, while in the other was a six-inch gleaming stiletto.

I wanted to piss myself; to curl up and die; to let my legs simply collapse under me.

But I did none of these things. Instead, as his eyes widened with an unpleasant glee and the slash-like smile twisted up at the edges, I smashed the soap dish right into it with every ounce of strength I had, knocking him backwards into the sink.

He grunted in pain and dropped the knife as a deep gash opened up on his cheek.

There was very little room for me to get past him but I didn't think about that. I was out of that bathtub like a greyhound out of a trap, and charging into the bedroom.

The big guy with the shaven head was standing on the other side of the trolley, in the same position he was in earlier, except now he was pulling a large knife from the pocket of his boiler suit and glaring at me with cold, confident eyes.

Yelling as loudly as I could in a desperate effort to panic him, I lobbed the soap dish at his face without even breaking stride. He threw up a hand to ward off the impact but it hit him on the elbow and he yelped in pain as it bounced off. Half a second later I charged into the trolley and slammed it into his lower abdomen, sending him off balance, though not quite knocking him down.

It was enough to buy me a second and a half, though, and that was all I needed as I ran at the half-open bedroom door, keeping my head down and dodging the knife as he lashed out wildly, charging through it and into the lounge, feeling a wild surge of hope. I was going to make it. I was going to get out of there.

'Leave him, he's mine!' came a barked command behind me. It was the Irishman with the saucer eyes, and there was an icy calm in his voice that made my heart lurch.

I jumped the coffee table, clipped it, and almost fell into the front door, grabbing at the handle and yanking it as hard as I could, only noticing at the last second that the chain was on. Incredibly, I didn't panic, just flicked the chain across in one movement, threw the door open and ran out into the corridor.

I felt something swish through the air behind me. The knife. It touched the material of my shirt but didn't break it. He was right behind me, just feet away. I could hear him breathing.

I started running, realizing as soon as I did so that I was going the wrong way from the lifts, and that the corridor ahead seemed to be a dead end. I yelled again, hoping someone would hear me, thinking that if I made enough noise my pursuer would panic and turn back; but there was nothing, just an intensely loud silence. It was like I was suddenly in the middle of a nightmare.

Behind me he kept coming, his breath almost on my neck, and it was his patient, predatory silence that terrified me the most.

There was a door at the end with a staircase sign above it, and I felt another surge of hope and accelerated, shouting as loudly as I could into the silence. I hit the door head on in a way that would have made Maxwell proud. Because it was a swing door, it flew open and I stumbled, almost losing my footing before swinging hard right and charging down the staircase, taking the steps three at a time, knowing that if I fell I was dead, no question.

Every part of me seemed to ache from the exertion of running, and in my semi-inebriated state I wasn't sure how long I could keep it up for. I could still hear him, ever so close, and I had a desperate urge to look round, but knew it might cost me a precious quarter second which might end up being the difference between life and death. Instead, I started taking the steps four at a time, praying that the doorman was at his desk so at least he might be able to help. Praying that I made it that far.

The knife suddenly appeared right in front of my face as he jumped on my back and I was flung forward, tumbling down the steps, doing a somersault, smacking my head painfully on the hard linoleum steps. I knew that any moment I was going to be stabbed. But then I heard the knife clatter against the wall as he was thrown clear.

He landed hard against the wall at the bottom of the steps but somehow he still had the weapon in his hands, and now he was in front of me and blocking my way while I was lying on my stomach on the steps, only five feet from the tip of his blade. His face was bleeding where I'd cut him with the soap dish and his wiry hair was slightly askew. But he still wore the cruel, predatory smile as if it had been etched permanently on the stretched skin, and the expression in his eyes was one of chilling confidence, as if he knew that whatever I did it would make no difference because, in the end, the outcome was inevitable.

But I wasn't finished yet. I used my hands to push me upright as if I was doing some kind of springing press-up. Somehow I managed the process slightly quicker than him, before vaulting over the banister on to the next set of steps, stumbling down them, ignoring the savage pounding in my head.

Once again he was right there with me, and I knew he wasn't going to give up, so, summoning up every last ounce of whatever feeble reserves of energy I had left, I jumped the whole of the next staircase in one, landed hard on my feet, swung round using the banister as support, and did the same thing on the next one, and the next, feeling a kind of delirious adrenalin-fuelled excitement at the prospect of escape.

And at that exact same moment the stairs stopped and I realized

I'd missed the ground floor, and possible safety. Instead, I was in the basement.

Panting, I looked back up just as my pursuer arrived at the top of the last flight of steps. 'Oops,' he said playfully, waving the knife in front of him like a wagging finger. 'Bad move.'

A small part of me felt like giving up there and then. Admitting the fact that I wasn't going to make it out of there and throwing myself at his mercy. Except that I knew there wouldn't be any.

And it was only a small part of me. Self-preservation won through, and as he jumped down the last of the steps I turned and ran for the fire door in the corner – the only way out. I had no idea whether or not it was open, or where it led to, just relied on my instinct to live to keep me going. Running right into it, I pulled down the metal handle, felt it give, and half fell, half scrambled through into a cold and cavernous underground car park.

He was still with me, almost as if he was glued to my slipstream, but this time I took the offensive and turned and slammed all my weight against the fire door, catching him by surprise and trapping his knife arm in it.

But before I could do any real damage, he pushed from the other side and, being one hell of a lot stronger than me and with momentum on his side, he sent it flying open, and me stumbling backwards.

I turned and ran through the dimly lit, silent car park, not know-ing where I could turn. Ahead of me was one of those big roller doors that I knew was either the entrance or the exit, but it was shut. My legs felt weak and I just couldn't seem to get the pace up to put any distance between us – the bastard was like some kind of automaton – and I'd barely gone twenty yards before he leapt on my back for a second time, sending me crashing into the concrete.

Sitting astride my back, he yanked my head up by the hair and I knew in an instant that he was going to cut my throat like some kind of animal. I bucked and thrashed as the knife suddenly appeared right in front of my face, and managed to pull free a hand. I immediately grabbed him by the wrist, forcing the blade away from me. I also jerked my head forward, trying to bite him, but his grip on my hair was too strong. This guy had the better of me, and both of us knew it. My arm was shaking with the effort of holding the blade away, and right then my life expectancy could be measured in seconds.

The sound of hydraulics interrupted our deadly duel, and a second later the roller door began to open. I think it surprised both of us because I felt his grip on my hair momentarily ease, which gave me the chance I needed. I sank my teeth into his knife wrist, biting down hard, knowing that while his arm remained in my mouth he couldn't use the blade on me.

He yelled and grabbed my hair again, tugging me backwards, but this time I wasn't letting go and I kept biting down, remembering something I'd once read about the strength of a human bite being something like two hundred pounds of pressure per square inch. I tasted blood and his yells became more urgent.

And all the time the roller door kept opening. It was now five feet above the tarmac and I could see the headlights of a big 4×4 just outside, waiting to come in. There was no way it wouldn't see us. I was going to make it. I felt a rush of hope, kept my teeth clamped on his wrist.

But then, in one swift, savage motion, he yanked his wrist free from my jaws. I clenched my teeth, waiting for the knife to slice across my flesh, but instead the weight lifted from my back, and a second later I heard his footfalls on the concrete floor as he ran back the way he'd come.

Exhausted and battered, I lay where I was, looking up at the 4×4 as it nudged its way inside before turning left and disappearing from view.

The driver hadn't seen me. Did this mean that my attacker was going to come back and finish the job? Was he just waiting?

I didn't hang around to find out. I ran wildly through the open roller door and up the ramp, hitting the fresh night air of the street and breathing it in as if my very life depended on it.

But my life depended on nothing any more. I'd saved it. Now I had to think about Jenny's.

I kept running up the dark, silent street until I came to an alley-way on my right. I turned down it and, exhausted, took refuge behind a pair of wheelie bins, leaning against a wall and slowly sliding down it until I was sitting down. I had to phone the police straight away and tell them what I'd just witnessed, so, after taking a few seconds to get at least some of my breath back, I reached into my pocket for my mobile.

And cursed. It was in my jacket, back at the apartment.

Something else too . . . my wallet. With all my ID in it.

Which meant they were going to know exactly who I was.

Four

A part of me wanted to keep running. To put as much distance between me and Jenny's place as possible, knowing how close I'd just come to death. Another part wanted to go back and keep watch on it, hoping that I might be in time to see the two men leave and pick up any vital clues I could then give to the police.

As it happened, I could do neither. I was too exhausted, and for a full minute I concentrated simply on getting my breath back.

As my panting began to ease, I was suddenly jolted back to reality by the sound of a car moving ever so slowly along the street. *Jesus, they're still here. Looking for me.*

I turned round, looking for a way out, saw only a high wall I was never going to be able to climb. I was stuck up a dead end. Knowing I was hopelessly exposed, I lifted up the lid of one of the wheelie bins and wriggled inside, landing loudly on a pile of stinking binbags.

The sound outside was muffled but I could hear the car stopping and knew that it was at the end of the alley.

A car door opened. Shut again.

I began to pray. I'd never really believed in God, but now that I'd arrived at this single most terrifying point in my life, I desperately begged forgiveness for any sin I may have committed and promised faithfully that if he got me out of this I would be a much better person. That I would give money to charity, help people . . . anything.

Stop. Don't breathe.

I could hear stealthy footfalls on the concrete. Approaching me. Something plastic in one of the binbags made a cracking sound beneath me and I clenched my teeth. The silence was killing me. Was one of them right outside now, knife in hand, getting ready to strike?

I strained, listening.

Silence.

The wait seemed to last for ever. Seconds ticking like dull, bored hours.

And then I heard the car door slam again and the car pull away.

I exhaled sharply, but didn't move. It could have been a trap.

Gradually I began to breathe more easily but I continued to lie exactly where I was, listening to the quiet of the night. At some point I think I even drifted off to sleep: I remember opening my eyes and getting a shock because I was still in darkness, and the smell was terrible, and my mouth felt like someone had been sand-papering it. At first I didn't know where I was. Then it all came back to me in a huge rush like some kind of horrible hallucination. Someone had tried to kill me, and they'd come very close to succeeding.

I took a couple of deep breaths to calm myself, then clambered to my feet and climbed out of the wheelie bin into far fresher air. The alley was quiet, even the night-time sounds of the city seemed strangely muted. I stretched, and looked at my watch. It had just turned twenty past one – over an hour since it had all happened. An image suddenly came to me of an unconscious Jenny being casually flung into the cleaning trolley, and I felt a renewed burst of anger and guilt. I could have done something to help her. And I hadn't.

Rubbing my eyes, trying hard to focus as I felt the first stirrings of an early hangover coming on, I walked back to Jenny's street and, recalling the route I'd taken earlier, turned left. I stopped in front of her apartment block. Nothing looked any different from when we'd arrived together, which now felt like a lifetime ago. Except that this time the doorman, a middle-aged man in a jacket and tie, was sitting at the front desk, reading a paper and eating a packet of crisps. It looked a perfectly natural scene, and, standing there, I had this bizarre feeling that maybe nothing had actually happened. Perhaps I'd dreamt it all.

But no. It had happened all right. I was sure of that.

I started towards the door, then stopped. There was no point trying to talk to the doorman. I looked and smelled pretty awful, having fallen asleep in a dustbin, and he hadn't even seen me earlier. He'd probably think I was mad. I had to speak to the police. But with no phone, no ATM card and only a handful of loose change in my jeans pocket, that was going to be a lot easier said than done.

I memorized the apartment address and walked out on to the main road, heading in a general southerly direction. There was still traffic around but most of the taxis ignored me, and those few that did stop pulled away again as soon as I told them I needed to get to a police station and almost certainly didn't have enough money for the fare. At last I found a driver charitable enough to give me directions to the nearest one, before advising me to take a bath as soon as possible and disappearing pretty sharpish.

It wasn't far, but I still managed to get lost several times, and it was past two o'clock when I finally walked through the door of Islington police station and straight into a scene of bedlam of the sort I suspected was played out in stations like this most nights and which reminded me graphically why I'd left England in the first place.

An overweight guy in a cut-off T-shirt and shorts that were falling down round his ample behind was being held face down in the middle of the linoleum floor by a total of four uniformed officers while he kicked and struggled and yelled that he wasn't drunk, even though the evidence strongly suggested otherwise. His girlfriend, meanwhile, was being pinned up against the wall with her arm behind her back by two female officers, both of whom were trying to dodge her spiked heels as she kicked out donkey-style and let out long, piercing, horror-film screams in a voice so high I actually had to put my hands over my ears. The place smelled of stale sweat and disinfectant. I felt a sudden, intense desire to be lying next to Yvonne in the still of the Burgundy farm-house we'd once shared, with only the sound of the owls for company.

I walked round the guy on the floor and stopped at the front desk where a world-weary custody sergeant with a long face and heavy black eye bags gave me a stare so intense in its disinterest that I could only assume he'd spent hours in front of the mirror per-fecting it. 'Put him in cell three,' he called out over my shoulder during a temporary pause in the screaming. He sighed, turning his attention back to me. 'Yes, sir?'

'I want to report a kidnapping,' I told him, putting on my most serious and earnest expression.

'Whose?'

'A friend of mine.'

'And when did this happen, sir?'

I looked at my watch. 'A couple of hours ago now.'

'And you've just seen fit to report it.'

'I had to walk here. I've lost all my money and my phone.'

'Have you been drinking, sir?' he asked, his tone annoyingly patronizing.

I knew there was no point in denying it. 'A little, yes. But not like him.' I pointed to the drunk whose shorts had fallen to his ankles now that he'd been lifted to his feet, revealing a sight none of us wanted to see.

'You know the kind of stories I hear from drunk people?' he continued wearily.

The girl screamed again. I waited for her to stop before continuing. 'Listen, officer, I'm being deadly serious. A girl I know was kidnapped tonight by two men and I need to talk to someone in CID urgently. I'm not making this up, I promise you.'

'Put her in cell five,' he called over my shoulder. 'So I don't have to listen to her.'

'Wanker!' she howled before being dragged across the floor behind her boyfriend and through a door to the cells.

'Please.' I looked at him imploringly. 'I'm not drunk, and I'm not mad. I know what I saw.'

He stared at me for a long second, then stood up, clearly deciding it was easier just to pass the buck. 'Take a seat and I'll see who's available.'

I sat down on a hard plastic chair in the corner and waited in the now empty foyer, staring at the posters warning against committing various heinous and not-so-heinous crimes that lined every spare inch of wall. I was absolutely shattered, but it struck me then that it might not even be safe for me to go home. If the kidnappers had searched my jacket, they'd have found my wallet. Then I realized with a sense of relief that there wasn't anything in there with my address on. I never took my driving licence out with me, so it would just be my credit and debit cards, plus my Blockbuster membership. So all they'd have was my name as it appeared on the cards: R. Fallon. Not exactly common, but in a city the size of London there were bound to be a few of us. So I was probably safe. But right then I could have done with something a little more concrete than 'probably'.

'Mr Fallon?'

I looked up and saw an attractive dark-haired woman in her early thirties emerging from the door opposite. She was dressed casually in jeans, a sweatshirt and trainers, but straight away I could tell she was a policewoman. There was a toughness and confidence about her that was immediately reassuring.

'I'm DS Tina Boyd,' she said as we shook hands, 'Islington CID. I understand you want to report a possible kidnapping?'

'Well, it's not a possible kidnapping, it's a real one. A friend of mine's been abducted.'

She nodded understandingly. 'Let's talk inside.'

She led me back through the door, up some stairs and into a small corner room, empty except for a desk with a chair on either side. There was an oldish-looking tape recorder on the desk and she switched it on, motioning for me to take a seat. 'I hope you don't mind. I want to record our interview.' She pulled a notebook out of her back pocket and sat back in the chair, regarding me with eyes that didn't look like they missed a lot. 'So, tell me what happened. From the beginning.'

I told her everything from the moment I'd met Jenny in the bar to when I'd turned up at the police station, keeping the details as brief and concise as possible. She listened patiently and didn't interrupt at any point, except to take descriptions of the two kidnappers. The thing about her was that she had the kind of face you automatically want to trust, and I felt myself warming to my theme as I continued, ignoring the little voice in my head that told me that what I was saying sounded outlandish.

'So she was alive when they took her?'

'I believe so, yes.'

'And did they make any attempt to molest her?'

'Not that I saw. They tied her up and they chucked her in the cleaning trolley.'

'And there's no reason you can think of why they would have taken her? Anything they might have said when you were listening in, for instance?'

I shook my head. 'From what I can gather they were trying to get her out of the apartment as fast as possible.'

'OK,' she said, writing something down in the notebook. 'And what's Jenny's last name?'

My mind suddenly went blank. I'd only ever known her as Jenny, although I had definitely been told her last name before. I racked my brains. 'It's . . . Brakestone, Brakeslip, something like that. No, Brakspear. It's definitely Brakspear.'

'You're sure about that?'

I nodded, way too vigorously, conscious of how unconvincing this must sound to a police officer. 'Yeah, I'm sure.'

'And you met her in a bar tonight? I'm assuming you'd had a few drinks?'

'I'd had a few, yes, but I knew what I was doing.'

'And you say Jenny's a friend of yours? But one whose last name you don't remember?'

'I don't know her that well, OK?'

DS Boyd shot me a hard look, the kind that told me in no uncertain terms to remember who I was dealing with. 'Listen, Mr Fallon, I'm just trying to establish the facts. So how exactly do you know her?'

'She went out with a friend of mine for a while.'

'And your friend's name is?'

'Dominic Moynihan.'

She wrote down Dom's contact details, then asked me when the two of them had split up.

'A while back. Maybe a year.' I thought about adding that he'd been in touch with her recently about getting back together but stopped myself, knowing that it wouldn't make me look good.

'What do you do for a living, Mr Fallon?'

'I'm a writer.' Usually I loved to say that to people, but now it sounded fatuous, and tinged with an air of unreliability.

'And what do you write about?'

'Does it matter? I'm trying to report a kidnap here. A young woman's been abducted and we need to find her.'

DS Boyd gave me another of those looks. 'I'm just trying to find out some background. It'll help us in our search.'

'I write crime,' I answered wearily. 'True crime.'

'And does it involve a kidnap?'

'No it doesn't. Jesus Christ! What the hell do I have to do to convince you I'm telling the truth? Do you think I want to be sitting here in the middle of the night talking to people who'd far rather I just went away?'

I fell silent, staring at her. Feeling at the end of my tether.

DS Boyd rested her hands carefully on the desk and looked at me closely. She had very dark eyes but it was difficult to tell whether they were brown or blue. 'OK, Mr Fallon,' she said, 'let me level with you. It may surprise you to learn that we get a lot of people coming in here reporting crimes that haven't actually happened, particularly when they've been drinking. We're also very busy dealing with the many crimes that do happen, so I have to ask a lot of questions before I'm in a position to judge what to do. Now I've heard what you've got to say and I'm satisfied that you genuinely believe an incident's happened—'

'It has. I promise you.'

'Then I'm going to give you the benefit of the doubt.' She stood up abruptly.

'Where are you going?'

'To the scene of the crime.' She gestured for me to follow her. 'I'm assuming you remember where that is?'

Five

'Kidnapping's nothing like as rare as people think,' said Tina Boyd as we approached the double doors at the front of Jenny's apartment block, 'but it's almost always drugs-related. People getting held to ransom by dealers over unpaid debts, that sort of thing. Could Jenny have been involved in the drugs trade, do you think?'

I couldn't honestly say for certain, but Dom had never mentioned anything about it, and he'd been anti-drugs since a friend of his had OD'd on a mix of coke and ecstasy back at uni, so I didn't think so. 'She's just a normal girl, you know,' I answered wearily.

'That's what I can't understand,' she mused, pressing her warrant card against the glass so that the doorman could see it. It was the same guy as earlier – grey-haired, middle-aged, ordinary looking. He buzzed us in.

I felt strangely sheepish as I followed Tina over to the front desk. She introduced us both and said that I'd been in the building about three hours earlier and had witnessed a possible abduction.

The doorman fixed me with a bemused expression. 'Really? Who was abducted then?'

'A Miss Jenny Brakspear. Apparently she lives on the ninth floor.'

He frowned. 'Blonde Jenny?'

'That's her,' I said.

He looked puzzled. 'That's weird. I haven't even seen her tonight. I thought she'd gone on holiday.'

'Hold on,' I said, unable to believe what I was hearing. 'You did see her. She called out to you. Your name's John, right?'

'Yeah, it's John, but I still didn't see her.'

'John what?' asked Tina.

'Gentleman,' he answered, 'and I'm telling you I didn't see her tonight.'

Tina wrote down his name in her notebook. Not that John Gentleman was one you were likely to forget. I couldn't believe the guy was lying.

'What's supposed to have happened then?' he asked Tina, giving me a distasteful look.

'We can't divulge any details at the moment, sir,' she answered smoothly. 'I'm assuming you've got CCTV cameras in this building?'

Gentleman nodded. 'We've got two. One's at the back, at the entrance to the underground car park, and there's another above the front doors where you've just come in. The one at the back's been on the blink for the last few days. We've got an engineer booked in for tomorrow. But the front one's working all right.'

'Mr Fallon says that he came in here at approximately midnight. Do you mind if we take a look at the footage for about fifteen minutes either side?'

'Sure,' said Gentleman, double-clicking on a mouse under the desk and turning round the PC monitor so we could see what was happening. 'We use DVR filming technology in the cameras so it records straight to the computer's hard drive. It means we can store

46

the film indefinitely.' He double-clicked again and a close-up aerial view of the area just outside the double doors appeared. He fast-forwarded through it quickly until the time in the bottom left-hand corner said 23.30. Next to it was Sunday's date. 'Right, I'm slowing down the search now so we're moving through the footage at sixteen times normal speed. Just let me know when you want me to stop.'

We watched in silence. For most of the time the area was empty. Occasionally, though, people appeared, and Gentleman slowed down the footage so we could get a look at them. He seemed very keen to be as cooperative as possible.

The time in the bottom corner of the screen hit 00.00 and Monday's date appeared. Gentleman kept searching. A handful of other people appeared, but not Jenny and me. It hit 00.15. Gentleman looked at Tina expectantly, and she looked at me.

'You said midnight didn't you, Mr Fallon?'

'It might have been a bit later,' I muttered, even though I knew it hadn't been.

I watched as the time moved inexorably towards 00.30.

'This is bullshit,' I said eventually. 'This film's been tampered with. I was here tonight. I can describe Jenny's apartment if you want me to.' I ran a hand across my forehead, feeling the exhaustion taking hold, trying to get a grip on what the hell was happening.

'Look, mate,' said Gentleman, 'I've been here all night and I haven't seen you, I haven't seen Jenny, and I haven't tampered with this. Nor's anyone else.'

I turned to Tina. Her expression was impassive. It was im-possible to tell what she was thinking.

'When was the last time you saw Miss Brakspear?' she asked the doorman.

'Yesterday, I think. She told me she was going on holiday.'

'Where?'

'Barbados. She's a bit of a world traveller, Jenny. I thought she said she was going tonight, but it might have been tomorrow.' He shrugged, his casual demeanour suggesting that my story was no longer even worth attempting to take seriously.

But credit to Tina Boyd, she didn't turn round and leave, even though I think I would have done. Instead she asked to see Jenny's apartment.

Gentleman didn't look too happy. He said he wasn't authorized, but Tina was insistent, so he located the keys and took us up in the lift.

As he unlocked Jenny's front door I scanned the woodwork for signs of forced entry but there wasn't a single scratch. I wondered how the hell the two kidnappers had got in. Jenny hadn't let them in. She'd been in the bedroom.

So, the chances were they'd also had a key.

I knew what the inside of the apartment was going to look like before Gentleman led us inside, and my suspicions were immediately confirmed. The front room was immaculate. The coffee table I'd clipped while running away was set at exactly the right angle between the two sofas.

Gentleman and Tina both looked at me expectantly. Unsure what to say, I walked past them and into the bedroom.

The bed was made. There was even a cuddly teddy bear with a sky-blue bow sitting perfectly symmetrically between the two sets of puffed-out pillows. The bathroom door was shut. There was no sign of the clothes Jenny had been wearing nor, more worryingly, my jacket. In fact, nothing was out of place. The room was so damn tidy it could have been part of a show home.

I flung open the bathroom door. It was perfect in there, too. No sign of any bloodstains from where I'd clouted the Irish guy with the soap dish. What I did notice, however, was that it smelled of disinfectant in a way it hadn't done earlier.

'Someone's cleaned this place up,' I said firmly, turning round.

'I can see that,' said Tina, coming into the room behind me. 'It looks great. But let me tell you something, Mr Fallon. In my experience, criminals never like to hang around after they've committed their crime. If these two men kidnapped Miss Brakspear, as you say, then it's extremely unlikely that they would have taken the time to make the bed and give the place a spring clean afterwards.'

'I know that,' I said, feeling like I was going mad. 'But that's exactly what happened. I promise you that. I'm not making it up.'

For several seconds, Tina didn't say anything. Gentleman appeared in the doorway of the bathroom. He was wearing an expression that was part way between irritation at being dragged all the way up here and the kind of patronizing pity usually reserved for the mentally ill.

What was worse was that in his shoes I'd have felt exactly the same.

Tina asked him if all the apartments on this floor were occupied.

'I'd have to check,' he answered, 'but I think Jenny might have been the only one living on this floor. What with the credit crunch, they've only sold about half the units in the building. Maybe not even that.'

Christ, that was all I needed.

We went back outside, and even though it was past three in the morning Tina knocked on the doors of the floor's other three apartments. No one answered.

I felt embarrassed and confused. Those events just hours earlier had happened – the fact that my jacket was missing was enough to prove that – but there was absolutely nothing I could do about it.

Tina got Gentleman to copy the footage from the CCTV camera on to a USB stick she was carrying and thanked him for his time. When we were outside, she told me she'd file a report and make some enquiries, but there was little enthusiasm in her tone.

'Someone's covering for these guys,' I persisted, trying to keep the desperation out of my voice. 'I swear it. That's why the camera for the underground car park wasn't working. Why there was no sign of forced entry. And why the place was cleaned up. I was there tonight and I know exactly what I saw. I bet if you check that footage through carefully enough, you'll see that it's been tampered with.'

Tina put up a hand to stop me. 'I'm sorry, Mr Fallon, but criminal conspiracies are a lot rarer than most of us like to think. Criminals just don't tend to be that clever. If two men did kidnap Miss Brakspear, it's highly unlikely that they were in cahoots with the door staff because the more people there are who know about something like this, the harder it is to keep it secret. Even you've admitted that Jenny's an ordinary girl with an ordinary job, and was acting perfectly normally when you met her earlier, so it's highly unlikely she's a victim of some kind of conspiracy. What I want you to do is to keep calm, try not to read too much into everything, and leave the investigating to me.'

'I bet if you check passenger lists for all flights to Barbados out of London Jenny Brakspear's name won't appear on them.'

'Mr Fallon, please.'

I wanted to keep trying to convince her that I was telling the truth, but I could see it wouldn't work. Instead, I asked her what she planned to do.

'I'll contact Jenny's place of work, and I'll contact her family to find out if they can shed any light on things. And when I've done that I'll be in a better position to decide what to do next.' She pulled out her car keys. 'You said you didn't have any money, didn't you?'

'That's right. My wallet was in my jacket.'

'Where do you live?'

'Colindale.'

'Do you want a lift home?'

I nodded, thankful at least for this kindness. 'Please.'

We drove back in silence. For a while I shut my eyes, but I didn't sleep. It was just easier than talking to DS Boyd. I knew she didn't believe me, and I could understand her scepticism, but it was an awful feeling to have witnessed a violent crime and know that a young woman's life was in danger yet have no one take you seriously.

Traffic on the road was sparse and it was barely twenty minutes later when Tina turned into my street.

'Whereabouts is your house?'

'Anywhere round here's fine,' I said, not wanting her to see my crappy little pad after Jenny's flashy apartment.

She pulled in a few doors down from Ramon's place and yawned. 'Get some sleep, Mr Fallon. And when you get up tomorrow have a good long shower. You're not smelling your best.'

I nodded. 'Thanks for the lift, and please, don't give up on this. There's a young woman missing. If we don't do something . . .'

'I'll make enquiries, I promise.'

'Can I take your number? Please. Just in case I think of anything else.'

She didn't look too happy but produced a business card from her handbag and handed it to me. 'I don't want you to take this as an excuse to keep calling me, Mr Fallon, because it won't help me locate Jenny. And I'm off duty in a couple of hours and I'll be sleeping. Understand?'

'Sure, thanks.'

Reluctantly, I got out of the car and stood in the darkness. DS Boyd pulled away with a small wave and her car quickly disappeared down the street, leaving me alone.

The night was dark and cool, and for a few minutes I stayed where I was. I thought about going to Ramon's place and asking if

I could stay there but there were no lights on in his flat and I really didn't want to have to recount what had happened to anyone else and endure their sceptical stares. So I slowly headed down the street.

Home for me was a rented one-bed ground-floor flat in one of the 1950s terraced houses that lined both sides of the road. I'd been there over a year but had never really got used to it. It was small and characterless, and I'd spent far too many lonely hours in it.

Approaching the front door now, I felt the tension rising in me, knowing it was possible that Jenny's kidnappers had already used the information in my wallet to find out where I lived. I looked over my shoulder but the street was silent. I checked the locks on the door but they were intact. Taking a deep breath, I opened the door and stepped inside.

That night at least there was no one waiting for me. I switched on the light and went through to the kitchen, where I poured myself a glass of water and drank it down in one. For the first time that night I noticed how awful I smelled and it amazed me that Tina had volunteered to drive me home. Her car must have reeked, yet she hadn't made a fuss. She struck me as a good-hearted person, even though she had an impressive line in cutting looks, and a good detective as well. There was an air of quiet confidence about her which I liked, and I really hoped she'd do something with this investigation.

I looked at the clock on the wall. It had just turned half past three. I needed my bed. But there was still something I could do before I gave up on Jenny for the night. Something that might shed some light on events.

Even though I really didn't want to have to do it, I located the landline receiver and, taking a deep breath, dialled one of the few telephone numbers I knew by heart.

Six

Dom Moynihan and I had been friends since school. After university, when I was temporarily unemployed, he'd helped get me my first job in the City, at the stockbrokers where he was working; and when, years later, my marriage had finally broke up and I'd returned to London, bitter and defeated, it was him I'd gone to for support. The thing was, Dom had always been there for me when I needed him, and although I'd always appreciated everything he'd done for me, and had told him so on many occasions, I'd never actually done any major favours in return. I would have if he'd ever needed one, but the fact that I hadn't always made me feel that I owed him, even though I knew he'd never call in the debt.

And when you owe someone, you really don't want to shit on them. Nevertheless, I picked up and put down the handset twice before finally forcing myself to make the call.

'Rob?' he groaned into the phone. 'Is that you? What's happened? You all right?'

'Yeah,' I said. 'Sort of.'

'Listen, I'm in Dubai on business. I've got a breakfast meeting in ten minutes. Let me call you back.'

'No, I need to talk to you now.'

'What's wrong?' he asked. 'Is it anything to do with Yvonne and Chloe?'

Dom, more than anyone, knew how hard I'd taken the break-up of my marriage and how much I missed the two of them. He sounded concerned, and I felt a rush of guilt so strong I almost burst into tears. But I forced myself to stay calm.

'They're fine,' I replied. 'The reason I phoned you was . . . It's about Jenny.'

'Jenny?'

'Jenny Brakspear. You know, your ex-girlfriend. When was the last time you saw her?'

'Christ, ages ago. Why?'

'She's a normal girl, right? She doesn't have any secrets or anything, does she?'

'Of course she's normal. Why are you asking me all this?'

I took a deep breath. 'She was kidnapped tonight. About three hours ago.'

'What? How do you know?'

'I was there.'

'Where?'

I paused before answering. 'At her apartment.'

He asked me what I'd been doing there, and then listened while I gave him a brief explanation.

'I'm really sorry, Dom. I didn't mean to do it. It just happened, you know? And when she told me that you were still trying to get back with her, that was it. I said I wasn't interested.' This was bullshit of course, but sometimes a lie causes far less harm than the truth.

There was a long silence on the other end of the phone and I waited, wondering if this meant the end of our friendship.

'Did she honestly tell you I was trying to get back with her?' he asked eventually.

'That's right, and when she said it, I told her—'

'Are you sure?'

'What do you mean?'

'Are you sure that she actually said it?'

'Of course I'm sure. It was only a few hours ago.'

'That's weird.'

'Why?'

'Because,' he replied, sounding strangely distant, 'I haven't spoken to her in at least six months.'

Seven

Unlike everyone else I'd spoken to that night, Dom didn't question my version of events, and he sounded genuinely worried about Jenny. But then, like me, he knew her personally, and I was beginning to realize what a difference that made.

He wasn't back from Dubai until Wednesday morning but said he'd do anything he could to help before then. Unfortunately, he didn't even have her mobile number any more, so I wasn't sure what he'd be able to manage from three thousand miles away. In the meantime, he told me not to give up pressing the police for action, and we agreed to talk the next day when I'd update him on where we were with things.

No mention was made of where all this left our friendship, but I knew that one way or another it was going to be affected. However, for the moment, it was going to be put aside while we tried to find out what the hell had happened to Jenny.

'I can't understand it, mate,' Dom said before he rang off. 'She's just a normal girl,' he added, using my exact description of her. 'Just like anyone else.'

Just a normal girl.

But she wasn't, was she? Jenny Brakspear was a liar. And if she'd lied about something like that, then what else had she lied about? It could have been the sort of white lie I'd just told Dom, but the thing was, I couldn't think of an innocent or beneficial reason for her telling me that he was trying to get back with her when he wasn't. Given the events of that night, something about it seemed suspicious, and I wondered what it was that Jenny had got herself involved in.

As I finally got into bed and pulled the covers over me, I was determined more than ever to find out.

Eight

DS Tina Boyd leaned back in her seat and yawned as she surveyed the morgue-like emptiness of the CID office – a drab, impersonal place littered with cheap furniture that always had that just-been-abandoned-in-an-awful-hurry look – and wondered what had happened to her career. Five years ago she'd been on the fast track to success – one of the new breed of female graduates who were destined for senior positions within the police service – the Met, if not the world, at her feet, yet here she was, stuck in the office alone at four a.m., desperate for a cigarette she wasn't allowed to smoke and a drink she wasn't allowed to drink. And with no one to talk this new case through with, because the other shift guy, DC Hunsdon, had done the sensible thing and phoned in sick with one of his all-too-regular bouts of 'the flu'.

Tina wasn't sure what to make of Rob Fallon's story. On the one hand it was truly outlandish, with no evidence at all to back it up. Yet her instincts were telling her that something wasn't right. First and foremost, he was acting too much like a man telling the truth. It was, of course, possible that he'd had some kind of episode and as a consequence did genuinely believe what he was saying, but

Tina had come across plenty of mentally ill people in her ten years in law enforcement, and even though Fallon had smelled pretty appalling, which was sometimes a sign of mental illness, he just didn't fit the bill. He'd been lucid and detailed in his account, had managed to give a plausible explanation for his unfortunate odour, and his details matched the layout of Miss Brakspear's building.

Even so, Tina might still have left it at that if there hadn't been a second reason for doubt. There are four million CCTV cameras in the UK – the biggest number per capita in the world – and at any time something like ten per cent are out of action due to technical faults; but in modern apartment complexes like Miss Brakspear's, where the cameras are new and state-of-the-art, that figure is almost certainly going to be less – five per cent at most. So it jarred with her that the one covering the back of the building had been out of use on the night a serious crime was reported.

Resisting the urge to sneak a cigarette in the toilet, she looked up Jenny Brakspear's name on the PNC.

If anyone had snatched her it was likely to be drugs-related. Tina was no estate agent but, even in the housing market's current parlous state, Jenny's apartment was going to be worth at least three hundred thousand pounds, which was a lot more than a girl who worked in a travel agent's could afford.

But it soon transpired that Jenny Brakspear didn't have a criminal record, and when Tina checked her address on the Land Registry, she saw that the apartment was owned by a Mr Roy Brakspear, who was probably her father. It wasn't uncommon for parents with a bit of money to buy properties for their grown-up children to live in, but it also represented a problem for Tina, because it took away an obvious motive.

It didn't take her long to get an address and telephone number for Roy Brakspear. He lived in a village just outside Cambridge. It was still the middle of the night, but she knew that if something had happened to Jenny then every minute wasted in the search for her could prove fatal.

He answered on the fifth ring, his voice sounding groggy. 'Hello?'

'Mr Roy Brakspear?'

'Yes.'

'This is DS Tina Boyd from Islington CID. I'm sorry to bother you at this time in the morning.'

'What do you want?' he asked, sounding nervous now.

'Are you related to a Miss Jenny Louise Brakspear of 9C Wolverton Villas in London?'

'She's my daughter. Why?'

'I don't want to unduly alarm you, sir, but we've had a report that she was abducted from her apartment in the early hours of this morning.'

'She can't have been.'

Tina was taken aback by the firmness of his response. 'Why not?'

'Because she phoned me from Gatwick airport at eleven o'clock last night. She was just about to board a plane to go on holiday. I could hear the noise in the background so she was definitely at the airport. Who was it who reported this?'

'A friend of hers,' Tina answered, aware of the doubt in her own voice.

'Well it sounds to me like her friend was playing some sort of joke. Jenny's been talking about this holiday for weeks.'

'Do you have a mobile number I can get her on? So I can speak to her just to satisfy myself that everything's all right?'

He came back to the phone a few seconds later. Tina wrote down the number and thanked him. 'I'm really sorry to have bothered you, sir,' she added. 'The person who made the abduction claim wasn't the most reliable source. As it happens, the doorman of her building said she was off on holiday to Spain, but unfortunately we still have to follow up every report otherwise we wouldn't be doing our job. I hope I haven't caused you too much distress.'

Brakspear said that he understood and that she hadn't, and Tina ended the call.

She immediately rang the number he'd given her for Jenny but an automated voice told her that the phone was currently switched off and that she should try again later. Somehow, she'd known that might happen.

According to everyone she'd talked to bar Rob Fallon, Jenny Brakspear wasn't missing, she was on holiday. Except it seemed she was holidaying in different places. The doorman, John Gentleman, had said it was Barbados, but when Tina had suggested to Jenny's father that he'd said Spain, Roy Brakspear hadn't contradicted her.

It could have been an innocent oversight, of course. After all, the poor guy had been half asleep. But taken along with everything else, her uneasy feeling remained, bolstered by the fact that Jenny's father had been so adamant that his daughter couldn't have been abducted. Tina wasn't a parent, but she was pretty damn sure that if a police officer had rung her in the middle of the night to give her the same news she wouldn't have been anything like as confident as him, and would have demanded further investigation.

But he hadn't.

And Jenny wasn't answering her phone.

Tina knew her boss, DCI Knox, wouldn't allow her to put too much time into this. They had way too much on at the moment, and without anything concrete to back up her case it was inevitably going to end up on the backburner. She'd keep trying Jenny's number, and would call her work too, when she got the chance, to see if they could verify the story. But right now that was the best she could do.

She yawned again and rubbed her eyes. Only another hour and a half of the shift before she finished and it became someone else's problem. Just enough time to file a report.

But first, there were a couple of things she needed to do.

Reaching into the bottom drawer of her desk, she pulled a stainless-steel hipflask from her make-up bag and slipped it into her jeans pocket, resisting the urge to take a slug then and there. Then, popping an unlit cigarette into her mouth, and ignoring the guilty voice in her head that told her she couldn't keep on like this, she got up from her desk and headed to the toilet.

Monday

Nine

I slept badly, and I slept late, not waking up for the final time until gone eleven o'clock. Straight away I recalled the previous night's events, but this time they felt like a bad, strangely distant dream. Bright sunlight filtered in through the curtains, and outside I could hear the sound of traffic. I lay staring at the ceiling for several minutes, relieved at the normality of the scene but still unable to extinguish the memory of the man trying to cut my throat in the underground car park, and the nagging question of what had happened to the girl I'd been planning to make love to only minutes before that.

I had a lunch meeting with my literary agent Murray scheduled for one p.m.: we were going to discuss the next ten chapters of my gangster masterpiece. But I didn't think I could take it today. I knew Murray was pleased with what I'd done because he'd already told me so, and normally I'd have jumped at the chance to leave the PC and the book behind and enjoy a long, boozy lunch, but there was no way I'd be able to concentrate on it today.

As I showered, all I could think about was Jenny Brakspear. Before the previous night I'd met her maybe ten, fifteen times socially. When she'd started going out with Dom I was already staying at his place, and I remember a couple of evenings when the three of us had lounged around drinking beers and watching DVDs. They were fun nights, reminding me a little of long-ago student days, and even though I felt a little like the odd one out, the two of them had always made me feel welcome. Jenny had talked to me about my relationship with Yvonne, and had tried to get me to think positively. That she partially succeeded was no mean feat.

Even after I'd moved out the three of us had met up for occasional drinks, and when I got my first post-wife girlfriend, Carly, the first people we invited round for dinner were Dom and Jenny.

I suppose it was true that I'd never really known her that well – not long after that dinner party she and Dom had split up and we'd fallen out of touch – but I'd spent enough time with her to be convinced that she was a level-headed girl with her heart in the right place. So why had she lied to me about Dom? And more importantly, why had she been kidnapped by two men who'd broken into her apartment without leaving a single sign of forced entry? I was sure now that the motive wasn't sexual. There'd been no lust in the eyes of either of the two men who'd taken her. Just a cold professionalism. If anything, they'd seemed totally uninterested in her as a person, if the way she'd been chucked into the trolley was anything to go by. There had to be another reason, and I couldn't stop thinking about what it might be.

I called Murray and postponed our lunch, feigning flu. He was disappointed – I think he was looking forward to a few drinks to start the working week – but said to call him as soon as I felt better and he'd absolutely make sure he found time in his diary. 'I know we're on to something extraordinary with this book, Robert,' he announced in that dramatic, vaguely camp manner of his.

'Maxwell's a horrible character. He'll sell millions. And the title, *Enforcer*. I absolutely love it.' To be honest, I thought the title was crap, but the whole thing now seemed hugely irrelevant.

As soon as I was off the phone to him I cancelled every one of my credit cards and ordered new ones before deciding to try to put everything to do with the previous night out of my mind and simply carry on with the book. I was currently on chapter twenty-two, almost two-thirds of the way through now, and at one of the most violent points, where Maxwell was in his armed robbery phase, just before he ended up on the wrong end of a Flying Squad ambush followed by a six-year stretch in Pentonville. In the real version of events no one had got hurt, but in mine, one of Maxwell's fellow robbers had been killed, while Maxwell himself had shot and badly wounded a cop (a legitimate target in Maxwell's eyes, because he'd been armed) before taking a bullet in the gut himself.

But the writing just didn't work that day. Suddenly, Maxwell didn't seem such an exotic and exciting character. For the first time I was seeing him for the thug he actually was, someone who made his money from intimidating people and, where intimidation failed, hurting them. No different, in fact, from the men who'd attacked me. I felt pissed off that I'd been in such thrall to him. I put it down to the fact that I'd never been the victim of crime before and so was far more inclined to glamorize it. I wondered if my view had now changed for ever, and what implications this was going to have for the book.

I sat staring at the computer screen for the best part of an hour before giving up and eating some lunch in front of the BBC news, which was the usual diet of doom and gloom and reminded me all too vividly why I avoided newspapers and news programmes these days. I was hoping that the break might provide some inspiration. It didn't. All I could think about was Jenny. Where she might be now and what I could be doing to locate her, because at that moment I was doing nothing.

Eventually I could hold back no longer. I called Islington police station and asked to be put through to CID. Without a crime reference number I found myself placed on hold, then sent through to an automated messaging service. When I tried again, the switchboard operator offered to take my details and get someone to call me back (I declined). It was only on my third attempt, when I told a different switchboard operator I wanted to report a murder but would only speak to someone in Islington CID, that I was reluctantly put through.

Incredibly, the phone still rang for a good minute and a half before it was picked up, which made me wonder what the hell you needed to do to get taken seriously by the police these days.

'DS Storey,' said a nasal voice, laced with a strange mixture of excitement and irritation. 'I understand you want to report a murder.'

'No,' I answered, feigning innocence. 'I'm following up on an abduction I reported last night.'

'So you're not reporting a murder?'

'No. I don't know where you got that from. There must have been some mistake.'

DS Storey sighed impatiently. In the background, I could hear a lot of noise. 'Have you got a crime reference number?' he demanded.

I told him I hadn't and started to explain what had happened but he stopped me dead, asking who I'd dealt with. When I told him it was DS Tina Boyd, he said she was who I needed to speak with, and she'd be back on duty at six o'clock.

I couldn't believe it. Jenny had been kidnapped and her kidnappers had tried to murder me yet no one appeared to be doing anything about it. 'This is an abduction I'm reporting,' I said, my patience finally snapping, 'not a fucking parking offence. Why is no one taking it seriously?'

'Listen, sir,' snapped Storey in return, snarling out the 'sir', 'if I don't know anything about it and you don't have a crime reference number then I can't help you. All right? Now, my advice is to contact DS Boyd direct when she comes in tonight because right now we have an emergency on at this station and I do not have the time to talk. OK?'

It wasn't OK, but there was nothing I could do about it, so I rang off.

I looked at my watch. It was half past two. I was angry with Tina Boyd. I'd thought she would take things seriously enough to pass the information on to her colleagues, but it was clear she hadn't. Figuring that I had nothing to lose, I dug out her mobile number and dialled it.

She answered after a fair number of rings and identified herself with a single hello, sounding half asleep.

'It's me,' I said, 'Rob Fallon. From last night. The kidnapping.'

A sigh of irritation echoed down the phone. 'I haven't forgotten you, Mr Fallon, but I was actually sleeping.'

'I'm sorry,' I lied. 'I didn't mean to wake you up.'

'You knew I was on night duty so I'd have thought it was pretty obvious that I'd be sleeping during the day.' She paused. 'What can I do for you now?'

'I want you to know I'm not bullshitting, DS Boyd.'

'You already told me that last night.'

'I've just been on the phone to one of your colleagues in CID, a DS Storey, and he didn't know anything about Jenny's kidnapping. Now I don't know why those men took her, or even if she's alive or dead, but the thing is, I cannot just sit here and do nothing while her life might be in danger.'

69

Tina gave another exaggerated sigh. 'I want you to forget about this, Mr Fallon.'

'Why? She could be in a lot of danger.'

'I spoke to her father before I came off duty this morning, and he told me that she couldn't have been abducted because she phoned him from Gatwick airport late last night on her way out of the country on holiday.'

'But she was with me late last night. And she never mentioned anything about a holiday. In fact, she said she'd just come back from somewhere, on business.'

'Well, that's what he said, Mr Fallon.'

'And have you managed to speak to her work? What have they said?'

'Ah, her work . . . that's an interesting one.'

I didn't like the way she said that.

'It took me a while to find the name of her employer with the limited information I had to work on, and I was off duty when I finally called them. I even put off my sleep for it, because I wanted to give you the benefit of the doubt. But I got through to her boss, a Miss Murton, and guess what?'

I began to get an ominous feeling in my gut. 'What?'

'She left three weeks ago.'

Ten

After she got off the phone, Tina found it impossible to get back to sleep. Eventually she got up and made herself a cup of strong black coffee. She knew she'd been a bit harsh on Fallon. Part of the reason for that was because she was always grouchy when she got woken up. The other part was because she still didn't know what to do about the investigation herself. A lot of Fallon's story made sense and there were some strange coincidences that appeared to back it up. Yet the fact remained that he was the only witness to this crime. And some things counted against him, like the fact that he'd been drinking heavily on the night and had had difficulty remembering Jenny's last name, as well as his claim that Jenny had told him she'd just returned from a business trip when, in reality, she'd left the company three weeks earlier.

She lit her first cigarette of the new day and tried Jenny's mobile number again – her fourth attempt – but like the other times, the automated voice told her the handset was switched off. This was turning into a real puzzle, one she was going to have to talk through with somebody. And she knew exactly who.

Tina had worked with Mike Bolt at SOCA, the Serious and

Organized Crime Agency, for more than a year before returning to the Met a few months earlier, and he was one of the few people whose opinion on criminal matters she trusted absolutely. But their parting of the ways had been difficult, which was what had stopped her picking up the phone to him earlier that morning.

During their time working together they'd become very close friends, and almost inevitably a mutual attraction had developed. One night he'd given her a lift home from a surveillance job and had made a pass at her. They'd kissed in the car, passionately, and she'd been tempted to let things go further, but she'd had a relationship with her boss in CID four years earlier, before SOCA, which had ended in tragedy, and she was desperate to avoid putting herself through the emotional mill again, especially with someone she was going to see so much of, so she'd pulled away from his embrace.

Mike had apologized and nothing more had been said about the incident, but their relationship had never been the same after that. To be fair, it hadn't been the only reason she'd left SOCA. She'd also grown tired of the long-drawn-out investigations into those shadowy figures running the UK underworld, which so often ended in abject failure. But Mike hadn't seen it like that. He'd thought it had something to do with him, and though she'd tried plenty of times to persuade him that wasn't the case, she knew she hadn't convinced him. And if she was entirely honest with herself, she wasn't convinced either.

They hadn't spoken since, which didn't help, and the longer time had gone on the harder it had become to re-establish contact. She regretted this because, despite the fact that she'd made the break, she missed him.

Now, though, seemed a good time to finally make that call. She speed-dialled his number, having never got round to relegating it to her standard contacts list.

She felt an unexpected jolt of nerves when he answered.

'Hey Tina,' he said, sounding pleased to hear from her, 'long time no speak. How's life back on the streets?'

'Same as it is in SOCA, I expect,' she answered, forcing herself to sound cheery. 'Too many bad guys. Too few of the good ones.'

'But you're enjoying it though, yeah?'

'There's plenty of action, that's for sure.'

In truth, it had been a big disappointment – something she really should have expected, given that she'd worked out of Islington before. Virtually all the crimes she dealt with, from domestic burglary right up to murder, were depressing, sordid affairs where the identity of the perpetrators was obvious immediately, and unfortunately there seemed to be a never-ending stream of them.

But she didn't say any of this to Mike. Instead, they made the usual small talk, and she was slightly saddened that it lasted only a couple of minutes before fizzling out.

'So, to what do I owe the pleasure of your call?' he asked when the inevitable silence arrived.

Tina told him about the kidnapping, going through the details methodically, trying hard not to miss anything out, and feeling better to be getting down to business. 'I don't know what to do, Mike,' she said. 'I still can't get hold of the girl, and Fallon doesn't strike me as a bullshitter. That's why I thought I'd run it by you.'

'You need to build on what you've got,' he replied after a few moments' thought, 'because it's nowhere near enough for the bosses to take seriously. First thing I'd suggest is to get the CCTV footage fast-tracked.'

'Easier said than done.'

'Well, you know Matt Turner works over at the FSS now?'

Matt Turner had been a colleague of theirs at SOCA until he was seriously injured during an operation the previous year.

'No,' she said, suddenly feeling very much out of the loop, 'I didn't.'

'He moved to their hi-tech unit a few months back. I think he got tired of the desk job at SOCA, and he's never going to recover enough for fieldwork.'

'It's a pity. He was a good guy.'

'He still is. Get your footage over there and tell him it's urgent. And if it turns out it has been doctored then you're definitely on to something, and by the sound of it, something big. And have you checked out the doorman at her apartment building yet? Because from what you're saying, they couldn't have done it without his help.'

'No, I haven't,' she said, knowing she should have thought of that. 'That would mean three people involved, which seems a lot.'

'True, but you can't discount it. See if he's got a record. That'll at least give you something to go on.'

'I will, but I don't think my boss is going to let me spend much time on it. We're snowed under at the moment.'

'But if it's happened – and from what you've told me my feeling is that it has – then he's going to need to act. Speak to him. See what he says. He might surprise you.'

Tina doubted that very much. Like most senior officers, DCI Knox was interested in hitting Home Office targets, and that meant dealing with the crimes that were right in front of them and easily solvable, not ones that required extensive resources and might not even have taken place. 'Thanks,' she said. 'I'll do that.'

'Let me know how you get on. Seriously. I'd be interested to find out.'

'Thanks. I will.'

'I'd help myself, but we're snowed under as well right now. I guess that's par for the course in our line.'

'It's all right, Mike, I wasn't after your help. Just your advice.

And you've been more than helpful.' He had too, but then he'd always been one of the best detectives she'd worked with.

'We aim to please,' he said, but this time the cheeriness in his voice sounded forced.

There was an awkward silence. Tina asked him what the team were working on at the moment.

'The usual,' he answered. 'Trying to bring down another of the Mr Bigs.'

'Who's it this time? Anyone I know?'

'Yeah,' he said, his tone sounding reluctant. 'Paul Wise.'

Tina swallowed hard. Mention of Paul Wise's name still made her jaw tighten and her stomach knot. If there was one person she could blame for doing so much to wreck her life, it was him, even though they'd never met. Wise was the bastard behind the murder of her former boss and lover John Gallan. A multi-millionaire businessman with his finger in all manner of unsavoury pies who'd managed to evade justice all his life and who was as close to untouchable as any criminal she'd ever come across.

'How come he's suddenly back on the SOCA agenda?' she asked, hearing the strain in her own voice. 'I thought everyone had given up on pinning anything on him.'

'No one's going to give up on Paul Wise, Tina.'

'And what's he doing now? I thought he was based out of the Turkish part of Cyprus, far away from the long arm of the law.' She knew damn well he was. She'd checked enough times.

'He is,' said Bolt, 'but he's been diversifying now that property development isn't as lucrative as it used to be. Now he's into large-scale heroin smuggling into the UK. That and prostitution.'

Tina snorted. 'As classy as ever. Are you close to getting him yet?'

'The honest answer's no. But that doesn't mean we stop trying. We've got a lot of resources aimed at him now. It's only a matter of time.'

She didn't know whether Mike believed this or not, but she didn't. Britain didn't even have an extradition treaty with the Turkish part of Cyprus, and the moment it got one Wise would be off somewhere else where he couldn't be touched. Men like him always seemed to be one step ahead of the law. She would still like to have been involved, though, and it suddenly irked her that she was out of it.

'If you do get the evidence to take him down, make sure you let me know, OK Mike?'

'You'll be the first I tell, Tina. I promise.'

She could hear the warmth in his voice, and she knew then that he would. 'Thanks. I appreciate that.'

'Take care. And don't give up on your case. Follow your instincts.'

I always do, she thought as she said her goodbyes. *And it usually gets me into trouble.*

Eleven

Have you ever felt that you're moving in a parallel universe to everyone else? Where everything you do takes on a dreamlike quality? I experienced it once before as a student when a group of us took magic mushrooms – my one and only foray into hard drugs – but even then I knew that what was happening wasn't reality. I was far less sure of that now, and for the first time in my life I began to question my sanity. I've had some tough times in my life, tremendous highs followed by leaden, black lows, but I've always felt in control. The things I was hearing now, however, were confusing me so much I was wondering whether last night had happened at all.

But I *had* been in Jenny's apartment because when I went back it felt completely familiar to me. And my jacket, along with my mobile phone and wallet, was definitely missing.

I needed to clear my head, so after I finished talking to Tina Boyd I drove up to Broxbourne woods and went for a much-needed walk, enjoying the solitude after all the drama of the past twenty-four hours.

I hadn't got very far when Dom called. He asked me if I'd had any news. 'I've been worried about it all day.'

'Some,' I said, and I told him what I knew.

There was a pause at the other end of the line, and I sensed what he was thinking. For a while, when I first got back from France, I'd gone into a real depression. I'd slept badly, found myself unable to work, and almost stopped eating entirely. At my lowest point I didn't get out of bed for three solid days, and I lost more than a stone in weight. I don't think it was a breakdown as such, but I know that Dom was worried about my mental health. He'd even talked to my dad about what he should do, without informing me. Eventually I fought my way out of the worst of it without need of outside help, but I was sure Dom was feeling the same concerns about me now. I hadn't seen him for a few weeks so in his eyes it was entirely possible, I suppose, that I had relapsed.

I knew he wanted to say something, so I beat him to it. 'Everything's been going fine in my life lately, Dom. This happened, I promise.' But I was conscious of the doubt in my voice.

'I just don't understand it,' he said. 'Why would Jenny's dad say she was on holiday if she wasn't?'

'What's he like, her dad?' I asked.

'I only met him a couple of times. He was a nice guy.'

'Is he rich?'

'He runs his own business and I think he's quite well off, but nothing spectacular. I doubt if he clears more than a couple of hundred grand a year. Not enough to kidnap his daughter for.'

It was a good point, and it closed another door for me, because now I had no obvious motive for Jenny's abduction. The nagging voice started in my ear again. *Did it really happen, Rob? Are you sure you're not imagining it?*

'What are you going to do now, Rob?' asked Dom.

'I don't know.' I sighed, unable to keep the sense of defeat out of my voice. 'Keep hassling my police contact, I guess. Get her to check the CCTV footage from Jenny's apartment block for any signs that it's been tampered with, because I know that it has been. Other than that, I don't know. I could try speaking to Maxwell, I suppose, see if he's got any ideas. You know, from a criminal's point of view.'

'That sounds a bit desperate.'

'It is,' I said wearily. 'But I'm beginning to run low on options.'

'Are you OK, Rob? Maybe I should come back.'

'Thanks, mate, but there's no point. Right now there's nothing you can do that I can't. You may as well stay where you are. I'll keep you posted.'

He tried to insist but I could tell his heart wasn't really in it. I wondered whether he did actually believe my story or whether he thought I'd finally gone over the edge.

Once I was off the phone I kept walking, enjoying being away from the city and its dangers, and it was gone six by the time I got back to the car. The shadows were lengthening as late afternoon turned into early evening, and the sunlight flickering through the beech trees took on a soft orange glow.

The last time I was up here I'd been with Yvonne and Chloe. Chloe had only just started walking, and I'd held her hand most of the way. It had been a sunny day like this, but that was the only similarity. Things had been very different then. We'd been discussing our move to France. The house there had been bought, our flat in London had been sold for close to double what we'd paid for it five years earlier, and I was preparing to hand in my notice at work. We'd had money in the bank and a brilliant plan for security, success and happiness.

I stood in silence for a long time, wondering how and why I'd let it all slip through my fingers, and wishing that I could have that time back again. I experienced a sudden, painful urge to phone and talk to Yvonne and Chloe. To chat to them about this and that and try to inject some semblance of normality back into my life.

But they were on a walking holiday in northern Sweden with Nigel, out of mobile phone contact. Instead, I got back in the car and began the drive home, thinking I desperately needed something to cheer me up.

Ramon might not have been everyone's cup of tea, but in the circumstances he'd do just fine.

Twelve

Agent Mike Bolt sat staring at the piles of paperwork on his desk, feeling a mixture of anger and frustration. His job at SOCA was disrupting the activities of the couple of hundred Mr Bigs who ran organized crime in the UK, an industry that was worth an almost unbelievable forty billion dollars a year, but he was pragmatic enough to know it was a war he and his colleagues were never going to win. The enemy was far too superior in numbers and resources for that. But the important thing was not to lose it entirely. You had to be patient and keep chipping away at their defences. Sometimes you had to wait months for a result. Sometimes you didn't even get one. A witness might suddenly retract his testimony, or a judge throw out the case, and all your hard work went up in smoke as the bad guys walked free with big grins on their faces and went back to making obscene amounts of money. But in Bolt's experience, there was always a chink in a target's armour somewhere, and if you kept going long enough, you'd eventually find it.

But even he had to admit that if Paul Wise had a chink in his armour, it was incredibly well hidden. Wise might have left the UK more than three years earlier to avoid the attentions of the law, but a large proportion of his income still came from criminal activities within his home country.

In the five months Bolt's team had been actively targeting him, they'd raided four brothels in which he had a controlling interest, freeing a total of sixty-seven trafficked women in the process. They'd also seized more than ten kilos of ninety per cent pure heroin belonging to him, most of it in a daring undercover operation during which two of his key operatives were arrested. All this activity had garnered plenty of positive press coverage, but unfortunately not a shred of evidence that could be used against Wise himself. The two operatives caught with the heroin weren't talking and had got themselves some seriously expensive legal representation (doubtless bankrolled by their boss). As for the people they'd arrested in the brothels, only two had been prepared to cooperate – a Turkish asylum seeker who managed one, and a local thug who ran security at another – and neither had met or even spoken to Wise, both having dealt with his middlemen.

Now, for the first time, Bolt and his team had turned to SOCA's Financial Intelligence Unit for help. The FIU's task was to discover where all the huge profits from organized crime were hidden so they could be traced back to the Mr Bigs who were making them, and subsequently used as evidence in any criminal proceedings. Bolt didn't have a huge amount of interest in the complex world of financial crime – it felt too far away from the action for him – but since nothing else was working he'd agreed with his bosses that going after Wise's money represented their best chance of truly hurting him.

However, after over a month of FIU involvement Bolt had only just received his first report from them in his email in-box that afternoon. It was forty-five pages long and read like absolute gobbledygook. So much so that he'd asked one of his team, Mo Khan, to take it away and decipher it for him in preparation for the meeting they were scheduled to have with the FIU representatives the next day. Bolt figured that with a B-grade A-level in applied economics Mo was probably the best qualified of all of them to make sense of it, but he'd been gone for more than two and a half hours now, so maybe he was having as much trouble as the rest of them.

Evening was drawing in, but Bolt wasn't thinking about going home. As he stood looking out of his office window across the park opposite and the high-rise buildings beyond, he was thinking about Tina Boyd, as he had been for most of the afternoon. He'd felt a real frisson of excitement when she called, even though they hadn't spoken or seen each other in close to a year, but then she'd always been able to get under his skin. The initial excitement had quickly turned to disappointment, though, when it became clear that the reason for her call was professional, and he felt bad that he'd had to tell her about the Paul Wise investigation, knowing the part that Wise had played in the death of her former boyfriend.

At least they'd agreed to stay in touch, and he knew that she'd want to hear about any developments on the Wise case, but he wished there was more to it than that. He'd pondered asking if she fancied meeting for a drink, but he knew it wouldn't work. He was still attracted to her, but the last time he'd followed his instincts when they were alone together, responding to signals he was sure had been there, had left him feeling embarrassed and depressed. It would be better simply to put her behind him completely.

There was a knock on the door and he turned round as a short, stocky Asian guy with a round jolly face and a frizzy mop of hair that couldn't decide whether it was salt or pepper ambled into the room. Mo Khan looked tired, his big bloodhound eyes sporting heavy bags, and Bolt noticed he was putting on weight round the middle – a result, no doubt, of his latest effort to give up smoking.

'Ah, the wanderer returns,' Bolt said with a smile, glad for the interruption. 'Any joy with that?'

'Some. It seems that Paul Wise is good at cleaning his money.'

'And it took them a month to work that out? He's been a criminal for thirty years. Of course he's good at cleaning his money.'

'Well, they've found out a bit more than that,' said Mo, as the two of them took seats opposite each other. 'They've worked out that he's making a gross annual profit of at least twenty-five million dollars, just from prostitution and drug smuggling. Most of the cash gets smuggled out of the country. Some of it gets sunk into his construction and leisure businesses, particularly the restaurants, where it's difficult to differentiate it from the legitimate takings. The rest of it ends up going through the usual laundering routes and into bank accounts in places like Iceland, Panama, and of course northern Cyprus, before it finally makes its way into Wise's pocket. He loses maybe thirty per cent of the total in turning it from dirty to clean, but he's still raking in huge quantities, and he's got some deal with the authorities over there where he's even managed to defer his tax payments.'

Bolt had long ago given up getting worked up about the personal wealth of the Mr Bigs, but he still whistled through his teeth at the size of these particular figures. 'And who said crime doesn't pay? OK, so how does the report help us?'

Mo shrugged. 'We might be able to disrupt the flow of the cash if we know how he's getting it out of the country and we can intercept it, but from what they say here, it's going to be a nightmare building a watertight money-laundering case against him. He spreads the stuff around too much for that, and the fact that he owns a lot of businesses where large sums of cash are used counts in his favour.'

'So they've been able to find out all these clever statistics and write this big flashy report, but it basically makes no difference.' Bolt shook his head irritably.

'That's about the size of it, boss. There is one piece of good news, though. The credit crunch is hitting Wise hard. Not only are all his legitimate businesses suffering, he's been putting millions into a hedge fund in the City run by some hotshot financier called Sir Henry Portman.'

'Where do I know that name from?'

Mo grinned. 'He was filmed by the *News of the World* dressed in stockings and suspenders snorting cocaine and cavorting with a succession of high-class prostitutes, one of whom was seen to spank his bare behind with a paddle.'

Bolt raised his eyebrows. 'And that's in the report?'

'No, I just Googled it now.'

'Jesus. But why would I remember that? Those kind of scandals are two a penny.'

'Well, one, he sued them successfully over it for breach of privacy, which made the news. Two, he's a big name in the City and his fund, HPP, has been one of the star performers of the last five years. Up until recently, that is. It's now down more than thirty-five per cent year on year. Which translates into losses in the millions for Wise.'

'Good. At least there's some divine justice. But it still doesn't bring us any closer to getting him. Is there any personal link between Wise and Portman?' Wise had had some good contacts with senior figures in the establishment, which in Bolt's view was one of the key reasons he'd avoided justice so far.

'Not that the report mentions,' said Mo. 'And even if there were, it wouldn't make any difference. The money Wise has been investing goes through a holding company of his, Ratten Holdings, and it's officially clean. According to him, he's just a businessman.'

As Mo spoke, Bolt Googled Sir Henry Portman on his PC and came up with several hundred matches. He clicked the first one and a report of his court victory against the *News of the World* appeared.

'Listen, boss, do you mind if I make a move? I wanted to take the kids swimming tonight, and time's getting on. I've written up a summary of the report for you to take a look at.'

Bolt smiled. Mo Khan doted on his four kids, and with the long hours they worked at SOCA, time was precious. 'Sure. We're done here. Have fun.'

For a fleeting moment he felt jealous of Mo having a family to go back to. His own wife, Mikaela, had died in a car accident seven years earlier, and he'd never remarried, or had kids.

He pushed the thought aside and turned back to the computer screen, inspecting the colour photo of the distinguished-looking gentleman with the silver hair and the pinstripe suit. In the picture, Sir Henry Portman was standing outside the High Court addressing reporters, alongside his blonde female lawyer, who looked a damn sight better than most of the ones Bolt had to deal with. He wore a serious expression, as befitted the occasion, but there was something vaguely rakish about him, a twinkling in the eyes, and it didn't take that much to imagine him enjoying the attentions of good-looking call girls.

Paul Wise was strongly suspected of being responsible for as many as twenty-five murders, including that of a teenage girl and at least one police officer, even though he used other people to do the actual dirty work, and Bolt wondered whether Portman knew where the money Wise was investing in his funds came from. Or whether he even cared.

After all, in Bolt's experience, when large amounts of money are involved, people tend to forget their morals very, very quickly indeed.

Thirteen

'What she lacked in obvious beauty, she made up for both in talent and enthusiasm,' announced Ramon, describing his conquest of the previous night, a credit controller called Cheryl. 'And I've got to tell you, my man, that even the great Ramon's libido has been temporarily tamed. I am, how you say, fair shagged out.' He grinned and took a toke on his joint, sucking in the smoke and holding it there for a good ten seconds before blowing out a thin stream towards the ceiling.

We were sitting in my bedroom cum living area, Ramon in the old armchair by my bed, me reclined on a couple of beanbags opposite him, a Peroni in my hand. An old Santana album (Ramon's choice) was playing on the iPod, and I was feeling relaxed for the first time in twenty-four hours. I was supposed to be cooking dinner for us both, but somehow I didn't think this was going to be happening any time soon.

'How about you, my man?' he said. 'There were a lot of women in that place last night. Did you attract one with your lethal combination of wit and good looks?'

'Incredible though it might seem, no.' I took a slug from the beer, surprised that I wasn't even tempted to tell him about what had happened to me. I guess at that moment I just wanted to forget about it.

'Ach Roberto,' he said, pointing the joint at me accusingly. 'A good-looking guy like you and you're wasting your youth. One day you're going to sit back and wonder where the time went. Let me tell you something, my man. No one ever regretted that they didn't spend enough time in the office.'

'I don't work in an office.'

'I know you don't. But you've still got to loosen up, my man. Here, have a puff on this little number. It's prime weed. Not any of that skunk shit.' He leaned forward with the joint.

Normally I'd have said no. I rarely smoked dope. It tended to make me both sleepy and incredibly horny at the same time, which was always a pointless combination, especially so when all I had for company was another man, but tonight I felt like throwing caution to the wind. I took it off him and inhaled deeply, enjoying the feeling of smoke in my lungs. I'd given up the cigarettes years back but, like most smokers, I still missed them.

'Everything's all right with you, isn't it, Roberto?' he asked, looking at me seriously.

I smiled. 'Sure, I'm good. It's quite a compliment to be told I'm wasting my youth when I'm thirty-four.'

'Yeah, but the man telling you that's forty-two.'

We both laughed, and I took another toke, beginning to get that lightheaded feeling.

'I want you to be happy, man, you know? You've had a few hard times, but you've got to remember that life's short, and it's there to be enjoyed. That's my philosophy and it's always worked.' He sat back in his seat, making himself comfortable, and fiddled with his bandanna (red tonight).

His philosophy had worked, too. Ramon might not have had a

lot financially, but he was one of the happiest men I knew. He had his dope, his dancing, his conquests, and one way or another he always perked me up, however black my mood was.

I drained my beer and pointed to his. 'Another one?'

'Do bears defecate in forested terrain?'

'Apparently so,' I said, and got up, handing him the joint.

As I pulled two more Peronis from the fridge, I had a sudden rush of guilt. Here I was enjoying myself, drinking and smoking dope without a second thought for Jenny. I looked at my watch. It had just turned half eight. I knew I ought to phone Tina and chivvy her into action, but I told myself that I'd do it later. If I hassled her too much she'd end up ignoring my calls.

'You know what I could do with?' I said, coming back into the room with the beers. 'A holiday. I've just realized I haven't been anywhere apart from France since before Chloe was born, and that was over four years ago.' I put Ramon's bottle on the bedside table beside his chair, and collapsed back into the beanbags. 'I'm thinking somewhere like Costa Rica. Have you ever been there?' I remembered that he'd always claimed to have been a bit of a world traveller.

Ramon didn't answer.

He didn't even move.

I tensed, experiencing a hollow feeling in the pit of my stomach. 'Ramon?' My voice cracked as I spoke his name.

He was slumped forward a little in his seat, like he'd fallen asleep, and the joint was no longer in his hand.

I put down my drink and got to my feet, moving too fast and getting a headrush as I walked over to him. 'Ramon? You all right, mate?'

I crouched down. Still no movement. The hollow feeling was spreading to every part of me. I lifted his head, not wanting to do it but knowing that I had to.

'Oh Jesus. Oh, Jesus Christ.'

There was a deep red hole where his left eye had been. It was pumping blood, a thick stripe of which ran slowly down his face and on to his neck, pooling in the fold there.

Straight away I knew he was dead. There was no question about it. His head hung heavy and useless in my hands, but it was still almost impossible to believe because I'd only been gone a few moments – thirty seconds at most – and when I'd left him he'd been laughing and talking and toking. Unable to quite comprehend what I was seeing, even though the blood was now running freely down his face, I felt desperately for a pulse that wasn't there.

A terrified panic ripped through me. 'Ramon! Ramon! Wake up! Stay with me!' I gave his face a gentle slap. 'Please,' I whispered. 'Stay with me. Don't go.'

And then I heard movement.

I froze.

'Who's Chloe?' said a voice behind me in a harsh Northern Irish accent.

Fourteen

My mouth went dry. My stomach tightened so much it was painful. More than anything else in the world, I didn't want to turn round.

But I couldn't keep staring at Ramon's blank, dead face either. Its utter lifelessness was tearing me apart.

Slowly, very slowly, I turned my head. Is this it? I kept asking myself. The end of my life? A lonely, bloody death in a cramped little flat miles away from the people I loved. I didn't want to die. *God, I didn't want to die.*

He stood between me and the bedroom door, blocking any possibility of escape – the grotesque-looking Irishman with the saucer eyes and the malignant smile permanently etched on the rack-tight skin of his face. He had one of his hands behind his back, while in the other he held the photo I kept by my bed of Yvonne, Chloe and me, taken in the garden a few weeks after we'd arrived in France, shortly before Chloe's second birthday, in the days when we were still full of optimism. Before everything went wrong.

It hadn't taken him long to find out where I lived, then.

'I asked you a question, Mr Fallon,' he said, his voice quiet and calm. 'Who's Chloe?'

He brought the hand round from behind his back, and I saw he was holding the stiletto he'd tried to cut my throat with the previous night, except this time it was stained with Ramon's blood. He tapped the tip of the blade against the photo. 'Is it her?' He turned the frame round so I could see it properly, rubbing the blade along the image of Chloe's innocent, smiling face.

'She's my daughter,' I said, my voice barely a croak.

'You don't want her to end up like your friend, do you?'

'No.'

'Good. Then you'll do exactly what I say.' He dropped the photo on to the carpet, and took a step towards me.

'You didn't have to kill him,' I whispered. 'He was nothing to do with this.'

'I know, but I enjoyed it.' He paused, taking pleasure in my fear, the pale saucer eyes lighting up with a childlike glee. 'Fear's a strange instinct, isn't it? It's supposedly there for self-preservation, yet right now it's preventing you from doing the one thing that will most obviously preserve your life – running.'

I didn't say anything. I didn't need to. He was right.

'Fear can make you weak and useless, but if you know how to control and channel it, it can be used to your advantage. I have that ability. I've always had it. But your problem right now is that you don't. Instead, your fear's going to make you do exactly as you're told.' He took another step forward so he was standing above me. I became aware of the scent of expensive aftershave. 'And what you're going to do now is drink this.' He produced a hipflask from the pocket of the raincoat he was wearing and threw it in my lap. 'Go on, drink.'

I picked it up but made no move to put it to my lips. Instead, I focused on the bloodstained blade only a few feet from my face. For the first time a real sense of anger began to overcome my fear. I couldn't believe this bastard had casually executed Ramon. And now he was threatening to do the same to my precious daughter, the one person in this world I would die to protect.

Some primal instinct kicked in. Remembering the way I'd caught him off guard the previous night, I leapt to my feet with a yell, blanking out the danger as I grabbed for his knife hand and lunged forward with the hipflask, using it as a makeshift club to slam into his face.

He moved aside easily and slapped the flask out of my hand, then drove a foot squarely into my groin.

I felt a searing pain travel up into my belly and the fight went out of me instantly. As I began to fall to my knees a gloved hand grabbed me by the throat and I was slammed back into the wall, stumbling over Ramon's corpse in the process. 'Don't fuck me about,' he hissed, and a split second later I felt the blade as he pushed it against my cheek.

For a second the room was silent, then he brought his face very close to mine. For the first time I noticed jagged patches of scar tissue round his chin that the plastic surgery had failed to get rid of entirely, and that he was wearing blusher to try to conceal them.

He ran the top of the blade along my cheek and into the pit just below my eye, pushing it against my eyeball. All the time his grip on my throat tightened, and I found it almost impossible to breathe.

'I once cut a man's face off with this knife,' he whispered gently, his breath warm on my skin. 'I started here.' He pushed the blade in harder and I began to moan, not daring to move a millimetre. 'And I sliced all the way down.' He slowly traced a line down my jawline to my chin. 'And when I'd finished, I had a fillet. Then I did the other side. His wife was watching at the time. I informed her that if she didn't tell me the whereabouts of her son – a man who owed a client of mine a very large sum of money – then I'd use a skillet to fry her husband's cheeks, and feed them to her. But she was strong-willed, as women so often are, so she ended up eating well that night. It was only when it was her turn to provide the meat that she relented and gave him up.' He let out a low chuckle, moving the blade down so that it was against my throat, revelling in my fear. 'I tell you this so you understand what I'm capable of if you lie to me.'

'I understand,' I whispered. All my anger had dissolved now and terror was back in the ascendant. 'I won't tell anyone, I swear it.'

'It's a little bit too late for that now, isn't it? You've already been blabbing to the police, telling them about what you thought you saw last night. Who else have you told?'

How the hell did he know that? Had he been following me somehow?

I knew immediately I couldn't betray Dom, but still I hesitated before answering, 'No one,' trying to look as confident in the lie as possible.

He spotted the hesitation. The whip-thin mouth curled up at either end in a knowing smile. 'I don't think you're taking me very seriously, are you, Mr Fallon?' he asked, placing an exaggerated emphasis on my name, driving home the fact that he was the one in control. 'Even though I've just executed your friend. I could cut you into little pieces right now, but you're lucky. Killing you might draw unwanted attention, what with the fact that you've been blabbing to the police, so for the moment it's easier to keep you alive. But if you keep bullshitting me, I might decide that it's easier just to be rid of you.'

I swallowed, the movement painful under the knife blade.

'I asked you a question: who else have you told? Answer it, cunt.'

'No one,' I whispered, meeting his intense stare, willing him to believe me.

He moved away suddenly, causing me to sway and almost fall, but I stayed where I was against the wall as he picked up the hipflask and thrust it into my hand again. 'You have exactly one minute to drink the contents of this bottle,' he announced calmly, moving the knife back and forth in front of my face. 'If you spill any, or hesitate at all for any reason, I'll begin to remove pieces of flesh.' He glanced at his watch. 'Starting now.'

I unscrewed the cap and caught the sickly scent of Scotch, a drink I'd despised since throwing up on it at a party aged sixteen. I took a deep breath and gulped a mouthful down, grimacing against the fiery taste. Visions of my own disfigurement danced across my mind, and my hands shook as I forced down more, thinking that if I had to suffer then I may as well be drunk. I wanted to throw up, but ignored the feeling and carried on. It's amazing what the threat of serious, life-altering violence can make you do. I even began to get used to the sour, fiery taste as I steadily emptied the flask. And all the time he stood watching me, the same calm, matter-of-fact expression on his face, and all the time I feared him completely because I knew that when he spoke of cutting pieces off me he was telling the absolute truth.

The room began to spin as I let the empty flask fall to the floor, and I worked hard to steady myself.

'Phone the police officer you dealt with,' he ordered, reaching into his pocket and pulling out the mobile phone I'd left in my jacket at Jenny's place. 'Tell her that you've been depressed lately and drinking too much, and that you made the story of the kidnapping up, and are sorry to have wasted her time. Say anything else and you'll be dead before you finish the sentence. Understand?'

I fumbled round in my pocket for Tina Boyd's business card, then dialled her number. She didn't answer, and after about ten rings the number went to message. I then said exactly what he'd told me to say, slurring out the words, still having difficulty standing up straight, before flicking the phone shut.

'So now you keep quiet, get on with your life, and never mention the girl's name again. That way, you and your family stay alive.'

I made no move to resist as he grabbed me by the hair and swung me round so I was facing the wall. The bile rose in my throat and I had to work hard to swallow it down.

'If you ever see me again,' he whispered, coming close to my ear, 'it means that it's your time to die. To lose every experience you ever had. For ever. Just like poor Ramon.'

And then he slammed me face first into the wall and the whole room exploded in pain and darkness.

Fifteen

Islington CID was bedlam when Tina turned up for duty that night. There'd been a serious stabbing incident that afternoon after two groups of kids from rival schools had clashed outside a fried chicken takeaway on the Holloway Road, leaving a fifteen-year-old in intensive care with life-threatening injuries. Most of her day-shift colleagues were still there, trying to collate the numerous witness statements and trawl through the CCTV tapes, and she was immediately roped in to help, only just finding the time to arrange a courier to get the USB stick containing the camera footage from Jenny's apartment over to Matt Turner at the FSS. She'd spoken to him earlier for the first time since visiting him in hospital over a year earlier, and though he really didn't owe her any favours, he'd told her he'd look at it straight away.

It was almost three hours before the place emptied and Tina was left on her own with a pile of paperwork, finally able to collect her thoughts. It had been a pretty awful day. To be reminded of the existence of Paul Wise and the fact that he was free and living it up in the Med after what he'd done to the man she'd once loved was bad enough, but she'd never have been reminded of it if it hadn't been for Rob Fallon. Not only had he sent her on a wild goose chase, wasting her time, but just to put the icing on the cake he'd also ruined her day's sleep. When she picked up his drunken voice-mail message she'd come close to throwing her phone against the nearest wall, such was her frustration. As if drinking heavily lately was some kind of excuse. Tina drank too heavily on occasion too, and had done so ever since Wise had had her lover murdered, but she made sure she kept it under control. She would never allow her-self to get to the stage where she blurred fantasy with reality.

She'd had a drink that night, something she never normally did before shifts. A large glass of red before she left her flat, gulped down, and two cigarettes in succession. It was a stupid move, and she'd cleaned her teeth twice to cover any smell. *Another thing to blame that prick Fallon for.* She felt like charging him with wasting police time but, to be honest, it wasn't worth the paperwork.

'No point crying over spilt milk, girl,' she said aloud, lighting a cigarette at her desk, against all the rules. She took a long drag and put her feet up on the pile of statements next to her PC, feeling rebellious. That lazy sod Hunsdon was still off sick, meaning once again she was all alone. It was, she thought bleakly, the story of her life.

Her phone rang. If it was Fallon again she decided she'd give him a real earful, but it wasn't. It was Matt Turner.

'Christ, you're working late,' Tina said, blowing a line of smoke towards the ceiling.

'How about you? Anything happening on the old night shift?'

'The usual. Murder, robbery and mayhem. Don't tell me you've managed to have a look at that stick already.'

'I certainly have.'

'I'm sorry, I didn't mean to waste your time. The whole thing was a hoax. I should have told you earlier.'

'Really? That's odd.'

'Why?'

'Because the footage you gave me has been tampered with.'

Tina removed her feet from the desk and sat up in her seat, frowning. 'Are you sure?'

'Course I'm sure. It wasn't even a very good job. It was just spliced and thirty seconds were taken out. I managed to retrieve it as well.'

'And what did it show?'

'A man and a woman coming up to the front door.'

'Describe them.'

'The man was an IC1, early thirties, with dark curly hair. She was late twenties, blonde, and very attractive if I may say so.'

Rob Fallon and Jenny Brakspear. So something had happened. Tina felt a stab of excitement. 'Thanks, Matt,' she said. 'You've been a great help.'

'So, it wasn't a hoax?'

'I don't know yet. I'll keep you posted.' She rang off and stubbed out her cigarette, wide awake suddenly.

Straight away, she did what Mike Bolt had suggested when she'd talked to him earlier that afternoon. She logged on to the PNC database and fed in the details of the man most likely to have doctored the CCTV footage.

Forty-seven-year-old John Lionel Gentleman, the doorman at Jenny's apartment building, had eight separate convictions, mainly theft-related, and stretching back twenty years. Definitely the kind of man who could be bought.

The question that was really interesting Tina now was, if Gentleman was bought, who had done the buying?

Sixteen

I wasn't sure how long I was unconscious for. It could have been a few minutes, more likely it was an hour or two. It was impossible to tell because when I did finally open my eyes and clamber slowly to my knees, I was still quite drunk. My head felt like lead, and when I touched my forehead there was a big painful lump there. I looked round, waiting patiently while the room came into focus. There was no sign of Ramon. Nor any sign that he'd even been there.

I got to my feet and staggered into the bathroom and over to the toilet, experiencing a wave of nausea. I fell to my knees and threw the whisky up into the bowl in violent spasms, staying in that position for a long time, head bowed, taking deep, painful breaths.

Finally, I staggered back into the bedroom, trying hard not to picture Ramon sitting there lifeless, and lay down on the bed, staring up at the ceiling, knowing that I was incredibly lucky to be alive. Twice now I'd come within a hair's breadth of death, and twice I'd been given another chance to carry on. I knew that I should simply accept that this was a battle I'd lost and do what that callous saucer-eyed bastard had told me to do, because it was clear that he wouldn't hesitate to kill me if it came to it, not to mention my family.

I'm the type of person who avoids confrontation. I've always preferred the quiet life. Maybe that's why I gave up the frenetic pace of the City and tried my luck as a writer. But I also have a strong sense of justice. I know that it's essential that people do the right thing, because if we neglect that basic tenet, then society collapses. Some people say that in the UK we've started doing it already: crossing the street to avoid the kids hanging around outside the shop, refusing to intervene to stop rowdy behaviour. I've done it myself. I once saw a school kid about twelve years old being mugged by a group of older kids. They were making him empty out his pockets and one of them looked like he had a knife. The kid seemed terrified. He looked over towards me, trying to get my attention, but I turned away and kept walking. I did phone the police, but only once I'd got round the corner where the muggers couldn't see me.

I'd hated myself for that. Truly hated myself. I remember Yvonne asking me if anything was wrong that evening, and I was too ashamed to tell her about what had happened, because I knew that however much she might understand my actions, she'd be ashamed of me too. And if I did nothing now, I knew I would never be able to live with the guilt. It was as simple as that.

For some reason, Jenny Brakspear had been snatched as part of a conspiracy (and whatever Tina Boyd had claimed, it was a conspiracy) involving a total of three people, the kidnappers and the doorman – four, if Jenny's father was in on it too. And if they'd gone to that much trouble to take her, and to cover up their crime, then there was a very important reason behind their actions. Which meant that, unlike Ramon, there was a possibility Jenny was still alive.

Things were different now, though. The people who'd snatched

Jenny had shown me how utterly brutal they were. And how well organized. They'd found me with no trouble at all, and they knew that I'd talked to the police, which meant that if I continued on the path I'd chosen I was going to have to be a lot more careful in my approach. I also needed to make sure that no one else close to me got hurt. Yvonne and Chloe were OK for the next two weeks at least because they were away in Sweden, but Dom might not be.

I drank a glass of water, then called him on the mobile. I had to make sure he was safe, and the only way I could do that was if I stopped him worrying about Jenny.

He was out at dinner with clients, but excused himself so he could take the call. Taking a deep breath, I told him that I'd been drinking very heavily the previous night, that I'd been on medication for depression, and that my imagination had ended up playing tricks on me because I'd heard from Jenny this evening and she was fine.

At first, Dom was furious with me, not only for causing him a night of needless worry but also for getting drunk when I was on prescribed drugs. Eventually, though, he became more sympathetic, asking me how long I'd been depressed for and whether I was getting counselling. Keen to get him off the phone, I answered his questions as best I could, and he told me that we'd get together when he got back and try to sort out my problems. 'You've got to put the past behind you, Rob. Yvonne's gone. Think of the future and don't piss your life away.' I promised him I wouldn't and he signed off by saying that unless I pulled myself together I'd end up dead in a ditch somewhere. Utterly unaware how close that had already come to being a reality.

But at least he'd bought the story.

Now that I'd got rid of the only person who'd actually believed me, I was effectively on my own, and as I was an investment analyst turned writer, not a detective, this meant I needed some expert help.

I was still thinking what I was going to do about this when the landline started ringing. I sat up suddenly and my vision blacked out temporarily, taking several seconds to return. Still feeling pretty awful, I looked at my watch for the first time since Ramon had been killed, surprised to see that it was almost half past midnight. I reached for the receiver.

'Mr Fallon,' said Tina Boyd. 'Have you sobered up yet?'

I almost laughed at the sound of her voice. Even after everything that had happened, Tina Boyd still gave me confidence. But I was also aware that the man who'd come here tonight was no idiot and might have left behind some kind of bug to record any calls I made. It was time to start thinking like them.

I knew from research I'd done for *Conspiracy* that it was almost impossible for a private individual to bug a mobile, so right then it was my best bet.

'Can I call you back?' I said. 'Five minutes?'

'I'll be waiting,' she said, and cut the connection.

Seventeen

Tina was sitting at her desk drinking her third coffee of the night when Fallon called back.

'Where are you speaking from?' she asked him.

'I'm walking down my street.'

'Is it safe at this time of night?'

'A lot safer than my flat. I had a visit tonight.'

'What happened?'

'One of the kidnappers broke in and threatened me with a knife. He knew I'd been speaking to the police and he was the one who made me call you.'

'Which of them was it?'

'The Irish guy. The one who'd had the plastic surgery.'

'Can you give any further description of him? Something you may not have mentioned last night?'

'He had scarring round his chin. It looked a bit like someone had cut him with a bottle, but it wasn't that pronounced. I think the plastic surgery must have got rid of most of it, which makes me think that at one time he must have been hurt pretty badly.'

Tina frowned as she wrote down this information. It all seemed so improbable somehow, yet her initial suspicions that Fallon had indeed been telling the truth were turning out to be correct. 'This man didn't hurt you, did he?'

'No, but he left me in no doubt that he would if I carried on searching for Jenny. That's why I'm phoning you from four hundred yards down the road. I don't want anyone else listening in.'

'And are you sure you're not being followed now?'

'I'm being extra careful, I promise.'

'Glad to hear it. And don't worry. We can offer you protection if you need it.' But even as she said the words, Tina wondered if they actually could.

Fallon sighed. 'I think I'm going to need it. What did you find out that made you call me?'

She told him about the doctored CCTV footage and the door-man's criminal record.

'So, the bastard was involved.'

'Almost certainly, and that makes it a major criminal operation. If they're going to this much trouble and planning, then there's a very specific reason why they kidnapped Jenny. Her father claims that nothing's happened to her—'

'He's lying. He's got to be.'

'I agree. And I think he's lying because he's under duress, which means the kidnappers are in contact with him. But we still don't know why.'

'It's usually money, isn't it?'

'Usually, but I'd be surprised if it was in this case. I've got some background on Roy Brakspear. He's a widower who lost his wife to cancer five years ago, and he's the director and part owner of a reasonably profitable mid-sized company based in Cambridge which supplies raw materials to the pharmaceuticals and tech-nology sectors. He takes a salary of one hundred and seventy thousand pounds per year and he holds fifteen per cent of the company's shares, which if he sold them tomorrow would net him about three hundred thousand. He's not going to be hitting the poverty line any time soon, but it doesn't make him a rich man. So there's something else, and I think we need to focus on Brakspear himself to find out what it is.'

'What do you need me to do?' asked Fallon, sounding eager to help.

'Right now, nothing. Go back home, get some sleep and leave the investigating to us.'

'Are you going to take finding Jenny seriously now? She's been gone twenty-four hours, and I'm really worried about her.'

'We've got enough evidence to move on this now so, yes, we are going to take it seriously. And I'll keep you informed of progress too, you have my word on that. But I want you to promise me you're not going to speak to anyone about this. Because if you do, it could jeopardize our inquiry.'

Fallon said he wouldn't, and she ended the call, returning to the pile of witness statements for the stabbing on the Holloway Road that afternoon.

It made the usual grim reading. A loud argument between a bunch of school kids, insults thrown, followed by a flurry of fists and feet, then suddenly one of them pulls a knife and plunges it into his nearest opponent. A single stab wound to the chest, delivered without thought of the consequences, and now a fifteen-year-old was in a hospital bed fighting for his life. Tina had never become inured to the casual violence she had to deal with and she found incidents like this – petty, pointless disputes that ended so horrifically and with so much attendant suffering – profoundly depressing. The only positive was that it wasn't going to be difficult to ID the perpetrator. This meant that CID resources could be freed up to look for Jenny. Tina had now decided to speak to DCI

Knox about it as soon as she finished her shift. With Jenny missing for twenty-four hours now, time really was of the essence. It crossed her mind to go straight to the Met's Kidnap Unit but she knew they were snowed under with drugs-related cases and probably wouldn't take what she had that seriously. It would be easier if Knox referred it.

She yawned and reached for her cigarettes, deciding that she could probably get away with having one more at her desk, rather than puffing out of the toilet window. But as she lit it she saw an exhausted-looking DCI Knox approaching along the corridor. She'd just thrown the cigarette into the dregs of her coffee cup and deposited it under the table when he opened the door and came inside.

Knox was usually annoyingly upbeat and full of motivational psycho-babble, but tonight he didn't look very happy at all. 'Bad news,' he said wearily. 'Our stabbing's just become a murder. The kid died at midnight.'

Tina's heart sank. Not just because a fifteen-year-old had lost his life and a family would now be grieving, but also because of what it meant for Jenny Brakspear.

Tina would never get the resources she needed now.

Tuesday

Eighteen

When Tina Boyd was nineteen years old and in her first year at university, she was out drinking one night in one of the student union bars with some of the rowdier elements of her psychology course when some bright spark suggested they have a competition to see who could down a pint of lager the fastest. Two minutes later, eleven people – nine men, Tina, and a girl called Claire – had lined up along the bar with their drinks in front of them, while another of the girls acted as timekeeper.

The winning time, achieved by a sixteen-stone rugby-playing former public schoolboy called Josh, was six seconds. Second was Tina, in eight. No one else came close and five of the contestants didn't even finish theirs. Claire ended up with the head spins and had to go home.

That should have been that, but when Josh started bragging about his drinking prowess, Tina's competitive streak kicked in and she offered him a challenge. She would match him drink for drink for the course of the evening, with each of them choosing what to have in alternate rounds. In hindsight, it was a mind-numbingly stupid idea, since Josh was close to twice her weight, but Tina could be like that sometimes. Almost self-destructive in her determination.

Over the next two hours they downed tequilas, sambuccas, pints of bitter, even a Malibu and pineapple (surprisingly, Josh's choice). Tina's boyfriend begged her to stop. She hadn't. Not voluntarily anyway. Eventually she simply passed out in her seat and had to be taken back to her hall of residence, where she spent much of the night throwing up.

The next day, her boyfriend, a slightly built intellectual called Vernon, finished with her, claiming with exasperation that he couldn't go out with someone like her because she was out of control and simply didn't know when to stop. He was right, of course. He could have added that she never did things the easy way, either. It was why she'd got into so many scrapes down the years, both in her police career and beyond. Why she'd once ended up being taken hostage by a gunman and being shot in the ensuing crossfire, cheating death only by the angle of his gun.

But that was also only half the story, because the thing about Tina was she tended to get results. The shot that had hit her in the hostage incident was only a flesh wound and the man holding the gun to her head – the one she'd tracked down herself – was killed. After all the trials and tribulations of her adult life (and there'd been plenty) she was still standing, and she was still catching the bad guys, which meant she had to be getting something right.

So when DCI Knox rejected her request for permission to concentrate on the Jenny Brakspear kidnapping, she'd decided to go it alone. She'd gone to him at one of the few quiet moments in the shift, but as she reeled out what evidence she had it was clear he wasn't really listening. He'd switched off altogether when she was forced to tell him that not only was Jenny's father adamant she wasn't missing, but the man who'd made the initial report had since phoned in to claim that he'd been lying. Tina could understand

Knox's scepticism. In the end, policework is a firefighting exercise. You have to constantly prioritize. And cases don't get much bigger than the murder of a schoolboy.

When she left the station just after six that morning, walking exhausted into a bright orange dawn, the name of the murder suspect was already known; it was now simply a matter of building the case against him. Tina could leave her colleagues to deal with that. More important for her was to formulate a plan to gather more evidence to get either Knox or the Kidnap Unit interested, because one way or another Jenny Brakspear's time was running out.

As she drove the short distance home, smoking a cigarette, she knew she was going to need to sleep first, otherwise she'd be useless. But Rob Fallon could still make himself useful.

It was time to give him his wake-up call.

Nineteen

'There's been a change of plan.'

'What's happened?' I asked, squinting against the brightness of the early-morning sun. It was 6.45 a.m. and I was walking down my street in the direction of the park, having been woken from an extraordinarily deep slumber ten minutes earlier.

'I can't get the help I need on the Brakspear case.'

'Why the hell not?' I asked, wondering what you had to do to get police assistance these days.

'One, we've got a murder inquiry on, and that takes precedence. Two, we still haven't got any concrete proof that anything's actually happened.'

I started to protest, but Tina cut me short. 'Listen, Mr Fallon, you're preaching to the converted. I don't like it any more than you do. But for the moment, we've just got to accept that we're on our own.'

This was the second occasion on which I really should have told her about what had happened to Ramon. The fact that he'd been killed in my house would definitely get police attention. The problem was, in the absence of a body, or indeed even a suspect, it might be attention of the wrong kind. Once again, it would be my word against everyone else's. Maybe even Tina wouldn't believe me this time. So I kept quiet about it. 'OK,' I sighed. 'So what do we do now?'

'I think Roy Brakspear's involved, and he's operating under duress. We need to find out why. When I phoned him early yesterday morning, he was at home. What I want to do is plant a listening device inside his house.'

'Is that legal?'

'Let me worry about that. I know someone who can get me the kit I need but it'll probably take me some time. In the meantime, I want you to drive up there.'

'How do you know I've got a car?'

'I checked you out, Mr Fallon. It pays to know who you're dealing with.'

You had to hand it to her. She was coolly efficient – the kind of person both Jenny and I needed. But it was still vaguely disconcerting to discover how easily she could access the details of my life.

'I want you to do some low-level surveillance of Roy's home – I'll email you the address and directions. That means finding a spot where you're not going to look conspicuous or out of place, and watching it. I want to know if he's there or not, and if he is, if there's anyone there with him. He drives a silver Audi A4 saloon. If there are any other cars parked on his property, or just outside, make a note of their numbers and call me back with them straight away. I haven't got a clue about the layout of the place but if you feel you can get close to the house and have a look inside, do it, but on no account get yourself caught.' Her tone hardened. 'Do you understand that? Do nothing too risky and make sure your phone's turned off. And something else too: I'm putting my neck on the line for you here, so if the shit hits the fan and you get caught trespassing, don't mention my name. If you do, I'll deny we ever had this conversation.'

'What are you going to do?' I asked, feeling weirdly like one of the characters in my old book, *Conspiracy*.

'Get a few hours' sleep, then I'm going to track down those listening devices.'

'If you do manage to plant one and you find anything out, how are you going to tell your bosses without getting yourself implicated?'

'I'll think of something,' she said evenly. 'I always do.'

She took my email address and hung up, leaving me wondering what kind of police officer I was dealing with. I was hoping above all else it was one who got results, because otherwise it wasn't just Jenny's life on the line.

It was mine, too.

Twenty

The Brakspear family home was an imposing detached house on the edge of a village not far from Cambridge that must have been pretty once but which had recently had a business park tacked on to the end of it. I drove past the front entrance but the security gates were closed and a high redbrick wall on either side prevented me from seeing much beyond, so I drove on another hundred yards and parked in a quiet tree-lined lane running off the main road.

It was ten past ten, the journey having been an extremely slow one thanks to heavy traffic on the M11. No one had been tailing me, or if they had they were damn good at it, and I felt a renewed sense of determination as I got out of the car and breathed in the fresh country air. At last it seemed I was actually doing something worthwhile in the hunt for Jenny, and if I could do anything to bring to justice the bastard who'd murdered Ramon, any risk I took would be worth it.

But they weren't the only things driving me. It was also the feeling that, after years of doing little more than existing, unsure about what direction I was heading in, I was finally actually living again.

Although the front of Brakspear's house faced the business park (which I imagine must have pissed him off when it was built), this was partly compensated by the fact that the property also backed directly on to an open field, which bordered the lane I'd just parked in. I climbed over the fence and made my way along its outer edge until I came to the wall at the back of the house. It was lower here, just over head height, with thick, impenetrable-looking leylandii hedges looming on the other side.

I was reluctant to trespass, particularly as there was no obvious exit route, but it was also clear that I wasn't going to find out anything from where I was standing. I tried the back gate but it was locked. So, checking that my mobile was switched to silent, I took a couple of steps back and did a fairly decent impression of a running jump, hauling myself over the top of the wall and sliding down the other side, getting scratched and snagged by the foliage all the way. It wasn't the most dignified of entrances, and I had to crawl on my belly commando-style under the hedge in order to poke my head out the other side.

The garden was mainly well-kept lawn with a stone patio running along the back of the house, complete with a table and chairs and a large Australian-style gas barbecue. It wasn't as big as I imagined and only about twenty yards separated me from the patio doors. They were shut, as were all the windows, even though the day was sunny and already warm – twenty degrees at least. There was something else too. The curtains were drawn behind all but one of the windows on the ground floor, which seemed odd, especially if Brakspear was there.

I lay where I was for several minutes, watching the one window with no curtains for any sign of activity inside, but there was nothing, and I quickly found myself becoming bored. I've never been the patient type, so I crawled out from under the hedge and, staying on my belly, made my way over to a neatly trimmed waist-height privet hedge that ran along one wall towards the house. I got to my feet and, using it as cover, walked, crouching, towards a wooden gate that provided access to the front.

I paused for a moment, listening for any sound coming from the other side. I heard nothing, so I slowly opened the gate. There were two cars in the driveway. One was Brakspear's Audi A4. The other was a dark blue Mazda. I took a couple of steps forward so I could read the number plate and took a photo of it on my mobile phone.

There was a scrape on the gravel behind me.

Then, before I could turn round, a hand grabbed me tightly by the shoulder.

Twenty-one

'Who the hell are you?' demanded a well-built middle-aged man.

It had to be Roy Brakspear. He had exactly the same eyes as Jenny as well as the rounded nose. Although a big man, with a shock of curly grey hair, the aggression he was showing didn't look like it sat there naturally. He looked, it has to be said, like a nice guy, a typical middle-class dad in his fifties whose only vice was a little bit of over-indulgence where food was concerned.

'I'm a friend of Jenny's,' I said as firmly as I could, pulling away from his grip. 'I've been looking for her since Sunday night.'

His expression softened. 'Are you the lad who reported her missing?'

'Yes, I reported it,' I replied. 'And the police told me you said she went on holiday to Spain. But she was with me.'

He nodded, looking concerned. 'I thought she had, but it seems I was wrong.' He took my arm again, gently this time. 'Listen, you'd better come inside.'

Something wasn't right. I could sense it. Roy Brakspear was smiling at me but a bead of sweat was running down his forehead and he'd developed a tic in the dark patch below his left eye. He looked like he hadn't been sleeping much lately.

I had an awful feeling that if I went inside that house I might not come back out of it again. But I kept my cool. 'You need to speak to the police again, Mr Brakspear. I'll call them now.' I flicked open my mobile phone.

His smile immediately disappeared, and his grip on my arm tightened again. 'Let's do it from the house. Come on.'

Then he did a strange thing. He silently mouthed a word at me: 'Run.'

I tensed as the adrenalin pumped through me.

'You've come a long way,' he continued. 'You probably need a cup of tea or something. Then we can talk about what to do next. OK?'

Someone else was here somewhere. It was possible they were creeping up on me right now. Behind me the security gates were shut, and probably locked, and they were way too high to try to climb. That meant going back the way I'd come.

Different, conflicting emotions continued to scud across Brakspear's face like clouds. Doubt. Confusion. Sympathy. Fear.

In one sudden movement, I broke free from his grip and bolted past him, heading for the back garden. He made a surprisingly violent grab for my shirt, ripping it, but there was no way I was stopping for anyone and I kept going, stuffing the mobile in my pocket, seeing the boot sticking out behind the wall at the last possible moment.

The big shaven-headed thug – the one with the London accent from Jenny's apartment – suddenly appeared from where he'd been hiding round the corner wielding a heavy-looking ball-peen hammer. But I'd had a split second's notice of his hiding place, and that was enough. Lowering my head and fuelled by a surge of adrenalin, I charged him like a bull, hitting him hard in the stomach. I felt a stab of pain in my lower back as he caught me with the hammer, but he stumbled back and I managed to knock him out of the way, flailing my arms wildly to try to keep him off balance. I found myself pointing in the direction of the privet hedge and I charged right through it, making for the end of the garden, head down, like a sprinter.

I took a quick look round. Shaven Head was running across the lawn parallel to me, moving particularly fast for a man so big. He held the ball-peen hammer like a tomahawk, a furious expression on his face. He was trying to cut off my escape. I clenched my teeth, willing myself to go faster.

The hammer flew straight at me, spinning through the air, the aim perfect. I ducked, and it skimmed the top of my head, actually parting my hair.

Immediately, Shaven Head began fumbling in the waistband of his jeans. I didn't know what he had down there, but I could guess. Shit! Shit! Shit! Staring straight ahead, I charged into the leylandii and, finding a strength and agility I never knew I had, literally scrambled up the wall, diving headfirst down the other side and doing a painful somersault on to the path.

This time I didn't turn round. I was on my feet in a second and racing for the car, and freedom.

Twenty-two

The call from Rob Fallon came through at 10.38 according to the alarm clock by Tina's bed, and it woke her from a deep slumber – for the second time in twenty-four hours.

He started talking as soon as she picked up. 'We've got a problem. I was caught at Brakspear's place. I only just got out.'

Tina listened in silence as Fallon poured out his story. He was talking ten to the dozen and it was clear he was still full of adrenalin.

'That's all we need,' she said when he'd finished. 'What did I tell you about not getting caught?'

'I know, but I've never done this sort of thing before. I did get a photo of the other guy's car on my phone, though. With the registration number.'

'Good. Text it to me as soon as you're off the phone.' She sat up in bed and stretched. 'How about you? Are you OK?'

'I've got a few cuts and bruises, but it could have been a lot worse.'

It almost had been. Tina knew she should never have sent him. It was always better to do these things yourself.

'Where are you now?' she asked him.

'About ten minutes away from Brakspear's house, heading back to the M11. Trying to put as much distance between me and them as possible.'

'I want you to go back.'

'What? Why?' He sounded stunned.

'Because now you've disturbed them they're probably going to want to get Brakspear out of there as soon as possible. If they haven't, and he's still there, then I think we're going to have to call in the cavalry.'

'Won't that put Jenny in danger, though?' he asked.

Tina sighed. It was a good question. 'Let me think about that,' she said, 'but right now, I want you to check if they're still there. Don't put yourself at risk or get out of the car. Just drive past and see if the Mazda's still at the front of the house. Then call me back straight away. OK?'

He said he would, although he didn't sound too enthusiastic about the prospect, and they ended the call.

Tina got out of bed and had a quick shower to wake herself up. She was pissed off with herself. This whole thing was running out of control. She was making decisions on the hoof because she was on her own and racing against the clock. She'd dealt with a kidnapping the previous year at SOCA when a fourteen-year-old girl, Emma Devern, had been abducted for ransom. That case had almost turned into tragedy, and that was with the full resources of SOCA concentrated on finding her. Now she was trying to do everything on her own and, to put it bluntly, she'd screwed up. The question was, what did she do now?

Fallon called back fifteen minutes later as she was making coffee. 'The Mazda's gone. Brakspear's car's still there.'

It was as she'd expected. There was no way the kidnappers could have stayed put with Fallon free. But it also made things harder.

'OK,' she said, weighing things up. 'Have you got anywhere you can stay for a few days? Somewhere you can lie low while we work out what to do?'

'Wouldn't it be easier if I just walked into a police station and asked for protection? This thing's getting too big for us now.'

'It would be if they believed you, but I'm not a hundred per cent sure they would.'

'Why not? We've got proof, haven't we? I saw one of Jenny's kidnappers at her father's house. Surely that means they've got her?'

'But you've already withdrawn your story once. If Brakspear was still at his house and we knew he was being held against his will, then we'd be able to get the police involved. But he's gone, and it's going to take a massive effort to convince the people who matter that they need to investigate. By that time, Jenny could be dead.'

'But we don't know for certain that the kidnapper took Brakspear with him. Maybe I could go back to the house and talk to him, persuade him to—'

'Mr Fallon,' Tina interrupted, 'do you honestly believe that after your unscheduled appearance the kidnapper hasn't taken Brakspear with him?'

Her words silenced him temporarily. When he finally spoke, he sounded weary. 'You say don't go to the police, just lie low for a while, but for how long? And what are we going to do in the meantime?'

'We need to change tactics,' she said quietly. 'Up the ante a little.'

'How?'

'Leave it with me. I've got a few calls to make, then I'll get back to you. In the meantime, stay away from home.'

'Don't leave it too long, DC Boyd.' Fallon sounded angry and frustrated, and Tina couldn't blame him. 'Pretty soon, the guy who threatened to kill me is going to know that I didn't heed his warning, and he's not going to give me a second chance. I'm a target now.'

'Killing you will only risk drawing attention to themselves, so try to keep calm.'

There was a long pause at the other end before Fallon said something about keeping calm being a lot easier said than done. Then he cut the connection.

Poor sod, thought Tina. She felt bad for putting him in such a precarious position, but knew too that what she'd said about the likely police scepticism if he requested protection was true. Even so, she felt she needed guidance on a way forward. She hadn't wanted to involve Mike Bolt but no longer felt she had any choice. He also had the resources to track down Brakspear's location, using either his mobile number or the registration plate of the mysterious Mazda that had been on his drive that morning, and which was soon going to be on Tina's own phone.

Mike wasn't answering. She left a message asking her to call him urgently, then lit a cigarette. She had a plan B, one that she'd been formulating in the shower, but it was risky, and she'd hoped she wouldn't have to use it.

She looked at her watch. It had just turned eleven, and the clock was ticking inexorably onwards. She'd give Mike until 11.30 to call her back. If he didn't, she knew she'd simply have to take her chances.

There was no other way.

Twenty-three

Where I was going to lay my head was a problem, and one I
thought about for most of the journey back to London. Under
normal circumstances I would have gone to Dom, but he was away
until the following day and I'd promised myself that I wouldn't
involve him now. There was always Yvonne and Chloe (and Nigel,
of course), but they were away too, and even if they'd been back at
home in France I'd never have risked hurting them by my presence.

There wasn't really anyone else. Not even family-wise. My mum
had died when I was fifteen after a long and protracted battle
against cancer. My older brother lived in New Zealand, where he'd
been for most of the last decade, and my dad now lived with my
stepmother (a pleasant woman, it has to be said) in South Africa.
So I was pretty much on my own.

It crossed my mind to try Maxwell, but he'd only ask too many
questions, and I really didn't want to have to tell him anything.

In the end, I decided to go online and find a cheap hotel somewhere in the sprawling anonymity of the West End, where I wasn't
going to be found.

First, though, I needed to eat. Hardly a thing had passed my lips in the last forty-eight hours, and anything that had had come straight back up again. I was in dire need of sustenance. When I got back into north London, I headed south until I found a suitably grimy-looking café on the Edgware Road where I consumed a huge fry-up of bacon, sausage, black pudding and just about anything else greasy and coronary-inducing they could fling on the plate, washed down with orange juice and two cups of strong coffee.

After I'd polished off the lot, I sat back and relaxed for the first time since all this started. True, I was in the most serious danger I'd been so far, because the people I was up against must now want me dead, whatever Tina Boyd might be saying to the contrary. But at that moment in time, in a busy café far from my usual haunts, it didn't feel that way. It felt instead like I was doing something good, something worthwhile. Maybe for the first time in my life.

Maybe this was the reason I was throwing myself so whole-heartedly into the hunt for a girl who, in reality, I hardly knew. Maybe, too, a part of me enjoyed the adventure. I've travelled the world and visited other cultures. Dived with sharks on the Barrier Reef; travelled up the Amazon in a steamboat; climbed to the summit of Kilimanjaro. But all those things are sanitized adventures. Now I was doing something that was truly risky – suicidal some might say, given that I was unarmed and untrained. But I didn't care. If I got through it in one piece and found out what had happened to Jenny, then at the very least Yvonne might think there was more to me than she'd always thought.

I was on the way back to the car, having paid my bill, when Tina called. I looked at my watch. Twenty past one.

'I want to escalate things, Mr Fallon,' she told me, 'and I'm going to need your help.'

There was a grim seriousness to her tone that I hadn't heard before. 'OK,' I said uncertainly, stopping by the car.

'I'll be totally honest with you. It's potentially going to put you in a lot of danger.'

'I'm already in a lot of danger,' I said, sounding braver than I felt. 'What is it?'

I listened as she gave me the details, and when she'd finished she asked me if I was prepared to go through with it. 'Right now, I believe this is our best way forward,' she added. 'I'll keep the situation under review and if we get any hard evidence of what's happened then I'll bring it straight to my colleagues, and get you full protection.'

I could hear my heart beating hard in my chest as I thought about what was being asked of me.

'You don't have to do it,' she said, then paused. 'The ball's in your court.'

I thought of Jenny. I thought of Ramon. I had no choice. 'Let's go for it.'

Twenty-four

John Gentleman, the doorman on duty at Jenny Brakspear's apartment building the night she was abducted, lived in a grimy-looking three-storey tenement building in one of the less attractive parts of Hackney which backed on to a well-used railway bridge. Unlike Jenny's place, there was no security door, and Tina walked straight inside.

Gentleman's flat was on the second floor and Tina didn't meet anyone on the walk up. The flooring in the corridor outside was cheap linoleum and she moved quietly along it, trying to remain as casual as possible. She stopped at his door and put her ear against it, hearing nothing beyond. The door was protected by three separate locks – no surprise in a place as rundown as this, where drug-related burglary was bound to be common, and no real obstacle to someone who knew what he or she was doing.

During her time in SOCA, Tina had learned to break into buildings quickly and efficiently. It was all part of the job. Most people didn't realize that it was perfectly legal for the authorities to break in and bug any property if they had grounds to believe that the individuals living there were committing serious crime.

But as Tina got to work on the new five-bar lock using a small set of hand picks from her SOCA days, she knew that what she was doing would cost her her job immediately if she was caught. It didn't deter her. Nor was it the first time she'd been in this position, breaking the laws she was meant to uphold. It wasn't that Tina didn't believe in the rule of law. She did – broadly speaking, anyway – but she'd also seen its weaknesses at first hand. Justice wasn't always done, and the wrong people sometimes walked free. Paul Wise, her lover's murderer, was a glaring example of this, and she used him as her justification whenever she bent the rules, as she was doing now. She hadn't wanted to go this far, though. It was only because she still hadn't heard from Mike Bolt, even though she'd left a second message on his voicemail, that she'd reluctantly concluded that she had to act on her own.

The five-bar took nearly two minutes to open. She was out of practice, and she also had to work hard to keep quiet and calm, knowing that she could be disturbed at any time. Across the corridor she could hear rap music playing and the sound of voices shouting at each other, and she was sweating by the time she finished.

The other two locks were older and less sturdy and took her thirty seconds between them. Then, after a final listen at the door, she opened it and slipped inside, feeling a rush of illicit excitement.

She found herself in a small, sparsely decorated living room. At the far end a door was partly ajar and beyond it she could hear soft snoring. John Gentleman was clearly out for the count. She shut the front door, spotting his landline handset on the mantelpiece next to a photo of a young girl of about five or six in school uniform, smiling at the camera. This would be his granddaughter, Tegan. Tina had done her research on Gentleman. He lived alone, having divorced eight years earlier. The sight of his granddaughter suddenly made her feel guilty, because it brought home to her exactly what she was doing.

Forcing herself to concentrate, she crept across the room and peered round the bedroom door. Gentleman was flat out on his back in a pair of baggy boxer shorts, the covers half off him. Tina glanced round the room, looking for any other handsets, but there weren't any. This was good. It made her task easier.

Retreating into the living room, shutting the door as much as she could, she picked up the handset from the mantelpiece and took the back off it. Then she reached into her jacket and pulled out a thin piece of plastic about three inches long and less than half an inch wide, which she inserted into a space inside. This was a handset tilt switch, a phone-tapping device with a tiny mike and its own power source which would activate automatically as soon as the handset was lifted up and would record every conversation made on it until the battery flattened. Tina had picked it up on the way over here. It wasn't exactly cutting edge, and could be detected easily by someone who knew what he was doing, but she knew Gentleman wouldn't know so it served her purpose well enough.

Having put the handset back together and replaced it on the mantelpiece, she took a pay-as-you-go mobile phone she'd picked up earlier from Carphone Warehouse from the same pocket. She switched it on and attached its hands-free kit before placing it in the corner of the room behind the TV, where it wouldn't be seen. This was her back-up listening device, in case the handset tilt switch didn't function properly. Although only a cheap standard phone, she'd made some alterations to the settings menu on the way over, turning off the ringer tone and setting it to auto answer, which would turn it into an open mike as soon as she called the number and allow her to listen in on anything said in the room. Even now, she was still taken aback by how easy it was to eavesdrop on people. Gentleman would no doubt discover the phone eventually, but by then she would have the information she wanted and there would be no way of tracing it back to her.

She left the flat as quietly as she'd entered it, using the picks to relock the door. Then, keeping her head down to remain as inconspicuous as possible, she walked back to the car. It was only when she was inside with a cigarette in her mouth that she allowed herself a small smile for a job well done.

She pulled out her mobile. It was ten to two, and still no call from Mike. Time, then, to put the plan into action.

She called Rob Fallon. 'Go for it,' she told him, before disconnecting.

Then she switched on the receiver, connecting to the handset tilt switch in Gentleman's phone, put in her earpiece and waited.

Twenty-five

I was standing in a phone box on the Edgware Road when I got the call from Tina. As soon as she'd hung up I picked up the receiver, took a deep breath, and dialled John Gentleman's landline number.

It rang for a long time before going to message. I didn't leave one, just counted to five and called again.

This time he answered, sounding groggy and pissed off. 'Who's this?'

I took a deep breath, then spoke clearly and slowly, as Tina had instructed. 'John Gentleman, I know that you're involved in the kidnap of Jenny Brakspear who lives in the apartment building where you work. You provided the kidnappers with a key to get into her apartment, you broke the security camera at the exit to the underground car park so they could get back out, you cleaned up after them—'

'I don't know what you're talking about!' he shouted, but there was uncertainty in his voice.

'You do, and if you admit it to me now and tell me who the kidnappers are, then I'll make sure your name doesn't get mentioned.'

'I told you: I don't know what you're fucking talking about!'

'You know they're going to kill her, don't you? And when they kill her, you're going to be an accessory to murder, and that means years behind bars. And you know exactly what that's like, don't you?'

'Who the fuck are you?'

'The one person who can help you. You've only got one chance to get out of this, Mr Gentleman, and that's to cooperate. Tell the police who you're working for, otherwise I'm going to spend every waking hour for the rest of my life building a case against you, and I'll make sure you go down for murder. Do you understand me?'

'You're that bloke who was with her, aren't you? Well, you listen to me! You can't prove a fucking thing! All right? And you're a dead fucking man messing around in stuff that doesn't concern you!'

'We'll see,' I said, and cut the connection.

Now there was absolutely no way back.

I called Tina. 'It's done.'

'I know,' she said, 'I heard you. Very menacing. Now we'll see what he does.'

Twenty-six

It didn't take Gentleman long to react. As Tina listened, he made a call out from the landline, just as she'd hoped. Unfortunately, she had no way of knowing the number he was calling, but that didn't matter. If necessary, she could contact the phone company and find that information out later.

There was no answer at the other end, just an automated voice asking him to leave a message.

'I've just had a call from that bloke who saw you at the flat on Sunday night,' said Gentleman breathlessly into the phone. 'The bastard's threatening to go to the law and turn me in. This whole thing's getting out of fucking hand. You've got to do something because I ain't taking the rap for it. Call me back ASAP, OK? I'm at home.' He reeled out the number. 'I'm getting very worried here, and if I don't hear back from you soon I'm going to go to the law myself!' He slammed the handset back in its cradle, and the tilt switch stopped recording.

Tina exhaled. She'd just heard the final proof that the kidnapping had actually occurred. Now she knew she had to do something. Unfortunately, by illegally tapping Gentleman's phone she'd put herself in a difficult position. If she went with the recording to DCI Knox, or the Kidnap Unit, she was going to have to answer some very inconvenient questions. But if she didn't . . . If she didn't, it might cost Jenny Brakspear her life.

Tina suddenly felt completely alone. She knew who she needed to speak to. But the one person who'd be able to get her out of this predicament and move things forward without her losing her job was currently off the radar.

'Where the hell are you, Mike?' she whispered, staring out of the windscreen towards Gentleman's apartment block.

She stubbed out her cigarette, took a drink from a bottle of mineral water on the seat next to her, and phoned Bolt for a third time. Once again he didn't pick up. Once again she left a message, except this time she said that the kidnapping had definitely occurred and that she needed his help desperately. She cursed herself afterwards for using that word. It made her feel weak. Yet, if truth be told, she was feeling pretty desperate.

She wondered what Gentleman was doing, and phoned the mobile she'd left behind his sofa, prefixing the number with 141, so that Gentleman wouldn't be able to trace the call back to her own mobile on the off-chance he discovered the handset before she had a chance to retrieve it. It auto-answered and went to open mike. She could hear movement inside the apartment. It sounded like he was pacing up and down, but the reception wasn't very good. He was definitely panicking, and it crossed her mind to knock on his door, show him her warrant card and wait to hear what he had to say. But there was no guarantee that he could help locate Jenny, or even ID the people who'd taken her.

So, sweating in the heat of the day, Tina sat in her car and pondered her next move while listening to Gentleman as he moved about in his apartment. He occasionally let slip an angry muffled curse, but soon she grew bored of listening to nothing and ended the call. The street was deadly quiet, only the occasional car and pedestrian appearing, and after a while she shut her eyes and dozed off.

She was woken with a start by the rumble of an engine, and as she opened her eyes she saw a dark blue Toyota Land Cruiser with blacked-out windows drive slowly past before pulling up on the other side of the road about twenty yards up from Gentleman's place.

A white man in dark glasses and a baseball cap got out the passenger side and took the briefest of glances up and down the street. The day was warm, mid-twenties and humid, yet he was still wearing a jacket, and even from twenty yards away Tina could see that the pale, almost translucent skin of his face was stretched tight from plastic surgery.

It was the kidnapper who'd threatened Rob.

She grabbed her Nikon camera from the seat beside her and started taking pictures. She managed to get several good ones in profile before the suspect turned and started walking in the direction of Gentleman's flat. She turned her attention to the Land Cruiser, getting a shot of its number plate as the driver accelerated away and disappeared under the railway bridge.

The suspect walked up to Gentleman's building, paused for just one second, and then went directly inside.

Tina tensed, listening. A part of her was pleased. She'd got a photo of one of the kidnappers, and given the way he looked it shouldn't be too hard to put a name to him. But another part of her was extremely concerned, because the manner of his arrival, and his demeanour and appearance, suggested he wasn't here to bolster Gentleman's morale.

She looked at her watch, made a mental note of the time – 2.45 – and phoned the mobile in the flat again, listening as it was auto-answered at the other end.

For the first few seconds there was silence. Then she heard a faint knock on the door, and the sound of footfalls. Gentleman said 'Who is it?' but Tina couldn't hear any reply. There was the sound of the door being unlocked, then Gentleman said something else, but this time it was unintelligible.

And then nothing. Not a sound for at least ten seconds. She thought she heard the door closing again, but couldn't be sure.

Tina frowned. Keeping the phone to her ear, she picked up the Nikon with her free hand.

Thirty seconds passed before she heard the deep engine rumble of the Land Cruiser. She watched in her wing mirror as it drove by her for a second time, heading back in the direction of the railway bridge. As the vehicle reached Gentleman's building, the driver slowed. A second later, the man in the cap and sunglasses walked out the front door.

Tina flinched. He was alone. Where the hell was Gentleman?

She dropped the phone, zoomed in with the Nikon and got off a couple more shots as he opened the passenger door, keeping his head down. As the Land Cruiser pulled away for a second time, Tina picked up the phone again and heard nothing but silence coming from Gentleman's apartment. She began to get an ominous feeling in the pit of her stomach.

She looked up at the second-floor windows. Nothing was moving up there. Cursing, she called Gentleman's landline. It rang and rang, finally going to message. She looked up his mobile number in her notebook and called that. It went to message too.

Either he was no longer at home or, far more likely, he was dead. Tina knew she'd miscalculated. If Gentleman had been killed, there was no way of avoiding the fact that it was her fault, because she was the one who'd set events in motion. 'Shit,' she whispered, 'what have I done?' She knew the answer: she'd acted like an amateur, and now the repercussions were going to be enormous.

She was still professional enough to know that she had some extremely valuable evidence in her possession, however. She pulled her laptop from under the passenger seat, plugged the camera into it, and watched as the photos she'd just taken downloaded. She then opened up her email account and sent the photos to Rob Fallon's and Mike Bolt's email addresses with the same message for both – Do you recognize this man? – before signing out and replacing the laptop under the seat.

There was no point phoning Bolt – she'd left enough messages for him already – so she called Fallon instead, asking him where he was.

'In the West End, looking for a hotel room. What's happening?'

'I'll give you a full briefing later. In the meantime, get into your email account. I've just sent you some photos. Download them on to a USB stick but don't show them to anyone until you hear from me. Understand?'

'Sure,' answered Fallon. He started to say something else but Tina said she'd phone him in an hour, and ended the call.

She stretched in her seat and sighed. What the hell was she going to do now?

Then the passenger door opened and the man in the cap and sunglasses climbed inside, holding a short-barrelled pistol with a silencer attached. 'Start driving now,' he said calmly, 'or you're dead.'

Twenty-seven

Mike Bolt was shattered. He hated inter-departmental meetings at the best of times, but when they dragged on and on, as this one with the people from the Financial Intelligence Unit had, they truly pissed him off. He, Mo Khan, his own boss, Big Barry Freud, and three other members of the team had gone into the meeting room at half past ten that morning and were only just emerging now, almost four and a half hours later, at five to three. Lunch had been sandwiches that tasted of plastic, eaten at the table while various people had continued to drone on, and now Bolt's back was aching badly and he was still hungry.

'Is it just me,' he asked Mo as they walked back to the team office, 'or are we in exactly the same place with Paul Wise as we were four hours ago?'

'I don't know,' answered Mo, sounding dazed. 'I'm too tired to think. But I wouldn't bet on an arrest being imminent.'

Bolt grunted, switching his phone off silent. 'My sentiments exactly.'

The meeting had been a hugely detailed rehash of what was in the report. There'd been the usual promises of greater cooperation between the various departments within SOCA, but aside from a few recommendations from the FIU people, who were going to put a degree of pressure on the various people involved in converting Paul Wise's money from dirty to clean, there was still no plan for bringing him to justice, or even curtailing his activities.

As far as Bolt was concerned, there were way too many meetings in SOCA and it was slowing them all down. Not for the first time in these past few months he hankered for a return to the good old days when he was part of the Met's Flying Squad, facing the comparatively straightforward task of chasing down armed robbers. At least you knew where you were with them.

The phone bleeped and he saw he had three messages, all from Tina Boyd. He wondered what was so urgent that she'd called that many times. As he listened to them, he realized that there had clearly been some major developments in the kidnap case she'd spoken to him about the previous day. Still, he was surprised she wanted to talk to him about it rather than her bosses at Islington CID.

He pressed call-back but it said her phone was switched off, which seemed odd if she was so keen to get hold of him. He sighed, hoping she hadn't got herself into trouble, knowing it wouldn't be the first time. Tina had a habit of relying heavily on her initiative and being prepared to go it alone on investigations, and occasionally she wasn't very good at judging when to stop. The positive side to this was that she usually got results. But, he thought grimly, it wasn't always such a positive if she was out there alone, dealing with the wrong kind of people.

'Anything the matter, boss?' asked Mo as they got back to the office.

'Nothing exciting,' Bolt replied, unsure about how much to tell Mo, who'd never got on that well with Tina, and who probably wouldn't approve of him encouraging her to follow up on her leads.

Although the team worked in an open-plan office, Bolt had his own small room at the far end. He went in there now and tried Tina's number a second time. Still switched off. He sat back at his desk and opened up his email screen on the PC.

There were ten new messages from various people, which was about average, but straight away he saw that the most recent one was from Tina, and that it had been sent just ten minutes ago. He opened it and read the message: Do you recognize this man?

There were five photos attached. He double-clicked on the first one. It was a profile shot of a man in a cap and sunglasses. The quality was good – Bolt could see that the skin on his pale face was tight, as if he'd had plastic surgery – but the subject was clearly well disguised. The second shot was similar but with less of the subject's face showing. The third was of the back of a Toyota Land Cruiser on a residential street. He took down its registration number, wishing Tina had given a bit more of an explanation in her email as to what this was all about. Then he opened photo number four.

This one was a close-up, full-frontal shot of the man in the cap and sunglasses from the chest upwards. He was trying to keep his head down and wasn't looking at the camera, but even so, there was something familiar about him. Bolt expanded the photo until it filled the screen, then focused on the pale face. It looked like the man had suffered burns at one time because the plastic surgery looked more like repair work than anything cosmetic. He zoomed in on the chin. The quality got worse, the picture beginning to blur, but a rectangle of skin lined with scar tissue remained distinctive. It was about half the size of a credit card and much fainter than it had been before, but unmistakable nonetheless.

Bolt felt a physical jolt. He took a deep breath and zoomed out again so that he was back to just the face. 'Jesus, it can't be,' he whispered. 'Not you.'

He turned away from the screen and called out to Mo.

'Is this who I think it is?' he asked, turning the monitor round as Mo came into the office.

Mo stared at the picture for a long time.

'It's him, isn't it?' said Bolt, zooming in again and pointing out the scar.

'It is,' said Mo at last. 'It's Hook. Who sent you this?'

Bolt's throat felt dry as he answered. 'Tina Boyd. About ten minutes ago. I'm guessing she was the one who took the photo.'

'Have you spoken to her yet?'

Bolt shook his head. 'No. Her phone's switched off. I just tried it.'

'Do you know when she took it?'

'No, but I'm guessing it was probably today. And here in London.'

Mo whistled through his lips. 'So Hook's back in town. There's got to be a very good reason why he'd risk his neck to be back here.'

Bolt dialled Tina's mobile again. It was still off.

'Well, whatever it is,' he said, 'I'm truly hoping he hasn't crossed paths with Tina. Because if he has . . .'

He let the sentence trail off. They both knew all too well what Hook was capable of.

Twenty-eight

Tina stared straight ahead as she drove through the streets of Hackney in the direction of the A12, as per the gunman's instructions, making absolutely sure that she avoided any eye contact, not wanting to give him an excuse to put a bullet in her.

She was trying to remain as calm as possible but it was damn hard, and she could feel herself sweating as she tried to figure out how to get out of this situation. She'd been in tight corners before, facing the wrong end of a gun, and had come out of them in one piece, but there was no guarantee that it would happen again, and she had a very bad feeling about the man next to her. Most criminals, even the well-organized professional ones, tended to exhibit signs of nerves, particularly when they were pointing a gun at someone, but this guy was sitting there with an almost Zen-like calmness, and in Tina's experience that made him extremely dangerous.

She stopped at a busy junction as the lights went red. Outside the car window the street was thronged with passers-by swarming around one another like ants, only feet away, yet as good as a million miles. No one looked at Tina, or caught her eye. A group of schoolchildren crossed in front of the car, one of them scraping his bag against the bonnet. They were so close she could hear their banter – heard one of them call his friend a name. She tensed, looking for the right moment to make her move.

'I know what you're thinking,' he said, and once again his thick Northern Irish accent sounded strange to Tina. It didn't really fit with the delicate, almost feminine features of his face. 'You're thinking that now's a good time to make a break for it. That I won't dare shoot you in broad daylight with a lot of people around. And I can understand that. But I'm afraid you'd be making a big mistake. You'd never even get a hand on the handle before I put a bullet in your heart. The rounds in this pistol are low-velocity so there'd be no exit wound, no smashed windows. And, with this suppressor, no noise. You know how impersonal London is, the way its citizens hurry on by minding their own business. I guarantee no one will have any idea that you've just been murdered.'

Tina didn't say anything. He'd read her thoughts. The lights turned green, and any chance she'd had (and in truth there had been none) was gone. She pulled away, indicating right.

'So, pretty lady, who are you? And what were you doing taking photos of me?'

She knew she was going to have to play this carefully. If she said the wrong thing, she was dead. 'My name's Tina Boyd, and I'm a police officer.'

'And what were you doing on that street? You can't have known I'd be coming by, so you must have been there for a reason. What is it?'

Tina knew there was no point lying. Not now. 'I was watching a property.'

'Ah, the one belonging to our friend Mr Gentleman, I'll wager.'

'That's right.'

'Interesting.'

'Look,' she said with as much confidence as she could muster, 'you may as well give yourself up. It's the best way.'

The man let out a low chuckle, his lips hardly moving. 'Now why would I want to do that? You appear to be unarmed and in no position to threaten me, and any colleagues you might have don't appear to be – how shall I put it? – beating a path to your door.' He turned round in his seat and looked through the back window. 'Do they?'

Again, Tina spoke with a confidence she didn't feel. 'My colleagues know where I am and they're on the way.'

'Is that right? And is it them you were talking to on your mobile phone just now?'

'Yes, so I really wouldn't do anything stupid. They'll throw away the key if anything happens to me.'

'I think, my love, that they would throw away the key if they caught me anyway. I've already killed one person today.' Out of the corner of her eye she could see him regarding her, his thin lips forming a tight smile. 'Our mutual friend, Mr Gentleman. How long do you think I'll get for snuffing him out?'

Tina stiffened. She thought of the photo of Gentleman's granddaughter on the mantelpiece.

'He was a pain in the arse,' continued the man with the gun, enjoying her reaction, leaning forward now so his mouth was right next to her ear, stroking the gun against her belly. 'I'd like to have finished him off more slowly – it's always more . . . satisfying that way – but I didn't have the time.'

He ran his lips across her earlobe, licking and nibbling it. 'Give me your phone,' he whispered gently. 'And don't hesitate or I'll kill you.'

Tina's skin was crawling but she refused to allow herself to flinch or pull away. Prising one hand from the wheel, she took it out of her pocket and handed it over.

As he flipped open the cover and began scrolling through the menu, Tina came to a halt behind stationary traffic at the next junction, and once again she thought about escape. It was a huge risk as this bastard definitely wasn't bluffing. But it was an even bigger one staying put, because she was pretty damn sure he wasn't going to let her live.

'Ah, so you weren't talking to your colleagues when I arrived. You were talking to another of our mutual friends, Mr Fallon. Now, he really is a pain in the arse. Are you sure you're a police officer? You wouldn't be joshing me now, would you?' His tongue flicked out like a lizard's, wetting his lips.

Then, without warning, he lunged forward, forcing the gun between her legs so that the end of the silencer was pushed hard against her groin. 'What's going on?' he demanded, his eyes boring into the side of her face. 'Tell me or I'll shoot you right here, right now.'

'I'm moonlighting,' Tina answered with an unavoidable flinch, staring straight ahead, only vaguely aware of the world outside. 'Doing work for Fallon.'

'Interesting. He really is very persistent.'

As the traffic began to move again, he switched the phone off, snapped off the cover with his teeth, pulled out the SIM card and pocketed it, then opened the window and threw out the pieces.

Tina cursed inwardly. This guy knew what he was doing, getting rid of the one item that could be used to trace her.

He picked up the Nikon. 'Now, these photos you took. Did you send them to Mr Fallon?'

'No,' she said firmly, hoping fervently that he hadn't been watching her car when she sent the photos on the laptop. She was just trying to stay alive now, hoping that if he didn't think she'd done that much to ID him he might let her go. It was a long shot, but when you've got a gun thrust between your legs, you tend to cling to long shots.

The man with the gun deleted the photos from the Nikon with his free hand and casually tossed it out of the window.

A bead of sweat ran down Tina's eyelid and into her eye. She blinked it away angrily. 'That camera cost me five hundred pounds,' she said coldly.

'If you hadn't been snooping around in other people's business, you wouldn't have lost it.'

She wiped her forehead, feeling a desperate urge for a cigarette. 'Do you mind if I smoke?'

'You've a gun pressed into your cunt and you're thinking about your next cigarette?' He chuckled again. 'You've got spirit, my love. I like that. Go on then.'

Tina reached down and pulled the pack and the lighter from where they were nestled in the cup holder. 'Do you want one?'

'No thanks. I prefer more enjoyable vices.'

He slipped the gun out from between her legs and rubbed it gently up and down her thighs, never taking his eyes off her.

Ignoring his gaze, Tina lit a cigarette and took a long drag, knowing that it was essential she keep talking to him. It was always more difficult to kill someone when you'd established a connection with them, although this guy sounded like he might well be the exception to the rule.

'Have you noticed something?' she asked him.

'What?' He sounded interested.

'I haven't looked at you once. I haven't seen your face.'

'You took those photos of me, didn't you?'

'From a distance, and with you wearing sunglasses and a cap. I can't describe you. Also, I've got no incentive to go to the police. I got Fallon to call Gentleman to try to panic him, so if you've killed him, then that's my fault. In other words, I'm going to keep quiet. So, rather than kill me and open up a whole world of shit, you might as well let me go. I'll get out of the car and I won't say another word to anyone. I promise.'

Out of the corner of her eye she saw his smile widen a little.

'Thanks for the advice,' he said, 'but it's OK.' He leaned forward again, running his nose softly up her neck. Sniffing. 'I'm quite enjoying the company.'

'What are you going to do to me?' she asked, trying hard to keep her voice even, more frightened than she'd been in years. Perhaps ever.

'Why, I'd have thought that was obvious,' he said quietly. Then he grabbed her by the chin, jerking her face round so she was looking directly into his pale face, even though they were travelling at close to thirty miles an hour. 'I'm going to kill you.'

Twenty-nine

It had just turned four o'clock when I finally found an internet café on a side street near Bloomsbury in the heart of the West End, and signed into my email account. The day was sunny, the streets were crowded, and I was hot and bothered, having been trooping round for much of the afternoon buying clothes and provisions and then looking for somewhere to check my mail, all the time waiting for news about what Tina was up to, because it was clear she was up to something.

I clicked open her email, saw the message, and downloaded the photos.

The first one stopped me dead. It was him. The strange-looking Irish kidnapper. I could only assume Tina had taken this photo outside John Gentleman's place. Seeing his face now made me go cold, bringing back black, terrible memories that I knew were going to stay with me for the rest of my days. I scrolled through more of the photos, finding it difficult to believe that this man had abducted Jenny and murdered Ramon in cold blood. He looked so much more ordinary in a cap and sunglasses.

I wear a four-gigabyte memory stick round my neck which

contains my most up-to-date drafts of *Conspiracy* as well as my book on Maxwell, and I copied all the photos on to it. I'm not the kind of person to rely too heavily on technology, though, so before I deleted them on the PC I printed them off in colour on one of the café's printers, paid the blank-eyed man at the desk, and headed out.

Now that the Irishman had finally come out into the open, I was itching for an update from Tina. In our last conversation she'd said she'd call in an hour, but that was an hour and twenty minutes ago, so I figured I could get away with hassling her.

Her phone was switched off. I waited five minutes, then tried again. Same message. I remembered only too well what this man was capable of – how he'd managed to conceal himself in my flat, listening to Ramon and I talking before striking silently and coldly in the space of seconds. If Tina had been taking photos of him, she'd have had to get close. Maybe too close.

I walked the streets of the West End for a while, trying her number, always in vain, waiting for a call that I had an ominous feeling was not going to come.

And it didn't.

My car was parked near Belsize Park Tube station and I took the Northern Line to get it. By the time I arrived, I had a plan. It was a fairly basic one, as most of mine tended to be, but it would have to do.

I'd picked up an *A to Z* some time earlier, and now I drove across north London through the choking rush-hour traffic until I came to a quiet rundown street of cheap 1960s housing. I've got a good memory for facts and figures and I remembered John Gentleman's address from when I'd been round to see him at the apartment block on the night Jenny was kidnapped. Since Tina's last known location was outside Gentleman's flat, I figured it was as good a place as any to start looking for her. Risky perhaps, but I was running low on options.

But as I drove under a railway bridge, hoping to see Gentleman's building come up on the right, I was forced to come to a stop. Ahead of me, police vans were parked on both sides of the road and lines of bright yellow scene-of-crime tape ran across it with a sign below saying POLICE NOTICE: ROAD CLOSED. A cluster of onlookers had gathered round the outside of the cordoned-off area, looking excited, while a group of men and women in top-to-toe white suits were trooping in and out of a clapped-out building with sludge-grey paintwork.

I knew without checking the number that this had to be Gentleman's place. And, like everyone else, I've seen enough crime programmes on the TV to know that the presence of this many police, particularly the ones in white suits, means that something extremely serious has taken place. Like murder.

As I sat staring at the scene, trying to take it all in, a uniformed cop approached the car, waving at me to back up. Heeding his instructions, I turned round and found a parking spot further back the other way before returning on foot, looking round for any sign of Tina.

I tried her number again. Still off.

'Do you know what's happened here?' I asked a couple of over-dressed old ladies who were tutting and shaking their heads as they watched the police at work.

'Murder,' growled one. 'Some poor sod killed in his own home.'

'Just keeps getting worse,' said the other, continuing to shake her head. 'You wonder when it's all going to stop.'

'They should hang 'em,' said the first lady. 'Bring back the death penalty. That'd sort it out.'

I thanked them and walked round the scene-of-crime tape and through the onlookers to the other side of the street. But still I couldn't see Tina. I went to the top of the road, checked the parked cars. They were all empty.

Where the hell was she?

I looked at my watch. It was nearly six p.m. More than three hours since we'd last spoken; two since the time she'd told me she'd ring. The sun's rays were weakening as evening began to draw in, and I got a leaden feeling in my gut.

Maybe I should have gone to the police there and then. In hindsight, it would have been the best move. But what stopped me once again was the fear that they wouldn't believe me, particularly my story about Ramon, and that I'd end up a suspect, even if I showed them the photos I had.

Instead, I decided to turn to the one man I'd avoided throughout all this. The subject of my book *Enforcer*, and my last resort.

Maxwell.

Thirty

Five years earlier, not long after Mike Bolt had joined the National Crime Squad, the organization that became SOCA, he'd found himself involved in a case that had ended up having a lasting impact on him.

It started when a three-man gang of Jamaican thugs based in Dalston took to holding up drug dealers at gunpoint and relieving them of their product and their money. These men were extremely violent and, on the one occasion they did meet resistance, they shot the dealer dead and seriously wounded his bodyguard, sending out an ominous message to all those who might defy them. In fact, so successful did they become that for a short while the supply of crack and heroin in the borough plummeted as the other dealers moved out to safer areas. The gang's luck, however, was always going to run out, and when they robbed two crackhouses belonging to Nicholas Tyndall, a high-level gangster in neighbouring Islington, getting away with tens of thousands in cash and drugs, it finally did.

Tyndall was not the type of man to let such blatant disrespect go unpunished. Because he had a great deal more power and influence than the dealers the Jamaicans had robbed in the past, it hadn't taken him long to identify them. Incredibly, it seemed they weren't even making much of an effort to hide their crimes, clearly thinking they were above retribution.

This changed when one of their number, Ralvin Menendez, was found dead on waste ground near his home, a bullet in his head and his severed penis and testicles stuffed into his mouth. A week later, a second member of the gang, Julius Barron, was discovered at home dead in bed, in exactly the same condition.

The two men's deaths generated only minimal publicity. Drug-related murders within the black community were common, and even though these killings were particularly brutal, there was still little that set them apart from the many others that occurred that year in London.

This all changed a month later when a third robber, Clyde Jones, met the same fate as his cohorts. Because when the killer turned up at his flat, breaking in through a window, Jones wasn't in there alone. Also present was his twelve-year-old niece Leticia, whom he was looking after for the night. No one knows for sure the exact sequence of events but it seems likely that Leticia came out of her bedroom and disturbed the killer as he was in the process of castrating her already dead uncle. If she screamed, no one reported hearing her. It was unlikely she got the chance. She was shot once in the head from a distance of about ten feet, and then twice more in the heart at point-blank range, so it was clear that the killer had deliberately finished her off.

In the ensuing public outcry, the National Crime Squad was called in to find the killer. Bolt had been part of the investigating team, and he remembered all too vividly visiting the Jones flat, a cramped, untidy place on the sixth floor of a tower block whose only views were of other tower blocks. There was a huge bloodstain on the living room sofa where Jones himself had died, and a smaller one on the threadbare carpet outside the bedroom where Leticia had breathed her last. Bolt had thought it such a cold, lonely place for a child to die. He'd been a police officer long enough to know how hard and unjust the world could be, but even so he'd been affected by what he'd seen, and he'd sworn then and there that he'd do everything in his power to find the person responsible.

With a reward of £50,000 on offer, the name of Nicholas Tyndall had quickly come up and the NCS had subsequently bugged his palatial Islington home. Listening in, they heard Tyndall refer repeatedly to someone he called Hook as the hitman he'd used for the murders of all three of the Jamaicans. It sounded like Tyndall was extremely annoyed that Hook had killed a civilian, and was even thinking about holding back on the balance of his payment because of the heat Leticia Jones's murder was generating. No one knows whether or not he did because shortly afterwards Tyndall ordered a professional bug sweep of his property which turned up all the listening devices. Incredibly, even with Tyndall's taped admissions, the CPS had somehow concluded that there wasn't enough evidence to charge him with anything.

Instead, NCS efforts were channelled into locating the mysterious man called Hook, and Bolt's team was given the task of finding out his real name. It took a hell of a lot of digging but eventually they identified him as one Michael James Killen, a thirty-seven-year-old former IRA gunman who was suspected of killing as many as eighteen people in a career spanning almost two decades. Having been released under the terms of the Good Friday Agreement from the Maze prison in 1999, where he'd been serving a life sentence for the murder of two RUC officers and a British soldier, he'd headed to the UK and become a gun for hire within the burgeoning London underworld, where reliable killers were always in demand.

Hook was spoken of with a quiet awe by those few in the criminal fraternity prepared to talk about him. It wasn't just that he was brutally efficient, with a breezeblock for a heart and a reputation for taking on any job and getting it done. There was also an air of real mystery about him. The son of wealthy Belfast accountants (father Catholic, mother Protestant), he was hardly your typical IRA gunman, and was remembered in the movement as someone who was more interested in the thrill of violence than furthering the cause of Irish unification. At one time he'd apparently been a good-looking man, but in 1991 he'd suffered extensive shrapnel injuries to his face and body when a bomb an IRA colleague had been working on exploded. He'd also lost two fingers on his left hand, hence the nickname: Hook.

Although he'd been arrested once by Met officers, in early 2001 on suspicion of murder, Hook had somehow avoided getting charged. Since then he'd kept an extremely low profile, and it was known that he'd resorted to plastic surgery on a number of occasions in order to change his appearance. So determined was he in this that hardly any of the people Bolt's team spoke to could physically describe him adequately (let alone say where he might be found). Those few who did attempt it came up with wildly different versions, none of which bore much resemblance to the badly scarred young man with the skin graft on his chin who appeared in the police mugshot taken when he was arrested in 2001.

Armed with all this information, the authorities had put out an all-ports alert for Hook and had every police force in the UK looking for him. But as the days turned into weeks, it became clear that he'd slipped the net, and eventually the public outcry died down as other heinous crimes vied for their attention.

Bolt, though, had never forgotten twelve-year-old Leticia Jones, a pretty little thing with a big gap-toothed grin who looked younger than her years. When, two years later, there was a series of high-level contract killings in southern Spain, including the murder of a Russian businessman in his Marbella villa along with three of his bodyguards, Bolt had suspected Hook's involvement. Whatever people might think, professional contract killers are few in number, ones capable of taking out four people at a time even fewer. Bolt had informed Interpol, and sure enough his hunch had paid off. A month later Hook was apprehended on a European arrest warrant as he boarded a plane at Madrid airport travelling under a false passport. Even the master of disguise could do little to conceal the fact that he was missing two fingers.

Less than a week later, Bolt and five colleagues from the NCS had flown out to Spain to bring him back to face trial for murder; but before they'd even touched down news had come through that Hook had escaped from custody, killing a police officer with his own gun in the process.

Hook was never seen in public again. Even though his name was high on Interpol's most wanted list, he disappeared completely. There was the occasional reported sighting, as well as daring contract killings carried out in different parts of the world which may or may not have borne his hallmark – a senior Indonesian politician slaughtered with his whole family; an American oil billionaire who'd disappeared off the face of the earth while on a hunting trip in the Yukon along with his son and two-man security detail, leaving a trophy wife thirty years his junior to inherit a fortune – but never anything concrete.

And now, three years on from his arrest in Spain, he was back again.

The first question was, why?

The second was what had happened to the woman who photographed him, and it was this one that Bolt was particularly concerned about as he sat in his boss's office at six o'clock that evening telling him about the Hook sighting. Because Tina was still out of contact.

It had to be said that SG2 Barry Freud, the SOCA equivalent of a DCS, was not best pleased with what he was hearing. A big, bald Yorkshireman with more than a passing resemblance to Humpty Dumpty, Big Barry, as he was universally known behind his back, constantly had one eye on promotion and as a consequence liked to run a steady ship, with risk-taking kept to an absolute minimum.

Usually Bolt could tolerate this type of environment (although he didn't particularly like it), but today things were suddenly very different. 'We can't just sit here, sir,' he said urgently. 'Hook's been on SOCA's most wanted list right from day one, and now we've had a sighting of him back in the country. We need to be putting all the resources we can into looking for him.'

Big Barry rolled his eyes and leaned back precariously in his seat. 'We've just spent half the day in a bloody great meeting with the FIU—'

'Which got us nowhere.'

'And we're right in the middle of a long-running case,' he continued, ignoring the interruption, 'against an extremely high-profile target.'

'You don't get much more high profile than Hook, sir. Ex-IRA gunman turned contract killer who murdered a twelve-year-old girl on one of his jobs. It would be a coup if we got him,' he said, appealing to his boss's ambitious streak.

Big Barry didn't look convinced. 'But where are we going to find him? That's the problem. We don't know when or where these photos were taken, do we?'

'No, but—'

'And you said Tina Boyd sent them to you?'

'That's right.'

'I thought she was back in the Met. Why's she sending them to you?'

Bolt told him about her call the previous day and the kidnapping case she was investigating.

'It all sounds bizarre, old mate,' he said, pulling a face. Big Barry Freud called every man he knew 'old mate'. It was supposed to be a term of endearment, but always sounded vaguely condescending.

'Bizarre it might be, but Tina's missing. And she has been since soon after she took those photos. Her mobile's off and we're still trying to trace where it lost power. And we're using the ANPR to try to find her car,' Bolt added, referring to the automatic number plate recognition system, a nationwide network of cameras used for tracking car movements.

'So you've already got people working on this? You haven't got the authority to do that, Mike.'

'Tina was one of ours for over a year, sir. Trying to help her is the least we can do. And if it helps us track down Hook, then we'll get a double result.'

'Have we got anything so far?'

Bolt sighed. 'Not much yet. I've got an all-ports alert out on Hook and the team are all chasing down their informants, seeing if any of them have heard anything on the grapevine about his return, and what he might be here for. Because one thing's for sure: it's not going to be a social visit.'

'What about the kidnapping Tina was meant to be investigating. Any leads on that?'

Bolt shook his head. 'I didn't write anything down when she phoned me about it. And it seems she was working on it unofficially. I spoke to Islington CID, where she's based now, and they've managed to get me the crime report that Tina filled out. It's not very detailed but it's got the name of the man who reported the kidnap initially: Robert Fallon, an unemployed thirty-four-year-old from Colindale. But he's not answering his home phone, and if he owns a mobile then it's pay-as-you-go because there's nothing in his name.'

'This isn't very promising,' said Big Barry with a marked lack of enthusiasm.

Bolt wasn't deterred. 'Tina also took a photo of a Toyota Land Cruiser which we think is connected to Hook, and we've got the ANPR people looking for that as well. We've got a lot of balls in the air and we only need one or two of them to come down for us to solve this.'

Big Barry Freud leaned forward in his seat, resting his elbows on his huge slab of a desk. 'All right, old mate,' he said, giving Bolt a suitably serious look. 'Because you've had results before, I'm pre-pared to cut you some slack. If any of these leads turn up something then we'll concentrate resources on trying to find Hook. It looks like we're already doing what we can to find Tina. But I can't just pull the whole team off what they're doing and send everyone off on a wild goose chase. And if you've put an all-ports alert out for Hook, then we've already done our bit. You under-stand where I'm coming from, don't you?' he added, his tone suggesting that he believed he was being hugely generous in his offer.

Bolt knew there wasn't much point saying anything else. It was the best he could have hoped for from his boss, so he said he'd keep him posted and headed back down the corridor to where his team were still flat out working to find their former colleague. Tina had never been hugely popular during her time at SOCA, mainly because she'd kept herself to herself and avoided social gatherings, but she was respected by everyone for her skills and determination, and there wasn't one person in the team who wasn't desperate to find her.

But the moment he stepped inside the main office he knew some-thing was wrong.

There were nine people in there – seven men and two women – gathered in a rough circle around Mo Khan, who was sitting down with a phone in his hand, his expression grim. No one was speaking, and as they heard Bolt enter they all turned his way.

Trying hard not to show the tension he was experiencing, he stopped and looked around. 'What's happened?'

It was Mo who answered him, his longest-serving colleague, and the most senior person in the room bar Bolt himself. 'Tina's car's been found abandoned near a village called Bramfield in Hertfordshire.'

'And?' Bolt knew there had to be an 'and'. The faces said it all.

Mo took a deep breath, his face tight with pent-up emotion. 'And the body of a young woman's been found nearby.'

Thirty-one

The man in the cream suit ran a comb through his thinning hair, straightened his jacket, and surveyed himself in the full-length mirror, pleased with the image that stared back at him.

He was not the best looking of men, he knew that. Physically, he was small and round in stature, with a large, hooked nose and thin, flinty eyes that hinted at an intelligence not entirely to be trusted. At school they'd christened him 'Shifty', and had tended to shun his company.

None of this bothered him unduly, however. After all, looks were transient. They disappeared eventually. He possessed something far more valuable. Power. There was a poise about him, a cool confidence in the way he carried himself, which had come from years of success in his chosen field. People treated him with respect. There were those who feared him too, knowing his reputation as a strong-willed man, unafraid of making tough decisions. Not the sort of person you would want to cross.

But what the man in the cream suit enjoyed the most was the fact that no one, not even those closest to him, had any idea of the true power he wielded. Nor the terrible secrets he harboured.

As he turned away from the mirror, the phone in his left trouser pocket began vibrating. He had a message. It was from a number he didn't recognize, but he knew the identity of the sender well enough. There was only one person in the world it could have been.

The message was in block capitals and just three words long.

STAGE TWO SUCCESS.

The man in the cream suit felt a tingling, almost sexual sensation running up his spine as he walked over to the window and looked out towards the darkening sea.

Events were moving fast now. All those months of planning were finally coming to fruition.

He looked at his watch and smiled.

Just twenty-four more hours . . .

Thirty-two

There were plenty of reasons why I'd deliberately avoided involving Maxwell until now, but chief among them was the fact that I didn't trust him. After all, he was a career criminal with a moral code that was skewed at best, non-existent at worst, so not the kind of guy you'd automatically turn to for help. But that also made him the kind of person best suited to tell me what the hell my next move should be, because as a criminal he would at least have some idea how other criminals think, and be able to advise me accordingly. And even if he wasn't feeling charitable, I figured that the fact that I was writing a book about him would give him some incentive to help me. After all, when it came down to it, I was more valuable to him alive than dead.

Maxwell (he didn't seem to have any other name) had retired from the London crime scene having made, in his own words, too many enemies – a feeling I was becoming all too familiar with. He now lived in deepest Berkshire, an hour's drive out of town on a good day, close to double that when you were doing it all the way from Hackney at the tail end of rush hour, as I was now.

I didn't phone ahead, deciding that it was easier to turn up unannounced, and it was getting close to eight o'clock when I pulled up outside the pretty picture-postcard cottage with the thatched roof that was his current abode. For a city boy who'd grown up on a sprawling east London council estate it seemed a strange place to end up, a good mile from the nearest house and almost dead quiet, except for the very faint buzz of traffic that you get anywhere in south-east England, and the occasional plane over-head. But that was one of the many paradoxes about Maxwell. He might have been one of the top London hard men in his day, but he also liked to grow his own vegetables and while away his days fishing for trout in the nearby streams.

I was relieved to see that the front door was open, and as I got out of the car and breathed in the fresh country air I felt a lot better. The city and all the danger it represented suddenly seemed a long way away and, if I was honest with myself, the idea of some-one like Maxwell being on my side came as a huge relief.

I could hear movement inside – a reassuring clatter of pots and pans coming from the kitchen – so I rapped hard on the door and called out his name, just so he'd know it wasn't one of his old enemies coming calling.

A few seconds later, Maxwell appeared in the narrow hallway, all five foot six of him, barrel-bodied and pug-faced, looking vaguely comical in an apron with a large cartoon pair of breasts on it. His grizzled face creased into a frown. 'All right, Robbie. Didn't expect to see you today. We didn't have a meet planned, did we?'

Maxwell always referred to me as Robbie – a term of address I'd always hated, but I'd never had the heart (or balls) to correct him.

'I need your help,' I said, looking straight into his narrow, hooded eyes.

The frown deepened, but he nodded. 'Better come inside then. Want a drink of something?'

I knew I needed to keep my wits about me, but the thought of a real drink proved irresistible. 'A beer, if you've got one.'

I followed him into the kitchen where a big pot was bubbling away on the stove. I didn't stop to look at its contents, but the smell was good, and I felt the first stirrings of hunger since lunchtime.

Maxwell opened two bottles of Peroni and handed me one, then led me through into his tiny sitting room where we always conducted our interviews, and which had clearly been designed for men of Maxwell's height rather than men of mine. I bent down, narrowly missing the overhead beam I'd almost knocked myself out on the first time I was here, and took a seat in one of the two old leather armchairs by the fireplace.

He sat down in the other one, placed the beer on the coffee table beside him, and lit a cigarette. If he was at all concerned about what I had to say, he didn't show it. But then that was Maxwell all over. He wasn't the kind of man to be easily fazed.

'OK,' he said through the smoke, 'what's happened?'

It seemed like I'd already told this story a thousand times, usually to a sceptical audience, but I had the feeling Maxwell would believe me. He'd inhabited the world where this kind of thing happened for a long, long time. So I told him everything, with the exception of Ramon's murder, every so often taking a big slug of my beer, while he listened in silence.

When I'd finished, he stubbed out his cigarette, rubbed a stubby, nicotine-stained finger along the side of his nose, and looked at me with a suspicion I wasn't expecting. 'You sure you ain't been smoking too much of the wacky baccy, Robbie? This is some fucking story and I know you've been prone to, you know, breakdowns.'

I met his gaze. 'It's the truth. I swear it.'

When the suspicious look didn't disappear, I told him I had the photographs to prove it and pulled the print-outs of the images Tina had emailed me from my back pocket.

'All right, let's have a look,' he said, and took them off me. He unfolded three of them and looked at them carefully. 'And these were taken today in London?'

'In Hackney. Why? Do you know the guy?' It was a long shot but, given Maxwell's previous career, not a complete impossibility.

He shook his head. 'You said he was Irish, right?'

'That's right. Northern Irish, I think.'

'I had dealings with some Belfast paramilitaries – UVF blokes – a few years back, but I never trusted them. The greedy bastards were always trying to put one over on you.' He sighed, handing the photos back.

'So,' I said, 'do you believe me now?'

He nodded slowly like some wise, thuggish Yoda. Maxwell never did anything in a hurry. 'Yeah,' he said at last, 'I believe you. Looks like you're in a lot of shit, mate.'

'Yes, Maxwell, I know that. What I'm after are suggestions about what I should be doing about it.'

'My advice?' Pause. 'Take a long fucking holiday. A month at least. Somewhere a long way away. And make sure you're on email as well. We'll need to speak about the book. Try to forget any of it ever fucking happened.'

'But what about Jenny? I can't just leave her at the mercy of someone who's going to kill her.'

Maxwell's features cracked into an unpleasant smile. 'Never really took you for the hero, Robbie. Thought you were more the sort who just liked to write about them.'

'Then maybe you don't know me that well. If someone's in trouble and I can help them, then that's what I'm going to do.' Two nights ago that hadn't been the case, but now I genuinely meant it.

'Well, that's real touching, Robbie, but you try poking your nose into something like this and you're going to end up with it sliced off, know what I mean? Let me give you a piece of advice,' he said, pointing his Peroni bottle in my general direction. 'Only get involved in something when you absolutely have to, or where there's money involved. Anything else, steer clear, because it ain't worth it. Especially in this case. If what you're saying's true, then it's possible they've killed a copper, which means they're prepared to kill anybody. Next time it could be you.' He settled back in his chair, having delivered his sage advice, and lit another cigarette.

I realized what Maxwell was truly like then. When I'd first met him I'd thought him glamorous – a hard man definitely, ruthless too – but because he liked a laugh, told a good story and was always nice to me, I'd got to thinking of him as a loveable rogue, someone who might hurt other criminals – people whose actions deserved it – but also someone who would stand up for the underdog, who wouldn't put up with bullies, who could be reasoned with, because underneath it all his heart was still somewhere close to the right place. But this was all bullshit. Maxwell was just another selfish thug, and it shocked me that it had taken my own experience at the hands of selfish thugs to understand this.

'Have you ever killed anyone?' I asked him.

Maxwell shook his head. 'I've come close a couple of times when people fucked me over, but no, I ain't.'

'What about kidnapping someone? Have you ever done that?'

He paused before answering. 'I've had to persuade people to pay back money they owe. Sometimes that meant holding them in places against their will, until their associates came up with the cash. Maybe even giving them a little bit of a kicking to ensure their cooperation. But no. Not like you're talking about. I never hurt women. I respect them too much for that.'

The way he was talking disgusted me, and I think that disgust must have shown on my face because his own creased into a fierce glare. 'Don't go all moralistic on me, Robbie. I've done some bad things. You know that. And I ain't particularly proud of some of them either, but I'm also a realist. And yeah, it's bad that this girl, whoever she is, has got herself kidnapped, but it ain't my business, and it ain't yours either. You hardly know her. And you're in a lot of trouble already. You've done what you can. Leave it.'

'I can't leave it.'

'Then I ain't gonna help you, mate. Sorry, but that's the way it is.' He shrugged his immense shoulders, as if to say there was nothing more he could do.

I felt terrible. I'd been a fool to expect him to help me. I thought about threatening to knock the book on the head unless he changed his mind but dismissed the idea immediately. I needed it as much as he did; and anyway, right then, the book seemed totally irrelevant.

I drank the last of my beer down in one, savouring its coldness.

'Do you want another?' he asked.

I did. Desperately. I really needed just to unwind, and the chair felt extremely comfortable. I could feel the indignation draining out of me. 'Yeah, please. And can I ask you a favour? I need a place to stay for a few days. To give me some time to lie low and think. Can you put me up here?'

'All right, but on one condition: you don't try and hunt for that girl while you're under this roof. Like I told you, I don't want to get involved.'

He fixed me with the kind of stare that dared you to defy him. I had a feeling not many people did, and I was no exception. I said that I wouldn't, and he headed back into the kitchen for more Peronis.

I knew I wouldn't be able to keep the promise, though. The events of the last two days might have frightened the shit out of me but I was still determined to locate Jenny and get her to safety. My life had changed. I'd changed. Never in my wildest dreams would I have expected to be risking my life to help a girl I hardly knew, but now that I was doing it, there was no way I was going to give up.

And for the first time, sitting there in Maxwell's house, I actually felt good about that.

But tonight . . . Tonight I was going to have to put my quest to one side. I was tired. I needed to rest.

When Maxwell came back with the drinks, I was already yawning. He told me I looked shagged out, and I didn't disagree. I drank the second beer fast while he spun one of his more amusing yarns about his days as a gangster. I wasn't really listening though, and when he offered me a third, I declined. 'I just need to close my eyes for a minute,' I said, feeling an overwhelming tiredness.

I remember him saying 'No problem', and something about having some chicken soup when I woke up, and I also remember him watching me closely as I drifted off, which I thought was a bit odd. Then sleep came and relieved me, at least temporarily, of all the burdens of the world.

Thirty-three

They'd driven much of the way in silence. Two men who'd been colleagues for almost six years, who'd had their ups and downs but who also, when it came down to it, were prepared to risk their careers and their necks for each other.

Bolt was conscious of the fact that Mo had done more of the risking over the years, that he'd covered for Bolt in some tricky situations, and he wouldn't have wanted anyone else in the car with him as they went to see if the woman who'd been found dead near Tina Boyd's abandoned car was in fact Tina herself. There'd been no identification on the body when it was found with gunshot wounds to the face by a dog walker two hours earlier, and the only description Bolt and Mo had was that it was a dark-haired woman in her thirties. But it was one that fitted Tina, and Bolt wasn't the type to believe in co-incidences. In the car he'd fought to keep an open mind and not jump to conclusions, but it was a battle he'd steadily lost.

He'd remembered the first time he met Tina, in a dive of a pub in Highgate one wet Saturday night. He and Mo had gone there to get some information from her about a case they were working on. It wasn't long after her boyfriend had died, and Bolt remembered how tired and vulnerable she'd looked, and how he'd had an immediate desire to take her in his arms and protect her. It was a feeling that had never really gone away during all the time he'd known her.

The victim's body was still at the crime scene when Bolt parked his Jaguar at the edge of the police cordon. Darkness was descending fast now, but the quiet stretch of wooded B-road just south of the village of Bramfield was a hive of activity. Two police patrol cars with their lights flashing blocked the road, a uniformed cop eating a baguette in one of them; a dozen other police vehicles and an ambulance were lined up on either side of the road. A plastic tent had been erected just inside the tree line, and a few yards behind it a red Nissan Micra that Bolt recognized as Tina's was parked up on the verge.

Bolt and Mo showed their ID to the uniform, who managed to finish chewing his baguette long enough to point them to a van where they could put on the plastic coveralls all officers were obliged to wear when entering crime scenes. Once they were kitted up, they slipped under the scene-of-crime tape and walked along a specially marked path lined with more tape in the direction of the tent.

Bolt was aware that his breathing had increased. He'd always feared death, right from childhood, because he'd never been able to believe – and God knows he'd tried – that there was anything beyond it. Unfortunately, because of his job, he'd had to see far more of it than most people, and almost always when the end had come violently. The sight of their empty faces was something he'd never got used to, and the prospect of seeing someone he knew and cared about lying there was much worse.

'I can do this if you want, boss,' said Mo quietly, turning his way.

Months earlier, when they'd been sharing one too many beers at a pub near SOCA's Vauxhall HQ, Bolt had told Mo about the night he made a pass at Tina, and about his feelings for her. It wasn't the sort of thing he usually shared; he preferred to keep matters of the heart to himself. But the drink had done what drink always does and loosened his tongue, and, with Tina having only recently departed from SOCA, he'd been at something of a low ebb. Mo hadn't approved, Bolt knew that, but he'd been sympathetic to his boss's plight, as he was now.

Bolt looked at Mo, saw the concern in his friend's eyes. He appreciated the offer but knew it was essential he didn't show weakness. 'No, it's all right,' he said. 'I'll be fine.'

One of the white-overalled officers peeled away from the throng and came over to them. 'Mo Khan?' The questioner was a woman in her mid thirties with an attractive, friendly face that didn't look like it needed much encouragement to break into a smile. Beneath the transparent hood she was wearing her hair, tied back, was a fiery red.

'That's me. And this is my boss, SG3 Mike Bolt.'

'I'm DCI Miller, the SIO on this case,' she said as the three of them shook hands. 'Thanks for coming. She's over here. The body was discovered by a dog walker approximately two and a half hours ago,' she continued as Mo and Bolt followed her to the tent. 'No real attempt to conceal the body.' She opened the flap and stood to one side. 'It looks like she was shot several times in the face and then just left where she fell.'

Bolt didn't flinch but his expression was granite as he stepped inside, barely conscious of Mo and DCI Miller filing in behind and standing either side of him.

She lay there alone, flat on her back in a halo of coagulating blood, arms neatly by her side, eyes closed. There were two small black holes in her face: one just below her mouth, the other high up on her cheek, like a large, out-of-place beauty spot. She looked asleep, peaceful, as if all the trials and tribulations of this world had been lifted from her shoulders. Which of course they had.

Bolt took a deep breath and turned to DCI Miller. 'It's not her,' he said.

Thirty-four

I'm going to kill you.

The afternoon had turned out to be the most terrifying of Tina Boyd's life. For what must have been close to an hour she'd driven her car at gunpoint along the North Circular Road, and finally out of London on the A10 heading north. During that time the man had spent much of his time asking her questions, often touching and stroking her as he spoke. Sometimes his tone was conversational. He would ask her about her background, her likes and dislikes, her work as a police officer. Other times his tone became cruel and he'd ask her quietly, playfully, what lengths she would go to in order to live, and whether she believed in life after death.

It was clear he was enjoying tormenting her, but she'd refused to play along, answering him defiantly (she'd do what it took to stay alive and, yes, she did believe in an afterlife), yet at the same time giving him enough information to keep him interested, and even asking questions of her own, although on these he tended to be evasive. Still, she was proud of herself for remaining calm, even when they'd left the noise and traffic of the A10 behind and moved on to quieter, more isolated roads. Even when he'd ordered her to drive off one of these quieter roads and down a deserted wooded lane.

It was only when he'd told her to stop the car and taken the keys from her that the fear really hit home. Tina's legs had buckled slightly as she was ordered on to the grass verge. This was it. The moment of truth.

You've seen his face! screamed a voice inside her head. *He's going to kill you!*

But she hadn't panicked. Instead, she'd turned to face him, knowing that it was harder for even the most brutal killer to shoot someone in cold blood that way, forcing herself to ignore the obvious fact that she was dealing with a sociopath.

He'd raised the gun so it was pointed at her chest and they'd looked at each other for a long, lingering moment.

And then he'd smiled, and said, 'Empty your pockets, and take off your watch.'

She'd done as she'd been told, pulling out her wallet and house keys. At his command, she'd thrown them into the bushes.

He'd come forward and given her a quick one-handed pat-down to check there was nothing left behind, then opened the boot and pushed her inside, slamming it behind her.

Despite being cramped and uncomfortable, for the first time Tina had felt a real surge of hope. He intended to keep her alive, for the moment at least, and this gave her a chance.

He'd also made a mistake: he'd missed the set of picks in the back pocket of her jeans, and failed to tie her hands. She'd immediately reached round, pulled them out and shoved them into her sock where they would be even harder to locate. She knew she was taking a big risk, concealing them and risking her tormentor's wrath later, but this was a time for big risks.

The car hadn't moved, and the engine had remained off for a long time. Tina had begun to wonder if he'd simply abandoned her.

Then, finally, she'd heard another car pull up next to her. She'd banged on the metal of the boot with her fist and yelled out as loudly as she could, excited at the prospect she might be freed. But when the boot opened she'd been greeted with the sight of the man with the gun again.

Without speaking, he'd pulled her out. She'd asked him what was going on but he'd told her to shut up, then shoved her roughly into the boot of the new car, a dark-coloured saloon. She'd had to push a couple of bags of grocery shopping aside before she could squeeze in, which had made her wonder where he'd got the car from. A few minutes later they were on the move again.

What was clear to Tina as she was driven along road after winding road was that the man who'd taken her was not only a sociopath but an extremely intelligent one who appeared to appreciate the tools available to the police for tracking down kidnap victims – hence his decision to get rid of her phone and her car. This was bad news, not only for her but also for Jenny Brakspear, because she was certain that this man was involved in her abduction too.

But what she couldn't understand was why he was choosing to let her live. 'Just be thankful he is, girl,' she'd whispered to herself, wondering at the same time why she'd allowed herself to end up in this position. Her desire to go it alone and bend the rules was, she'd always believed, borne out of a need to see justice done, yet there was more to it than that. There was also something self-destructive about the impulse, as if she were driven by a need to court danger, even in the knowledge that eventually she'd come unstuck.

However, now that her life truly was on the line, she realized, almost with a sense of surprise, that she desperately wanted to live. To try to return to the happier days that had been absent for far too long. Lying there frightened and hunched uncomfortably against the bags of shopping, she told herself that if she got through this she'd kick the booze – that monkey had been on her back for far too long now – and maybe even quit the force altogether and go off travelling somewhere new. South America, or southern Africa.

After what seemed an age the car slowed and made a sharp turning, then after a further hundred yards or so she heard the sound of gravel crunching under the wheels before it finally came to a halt. They'd already stopped a while back for about ten minutes, but this time she instinctively knew that this was their final destination.

She heard footsteps on the gravel and the sound of muffled voices, then the boot was flung open and the man with the gun shouted at her to shut her eyes, threatening death if she disobeyed.

There was no danger of that. She squeezed them shut like a young kid playing hide and seek as a hood was pulled roughly over her head. She was then led along the gravel by two men, each holding an arm, and dragging her, so she had to move fast. She was taken through several doors, then up some stairs and through yet another door, before finally being pushed roughly into a chair.

In silence they handcuffed her wrists behind the chair and strapped her to its back from stomach to neck with a roll of masking tape. She couldn't move an inch, and her hope began to evaporate. She still had the set of picks in her sock but there was no way of getting to them now.

The man with the gun told his colleague to leave, and there was a throaty edge to his voice as he spoke. Then he pulled off Tina's hood. His lips cracked into a smile, a look of undisguised lust in the big staring eyes, and she felt her heart sink. She knew then that this bastard had been telling the truth when he said he was going to kill her.

But it was clear that he wanted to have some fun first.

Thirty-five

When they were back in the Jaguar, having finished at the crime scene and having briefed DCI Miller about their hunt for Tina Boyd, Mike Bolt let out a long, deep sigh. 'I tell you, Mo, sometimes this job really gets to me.'

'It gets to all of us, boss. You know that.' Mo turned, and Bolt could see the lines of tension on his face. This had been tough for him, too.

'You know, I haven't seen her in more than a year, but if it had been her I think I would have fallen apart. I never knew she'd had that much of an effect on me.'

'But it wasn't Tina, was it? Which is a good sign. That's the way you've got to look at it, boss. Accentuate the positive. Keep the faith.'

'But where the hell is she?' said Bolt, staring out of the window at the trees.

The fact was, they'd run out of leads. The Land Cruiser Tina had photographed earlier had disappeared off the ANPR's radar, having last been spotted thirty miles away in Essex, and now Tina had disappeared too. All that remained was an anonymous woman shot dead in what appeared to be a professional hit. One that bore Hook's hallmarks – and Bolt could guess his motive: to hijack the victim's car and make it as hard as possible for him to be followed. As always, he seemed to be one step ahead.

'We're not going to stop searching for her,' said Mo eventually, his voice weary. 'Of course we're not. But I don't think there's much more we can do tonight.'

Bolt nodded. Mo was right. There really wasn't much else they could do. An alert had been put out to all the UK's police forces and now it was simply a matter of waiting. Without another word, he started the engine and pulled away.

But they'd barely been driving five minutes when Bolt's mobile started ringing.

'Who is it?' asked Mo, as he picked up the handset and examined the screen.

Bolt frowned. 'An old informant of mine. Strictly small time. His name's Maxwell.'

Thirty-six

When I woke up, I didn't have a clue where I was. Then I saw the empty armchair opposite me and the coffee table with the half-full ashtray and the Peroni bottles beside it, and I remembered I was at Maxwell's place.

I sat up, rubbing my eyes. The lights were on in the sitting room and the curtains were pulled but I could tell it was dark outside. I looked at my watch. Twenty past ten. I'd been out for an hour at least, probably longer. I got to my feet. The door to the kitchen was closed, but I could hear Maxwell in there. I needed a drink of water, then I needed to get to bed.

But I only took one step before the door opened and I realized with a single jolt of sheer terror that it wasn't Maxwell in the kitchen at all.

'Hello again,' said the Irishman, coming into the room, a gun with silencer raised in front of him. He was dressed in a black boiler suit and black boots, the saucer eyes cold and angry.

My stomach churned, and my legs felt like they were going to go from under me. All my optimistic thoughts of carrying on until I found Jenny, of defying the men I was up against – so attractive when I'd been sitting in the comfort of Maxwell's cottage with a large beer in my hand – turned immediately to dust, and I was once again what I'd always been: a terrified man out of my depth.

I didn't even think about running. There was no point. I was trapped. I tried to think of something to say, something that might stop him from doing what I knew he was about to do, but nothing came out.

'Didn't you believe me when I said I'd kill you if you carried on with your foolishness?' asked the Irishman, his harsh accent tinged with incredulity that I could be so stupid.

And the thing was, he was right. I had been stupid, utterly stupid, ever to have got involved. In that moment, I cursed Jenny Brakspear. And I cursed Maxwell too. I couldn't believe he had betrayed me like this. I knew he'd not been the most morally upright guy in the world, but I'd trusted him.

'Now it's time to pay for what you've done,' he said, grabbing my arm in a tight grip and pushing me back into the kitchen with the butt of the gun.

I could smell the chicken soup as I was shoved through the door. I saw Maxwell in there with the second kidnapper, the big lumbering guy with the shaven head. Both men had their backs to me, and even in my fear I felt a burst of rage. 'What's the matter, Maxwell? Can't you bear to face me, you treacherous bastard?'

Maxwell and Shaven Head turned round almost as one, which was when I realized that Maxwell wasn't a part of this at all. His face was bloodied and he had a deep cut above one eye. A rope had been pulled tight round his neck, the pressure making his eyes bug out. Shaven Head held one end of it in a gloved hand while his other held a gun, which was pressed hard against Maxwell's side. Maxwell, who was dwarfed in size by his captor, looked exactly like I felt: terrified. He wasn't even making any attempt to hide it, and this more than anything else extinguished any hope that I'd had. If even a hard bastard like Maxwell could be overpowered by these people, what the hell chance did I have?

'All right, let's go,' said the Irishman impatiently.

Shaven Head nodded and dragged Maxwell out into the hallway. I was given a shove and made to follow.

They seemed to know where they were going because they took us through the hall to the cottage's back door. I wondered immediately why they were taking us this way. It was only Maxwell's beloved vegetable patch that was out there.

The answer became obvious as soon as we were outside: the Irishman picked up a pair of shovels that were leaning against the door and handed one to each of us.

My heart beat savagely in my chest as I took mine and watched Maxwell take the other. Then I heard him groan because he too knew what we were going to have to do now.

I can't adequately describe the fear I experienced then. It was total and all-encompassing. My life didn't flash before me. Nothing like that. There was only the sure, solid knowledge that this was the end, that soon there would only be black nothingness. I wished I was religious, that I could have some small hope of salvation to cling on to, but I hadn't believed since I was a child, and death had always seemed too far away to care about.

But now . . . now it was right there at my side.

I felt dizzy as we were taken across Maxwell's small but well-kept lawn. I started to fall, but the barrel of the Irishman's gun pressed tighter into my spine, forcing me forward. I straightened up, desperate to delay the inevitable as long as possible, and kept moving.

Maxwell's vegetable patch was as big as the lawn itself and was bisected by a path that ran up to where his land ended and the woods began. We walked in dead silence up the path and then on to the soft soil so that we were standing side by side, facing the tree line. The night was warm and silent, and I was conscious of drops of light rain beginning to fall on my head. I swallowed and stood stock-still, staring blankly into the pines, ignoring Maxwell. Ignoring everything.

The Irishman stood on the soil behind us, while Shaven Head remained on the path and produced a torch from his pocket. He shone it on the side of my face and I thought I heard him snigger. My bowels felt like they were going to open and I clenched my buttocks together, not wishing to humiliate myself completely in my final moments.

'Time to dig, gentlemen,' said the Irishman, a genuine enjoyment in his voice.

I didn't hesitate, slamming my foot down on the shovel with more strength than I thought I was capable of, and hurling up a pile of dirt.

Out of the corner of my eye, I saw that Maxwell hadn't moved, and I felt a sudden slither of hope. Was he going to make some kind of move? Do something that might save us?

Then he spoke. 'Listen mate, please. I'm nothing to do with this. He's the one you want. I don't know anything. He just came here tonight for a drink, that's all.'

'You know you're going to die,' said the Irishman, addressing Maxwell. His tone was calm and even, almost reasonable. 'But there are different ways that you can meet death. It can be quick, and comparatively painless. Or it can be slow and agonizing.' He emphasized this last word, letting it slide almost playfully out of his mouth. 'It's your choice which way it is, but I can promise you that if you don't do exactly as you're told, then by the time I'm finished with you you'll be begging me to finish you off.'

Maxwell at last got the message, and began digging.

And so we dug together. Dug our own graves. The adrenalin coursed through me as I worked, and the rain grew steadily harder. I was terrified, but the act of thrusting the shovel into the soil gave me something to concentrate on, and even though I knew that the moment I finished it would spell the end, I kept on going, if anything increasing my pace, as I concentrated my fear and impotence on the task at hand. It was as if I wanted to make sure my final act in this world was done in the best way possible so that I could leave it with my head held high.

'What's your name, my friend?' the Irishman asked Maxwell when his hole was half dug and mine two-thirds done. Shallow, but almost long enough for me to fit in. I pictured myself lying face down in it, a bullet in the back of my head, the rain drumming down on my corpse. Never to be found, or properly mourned by the two people I cared about most in the world: Yvonne and Chloe.

'They call me Maxwell,' he answered listlessly.

'And is that your real name?'

This time he didn't hesitate. 'No,' he said. 'It's Harvey Hammond.'

I almost laughed out loud. *Harvey Hammond*. What sort of name was that? How could you have a gangster going by the name of Harvey? I was beginning to realize now that the man whose violent past I was meant to be chronicling might not be all he had cracked himself up to be.

'And what has Mr Fallon told you, Mr Hammond?'

Out of the corner of my eye I saw Maxwell, Harvey, whatever the hell his name was, stop digging and stand up straight, turning round so he faced the Irishman. 'Everything,' he said, figuring no doubt that there was no way he'd be believed if he tried to lie. 'But I promise you, there's no way I'd tell a fucking soul about it. I'm not that kind of bloke. I don't get myself involved in things that don't concern me. And I'd rather die than talk to the law. I've never said a word to them in my life. Honest.' He wiped the rain from his eyes and I could see that his shoulders were shaking. 'Please,' he whispered. 'He's the one you want. Not me. I'll keep shtum. Not a word. I promise.' And then, louder, almost wailing with desperation, 'I fucking promise!'

I realized he was crying. Sobbing softly. And I felt sorry for him. I couldn't help it, even though he was trying to get them to kill me rather than him.

I kept digging, staring now at the sodden hole in the ground I was standing in, trying to remain as anonymous as possible, letting Maxwell get all the attention. Knowing, even without seeing it, that the Irishman had lifted his gun and was preparing to kill him.

'Please!' begged Maxwell – Maxwell the growling hard man with the scar on his face; Maxwell who was never fazed by anything; Maxwell who was now shivering and shaking like a wet kitten. 'Please don't kill me. I won't say a word. I swear it. I fucking swear it!'

'Turn round,' said the Irishman. 'Face the trees.'

Maxwell made a weird moaning sound, and didn't move.

I gritted my teeth and dug furiously, ignoring the burning feeling in my biceps as I tried in vain to shut the world out.

There was a sound like a cork being popped from a champagne bottle, barely audible in the rain, and Maxwell's legs went from under him. He fell on to his behind and remained sitting upright, his grizzled face a mask of pain, both meaty hands clutching at his injured knee.

The Irishman took two steps forward, stopping in front of Maxwell, the smoking gun barrel pointed down at his head.

I stopped digging, stood up straight, eyes fixed on the scene in front of me.

Maxwell looked up at his executioner and just for an instant his expression became calm as he accepted the inevitable. Then the popping sound came again and a line of blood sprayed from the back of Maxwell's head as the bullet hit him in the face. He stayed stock still for an incredibly long moment, then tipped over backwards, his eyes still open. A spent shell landed in the mud beside me as the Irishman casually pumped two further rounds into his body. Maxwell juddered violently, threw one arm uselessly into the air, then, as his fist hit the sodden ground with a loud slap, he lay absolutely still.

The Irishman turned my way, grinning at me. He briefly glanced at the hole I'd dug and seemed satisfied that it was adequate. Then he lifted the gun so that the end of the smoking barrel was pointed directly between my eyes. 'So, my friend, your turn. Same as before. I can do it quick, or I can do it slow. Now, be honest with me. Aside from Miss Boyd, is there anyone you've told about Miss Brakspear?'

If I answered him, I died. If I didn't answer him, I'd get kneecapped like Maxwell, and possibly worse. Either way my life was completely over, and for several seconds I was utterly incapable of speaking. I simply stared at him, unable to avoid seeing Maxwell's body as it lay bleeding in its shallow grave, conscious of the warm trickle of urine running down my leg. I hunted desperately for any possible sign of mercy in the cold, staring eyes, knowing there would be none. But still you look, because in the end it is your only hope as you scrabble around for any chance of staying alive for a few moments longer.

A stark choice. Give up Dom and enjoy a few more precious seconds, even though the end result would be the same. Or say nothing and go to my grave right now.

'Tell me,' he said, lowering the gun so it was pointed at my kneecap.

I opened my mouth. It felt as dry as a bone. The urge to give up Dom and stay alive just one more moment was almost unstoppable.

But then he turned his head in the direction of the cottage.

I turned my head too, because I'd also heard it. The sound

of a car coming up the lane, its headlights illuminating the woods.

It stopped. Directly outside the cottage. And I heard the doors open.

Which was the moment I snapped out of the stony trance I'd been in and, with an angry shout, threw my shovel at the man who was about to kill me.

Thirty-seven

I didn't even look to see how my would-be killer had reacted. I saw the shovel hit him somewhere in the midriff while he was still turned the other way, and I heard him let out a surprised grunt, but by then I was charging for the tree line, splattering mud everywhere, knowing that salvation was only feet away.

I half dived, half slid into the trees, rolling on the pine needles and scrambling to my feet. Behind me I heard the pop of a shot fired through a silencer, then the sounds of barked orders and pursuit.

Sensing freedom, and with adrenalin coursing through me, I ran into the welcoming darkness, ignoring the branches that tore at my skin. I stumbled once, almost fell, but my sheer momentum, coupled with a desperate, exhilarating will to live, drove me onwards.

A powerful torch beam moved in a steady arc through the sodden foliage, trying to focus in on me, and as I weaved to avoid its glare a bullet hissed quietly past my head and popped into the trunk of a pine just ahead of me, leaving a small round hole and a thin trail of smoke. I caught the whiff of cordite as I passed and tried to accelerate but my legs wouldn't go any faster and my lungs ached with the strain of all my exertions. I wasn't fit, and it was beginning to show. But I knew without doubt that the men following me would be fitter, so either I continued to run or I died.

Without warning, the ground ahead of me simply disappeared, and before I knew it I was tumbling down a slope. I somersaulted once, hitting my head on something hard, and then I was immersed in water.

I scrambled to my feet, saw that I was knee deep in a shallow stream, then charged across it and scrambled up the slope on the other side. As I reached the top, gasping for breath and blinking the rainwater out of my eyes, I dared for the first time to look over my shoulder.

And saw him there. Standing in the darkness, at the top of the slope on the other side of the stream, barely twenty yards away, the snarling wolf face skewed slightly where it had taken a knock, but with the gun held outwards in both hands, taking aim.

I dived forward into the mud as he fired, making myself as small a target as possible. The shot sailed somewhere above me and I crawled assault-course style on my belly until I had cover from the trees. Then I got to my feet and was running again, hearing him splash through the water of the stream as he continued his pursuit.

I was tempted to drop down and hide in the thick undergrowth, knowing that it would be extremely difficult to find me there, but in the end my instincts told me that my best hope of survival was to put real distance between us and reach some kind of civilization.

I could hardly breathe now – my lungs felt like they were about to burst – but my legs somehow kept going and I'd covered maybe another fifty yards when I finally saw a gap in the trees ahead. The sounds of pursuit had faded and I had this sudden elated feeling that they'd given up, having decided that I was proving too difficult to kill.

The opening in the trees gave on to a quiet country road flanked on the far side by an impenetrable-looking hedge. As I ran on to the lane I saw the lights of houses about a hundred yards further down.

Freedom. As soon as I got there I knew I'd be safe. And this time I'd go straight to the police, regardless of what they believed or didn't believe.

But a hundred yards is a long way when every muscle in your body aches and each breath comes in a shallow gasp.

And when there are two men chasing you with guns.

I caught a flash of the torch beam in the trees to my right, but this time it was further ahead, between me and the houses. The bastards were trying to cut me off.

I took off again, arms flailing, my gait little more than an exhausted, drunken stagger.

A hundred yards. Eighty. Fifty. The torch beam had disappeared, and as I rounded a slight bend in the road I could see a red pub sign hanging outside one of the buildings. All the lights were on inside and there were several cars parked next to it. The rain was easing now.

Thirty yards. Twenty. I could hear the clink of glasses, the welcome buzz of conversation. Safety.

The pub door opened and a middle-aged man stepped out, turning his head to call out a final goodbye to those inside.

'Help me!' I managed to shout, the effort physically painful. Barely ten yards away now. 'Please help me!'

He was still grinning when he turned my way. I was, too. I'd never been so happy to see someone in my whole life. To have been so close to death and to be given a second chance at life is the sweetest, most incredible reward imaginable.

The bullet struck him in the eye with a malevolent hiss and blood splattered the pub window. He tottered on his feet for a full second, his expression one of mild surprise, then he lost his footing on the pub step and went down hard, his head hitting the pavement with an angry smack.

I stopped, all hope sucked out of me, and turned round slowly.

The Irishman was twenty yards away from me, the gun raised and pointed at me.

Strangely, I felt nothing. I think I was too exhausted for that. I'd tried everything. I'd done my best, and in the final analysis it simply hadn't been enough.

And then there was a roaring sound, getting closer and closer, and the Irishman was suddenly bathed in bright light.

A car. Coming fast, skidding now.

Instinctively I swung round to meet it, blinded by the headlights as it bore down on me, realizing at the very last second that I was right in the middle of the road; and then I was flying through the air, flailing like a madman, seeing the ground come up to greet me.

And then, bang.

Nothing.

Thirty-eight

Mike Bolt took the corner way too fast. There were plenty of reasons why: it was dark; it was pissing with rain; the road was unfamiliar, winding and very narrow; and, most important of all, he was a man in a serious hurry.

He slammed on the brakes, conscious of Mo Khan smacking a hand on to the dashboard to steady himself as he shouted instructions for back-up into his airwave radio, but the car was already going into a skid. Bolt turned the wheel hard, trying to straighten up before he hit the house looming up in front of him. He missed it narrowly, but the wheels locked and the car was temporarily out of control as it skidded along the rain-slicked road. A red pub sign appeared through the slicing of the wind-screen wipers, and then suddenly Mo yelled out, his voice almost deafening him: 'Boss! Watch out!'

A guy standing in the middle of the road facing them. Frozen like a deer in headlights.

The car was slowing down thanks to Bolt's pressure on the brakes, but nowhere near fast enough. He could see the fear on the guy's face, the way his eyes were widening, recognized him from the photo he'd seen at HQ earlier that day as Rob Fallon, the man they'd gone to Maxwell's place to see, the one man who might help them locate Tina.

And then, bang, they hit him.

He flew over the bonnet, smacked bodily into the windscreen, cracking it, then bounced off and into the darkness.

The tyres screamed, the car wobbled, and then, at last, it stopped. The two men lurched forward in their seats, Bolt's head narrowly missing the windscreen.

That was when, through the rain, he spotted another figure standing in the road only a few yards in front of them. It was a man, but Bolt didn't get a good look at him, because he was pointing a gun straight at the car.

'Get down!' he shouted, dragging Mo down by the collar as he ducked beneath the steering wheel.

There was the sound of breaking glass as a bullet whistled through the car, followed by a second crack as it exited through the back window.

Keeping his head below the level of the damaged windscreen, Bolt floored the accelerator and the Jaguar shot forward. Two more bullets smashed through the window in rapid succession, both missing their targets, and then out of the corner of his eye Bolt saw the gunman jump to one side as they passed him, then disappear from view. He lifted his head above the steering wheel, saw the guy running for the trees, but he was trying to do far too many things at once and before he had a chance to turn the wheel and give chase the Jaguar mounted a bank at the side of the road and ploughed into a hedge, before coming to a halt at a forty-five-degree angle to the tarmac.

For a moment, Bolt was too shocked to say anything. Barely five minutes earlier he'd been driving to his informant's house to follow up on a lead. Since then he'd discovered his corpse, done a mad dash to try to intercept his killers, run over Rob Fallon, probably written off his second car in a year, and narrowly avoided being shot dead.

But there was no time to dwell on any of that now. Shaken but unhurt, he jumped out of the car and, using the door as cover, scanned the trees ahead for the gunman, wondering for the first time if it had been Hook. Because if it had been, and they could catch him, then maybe they could find out what had happened to Tina.

But it was clear he was gone.

Bolt leaned back inside the car. 'Are you OK?' he asked Mo, who was scrabbling round on the floor for the radio.

'Just peachy,' Mo replied, picking it up, but his thick wedge of greying hair was standing upright and he looked like he'd seen a ghost. 'I think you might have saved my neck.' He pointed at one of the bullet holes in what was left of the windscreen. It was at head height on the passenger side.

There wasn't time for Bolt to acknowledge the gratitude in his colleague's voice. 'Get on that radio and tell them to get helicopter support here as soon as possible. We need to track down that shooter. And get ambulances here too. ASAP. I'll go check on our casualty.'

Leaving Mo in the car, Bolt ran back in the direction of the pub, the adrenalin-fuelled excitement he was experiencing tempered by the fact that he'd run down the one man they desperately needed to speak to.

A crowd had gathered outside the pub – about a dozen people in all, mostly men. Most appeared to be milling around, seemingly unable to take in what had just happened, but one was bent down beside a man lying on the ground, giving him what appeared to be an increasingly desperate heart massage.

Bolt's heart sank. Surely he hadn't killed Fallon. That would be the most terrible irony of all.

One of the men saw him coming. 'There he is, the one who hit him!' he shouted in a loud upper-class voice that carried all the way down the street.

Bolt pulled out his warrant card and waved it at the group. 'I'm a police officer,' he called out with as much authority as he could muster, knowing he needed to take control of this situation. 'Move out of the way please.'

The crowd parted a little, letting him through, although they aimed angry mutterings at his back.

'He's dead,' said the man giving the heart massage, looking up as Bolt stopped next to him, his expression one of utter disbelief. 'Jim's dead.'

Bolt looked down and felt a guilty surge of relief. Jim was a well-built man in his fifties, wearing a check shirt and corduroy waistcoat. There was a blackened, coin-shaped hole where his right eye should have been.

'This man's been shot,' he said firmly so that everyone could hear him. 'An ambulance'll be here in a few minutes. We're trying to locate the killer right now, but there's another casualty round here as well.' Then, wiping away the raindrops on his face, he pushed through the group, looking for Fallon, praying he was OK.

He found him lying in a narrow alleyway just up from the pub. He was on his side in an approximate fetal position, and he wasn't moving.

Cursing, Bolt crouched down beside him, feeling for a pulse. 'Mr Fallon, Rob . . . can you talk to me?'

Sirens began wailing in the distance, coming from more than one direction.

Fallon moaned. He was bleeding from the mouth, but he also had a strong pulse. Slowly his eyes opened and he rolled over so he was staring up at Bolt, his face a mask of numb shock. There was a gash above his eye that was weeping a thin trail of blood down one cheek and he had a cut on his head as well.

'It's all right, Rob, you're safe now. I'm a police officer, and an ambulance is on the way.' He showed him his warrant card. 'Can you speak?' he asked, conscious that the sirens were getting closer, and that he had only a short time to talk to Fallon before he was taken to hospital.

'Yeah,' he said weakly, 'I can speak. But I think I might have broken my arm.'

Bolt looked down. His right arm was on the ground beneath him, and for the first time he saw that it was bent at an unpleasant angle.

'The doctors'll fix that. But I need to know about Tina Boyd. Do you have any idea where she is? We need to find her urgently.'

Fallon managed to shake his head a little. 'No. I was trying to get hold of her earlier.'

'Have you been in contact with her today?'

'Yes.'

'Where was she when you last spoke to her?'

Fallon winced in pain. 'Outside the doorman's place. John Gentleman.'

'Doorman?'

'The one at Jenny's place. Jenny Brakspear.' Fallon struggled to sit up, but failed. 'Listen, you've got to find her. The Irish guy, the one with the gun . . . I think he's got her.' He started to say something else but his words were drowned out by the blaring sirens as the first of the emergency services vehicles came to a halt on the road behind them.

Through the noise, Bolt told Fallon once again that he'd be OK now and squeezed his good hand. But inside he was in turmoil.

Where the hell was Tina Boyd?

Thirty-nine

When the phone in his left pocket began to vibrate, the man in the cream suit excused himself from his conversation with the mayor and his wife – a mountain of a woman who'd single-handedly polished off two plates of canapés – and weaved his way through the clusters of guests lining the swimming pool over to the cobbled steps leading down to the beach.

'Where are you calling from?' he demanded, walking along the sand away from the party.

'A phone box,' answered the man he knew only as Hook. 'We've got a problem. The witness I told you about. Fallon. We didn't get him.'

The man in the cream suit hissed through his teeth. It was a sound he made whenever he became angry or frustrated. In this case, he was both. 'I thought I told you specifically to get rid of him.'

'You did, but he managed to evade us.'

'If you'd dealt with him in the beginning, as I wanted you to do, we wouldn't have this problem, would we? Right now, he's a major threat to everything. I want him dead. Put all your resources into it.'

'It's too late. He's in the hands of the police.'

The man in the cream suit hissed again. 'I can't afford problems on this. There's too much riding on it. Neither can you. I'm sure I don't need to remind you that the two million you're being paid is conditional on events reaching a successful conclusion. If Fallon talks, that's not going to happen.'

'He's hurt. I'm not sure how badly, but he was hit head-on by a car travelling at speed which knocked him high into the air. I saw it happen. It's possible he might even be dead.'

'It would be useful if he was, but we can't leave it to chance. Can you get to him in the hospital?'

'It's possible, but it might be too risky.'

'I didn't think you were the kind who scared easily, Mr Hook.'

'I'm not, but I'm no fool either. That's why I'm still here.'

The man in the cream suit thought about pushing him further but decided against it. He was used to getting his own way, but he was also pragmatic enough to know that Hook had a point. 'Do what you can, but events are very close to fruition and nothing can go wrong now. There's too much riding on it. How far away are we from receiving the goods?'

'A matter of hours. As soon as we have them, no one's going to be able to stop us.'

'So everything's in place?'

'Absolutely.'

'Good. Kill Fallon. I'll sleep easier with him gone. And keep me posted on developments.'

He hung up and stopped walking, looking out to sea at the squid boats on the horizon. As with everything in life, there were complications, but the man in the cream suit was not the type to worry unduly. He was a gambler by nature. This was just a bigger gamble than usual. Even if it failed he would still be insulated from its repercussions, because he was also an expert at covering his tracks.

As he returned to the party, he heard his wife's high-pitched, faux upper-class laughter rising above the buzz of chatter as she talked to two middle-aged men in suits, one of whom was gazing unashamedly at her new breasts. The party had been her idea. Charmaine liked to act the glamorous hostess, and the man in the cream suit was happy to go along with it. She was a useful trophy, but little else. His real interest lay in much younger company, and he tended to travel overseas for his gratification, to Phnom Penh, Saigon and Manila.

Charmaine caught his eye as he took a glass of Krug from one of the waitresses, and flashed him an expensive smile. 'Darling, where have you been? I wanted to introduce you to some friends. This is Mohammed.' She pointed to the one focusing on her cleavage. 'And this is Atul. They're in import/export.'

The man in the cream suit came over and put out a hand to each of them in turn. 'Paul Wise,' he said, flashing a smile of his own. 'Very pleased to meet you.'

Forty

Mobile reception in the village was almost non-existent so Bolt found himself shouting into the phone as he walked away from the jumble of emergency services vehicles clustered around the pub. 'I need an armed guard on Robert Fallon. A minimum of three officers. He's currently en route to Wexham Park Hospital in Slough. This is absolutely top priority. He's the only live witness we have to what's been going on here.'

The man Mike Bolt was talking to was Frank Carruthers, the assistant chief constable of Thames Valley Police, currently in charge of the force while his boss was sunning himself on the Algarve, and who up until a few minutes before had been relaxing at home in front of the television. He sounded shell-shocked to find himself suddenly presented with a double murder investigation and absolutely no sign of any suspects.

'It's going to take me time to get a team over there,' explained Carruthers. 'All our ARVs are currently hunting for the gunmen involved in this incident, and we just don't have the resources you lot have got in London.'

'We haven't got time, sir. Mr Fallon was the gunman's target tonight. He managed to get away, but we believe that the gunman is a professional shooter called Michael James Killen, also known as Hook. He's currently wanted for a number of murders, and may well have another go at Fallon.'

'And we're trying to find him now, which is our first priority.'

'Well, you could do worse than try the hospital.'

'There are procedures to follow, Mr Bolt. You know that. I've got to make sure that the area's secure and that there's no immediate threat to members of the public.'

Bolt could have predicted this kind of reaction. Police officers, at senior and junior level, tended to play things far more by the book these days and were discouraged from using their initiative too much. He could sympathize with Carruthers. Everything was target- and procedure-related now, and as one of the brass, if he didn't do everything the right way, he was in trouble.

So he changed tack. 'As I said, Fallon's pretty much the only witness to what happened here tonight. If we do catch Hook and charge him with the murders, we'll need Fallon to give evidence. It's essential he's protected.'

'How serious are his injuries?' asked Carruthers.

'He's hurt, but he's also conscious and talking.'

'And why is he a target exactly?'

'I'm not sure yet, but as soon as I find out anything I'll let you know.'

There was a short silence at the other end. 'OK,' said Carruthers eventually. 'I'll get people over to the hospital as soon as I can.'

Bolt thanked him, knowing he'd done all he could. He wasn't going to leave anything to chance though, and he hurried back to where Mo was leaning against a marked patrol car next to the police cordon, drinking a mug of coffee and talking into his mobile. He still looked shocked, which Bolt could understand. He wasn't feeling it so much himself, partly because he'd been shot at before on more than one occasion, and was better prepared to handle it. Perhaps later, when he was alone, it would hit home. Right now it was something he didn't have time for.

The rain had eased to a light drizzle, and the lane was busy with a mixture of curious onlookers, horrified witnesses and swarms of local uniforms who seemed to have materialized in huge numbers, and SOCO, busy kitting themselves up to begin the fingertip search of the crime scene. Above their heads, a police helicopter circled steadily, although already its presence was obsolete. Hook – and Bolt was now convinced it was him – was long gone.

As Bolt reached him, Mo came off the phone. 'That was Saira,' he said, referring to his wife and the mother of his four children. 'I was telling her not to wait up for me. I didn't have the heart to tell her that someone just tried to shoot us.'

Bolt smiled grimly. 'Probably just as well.'

'You know, boss,' he said, sounding subdued, 'I'll vouch for you that Fallon was in the middle of the road, and you weren't driving erratically when you hit him. In case they bring the IPCC in.'

'Thanks, I appreciate it.' He gave Mo's arm an affectionate pat. 'Right now, though, it's the least of our worries. We need to get over to the hospital. The armed guard's not set up yet and I want to make sure nothing happens to Fallon.'

'How are we going to get over there? We've lost our transport.'

'No we haven't.' He motioned for Mo to follow and set off through the mêlée, conscious of the fact that he had to keep his colleague distracted so that the shock didn't begin to overwhelm him. Right now, he needed Mo.

The Jag was still parked halfway up the bank at the end of the village, temporarily forgotten. A single uniform stood guard over it, since technically it remained part of the crime scene. Pulling out his keys, Bolt flashed his warrant card, said he had permission from

Assistant Chief Constable Carruthers to remove the vehicle, and carried on walking.

'I don't think we should do this, boss,' said Mo once they'd climbed in. 'We have the slight problem that we can't actually see anything out of the windscreen.'

Bolt would never have described himself as impulsive, but he took a huge amount of satisfaction from his next move, which was to reach down behind the driver's seat, lift up the Enforcer – the heavy cylindrical tool used for breaking down doors – and smash it through the ruined windscreen. The driver's half disappeared completely as glass flew across the bonnet and on to the grass below. 'We can now,' he said.

He manoeuvred the car back on to the road with a loud bump so that it was facing away from the murder scene, relieved to realize that the vehicle was still in good working order. In his rearview mirror, Bolt saw the uniform staring at him aghast. Bolt had a moment's doubt too, but it didn't stop him from accelerating away, weaving around the Road Closed sign and heading in the direction of Slough.

Forty-one

The room was small, square and empty, save for the heavy office chair Tina Boyd was strapped tight to. She was cold and tired – naked too, apart from her blouse and socks.

He'd removed all her other clothes when they were alone together earlier, slicing them off with a knife before tossing them casually into the corner. Tina had been expecting him to rape her, but strangely he hadn't, preferring to use his hands to stroke and paw her, every so often breaking off and pacing slowly around the chair, taunting her in cruel little whispers.

Are you ready to die yet?

Do you want me to fuck you now, or should I wait for the others?

She'd said nothing, enduring his attention in cold, defiant silence, trying to ignore the way her skin slithered and crawled under his touch, preparing for the inevitable.

But the inevitable had not yet come. It was as if he'd suddenly lost interest, replacing the hood on her head and leaving the room with a final, almost half-hearted taunt.

Later, bitch.

That had been hours back now; since then there'd been nothing but silence. She couldn't even hear anything outside. She was freezing cold and starving hungry, and worst of all she was utterly alone, with no prospect of help.

The thought scared her. Her life had been hard these past four years, and in some ways it had been getting worse, particularly the constant fight with the booze, but she wasn't going to give it up without a fight. In a fit of sudden desperation she struggled against her bonds, howling her frustration from behind the gag as the realization that her efforts were utterly pointless hit her once again. The only part of her body she could move was her head. It was as if she was paralysed from the neck down. Her ankles were tied to the chair's base with ropes, and her hands and elbows were lashed to the arm rests. Several rolls of thick masking tape had been wrapped round and round her chest and stomach, giving her the appearance of a half-dressed mummy. Thankfully, the set of picks in her sock hadn't been discovered. She might not have been able to reach them but they still represented some sort of hope, however faint.

Suddenly she heard something. It was a muffled cry, coming from beyond the wall.

For a second, she thought she'd imagined it. Then it came again. Someone was trying to call out to her but whoever it was was gagged too.

Jenny Brakspear! It had to be her. So she was still alive . . .

Tina made a noise in return, using her weight to try to force the chair nearer to the wall. But the damn thing wouldn't budge. Someone had removed the wheels, and it was way too heavy. She made more noises, wanting to let Jenny know that she wasn't entirely alone. Relieved herself, that she wasn't the only prisoner here.

Tina waited for a response, but the cries from beyond the wall had stopped. Then she heard something else, much fainter this time. The sound of weeping.

Tina made some supportive noises, hoping this would encourage Jenny to stop, but the weeping continued, then finally it stopped altogether, and the cold silence returned.

She wondered what Jenny had had to put up with from the man who'd kidnapped her, what kinds of torments he'd put her through. She also wondered what it was that was going on here. They'd kidnapped Jenny two days ago and were clearly keeping her alive. They were keeping Tina alive, too.

The burning question was, for how long?

Wednesday

Forty-two

I was feeling groggy, having been given painkillers by a harassed-looking doctor who couldn't have been long out of medical school, and they must have been pretty damn strong because the terrible burning sensation in my right arm had been reduced to a dull throb. I still ached all over, and my mouth was bone dry, but I felt a vague euphoria. I was alive. Against all the odds, I was alive.

My hospital room was small and bright, and I was lying in bed. Outside I could hear voices and people moving about. Comforting sounds. People meant safety. The clock on the wall read ten past midnight.

As I lay there, I remembered with intense clarity digging my own grave in the rain, and watching Maxwell die. I'd never seen someone die before, even though I'd written about death vividly enough in *Conspiracy*. The sight of Ramon sitting lifeless in my bedroom had been awful, but seeing Maxwell actually murdered in front of me had been a whole lot worse. I remembered running through the trees, hearing the men behind me, thinking that this was it, the end; then the headlights, the sound of screeching tyres, and the car slamming me over its bonnet and sending me flying into the dirt.

Jesus. I'd been so damn close to death. For the second time in less than forty-eight hours. It was as if I was involved in an intense, never-ending nightmare that seemed to get worse and worse.

But it looked at last like it might be over.

I was desperately thirsty. I hadn't drunk a thing since the two Peronis at Maxwell's, close to four hours ago now, and no water since the middle of the afternoon. There wasn't a glass on the bed-side table so I climbed out of bed, my hospital-issue pyjamas crinkling in time to my movement. My head began to spin and I had to stand still and shut my eyes for a few moments.

When I felt normal again, I opened the door and was surprised to see there was no police guard outside. The guy who'd come to me when I was semi-conscious had said he was police and that I was safe now. So, where were they?

I stepped out into the corridor.

And saw him immediately.

He was about ten yards away, talking to one of the nurses. He was dressed in the black jacket and jeans he'd been wearing back at Maxwell's place earlier, and his boots were still muddy with the soil from Maxwell's vegetable patch, but he was wearing a baseball cap again now, and horn-rimmed glasses.

For a split second I froze, unable to move, then he slowly turned my way and our eyes met. His lips curled in a tight, triumphant smile and, ignoring the nurse now, he put a hand inside his jacket.

And that was it. I ran.

But it was like wading through treacle. The painkillers, my injuries, my pure exhaustion, they were all slowing me down, making each step seem like an incredible achievement. And all the time I could picture him in my mind, raising the gun, aiming, pulling the trigger . . .

I swung a hard left, narrowly missing a cleaner with his trolley coming the other way. Behind me, I could hear his footfalls as he gave chase. Someone yelled for security. Someone else screamed the words I was dreading: 'He's got a gun!'

In front of me, the corridor stretched for thirty yards. A pair of orderlies were coming the other way, with a patient on a stretcher. Apart from them, it was empty. I was never going to make it. No way.

In one instinctive movement I shoved the cleaner out of the way with my good arm, then, as my pursuer came round the corner, a calm, determined expression on his face, the gun he'd used to kill Maxwell by his side, I kicked the trolley straight at him.

He was caught by surprise and crashed right into it, his momentum sending him sprawling in a heap.

Ignoring the nausea rising up in me, and the throbbing in my head and arm, I kept running. My heart hammering relentlessly.

The two orderlies stared at me aghast, then they both ducked down, using their gurney as cover.

I didn't wait for the bullet. I saw a door coming up on my right and scrambled through it, slamming it shut behind me.

I was in a small ward. A handful of beds were lined up against the opposite wall. But they were all empty. The whole place was empty. Outside, I could hear panicked shouting. More footfalls.

I was trapped. Jesus, I was trapped.

Looking round quickly, I located the light switch, flicked it off and plunged the room into darkness. Then, as quickly as I could, I slipped under one of the beds furthest from the door, and lay there on my back, staring up at the mattress several inches above me, knowing this was no cover at all, trying to calm my breathing. Waiting . . .

The door opened and shut again, and the lights were switched back on.

I held my breath. Outside, the noise seemed to have died away. Where the hell was everyone?

The footsteps were quiet as the man moved through the room, coming steadily closer. My guts churned, my heart beat furiously in my chest. I tried desperately to think of an escape plan, my mind whirring and leaping but coming up with nothing, because of course there was nothing to come up with.

The footsteps stopped. Right next to the bed. My lungs felt like they were going to burst. I had to breathe soon, had to—

'Mr Fallon?'

I recognized the voice. It was the police officer from earlier, the one who was with me after I'd been hit by the car, before the ambulance came.

'My name's Mike Bolt, and I'm from the Serious and Organized Crime Agency.'

He helped me out from under the bed and I got a proper look at him for the first time. He was tall and well built, with close-cropped silver-blond hair and piercing blue eyes, and there were three small scars on the lean, slightly lined face, one of them a vivid C-shape gouged into his cheek, that gave him an appearance that was close to, but not quite, thuggish. Right then he inspired confidence and I was glad he was on my side.

'You lead a charmed life, Mr Fallon,' he said, leading me out into the corridor, where a number of medical staff had gathered to see what was going on.

'Have you got the guy who was after me?' I asked him.

'We're looking for him now,' he answered as we walked back to my room. 'But there's no need for you to worry. We've got armed officers all over the building.'

I felt like saying that this could be construed as being a bit late, but didn't bother. I was pleased just to be safe, a feeling that was reinforced when I saw the three black-clad Robocop lookalikes standing outside the door of my room, wielding machine guns.

Standing off to one side of them in jeans and check shirt was a short, squat Asian guy with a thick head of hair like a badger's, talking animatedly to the harassed-looking junior doctor who'd examined me earlier.

'This is my colleague, Mo Khan,' said Bolt as the Asian guy turned round. 'We'd like to ask you some questions quickly if that's OK? It's extremely urgent.'

'I don't think this is a good idea,' said the doctor, pushing past Mo Khan. 'This patient needs rest,' he added firmly, addressing Mike Bolt.

'It's OK,' I said, pleased for the opportunity to finally tell my story in full. 'I'll speak to them now.'

A few minutes later I was back in bed with a glass of water in my hand, feeling a little more relaxed as they took seats on either side of the bed.

'OK,' said Bolt as Mo Khan produced a tape recorder, 'we understand you witnessed a kidnapping. Take us through everything from the beginning. And please don't leave anything out.'

So this time I didn't. I told them everything, including what had happened to Ramon, knowing that there was no longer any point in holding anything back. Neither of them seemed fazed by my revelations. Instead they took me through every important detail of the past forty-eight hours, slowly and carefully, asking questions where necessary, but otherwise allowing me to talk.

When I'd finished, I felt numb and spent. I took a big gulp of water and sat back against the pillows, hoping they believed me, but not sure what else I could say.

'You're extremely lucky, Mr Fallon,' said Bolt, leaning forward in his seat. 'The man who's been after you is a professional killer.'

'You know him, then?'

'I know of him. His name's Michael Killen, and he's extremely dangerous.'

Hearing his name took away some of the mystery surrounding

him. It had a diminishing effect, making him smaller and pettier, somehow less immortal. 'I know I'm lucky to be alive,' I said, suddenly feeling deflated. 'But does this mean you'll be able to find Jenny now? And Tina? She's still missing, isn't she?'

Bolt nodded, an expression of concern crossing his face. It was clear he knew her. 'Unfortunately she is, yes,' he answered. 'We're in a better position to find both of them now we've talked to you and you've filled in the gaps, but I've got to be honest, we're still short of leads.'

'So, Killen's escaped then?'

'It looks that way. And I've got no doubt he knows where both women are.'

It was Mo Khan who spoke next. 'Is there anything you can think of, Mr Fallon, any clue at all that might help us find them? Something you saw or heard that you haven't yet told us about?'

'I've still got those photos that Tina sent me.'

'We've already seen them,' he said.

I wondered how this could be but didn't say anything. I was too busy racking my brains, but unfortunately to no avail. 'I'm sorry,' I told them at last, 'I can't think of anything.'

They looked disappointed but thanked me for my help and got to their feet. It was clear they were finished with me for now.

'One thing before you go,' I said. 'You turned up out of the blue at Maxwell's place tonight. How did you know I was there?'

'Maxwell – Harvey Hammond – was a police informant of mine for a number of years,' Bolt answered.

That caught me out. 'I was writing a book about him,' I said. 'I thought he was some bigshot criminal.'

'No, he was small-time. He used to know a lot of people on the fringes, and he was good at keeping his ear to the ground, but he was no Ronnie Kray.' He gave me a sympathetic look, seeing that this news represented something of an unpleasant surprise.

In truth, it was one of the biggest shocks I'd had in the last few days. I'd really believed in Maxwell, had been totally taken in by his tales of villainy. To find out that he was nothing but a lowlife snitch made me feel like a gullible prick.

'One thing I've learned in twenty years as a cop,' continued Bolt, 'is that the real bad guys don't tend to talk about what they do, only the wannabes. Look at it this way, though. If it hadn't been for Maxwell calling me to let us know you were at his place, you'd be dead now.'

As they turned to leave, something else occurred to me. 'And how did Killen and his mate manage to track me down to Maxwell's cottage? I'm positive I wasn't followed there and no one knew that was where I was going.'

They exchanged glances again, and it was clear that neither of them had thought about this.

There was a pause of a couple of seconds before a look of realization crossed Mo Khan's face. 'You said Killen gave you back your phone when he came to your place on Monday night, didn't you?'

I nodded.

'Where's the phone now?'

'In my jeans pocket.' I pointed to where my clothes were hanging over a chair in the corner.

He went through them until he found it and then, as I watched, he took off the back and started fiddling round inside. A couple of seconds later he removed a small round object, about half the size of a penny piece. He held it up for me to see. It emitted a tiny flashing red light. 'A GPS tracking device. Simple, yet highly effective.' He gave me a look that might have been sympathetic, or was possibly just pitying. 'It seems, Mr Fallon, that they knew exactly where you were the whole time.'

Forty-three

Bolt stood in the hospital car park, breathing in the cool night air. The rain had stopped completely now, leaving behind the smell of late summer foliage. He'd just finished paying the man from Autoglass, who'd put a new windscreen on the Jag, and he was pissed off.

To have come so close to Hook – the man he'd been after for five years – and then lose him wasn't easy to stomach, particularly with Tina unaccounted for. But it could have been worse. They'd almost lost Fallon as well. When they'd arrived at the hospital earlier and run into the ARV team tasked with guarding Fallon at the entrance, they'd heard the commotion and had run through accident and emergency, disturbing Hook, who'd abandoned his pursuit of Fallon and fled, using two orderlies and their gurney as cover. Bolt had even caught a glimpse of him, thirty yards away down the end of a corridor. So near, yet so bloody far.

His mobile started ringing.

It was Big Barry Freud. 'What on earth's going on, Mike?' he demanded. 'I've just had a call from the assistant chief constable of Thames Valley Police. He says you've been involved in a shoot-out in Berkshire, ran someone over, and drove off in a car that was being treated as crime-scene evidence. Care to explain?'

When he put it like that, it didn't sound too good, but Bolt was fairly certain that his actions had helped save Fallon's life, which was going to earn him some sort of credit. He gave Barry a brief rundown of the situation.

'So you're saying it's all to do with this bloody kidnap that Tina Boyd's been investigating?'

'It looks that way. Hook's definitely trying to do everything he can to shut up Fallon. And he's taking some massive risks. Like coming here tonight.'

'Blimey. It must be a very lucrative kidnapping to be worth all this effort and this many murders. What do we know about this girl?'

'Her name's Jenny Brakspear. And it's not a lot, but according to Tina, her father denied that any kidnapping had actually taken place. He said she'd gone on holiday. I had one of the team check up on Jenny's and her dad's backgrounds earlier, but everything ended up being put to one side when we got the call about Tina, and I haven't got the results back yet.'

'I heard that the body wasn't Tina's.'

'No.' Bolt knew he should have phoned Barry and told him it wasn't, but things had been happening so fast that night there'd been hardly a moment to stop and think.

'And you still haven't heard from her?'

Bolt sighed. 'No we haven't. But we've talked to Fallon.'

'Was he any help?'

'He's filled us in on what happened, but the problem is he didn't really know Jenny that well.'

'Great.' Big Barry exhaled loudly down the phone. 'Which of the team was looking into Jenny's background?'

'Kris Obanje. I think Mo's on the phone to him now.' Bolt

looked across to where his colleague was standing on the hospital steps, talking animatedly into his mobile and taking notes at the same time.

'Good. Find out what you can and keep me in the loop. I'm at home.'

Bolt said he would, and ended the call. It was 1.20 in the morning, and he was exhausted. But he had a feeling neither he nor Mo Khan were going to be sleeping any time soon.

Forty-four

'According to Obanje, Jenny Brakspear's a complete unknown,' said Mo, pocketing his phone. 'Currently unemployed. She worked for an internet travel company based in Islington until about three months ago but got made redundant because of the credit crunch. No criminal record. Just an ordinary middle-class girl.'

'Her dad's the key,' said Bolt. 'He's the one they've got to be blackmailing. What did Obanje find out about him?'

'He's a company director of a gas wholesaler based in Cambridge. Good salary, and he's a part owner of the company, but there's not enough to hold him to ransom over. If he liquidated all his assets tomorrow then Kris reckons he could probably raise a few hundred thousand, but he hasn't even attempted to do that. The company's listed on AIM, the small company stock exchange, and there've been no share transactions this week, which there would have been if he'd been trying to raise money by selling his shares.'

'So it's something else.'

They both stood in silence for a minute.

Then a thought struck Bolt. 'You said Brakspear's a director of a gas company. What type of gases do they deal with?'

Mo shrugged. 'I don't know, and I don't think Kris looked into it in too much detail. But they wouldn't be ransoming her for gas, would they? It can't be worth that much money.'

'But if it's not money, I don't know what else it could be. Have you got a name for the company?'

He flicked open his notebook. 'Mainline Gas Services.'

'Let's look them up.'

Mo Khan always kept his laptop with him on jobs. It was currently under the seat in the Jaguar. They got inside the car and he looked up Mainline on the net, using a plug-in stick.

The company's website was pretty basic. It gave a brief history and an even briefer description of the services offered, and the gases they dealt with, none of which looked particularly controversial, although Bolt knew that this didn't mean much.

Mainline had two directors. One was Roy Brakspear, and when Mo double-clicked on his name the photograph of an ordinary-looking man in his fifties with grey hair and an avuncular smile appeared. His background was equally ordinary. A Masters degree in Chemistry from Cambridge; twelve years as a chemist at ICI before founding Mainline with an ICI colleague in 1987; one adult daughter. No mention of a wife. The ICI colleague was Miles Cavendish, now managing director, a younger-looking guy with red hair in a side parting and a much more confident, go-getting smile in his website photo.

'We need to speak to this guy,' said Bolt, pointing at Cavendish's mug.

'He's not going to be pleased being woken at this time in the morning.'

'It's an emergency. We've got no choice.'

It only took a few minutes to find Cavendish's number. SOCA

had access to every registered telephone number in the country, but in this case Bolt bypassed HQ and phoned directory enquiries, immediately striking gold.

'This guy must be one of the last people in the country listed in the phone book,' he said as he wrote down the number. 'I'd never have my number there for every Tom, Dick and Harry to see.'

Mo shrugged. 'Saira insists on it. Just in case any of her old friends are trying to look her up.'

'And do any?'

'No. All we get are calls from Indian call centres.'

'I think when he finds out what this is about, Cavendish is going to wish we were an Indian call centre.'

He dialled the number. The phone seemed to ring for ever. Bolt was just about to give up when a hugely irritated male voice came over the line. 'Yes?'

'Miles Cavendish?'

'That's me,' he answered, still not sounding quite awake. 'Who am I speaking to, please?'

Bolt introduced himself and heard the audible intake of breath. No one likes a call from SOCA.

'How can I help you?' There was concern in his voice.

Bolt knew he had to choose his words carefully. He needed answers but he didn't want to have to give too much away. 'Can you tell me if your company, Mainline, handles any gases that could be described as expensive? Or dangerous?'

'Excuse me, can you explain what on earth this is all about? It's half past one in the morning.'

'Can you please answer the question, sir?'

'Look,' snapped Cavendish, 'how do I even know you are who you say you are? You could be anyone. Let me call you back.'

'I'm on a mobile.'

'In that case, goodbye. I'm not talking to people whose credentials I can't see.'

Bolt started to say something else but he was talking into a dead phone, and when he called back it was engaged. He shook his head angrily. 'Arsehole,' he cursed.

'You can't blame him, boss. You wouldn't give out information to someone who called you at home, would you?'

Bolt sighed. 'We're going to have to get his address and drive up there.'

'We could arrange for local CID to go round there if we told them what we needed to know. It would save us a long journey.'

Bolt looked at his colleague. There were big black bags under his eyes and he looked shattered. 'I'd rather do it myself, but there's no need for you to come with me. Honestly. I can drop you back home on the way. It's different for me. It's personal.'

Mo frowned. 'I was never a major fan of Tina Boyd, boss, but I still want to find her. And I want Hook just as much as you do. I worked the Leticia Jones case as well, remember?'

'I just thought maybe you could do with the rest. You look pretty whacked out.'

'I am. But look in the mirror. You do, too. We're in this together, boss. And also, there's still the matter that you saved my neck tonight, whatever you might think. So I owe you. Make the most of it. It won't last for ever.'

Bolt smiled. He felt touched, but didn't know quite what to say. In the end, he turned on the Jag's engine, backed out of the parking space, and once again they were on the move.

Forty-five

Miles Cavendish lived in the village of Stretham, about ten miles north of Cambridge on the A10, and it wasn't far short of three in the morning when Bolt and Mo finally pulled up in front of an attractive barn conversion set back a hundred yards from the road down a quiet lane.

Security lights illuminated the whole of the well-kept front garden, and as they got out of the car more lights came on in the house. By the time they got to the front door it had been opened on a chain by the man from the website photo. He was in a dressing gown and striped pyjamas and his hair was a mess. He eyed them with a mixture of suspicion and concern.

'Mr Cavendish, we spoke earlier.' Bolt placed his warrant card in the gap so that Cavendish could examine it as carefully as he wanted.

'Oh God,' said Cavendish, releasing the chain and opening the door. 'So it wasn't a hoax.'

'I'm afraid not,' answered Bolt as he and Mo stepped inside.

They followed Cavendish through to a traditionally decorated lounge and he invited them to sit down. 'I'm sorry about earlier but

I've been the victim of identity fraud before and I'm very careful what I say on the phone to people I don't know. Could you please tell me what this is about?' He looked at them anxiously.

They'd decided on the way up to treat Cavendish as if he was a suspect. Which meant not giving much away.

'We can't tell you very much, I'm afraid,' Bolt replied. 'Right now, we just want you to answer our questions.'

Cavendish went white. 'We're a very respectable company, officers. We've got nothing to hide, I promise. We pay our taxes on time—'

'Firstly,' said Mo, 'can you tell me what your organization does?'

'We're a gas wholesaler. Basically, we buy certain specialist gases, directly from the manufacturers in this country and Europe, and sell them on in smaller quantities to our clients, who are mainly in the pharmaceutical and technology sectors.'

'And are there any gases your company handles that could be classed as highly expensive?'

'Yes. Some of the loads are worth a lot of money. A mixed batch of, say, xenon, tungsten hexaflouride, helium-3 isotope, could be worth as much as a hundred thousand pounds.'

That seemed to Bolt to be a lot of money for gas, but it wasn't the kind of figure worth killing people for. 'And do you handle dangerous gases as well?'

'Numerous. We deal in toxics and flammables. You'll have to be more specific.'

'What about radioactive materials?'

'No, we don't deal with radioactives. That's a very specialized area. Please, Mr Bolt, can you tell me what you're getting at?'

Bolt couldn't help feeling sorry for the guy. Unless he was an extremely good actor, it was clear he wasn't involved in Jenny Brakspear's abduction. But it was still essential that he take their enquiries absolutely seriously.

'Could you tell me if any orders for dangerous gases have been made in the past three days? Is that possible to check?'

Cavendish looked at them both in turn. 'All orders of hazardous gases or chemicals need a director's signature,' he said eventually. 'And there are only two directors. Myself—'

'And Roy Brakspear,' said Mo, finishing the sentence off for him. 'When was the last time you spoke to him?'

'Monday morning,' he answered. 'Roy wasn't feeling well. He said he'd been getting stomach cramps over the weekend. We discussed a client proposal we've got coming up but we didn't talk for long.'

'Has he been into work at all this week?'

Cavendish shook his head. 'No, we agreed it was better for him to work at home until he felt better.'

'So you haven't seen Roy at all this week?'

Again he shook his head. 'No. I tried to call him earlier on tonight to check that he was OK but he didn't answer. I assume he was sleeping. He's like me. He lives on his own.'

'But he has a daughter,' said Bolt.

'That's right. Jenny.'

'So he was married once?'

'He was. Celia passed away five years ago. She had stomach cancer. It was very tragic.'

Bolt felt a twinge of sympathy for Brakspear. He'd lost Mikaela seven years ago, yet still thought about her every day. A loss like that never really goes away, and for Brakspear to now face losing his only daughter must be unbearable. He would do anything to keep her alive. The question was, what had he done?

'Can you tell me if Roy's placed any orders for gases or chemicals this week?' he asked. 'Particularly anything out of the ordinary.'

Cavendish frowned. 'Mr Bolt, I've worked with Roy Brakspear for over twenty years now and I can assure you that he's as straight as a die. I can promise you he's done absolutely nothing wrong.'

Bolt leaned forward in his seat and fixed Cavendish with a hard stare. 'Can you just check for us, Mr Cavendish? Please.'

'OK,' he said reluctantly, getting to his feet. 'If he has, it'll be recorded on our system. I can access it from the study.'

They followed him through the lounge to a wide airy room at the back of the house where a mahogany desk faced out into the back garden, and waited in silence while Cavendish booted up his PC. When it was up and running he sat down and began typing.

Bolt rubbed his eyes and thought about Tina, wondered where she was and whether she was even still alive. He hadn't wanted to admit it to himself but, though the kidnappers might have a good reason to keep Jenny alive if they wanted her father to do something for them, they had no obvious reason to do the same with Tina. In fact, quite the reverse. She'd been investigating them, so clearly it would be better if she was out of the way. The only thing giving Bolt hope was the fact that her body hadn't been found yet, even though her car had. It wasn't much, but until he heard otherwise he'd keep searching for her.

'Nothing yet,' said Cavendish, without looking round, still tapping away on the keyboard. 'As I've said to you already, Roy's as straight as a die. He won't have made any significant orders – anything out of the ordinary, as you put it – without telling me.'

Bolt leaned against the wall, feeling frustrated. Roy Brakspear was being blackmailed, he was absolutely sure of it. No other explanation made sense. But if it wasn't something to do with his work, then what the hell was it?

'Christ.' Cavendish had stopped tapping on the keyboard and was now staring at something on the screen.

'What is it?'

Bolt and Mo hurried over to where he was sitting. On the screen was an invoice that appeared to be in German.

'I don't understand it,' said Cavendish distantly. 'Roy has put in an order. For a whole lorry load of phosgene. Now why on earth would he do that? We only ever buy it one pallet at a time.'

'What is phosgene?' asked Bolt.

Cavendish turned to face him. 'It's a component for pharmaceutical products, and it's more commonly used name is mustard gas.'

Bolt was confused. 'Mustard gas? The stuff they used to use in the First World War? And Roy Brakspear was able to order it? Just like that?'

'It's a legal product, Mr Bolt, manufactured in Germany. And we're authorized to import it. This quantity is unusually large, but it won't have been queried because the company has been dealing with us for years.'

'When was this order placed?' asked Mo.

Cavendish typed a command. 'Seven a.m. on Monday morning, so he must have done it remotely. I spoke to Roy about two hours later and he didn't say anything about it.'

'Is there time to cancel the order?' snapped Bolt.

Cavendish typed another command, and Bolt heard him swallow. 'No,' he said quietly. 'According to the system it was picked up at the factory in Germany at two o'clock yesterday afternoon. It must have been a rush order, but I've got no idea who it could be for. Roy hasn't listed who the end user is.'

He didn't need to, thought Bolt. The end user in this case was going to be Hook. But what the hell was he going to do with a lorry load of mustard gas?

'What would happen if the gas was released?' he asked Cavendish. 'What sort of damage would it do?'

Cavendish turned in his seat so he was facing Bolt. He looked stunned. 'But who's going to release it?'

'Just answer the question.'

'It depends on the weather conditions and how it is released. It's carried in light steel cylinders and you can't simply blow them up because that would render the gas ineffective. However, if there was very little wind, the gas was dispersed in a crowded area, and the people who carried out the dispersal somehow managed to break the valves on the cylinders simultaneously without damaging the phosgene, then . . .' He paused, and when he spoke again, his voice cracked a little. 'I dread to think. The death toll would be hundreds at least. Possibly even thousands.'

Bolt looked at Mo, whose face was draining of colour. Bolt was shocked himself. He knew what Hook was capable of. They both did. There were only two reasons why a man like him could possibly want something as lethal as this. Either to blackmail some other organization, the government perhaps. Or to commit a terrorist act.

Bolt forced himself to remain calm. 'We need to locate the load urgently,' he said. 'How do we do it?'

'I don't know which driver we used. Roy didn't fill his name in on the order form. There'll be a signature on the paperwork though. That should tell us who it is.' He began typing again, and a copy of the German invoice reappeared on the screen. 'There's the signature,' he said, pointing to an illegible squiggle in the bottom right-hand corner. He examined it closely, shaking his head. 'I'm afraid I don't recognize it.'

'What the hell is this?' demanded Mo, his face red with anger. 'You don't know who the hell's driving a deadly cargo on your company's behalf?'

Bolt could understand his friend's reaction. He had a wife and four children at home in London. If Hook was plotting a terrorist outrage then it was a fair guess that the capital would be the target, which put a hugely personal slant on the case.

'It's not my fault if Roy didn't fill out the information,' said Cavendish defensively.

Mo wasn't mollified. 'What about the checks and balances?' he asked. 'You should have known about it. You're a director of the company, for God's sake.'

'Roy's a director, too. He's in charge of the bloody checks and balances. How was I to know he'd do something like this? I can't understand it. What the hell did he think he was doing?' Cavendish put his head in his hands and stared down at the desktop.

Bolt put a hand on his shoulder. 'OK, Mr Cavendish, no one's saying it's your fault. But we really do need to locate the lorry carrying this load.'

Cavendish slowly lifted his head and looked up at Bolt with frightened eyes. 'That's the problem, Mr Bolt. We don't have any of our own drivers. We use agency ones, and they come from all over the place. That bloody gas could be anywhere.'

Forty-six

Mike Bolt was an optimist. He'd had some hard, hard times – the death of Mikaela being the hardest of all – but he remained conscious of the fact that if he kept a level head and rode the punches thrown at him, eventually he'd come through the other side, and things would get better. Because if you let them, they always did.

But at that moment he was having to work hard to keep his spirits up. Finding the mustard gas and, by extension, Tina and Jenny Brakspear was looking like an impossible task. In Hook, they were up against a highly professional operator who'd only remained at liberty for so long because he kept ahead of the game. But it was still possible, he told himself. It was just a matter of staying calm and working through the leads they had, and for that they needed resources.

It was twenty to four when Bolt stepped outside into Cavendish's back garden, leaving Mo inside with him. He dialled Big Barry's home number. The case had changed dramatically now that national security was threatened, and Bolt needed his boss's help.

Big Barry still sounded asleep when he answered the phone, but that didn't last long. 'How could this happen?' he demanded when Bolt told him about the mustard gas.

'All too easily, by the sound of things. Obviously, the important thing is to find the bloody stuff. Cavendish is in a bit of a state of shock.'

'I'm not bloody surprised. He'll be in even more of a one if it gets let off and it's his firm that's responsible for it. How bad could it be if it's released?'

Bolt told him.

'Christ.' There was silence on the other end of the line as Big Barry took the information in. 'I'm going to have to get the director involved. The PM's going to have to know about this as well. This is government-level stuff.'

'I know,' said Bolt, moving further into the garden. 'Cavendish has given us a list of agencies in the UK and Europe that Mainline have used before to hire drivers. But there are a lot of them. Eighteen altogether. And as Brakspear was trying to hide what he was doing, it's possible he could have gone to someone else.'

'How do we know that he even hired a driver? What's to stop him sending one of the kidnappers over to pick up the order?'

'I asked Cavendish about that. All drivers carrying hazardous goods have to have something called an APR licence, which has photo ID on it. They give them out to plenty of people, but it's unlikely the company manufacturing the mustard gas in Germany would have given the order to someone who didn't have a valid one. One could always be faked, I suppose, but my guess is Hook's going to try to intercept the load somewhere between the factory and the final destination, which is a secure facility that Mainline have just outside Cambridge.'

'If he hasn't done it already.' Big Barry sighed. 'OK, email me that list and the name of the company in Germany. I'll get resources lined up to contact everyone, but it's all going to take a while at this time of the morning.'

'There might be a quicker way,' said Bolt.

'What?'

'I'm pretty sure Brakspear was being imprisoned in his home shortly after Jenny was kidnapped. He was there on Monday because Tina and Cavendish both told me they called him at different times, and he was there when Fallon turned up yesterday morning. So it's possible he called the agency to hire the driver from his home phone. If we check the records, we might be able to find out who it is.'

'Good thinking,' said Big Barry, suddenly sounding a little happier. 'Good work, old mate. I tell you: if we stop this stuff falling into the wrong hands, it'll be a real result for SOCA. A high-profile one, too.'

Bolt knew that his boss was always on the lookout for the big result that would get him on to the next rung of the SOCA ladder, and nearer to his final goal of directorship. Ordinarily, Bolt would have let it go. He was used to Barry's attitude, and because he was a decent enough boss he could generally tolerate it, but these weren't ordinary times. 'I'll be happy when we get Tina and Jenny Brakspear back,' he countered, making little attempt to disguise the irritation in his voice.

'Of course, of course,' said Big Barry, backtracking. 'And what about Roy Brakspear? You said he was at home yesterday morning. Is it possible he's still there?'

'I doubt it, sir. My gut feeling is that Hook would have moved him after Fallon turned up, just in case Fallon raised the alarm. And if not then, they'd have moved him by now because Hook must know we've spoken to Fallon.'

'Hook's got a lot on his plate at the moment and he can't be operating with that many people. He might not have had the chance. Can you get down to Brakspear's place and take a look around? You're up that way, aren't you? In the meantime, I'll get a full surveillance team with armed back-up, and a search warrant sorted out. We might have to break him out of there.'

'I don't want to do anything that endangers Tina, sir. Or Jenny.'

'We'll do what we can to bring them home in one piece, but I'm sorry to have to say it, old mate, but as of now they've ceased to be top priority.'

Forty-seven

Bolt and Mo were exhausted, operating purely on adrenalin as they drove to Brakspear's place.

'I want to tell Saira to take the kids out of London for a couple of days,' said Mo after a long silence. 'Her sister's in Leicester. They can go and stay there. There's enough room.'

'Don't do anything yet,' Bolt told him. 'We don't even know the current whereabouts of the gas, and it's important we keep things under wraps as much as possible. We don't want to start some kind of panic.'

'That's easy for you to say,' Mo snapped. 'You don't have a family.' He stopped himself from going on, a look of anguish crossing his face. 'I'm sorry, boss, I didn't mean it like that. It's just, you know . . .' He shook his head. 'All this is a lot to take on board.'

'It's all right,' said Bolt. He knew he'd almost certainly have done the same if Mikaela was still alive: made a call, told her to keep quiet but to get out of the city. Now that he lived alone it was hypocritical for him to deny others the chance to put the safety of the people they loved first. 'Do what you think's right, Mo,' he said eventually. 'I won't stand in your way.'

Mo nodded, and fell silent again.

It had just turned quarter to five when they reached Roy Brakspear's house. Bolt slowed down a touch as they passed the front entrance. The wrought-iron gates were shut but he caught a glimpse of Brakspear's car on the driveway.

They parked next to a terrace of whitewashed cottages nearby and got out of the car. The first signs of light were appearing on the horizon and the early morning was peaceful and silent. Big Barry had called back to tell Bolt that a surveillance team wouldn't be available for at least an hour, but he'd also said that if he thought the place was empty then they should go inside and worry about the consequences later. Which suited Bolt just fine.

A footpath at the end of the terrace ran parallel to the exterior wall of Brakspear's property to a cornfield beyond, and they moved up it in silence. The side gate was locked, but as long-term surveillance officers they were used to getting into places they weren't supposed to, and they helped each other over the wall and into the garden.

The house was quiet, with all the curtains drawn, and they crept quietly across the lawn until they reached the back door. Bolt listened at the glass but heard nothing beyond. He tried the door handle but it was locked. The lock was old, though, and could be picked in seconds.

He and Mo exchanged glances. It was likely Brakspear wasn't there, but it was also possible he was, and that whoever was baby-sitting him would be armed.

'Let's do it,' whispered Mo.

Bolt nodded, produced his picks, and a few seconds later they were inside an old-fashioned utility room with a washing machine and fridge freezer. Both men produced their standard-issue pepper sprays – the only weapons they had, and woefully inadequate if they encountered trouble. Holding his out in front of him, his finger on the nozzle, Bolt crept through the silent house, conscious of Mo right behind him.

The utility room gave way to a spacious kitchen with a breakfast bar in the middle that had obviously been refitted recently. Unwashed pots and pans filled the sink and there was a faint odour of fried food.

They moved into the silent gloom of the hallway. A dying moonlight filtered in through the window above the front door illuminating a framed poster-sized photograph on the opposite wall. Bolt stopped and inspected it.

The photo was a family shot of a younger Roy Brakspear standing between an attractive woman in her thirties and a cute-looking girl of about ten, which must have been Jenny. All of them were smiling at the camera, and even in the gloom Bolt could see that Brakspear looked genuinely happy. A man with his family. The photograph resonated with Bolt. It also angered him because it demonstrated so perfectly the casual evil of the men who were putting him through this. Bastards. A sudden desire for vengeance ripped through him, so intense that it made him shiver.

He turned away and padded silently across the hallway to the staircase.

That was when he caught a faint stale smell coming from upstairs. Like rancid meat.

He stopped, turned. Mo had caught it, too. He was wrinkling his nose. They both knew what it meant.

Bolt headed up the stairs and out on to the landing. The door opposite was shut, but the smell here was much stronger and hung heavy in the air. The murky silence seemed loud in Bolt's ears.

Holding the pepper spray in front of him, he slowly opened the door and stepped inside.

Roy Brakspear was lying face down on the bed, sideways on, his legs dangling off the edge. He was wearing casual middle-aged clothes – a pair of slacks and a navy sweater – tan brogues on the feet. His arms were outstretched on either side of him where he'd fallen and a small pool of blood had formed round his head. Further drops speckled the sheets where the bullet that had been callously fired into the back of his head had exited.

Mo came in and stood beside Bolt. He didn't speak.

'Poor sod was just a loose end to them,' said Bolt, looking down at the body. He thought about the smiling husband and father in the downstairs photo. Two of that family were now dead. It was possible the third member, Jenny, was too, and if she wasn't yet she would be once the mustard gas was in Hook's hands.

They searched the rest of the house, throwing all the lights on, no longer needing to keep quiet, but there was no obvious evidence pointing to either the identity or the location of the kidnappers. The place would have to be searched a lot more thoroughly but this would now be done by scene-of-crime officers.

They left the way they'd come in, and Bolt put a call in to Big Barry. 'Bad news,' he said when his boss answered, and he told him what they'd found.

'Poor bugger,' sighed Barry with only the barest modicum of sympathy. 'I've got news for you as well. There's good and there's bad.'

'What's the good?'

'Your hunch paid off. We checked Brakspear's phone records, got the number for the drivers' agency he used, and we've finally got the name of the driver picking up the load, and the registration of his lorry.'

'What's the bad?' asked Bolt, even though he could guess what it was.

'He's not answering his phone and the tracking device on the lorry isn't picking up. The bugger's disappeared into thin air.'

Forty-eight

Frank O'Toole watched from his position in the gap behind the steps leading down to the ferry's lower parking level as the man he was tracking weaved his way through the stationary vehicles until he came to the lorry. The man's name was Trevor Gould. He was in his early fifties, with a ruddy complexion suggesting high blood pressure and an immense pot belly which made him look like he'd swallowed a beach ball. He stopped by the lorry and clicked off its central locking, unaware that its plates had been changed.

Another guy in a suit, looking exhausted, made his way to his own vehicle, and from the top of the steps O'Toole could hear more voices. It was time to move.

As Gould opened the driver's door and heaved himself up on to the step, precariously balancing the half-eaten baguette he was carrying, O'Toole slipped from his hiding place and strode over to him, keeping his head down and watching the man in the suit out of the corner of his eye as he got into his own car.

Gould was so busy squeezing himself into the driver's seat that he didn't spot a thing until O'Toole was leaning into the cab and jabbing the hunting knife into his side.

'Move over,' he hissed, 'and don't look at me or make a sound. Otherwise you're dead.'

'I don't want any trouble,' said Gould, who was sensible enough to do what he was told. It was a real effort for him to clamber over the handbrake and the gearstick, and O'Toole noticed with wry amusement that he continued to clutch the greasy baguette as if it was the crown jewels.

'Where's the tracking device in this thing?' O'Toole demanded.

'Under my seat,' replied Gould, making an exaggerated effort not to look at him.

'Disconnect it.'

As Gould leaned down, O'Toole slipped a hypodermic syringe from the inside pocket of his leather jacket. He removed the stopper and, as Gould sat back up again, jabbed the needle into his arm.

Unlike the man he was currently working for, Frank O'Toole didn't enjoy killing people. He'd only done it once before and that was fifteen years ago now. A tout who'd been selling information to the Brits. O'Toole and another man had kidnapped him from the street outside his home and taken him to an abandoned warehouse just outside Newry where he'd been tried by an IRA military court and found guilty of the crimes of which he was accused. There was only ever one sentence for touting: death. O'Toole had been given the task of carrying it out, something he'd done without hesitation, putting a bullet in the back of the man's head as he knelt down, blindfolded and begging for his life. O'Toole had had no sympathy for him – touts deserved what was coming to them – but he hadn't gained any satisfaction from doing it either. It was a job, nothing more. Just as it was a job now. And this time he was being paid a hundred grand for his troubles – more than he'd earned in the last ten years – which meant there was no place for weakness. Or too many questions.

Trevor Gould grimaced as the poison flooded into his system, and his eyes bulged. O'Toole slapped a hand over his mouth and pushed him back in the seat as he juddered and writhed. He could have killed him with the knife but that would have been way too messy. O'Toole wasn't squeamish, but he was going to have to drive this thing for the next hour and he didn't want it looking or smelling like a slaughterhouse.

Gould took several minutes to die, but his demise was silent and attracted no attention from the people who were now milling about their cars as the ferry made its way slowly into Harwich docks. When he was finally still, his face puce, O'Toole reached into his pocket, pulled out the APR licence badge that had been made for him, and attached it to his own jacket. He then squeezed Gould's body into the sleeping area behind the front seats and chucked a grimy-looking duvet over it. Ignoring the smell that was already beginning to permeate the cab, he polished off Gould's baguette, then started the lorry's engine as the ferry drew into the docks.

Barely five minutes later the ferry's iron doors opened, and O'Toole joined the long line of traffic snaking its way towards passport control. He sighed with relief as he was waved through with the merest hint of a glance by a kid barely out of his teens. He didn't even have to open his window. Just waved his false British passport in the kid's general direction. It amazed him that there was so little security, although he guessed that these days men like him, white and middle-aged, were no longer considered suspicious.

He chuckled to himself. Once upon a time he was one of Scotland Yard's most wanted men, with his own file at MI5. Now he was considered part of a long ago, irrelevant past.

Such complacency was going to prove a huge mistake.

Forty-nine

'Nigel's gay,' said Yvonne with an exaggerated sigh, looking up at me, her expression a strange mix of disappointment and naked lust. 'I caught him with the local blacksmith.' Her hand slowly stroked my arm, and I found myself getting aroused. 'I think we should get back together, Rob. It's been too long, and I haven't been happy without you, I really haven't. You were always the man for me.'

I almost cried out with joy. This was what I'd wanted for a long time. The three of us back together again. It was as if a complex plan had finally come together.

Then I woke up.

Dazed, and with my arm throbbing painfully, I sat up in bed and picked up my watch from the bedside table. It was half past ten. I'd been asleep for the best part of ten hours. Sunlight flooded in through the window, and through the glass in the door I could see the silhouette of a man with a machine gun standing guard. After the most hectic and terrifying few days of my life, I was finally safe.

But, strangely, this knowledge didn't make me feel as good as it should have. Instead, I was enveloped by a feeling of real melancholy. This was partly to do with the dream I'd just had. It might have been pretty bizarre but it had also offered me a little hope, which had now been snatched back by reality. But it wasn't just that. With the drama of the last few days over, I was suddenly completely alone, no longer part of the events whirling round me.

I thought of Jenny and Tina Boyd and wondered if they were still alive. Somehow I couldn't imagine that bastard with the saucer eyes letting them go. He didn't seem the kind of man capable of showing any mercy. I wished I'd been more help to the cops who'd come to see me the previous night. They'd seemed like pretty intelligent on-the-ball guys, but it all depended on the quality of the leads they had to work on, and since most of them had come from me I wasn't at all sure they were that good.

The business card of the one in charge, Mike Bolt, was on the bedside table, and I picked it up now, wanting to call him for an update but knowing he wouldn't appreciate it, especially as I had nothing new to tell him.

There was a jug of water by the bed and I filled my glass and drank deeply, racking my brains for something I might have missed out in my account of those frenetic forty-eight hours.

It was only when I'd refilled my glass and picked up my mobile phone – the one that had advertised my whereabouts to the men who wanted to kill me – that it struck me. When I went to Jenny's father's place I'd photographed the unidentified car on his driveway on my mobile before he disturbed me. For some reason – it must have been the fact that it was sandwiched between far bigger, more terrifying events – I hadn't mentioned it to Bolt and his colleague, yet the car had almost certainly belonged to the shaven-headed kidnapper who'd chased me across Jenny's dad's lawn. And he might still be using it.

I didn't know whether or not the police had already visited her dad's place, or whether they'd located the car, but it had to be worth telling them about.

Hoping that he had some good news for me, I dialled Mike Bolt's number.

Fifty

Eamon Donald stubbed his cigarette underfoot and watched as the lorry drove through the open double doors and into the cavernous barn, stopping at the end. The driver exited the cab and Donald immediately recognized him as Frank O'Toole, a volunteer from the old days. They'd spent a few months together in the Maze in the early nineties, before the first ceasefire, and Donald remembered that he'd been well thought of by his commanding officer. 'Reliable' was the word he'd used. Exactly what was needed for a job like this.

He was less sure of the other guy Hook had hired, a big shaven-headed thug from south London called Stone, who was currently at the far end of the barn sawing up long tubes of drainpiping into pieces six feet long. Stone didn't speak much, nor did he ask any questions, such as 'What am I doing sawing up tubes of drain-piping?' He did exactly what he was told without fuss or comment. In Eamon Donald's view, men who didn't ask questions shouldn't be trusted. Either they were immensely stupid or, worse, they were pretending to be. Hook had said that he'd worked with Stone in his days as a freelance London hitman, and it had been a success.

Donald trusted his current employer's judgement, but he still had his doubts about the Londoner.

'Hello Eamon,' said O'Toole, coming over. 'I had an idea I might run into you at some point on this op. How are you doing?'

'I'm fine,' answered Donald, smiling thinly as they shook hands. He hoped that other people wouldn't jump to the same conclusion. As one of the IRA's most seasoned bombmakers, with more than twenty-five years' worth of experience with explosives under his belt, some of which was still very much up to date, Donald had to be very careful that he covered his tracks on this op. 'So, you know what the load is you're carrying, then?' he asked.

O'Toole nodded. 'Aye, I do. I don't think he does, though.' He pointed at Stone, who had his back to them, sawing away.

'No, and we're not going to say anything to him either. The fewer people who know about this, the better. And he might not be too happy if he thinks we're going to bomb his home town.'

'Are we?' asked O'Toole, looking interested. 'Do you know what the target is?'

'No, I don't.' This was a lie. Donald knew exactly what, and who, the target was going to be. 'All I know is it's got to be ready by ten o'clock tonight, so we're going to need to get going. I don't want Hook on my back telling me to hurry things along. You can't hurry something like this.'

'Where is Hook?' asked O'Toole, looking round.

'He's about here somewhere. Probably with the hostages.'

'They're still alive, are they? I thought he'd have wanted rid of them by now.'

Donald shrugged. Hook had always had an eye for the ladies. In the old days he'd had a lot of success, but that had all changed when his face had been ripped apart by the bomb. Now he just looked like a freak. But Donald had no doubt that he would have taken advantage of the current situation, and that both the women upstairs would have been on the receiving end of his unwanted advances by now. As a father of two adult daughters himself, Donald didn't approve. He was notoriously prudish in matters of the flesh, but as long as it didn't interfere with the op, and they were both disposed of before the end of it, he was prepared to turn a blind eye.

Deciding it was time to bring the small talk to an end, he walked over to the back of the lorry. 'Keys,' he said to O'Toole, putting out a hand.

O'Toole handed them to him, and Donald unlocked the rear doors and pulled them open.

In front of him, stacked two high, were open-ended wooden pallets containing neat, straight rows of plain aluminium cylinders – 236 in all. But Eamon Donald didn't see plain aluminium cylinders. He saw great gouting plumes of fire and jagged clouds of shrapnel. Destruction. And, of course, revenge. The IRA's struggle might have officially ended more than a decade earlier but Donald retained a deep hatred for the British. They'd imprisoned him in the Maze for a total of fourteen years, as well as shooting dead his brother, Padraig. He'd made them suffer too, of course, with a string of bombs that had left more than fifty members of the Brit establishment and their allies dead down the years. The innocent had died too, several dozen at least, but they were unavoidable collateral damage in a war that, for Donald, would never be over.

When Hook had approached him a few weeks earlier with his offer of work, Donald had almost said no. The job was risky in the extreme and likely to attract a lot of heat. But he'd gone for it, and it had had nothing to do with the hundred and fifty grand he'd be receiving. It was because Hook was providing him with the opportunity for a bloody, crippling victory over his old enemy that would eclipse everything that had gone before.

O'Toole must have read his thoughts. 'It's going to be a big one, isn't it?' he said quietly.

Donald caught the vaguest flash of doubt on the other man's face as he turned his way and fixed him with a hard stare. 'Whatever it is, it's no less than the bastards deserve. Remember that.'

Fifty-one

Bolt was woken by his mobile phone. He sat up suddenly, groggily patting his pockets, before finally locating it. He didn't recognize the number and for a split second he wondered if it was Tina.

But it wasn't. It was Rob Fallon, and he was asking if they'd made any progress on the hunt for her and Jenny.

Bolt had snatched some sleep in his office while all around him his colleagues had been working flat out, but so far Operation Medusa, the massive police operation to find the missing consignment of mustard gas and, by extension, the two women, hadn't been successful on either count. They knew that the lorry was in the UK, and that it had come in on the overnight ferry from Zeebrugge to Harwich, but they were also sure that its number plates had been changed en route because an emergency trawl of all the traffic cameras in the greater Harwich area had failed to turn up anything. Like Hook, it had disappeared into thin air. A complete news blackout was in place while the full resources of the British state were diverted to the hunt, but he was all too aware that even this might not be enough, because time was not on their side.

Bolt cleared his throat, fighting down his disappointment, and gave Fallon the stock answer that they were following up a number of leads and that he'd give him news as soon as he had any. He felt like crap, and hoped Fallon would get the message and get off the phone.

'I might have a lead for you.'

Bolt perked up a little, but not much. Things had moved on, and Fallon was the least of their problems in a case as big as this. But he asked what it was, then listened with growing interest as Fallon explained about the car on Roy Brakspear's drive the previous day and the photo he'd taken on his mobile. 'I don't know how much help it is,' he continued uncertainly, 'but I thought you ought to know about it.'

Bolt pulled a notebook from his jacket and wrote down the car's make, colour and registration number, then he hung up, feeling a little more hopeful suddenly. Fallon had told him that the car wasn't there when he'd returned to the property, so it had clearly been used by the kidnapper. If they could find the car, it was possible they could find Hook.

He put the mobile back in his pocket and got to his feet, still feeling pretty crap, but Fallon's information had given him enough of an adrenalin buzz to keep him going for a few hours longer.

Big Barry Freud was temporarily off the phone and looking exhausted when Bolt walked into his office.

'You know,' he said as Bolt sat down, 'even with all this bloody stuff going on, I've still got Thames Valley giving me crap about you driving off from the murder scene last night. I've had their assistant chief constable on the phone twice this morning. He sounds like a right old woman. He wants you interviewed in connection with their inquiry but I've told him you're not available at the moment. I won't be able to put it off much longer, though.' He paused in his monologue to wipe sweat from his brow with a handkerchief that looked like it had had a fair amount of use already that day.

'I've got a lead,' announced Bolt, and he told Big Barry about the dark blue Mazda Fallon had photographed at the Brakspear residence. 'If the kidnapper doesn't know that Fallon got a shot of the number plate, he might still be using it now. If we can find him, we might be able to find Hook and the gas.'

Big Barry grinned, seemingly pleased with this new information. 'Got to be worth a try, hasn't it? I'll get on to the ANPR people.'

The automatic number plate recognition system was the latest technological tool available to the police in the twenty-first-century fight against crime. It used a huge network of CCTV cameras which automatically read car number plates to log the movement of vehicles along virtually every main road in Britain. These images were then stored on a vast central database, housed alongside the Police National Computer HQ. If the Mazda had been driven in the past twenty-four hours, the ANPR would have a record of its journey.

Big Barry picked up the phone and two minutes later he was giving the Mazda's registration number to one of the senior officers in charge of the database, and telling him in no uncertain terms that his team could put everything else aside because tracing this car was the absolute number one priority. 'And that comes right from the very top, old mate,' he added, putting a faintly ludicrous emphasis on the word 'top'.

Big Barry Freud was the kind of man who liked to throw his not inconsiderable weight about, particularly during major inquiries. He believed that it was just part of his decisive take-charge personality, but to most other people, including Bolt, it was just plain rudeness.

Still, it seemed to work, and when he got off the phone he gave Bolt a decisive nod. 'He's going to call back in five minutes.'

'Any more progress on finding the lorry?' Bolt asked him. There were currently officers from three different police forces re-examining the camera footage from Harwich to see if they could identify it using just its physical description.

'Nothing yet,' said Big Barry. 'We must have two hundred bodies working on it, but Gould's wife hasn't been a lot of help. She says the lorry's big and white, with black writing down the side saying Banton Transport, which apparently isn't even that big. Oh, and that he's got a West Ham banner in the back of the cab, but she doesn't think you can see that very easily from the outside.'

'Shit. It's not a lot, is it?'

'No, it isn't. And you know what these CCTV images are like. They're blurry at the best of times. It's like the proverbial needle in the haystack, old mate.' He sighed. 'If we had some idea of what the target was going to be, it would help, but we haven't got a bloody clue.'

'Something like mustard gas is only going to be used for one thing: to cause mass casualties. Have we got any idea who Hook might be working for?'

Big Barry shook his head. 'Nothing. But I have had a briefing on the gas's properties and how it might be released. Apparently, if it gets ignited, mustard gas loses its potency, so they can't blow up the load with a conventional bomb. It's possible they can get someone with a decent gas mask to release it manually by opening up the cylinders one by one, but there are more than two hundred of them, so it would take ages, and as soon as people got a whiff of the first few they'd be off in no time, so it wouldn't be very effective.'

'So what are they going to do?'

'No one knows. But I've got a feeling they'll find a way.' He sighed again, and Bolt could see the pressure his boss was under. 'If they somehow get it out into the atmosphere, it'll be a bloody catastrophe. It's a sunny day with a light breeze, which is meant to be perfect conditions for releasing it. I don't mind telling you, I'm glad my missus isn't up in town today.'

Bolt was surprised at his honesty. Big Barry Freud usually towed the party line, but these, it seemed, were unprecedented times. 'Plenty of peoples' wives are,' he said, thinking about Mo and Saira, and their four children. He'd dropped Mo back at home on the way here earlier so he could grab a bit of sleep and they could spend some time together, and he wondered whether he'd sent them out of town as well.

'If the powers-that-be think there's a need to evacuate, then they'll do it,' said Big Barry, 'but they're setting up roadblocks coming into town and the congestion charge cameras are tracking any white lorries.' He was trying to sound confident but it wasn't really working, and he was saved from further conversation by the ringing of his phone.

It was clear the caller was from the ANPR. Barry wrote something down on the giant notepad that covered half his desk before hanging up.

'The Mazda was last caught on the ANPR yesterday afternoon at 2.47 p.m. just north of Saffron Walden in Essex on the B1052 at Linton in Cambridgeshire. If it's been used since, then it hasn't gone far because it would have been caught on one of the other cameras. They're going to send us a map showing the area where it might still be.'

Bolt smiled. 'That should narrow it down a bit.'

But when the map was emailed through to Barry's PC ten minutes later, it was clear that it hadn't narrowed things down as much as either of them would have liked. Although the Mazda's last location was surrounded by cameras, it was a largely semi-rural area of northern Essex, with hundreds of back roads and villages, bordered by the M11 to the west, and the computer-generated map calculated that the car could be anywhere in an area of almost 190 square miles.

'Christ, that doesn't help us much, does it?' said Big Barry as they pored over the printout. 'I've got a tag on those plates, so if the car starts moving again we'll know as soon as it's picked up by a camera. Until then, though . . .'

Bolt wasn't entirely deterred. 'You say the gas can't be released very easily manually, right? So, if they're going to come up with a way of releasing it effectively, they're going to have to take it somewhere to get it ready, don't you think?'

Big Barry shrugged. 'I don't know. It's possible, I suppose.'

'Well, maybe the car's gone to the same place. Hook hasn't got a big team. So far we only know of one person working with him.'

'I still don't see what you're getting at, Mike.'

'I'm thinking that maybe they've got a base round there somewhere. A centre for their operations.' He ran a finger in a wide circle on the map. 'A place they would have rented. If you can let me take a couple of people from my team off the CCTV trawl, we can look up all the estate agents in the area, see who's rented out property recently. It's a long shot . . .'

'An extremely long shot. We don't even know that the car hasn't just been abandoned in a wood somewhere.'

'But it's got to be worth a look. We've got two hundred people working on the CCTV. Surely we can spare a couple of them?'

Big Barry looked doubtful, but he was the sort of guy who always liked to cover all his bases, just in case there was an opportunity for personal advancement in one of them. 'OK, take one person.' He looked at his watch. 'It's eleven now. We'll review how you're getting on at two.'

Bolt thanked him and walked out with the map before his boss had a chance to change his mind. It was still a case of searching for a needle in a haystack, but at least the haystack was getting smaller.

And any effort was worth it if it led to Tina.

Fifty-two

The interior of the lorry's cab still reeked of death, even though they'd removed the driver's body more than an hour earlier, and Eamon Donald was pleased when he'd finished drilling the holes through to the back that were needed for the bomb's wires, and could finally get out into the comparative fresh air for a much-needed smoke. He'd been trying to give up for the best part of a decade now, a process that had started when his old man, a lifelong smoker, contracted terminal lung cancer, but he'd never managed to last for more than a week, and for the time being at least he'd given up giving up.

He lit a Marlboro Light and approached Stone and O'Toole, both of whom were hard at work among the pieces of drainpiping Stone had been sawing up earlier. O'Toole was using a large measuring jug to fill up each tube with a ready-made explosive slurry mix of ammonium nitrate and fuel oil that he was getting from a barrel next to him, while Stone was on his hands and knees attaching handfuls of six-inch nails to the tube exteriors using thick rolls of industrial masking tape. Every ingredient they were using could be bought legally by people who knew what they were doing.

'How's it going, lads?' Donald called out, making sure he stood well back from them with the cigarette.

'Another hour, I reckon,' answered O'Toole. 'Then we're going to need a break.'

Stone grunted something that sounded like agreement.

'And when you're done you can have one, don't worry.'

Donald looked at his watch. It had just turned half past twelve and they were well ahead of schedule. He was also beginning to get hungry, and hoped that Hook had got in some supplies. Donald liked his food, and he'd always found it difficult to function on an empty stomach. Somehow, though, he knew Hook wouldn't have anything tasty on offer. He wasn't the kind to get pleasure from eating. He wasn't really the type to get pleasure from anything bar, it seemed, rape and murder.

As he thought these unkind thoughts about his current employer, the barn doors opened and Hook appeared in his *Friday the 13th*-style boiler suit and gloves, his anaemic face looking like something out of a 'plastic surgery gone wrong' documentary. Donald wondered how the guy ever managed to blend into a crowd, as he was reputed to be able to do. To him, Hook blended in like a go-go dancer in a nunnery.

As Donald took a long, much-needed pull on the cigarette, Hook came over and guided him towards the front of the lorry, well away from Stone and O'Toole, and out of earshot.

'How's it coming along?' he asked.

'We're doing fine. Your bomb'll be ready on time.'

Hook nodded. 'Good. That's what I want to hear.' But there was something tense about him. He wrinkled his nose, glancing at the cigarette, and Donald remembered that he didn't like smoking.

Tough titty. He took another drag, savouring the taste.

They stopped at the cab, and Hook fixed him with a probing

stare. 'I hear that when mustard gas ignites it loses its effect. How are you intending to fix that?'

'Ah, I see you've done your homework.'

'I always do my homework, Eamon.'

'Well, it's very simple really,' he said, unable to mask the enthusiasm he always felt when talking about bombs. 'When those two over there have finished filling the tubes with explosive mix, I'm going to put a detonator in each one and run them through the gaps in the pallets holding the gas. By my calculation there should be two tubes for each pallet. Then we wire them up to a connector box, which is basically the bridge between the explosive-filled tubes and the main detonator in the cab. When we set off the main detonator, the connector box will send a signal through the wiring and our thirty-two mini bombs will explode simultaneously, sending the nails attached to the outside of the tubing flying everywhere, and with enough force to puncture all the cylinders.

'But' – and here Donald paused for effect, feeling especially pleased with himself – 'the beauty of the design is that, because the tubes are made from toughened plastic, the power of the blast will be contained within each tube itself – think of it like a blanket smothering the flames – so the cylinders will get peppered with holes and thrown all over the place, but the gas itself won't get ignited. We might lose a couple, because it's not entirely foolproof, and a few won't get punctured, but I'm reckoning that ninety-five per cent of the cargo will be released into the surrounding air undamaged. With a little bit of a breeze and no rain, everyone in a mile radius will be breathing in pure poison. It'll be the most lethal terrorist attack in UK history. The Brits won't know what fucking hit them.'

'And you've put in the modifications we talked about?' asked Hook quietly.

When he'd hired Donald, Hook had stipulated that the bomb

had to explode no matter what, even if the lorry was intercepted by the security forces, otherwise none of them would get their money. Technically speaking, this wasn't a problem at all, as Donald had explained. All it required was a pressure pad placed under the driver's seat connected to the bomb's battery pack. Once the bomb was live – and it could be made live with the flick of a switch before the lorry had even begun its journey – then the moment the driver lifted his weight from the seat, the movement from the pressure pad would set off the bomb, so even if he was shot dead while driving and toppled over, it would still explode. It was a tactic used by terrorist groups with vehicle bombs across the Middle East to ensure that, even if their suicide bombers experienced a sudden loss of nerve, their deadly cargoes would still detonate.

There was only one problem. When Donald had agreed to do the job, he hadn't realized that the driver was going to be a volunteer from the old days.

'They'll be put in before the end,' he answered. 'It's only a five-minute job. But does it have to be O'Toole who drives? He's one of our people. Why not use Stone? He's nothing to us.'

Hook stared at him blankly. 'Stone's too stupid. We need some-one reliable. It's going to be O'Toole.'

Donald dragged hard on his cigarette, looking over Hook's shoulder to where O'Toole and Stone were working away. O'Toole would never suspect that his old comrades would betray him, and the fact that the man who'd hired him couldn't give a shit pissed Donald off.

'You never really believed, did you, Michael?' he said rhetorically, using the other man's real Christian name. 'In any of what we were doing.'

'That's none of your business.'

'You know, what I can't understand is why you're doing this. I'm doing it because I hate the Brits. Because I owe them for four hundred years of oppression, and because they never baulked at killing innocents, so why the hell should I? But what do you get out of this? I mean, I know your client, whoever he is, is bound to be paying you a lot of money, but it strikes me that a man like you has already got plenty of cash, and this kind of job, leaving so many dead and every cop in the country hunting you down ... No amount of money's worth that.' He took a last drag on his cigarette and crushed it underfoot. 'So, what's your motivation?'

Hook leaned forward and his whole face seemed to darken. 'Because I fucking can,' he hissed, eyes sparkling maliciously. 'Now, do me a big favour, Eamon Donald, and get back to work.'

The two men eyeballed each other for several seconds, but it was Donald who backed down and turned away, immediately regretting that he'd seen fit to rile the other man. Regretting, too, that he'd ever agreed to work with him in a freelance capacity. The pay was good – a hundred and fifty grand, fifty already in his hands, the other hundred following as soon as the job was finished. But for the first time he wondered if he was going to actually receive this last instalment. If Hook was prepared to leave O'Toole dead, why not Donald himself as well?

He decided he was going to have to watch his back.

Fifty-three

I was sitting up in bed, thinking about Jenny Brakspear, when there was a knock on the door and who should step inside but my old friend Dom, holding a box of chocolates in one hand and a Waterstone's book bag in the other. He was dressed in an open-neck shirt and well-cut suit, and his face was lean and tanned. He'd lost weight and it looked like he'd been working out.

I grinned, pleased to see him, but a part of me was also jealous. This was Jenny's boyfriend, the man she'd been with for close to a year, and who'd been living it up in Dubai when she'd needed him most. Unlike me. I'd been there when it mattered.

'Hello mate,' he said with a supportive smile. 'How are you? Brought you a few bits and pieces.' He laid the chocolates and the book bag on the table beside the bed and shook my good hand. His grip was weak. Usually it was tight and confident, but I guess I didn't look like I could handle a firm handshake.

'Thanks, mate, it's appreciated.'

He pulled up a chair and sat down, looking at me with a mixture of sympathy and awe. 'I can't believe what's happened to you. I really can't.'

'The evidence is here.' I gestured at the police guard still outside the room. 'It happened.'

'I heard Maxwell's dead.' I'd introduced Dom to Maxwell a while back because he'd always wanted to meet a real live gangster. Maxwell had told me he thought Dom was an arsehole.

I nodded. 'I saw him die.'

And then it all seemed to hit me in one go, a huge rolling wave of shock: how close I'd come to death, not once but twice; the crystal-clear image of Maxwell's corpse in that muddy grave . . . For several seconds I couldn't speak.

Dom looked worried and asked me if I was all right.

'Yeah, I'm fine. I just need a moment.' I ran my good hand through my hair, amazed that my body didn't ache more than it did, although I suspect that was the drugs, then took a slug of water. 'I don't know what's happened to me, Dom. It's like I've stepped into some kind of nightmare.'

'I can't believe anyone could get to Maxwell.'

I grunted, remembering the way he'd begged for his life. 'These people are way out of Maxwell's league. They're way out of anyone's league. And the worst thing is, they've still got Jenny.'

'I know,' he said.

'Why would anyone kidnap her? And kill so many people to cover it up? That's what I can't understand.'

'Have the police not given you any ideas why she might have been snatched?'

'Not that they've told me, but I'm out of the loop now. I've asked them to keep me posted, but I'm not holding my breath.'

'What are you going to do now?'

It was a good question. I couldn't go home as my flat was now a crime scene – not that I wanted to go back there anyway. To be honest, I never wanted to go back there again. 'I don't know,' I told him. 'I don't want to stay here any longer, and apparently they're removing my police guard because I'm no longer considered to be in danger, so . . .' I let the sentence trail off, hoping it would act as a hint.

It did. 'Why don't you come and stay with me for a few days?' he suggested, looking like he meant the offer. 'I took today off. I should be able to get the rest of the week too.'

'Are you sure?' I asked, hoping he was.

'You're my mate, Rob. Course I'm sure.'

I was touched. So much so I felt like shedding a tear, though thankfully I managed to stop myself. Instead I immediately climbed out of bed, desperate to get out of the place. Hospitals aren't much fun at the best of times, but when someone's tried to kill you in one, it acts as a pretty sizeable incentive to leave.

However, what with my somewhat unusual circumstances, coupled with the British penchant for bureaucracy, it didn't prove all that easy. First of all, I had to get permission from Thames Valley Police, who were in charge of guarding me, who had to phone Mike Bolt, who agreed in principle with me leaving but wanted a forwarding address in case he needed to reach me, before the assistant chief constable finally rubber-stamped my request. It was then the turn of the hospital itself to be convinced that I was in a fit state to be released from its care, and for some reason they were even more reluctant to see the back of me than Her Majesty's finest, insisting that I wait for the duty doctor to give me a thorough going-over, even though he was only a third of the way through his rounds. So it was well over an hour before I at last got into Dom's car for the journey back to London, laden down with enough painkillers to knock out a football team.

We didn't speak much. I was still a little shell-shocked by events, and all the drugs I'd had were making me dopey. But when we reached Dom's palatial pad in Wanstead and he cracked open a bottle of Sauvignon Blanc and told me to relax while he cooked a late lunch, I began to perk up. Dom had never been the best cook in the world – takeaways were our main dietary staple when I was living there – but this time he actually put together a half-decent king prawn stir fry, although given the lack of food over the last few days I'd have devoured pretty much anything.

After we'd eaten, we retired to the front room with the wine and talked about what had happened. Dom asked me plenty of questions but he seemed to take particular interest in the actions of the pale murderous Irishman. 'He sounds stone cold,' he commented after I'd told him about the casual murder of Ramon in my bedroom, and I thought I caught just the slightest hint of admiration in his voice. 'Maybe now Maxwell's gone you should consider writing a book about all this. It'd probably sell millions.'

Dom had always bought into the glamour of the criminal under-world, which was why his bookshelves were full of sensational true crime books, and why he'd been so keen to meet Maxwell. His attitude irritated me, but then I'd been seduced in exactly the same way.

'He was an animal,' I said with a conversation-ending finality.

'Shit, I'm sorry mate, I didn't mean it to sound flippant.' He looked genuinely remorseful. 'It's just, you know, I didn't know people like that really existed.'

The drink continued to flow and we moved on to happier subjects. We began to reminisce about the old days: the laughs we'd had in school; the disastrous teenage double date we'd been on with the twin Queen sisters, when Dom made his date Sam cry and mine, Justine, attacked him with her shoe; the disastrous camping holiday to the south of France when the two of us, aged seventeen, got on the wrong train at the Gare du Nord in Paris and ended up spending four rainsoaked days in Belgium . . . Good times, too long ago now, when the world was a fun and easy place, one in which stone-cold killers had never roamed.

As we laughed and talked, I genuinely forgot my troubles in that soft, comforting embrace of alcohol, but then I remembered that Jenny Brakspear was still out there somewhere, and the thought made me feel guilty.

Seeing the change in my expression, Dom asked me what was wrong, and when I told him, he too grew serious. 'I know how you feel, mate, and if it's any consolation, I feel the same way. But neither of us can beat ourselves up about it, especially you. You did all you could to find her, and now, thanks to you, there are plenty of people out there looking.'

'That doesn't mean they're going to find her, though, does it? Not if she's well enough hidden.'

'You can't think like that, Rob. You've got to be positive. You know with all the technology they've got these days, they can find anybody. Shit, look how easy the Irish guy and his mate found you. One tiny GPS transmitter and they can trace a person down to the nearest metre.'

'I suppose so,' I said, not really sharing his confidence.

He picked up the empty wine bottle from the pine coffee table. 'Shall I crack open another one?'

'I don't know. I'm feeling it already with the painkillers.'

He gave me a sly smile. 'Come on. Drown the sorrows. You can always sleep it off later. Remember, you've done your bit.'

Like a lot of City boys, Dom had always drunk a lot. It was an easy way to handle the pressure and the long hours. I'd never caned it to quite the same extent, but I figured another bottle probably wouldn't do a huge amount of harm. There was nothing else I could do to find Jenny, so I might as well forget about it for a while. 'Go on then,' I said. 'In for a penny and all that.'

He looked pleased – after all, no one likes to drink alone – but as he left the room I realized that something was bugging me, although in the fog of the booze it was difficult to identify what it was.

Then I remembered.

I hadn't told Dom about the GPS transmitter in my mobile. I went back through the conversation we'd had, trying to work out if I was mistaken.

Then something else hit me, its ramifications so immense and terrifying that I suddenly sat bolt upright on the sofa.

Maxwell didn't have mobile reception at his place.

He used to say he was happier without it because only a handful of people had his landline number, which meant only people he wanted to speak to could get hold of him. It meant that when I interviewed him for the book, I never got interrupted.

So the kidnappers couldn't have used the GPS to find me there. Which could only mean one thing: they'd had inside information from somewhere.

And as I turned towards the door, I knew immediately where it had come from.

Fifty-four

The smile on Dom's face died the moment he came into the room and saw my expression. I think in that moment he knew that I'd found him out.

'What is it, Rob?' he asked with a casualness that seemed forced as he put the bottle of Sauvignon Blanc down on the table.

'Where's Jenny, Dom?' I demanded.

'What are you talking about? How should I know?'

I told him about the lack of a mobile reception at Maxwell's place.

'What the hell's that got to do with me?'

'You knew where Maxwell lived, didn't you?'

'Well, yeah, but so did quite a lot of other people.'

'But none of them were intimately acquainted with Jenny, were they?'

Part of me couldn't believe I was saying what I was saying. After all, Dom was my friend of more than twenty years, a normal guy who'd lived a normal life and who'd never been in trouble before. Yet when I'd spoken to him on the phone in Dubai the other day, something hadn't rung true. It was the way he'd denied that he'd talked to Jenny for months, even though she'd told me he'd been calling her, trying to get back together. Because why on earth would she have made something like that up?

'You were lying when you said you hadn't spoken to Jenny for months, weren't you? So tell me,' I said, raising my voice now, 'where the hell is she?'

'Christ, Rob, don't be so fucking stupid. Why the hell would I ever get involved in a kidnapping? I'm a businessman, not a criminal. You're delirious, mate. You need some rest.'

He tried staring me out, wearing an expression of righteous indignation and surprise that I'd seen him use plenty of times, usually when he was trying to convince someone he was telling the truth. It usually worked, too, and was doubtless one of the reasons he'd been so successful in business. Back in the old days it had always convinced our teachers he was telling the truth. But I knew him too well. Most of the time he did it when he was lying.

As if to confirm my suspicions, the skin beneath his right eye began to twitch, a long-standing habit that invariably occurred when he was under stress.

I felt the rage building in me. 'You bastard! Where is she? Where's Jenny?'

'What the fuck are you talking about?' he shouted, his voice filling the room. 'You're fucking delirious, Rob, so don't say stuff you don't mean, all right? Why don't you just go for a lie down or something? OK?'

'Where is she? Is she still alive?'

'Shut the fuck up!' he hissed, the guilt coming off him in waves.

'I'm going to call the police, Dom. Right now. I've got the number of one of the senior guys on my phone. Maybe you can convince him you don't know what's happened to Jenny, because you know what? You're not convincing me.'

I stood up and pulled the phone from my pocket with my good

hand, still finding it almost impossible to believe that this was happening. Of all the shocks I'd had recently, this was undoubtedly the biggest of all. Which was why, I suppose, it had taken me so long to work it out.

'Put the phone down, Rob,' said Dom with an icy calm. 'Now.'

'No.'

The punch came out of nowhere, connecting perfectly with my jaw and sending me crashing back on to the sofa. The phone flew out of my hand, thudding on to the carpet somewhere out of sight.

Before I could react, Dom grabbed a cushion from one of the sofas and sprang across the coffee table, his face contorted with an angry panic I'd never seen there before. He landed on top of me, one leg digging into my broken arm, and I cried out in pain, trying to avoid the blows raining down on me. Then suddenly the cushion was being pushed into my face and I could no longer see anything. I struggled under him, but he was an ex-rugby player, and even though he'd lost weight he was still a big guy, and in my condition it was always going to be an unequal battle.

I heard him grunt with exertion as he forced the pillow down hard and I felt the panic surge in me as my breath became trapped in my throat. I grabbed his thigh with my good hand, squeezing it as hard as I could. I wanted to beg him for mercy, to tell him that if only he let me go I wouldn't say a word. But only muffled gasps came out as I fought for air.

Without warning, the cushion was pulled away. Dom was staring down at me, tears in his eyes. 'You fucking prick!' he shouted, bringing back his fist. 'Why did you have to get involved? Why couldn't you have just kept out of it and got your own fucking girl-friend? Then none of this would have happened!'

I started to say something but he punched me again, full in the face, although this time there was less power in the blow. I could tell then that he was incapable of killing me. I could hardly move, and my arm was in so much agony I thought it might have been broken again. Even so, I felt hopeful, because it seemed that Dom still possessed some kind of conscience.

He stood up, breathing heavily, clenching and unclenching his fists. Thinking.

Spitting blood from my mouth, I spoke through gritted teeth. 'If you tell me where she is, Dom, I'll call the police anonymously and give them the location. I won't mention your name, I promise.'

'I don't fucking know, all right!' he shouted, pacing the room. 'I haven't got a clue where she is!'

'So what's going on, Dom? Tell me. Please. I'm your mate.'

He gave a sort of groan. 'You were, Rob. But not any more.'

'I can help you. Honestly.'

'No, you can't. You most definitely fucking can't. The only people who can help me are not going to want you shooting your mouth off.'

'I'm going to leave now,' I said, getting unsteadily to my feet, ignoring the way the room was spinning. 'I won't say a word. I promise.' But my plea sounded hollow, and we both knew it.

Dom shook his head firmly. 'I'm sorry, mate, but I can't allow you to do that.'

Knowing I had no choice, I started towards the door, giving him the kind of anguished, vulnerable look I hoped would make him feel sorry enough for me that he wouldn't intervene.

He blocked my path, and I saw that his expression was hard and determined.

I went for the bottle of Sauvignon Blanc on the coffee table, but the booze and pills had made me way too slow, and he knocked me out of the way and grabbed it himself.

'Don't!' I yelled, throwing up my hands to protect myself but unable to stop the bottle connecting with my temple.

Something in my head seemed to explode, and my legs went from under me. I landed hard on the sofa, the back of my head smacking painfully against the armrest, the blood already pouring into my right eye while the vision in my left began to swim.

I saw a wobbling, swirling image of Dom take a mobile from his pocket and, just before unconsciousness finally enveloped me, I heard him speak four words to the person on the other end with an eerie, unnerving calm that chilled my bones.

'We've got a problem.'

Fifty-five

There was movement outside the door, and Tina tensed as it opened, the hood over her head preventing her from seeing who it was.

For several seconds there was silence. Then she heard a sniffing sound close by her.

'Hmm, it smells like someone couldn't control herself.'

It was him. The man who'd abducted her.

Then, in one sudden movement, the hood was ripped off. Squinting against the brightness of the light, Tina saw him standing in front of her, dressed in a boiler suit and gloves, a mocking half-smile on his thin lips, a pistol with silencer in his hand.

He yanked the gag from her mouth, but she barely noticed the pain. Her raging thirst overcame everything. 'Have you got some water?' she asked, her voice a dry rasp.

Without answering, he pulled a bottle of Evian from one of the boiler suit pockets and pushed it into her mouth.

Tina drank thirstily, consuming the whole bottle in one go.

Almost immediately she experienced a powerful urge for a real drink, something that would make this horrendous situation more tolerable. 'Have you got anything stronger?' she asked before she could stop herself.

He brought his face close to hers, the saucer eyes inspecting her with interest, and she cursed herself for letting him see her weakness. 'I'm afraid not, Tina Boyd. But then, I wouldn't want you drunk for what I'm about to show you.'

She felt the fear coming then, in hard waves that tightened every muscle. 'What are you going to show me?'

He leaned down so his cheek was touching hers. It felt like rubber. 'It's a surprise,' he whispered into her ear.

A knife appeared in his free hand. He crouched down and used it to cut her free of the masking tape and the ropes, slicing them roughly yet thoroughly, yet somehow managing to avoid cutting her. When what was left of her bonds was scattered in several piles around the chair where she'd spent most of the last twenty-four hours, he stepped back and told her to get to her feet.

She did as she was told, so stiff she almost fell straight back down again. It felt strange being free. But not good, because somehow she knew that he wouldn't be tying her up again. Some time soon, maybe even in the next few minutes, he'd be finished with her. And when he was, that would be it.

'Put your hands behind your back, palms outwards,' he commanded, putting the knife away and coming round behind her. 'And don't try anything stupid, otherwise I'll make you scream.'

Tina moved her hands behind her and waited as he fitted a pair of new-style police restraints. Then finally she stood facing him, still dressed only in a blouse and socks. 'Do you mind if I put some clothes on?' she asked him. 'I'm very cold.'

He smiled. 'No. I like it when you suffer a little.'

He took her by the arm and pushed her in the direction of the open door, following behind her as she walked unsteadily through it, wondering if these would be the last steps of her life. She tried not to limp as she stepped painfully on the set of picks, which were pushing against the sole of her foot, hoping he wouldn't notice there was anything amiss.

The door led out on to a narrow balcony with stairs leading down to the ground floor on her left, and another door directly opposite.

'Keep going,' he said, pushing the silencer into the small of her back.

'Where?' she asked, standing at the top of the staircase, hating the uncertainty in her voice, because that would show him she was scared, and she couldn't have that.

'In there,' he said, pushing the door. 'Go on, it's open.'

Taking a deep breath, she went in, wondering what on earth was going to greet her.

What did was something far worse than she could have imagined.

The room was dark and fetid, lit only by a dim overhead strip light, the smell of human filth like ammonia in Tina's nostrils. A young woman, bruised and naked, with unkempt blonde hair and terrified eyes, whom she immediately recognized as Jenny Brakspear, was spreadeagled and chained to a black bondage-style contraption that had been attached to the far wall, completely covering the room's only window. A spiked collar kept her head in place and a plastic ball gag had been stuffed into her mouth to prevent her crying out. As Tina took a step closer, she saw that there were long dried rivulets of blood running down one arm. She followed them to their source and flinched when she saw that the tip of the little finger on her left hand was missing. An expensive-looking video camera on a tripod had been set up with the lens facing her to record her torment.

As the man responsible for it came into the room behind her, Jenny Brakspear moaned, and Tina recognized the sound as the one she'd heard the previous night. Trying not to gag against the room's stench, she looked at Jenny who was staring at her with pleading, beaten eyes, and mouthed to her that it was going to be all right, even though it was obvious that it would never be all right for her again.

'What do you think?' he whispered, coming close to Tina's ear. 'Aren't you lucky you're not being kept in accommodation like this.'

'Why are you doing this?' Tina asked, feeling a mixture of anger and black despair. It was difficult to believe that people as heartless as the man next to her existed. 'What's she ever done to you?'

'Would you rather I put you up there instead?'

'Just let her go, for Christ's sake!'

He chuckled. 'Ah, like I said earlier, you've got spirit, Tina Boyd. You interest me. That's why you're still alive. But this one . . . She's got no spirit at all.' He gave a melodramatic sigh. 'So she has to die.'

With a sudden movement he kicked Tina's legs from under her. As she fell to the floor, he raised the gun, took aim and, as Jenny Brakspear's eyes widened for the last time, shot her once in the groin, then once in the forehead.

Blood sprayed the board and Jenny's body shivered violently for several seconds before finally her head tilted forward and she was still.

'You fucking bastard!' screamed Tina, trying to scramble to her feet.

Stepping easily to one side, he kicked her in the side of the head, sending her sprawling, then grabbed her by the hair and dragged her to her feet. 'Do you want to die too, Tina Boyd?' He laughed, a mad, sadistic ecstasy in his voice. 'Do you, darling? Like her?' He dragged her forward so she was right in front of Jenny's corpse and could see the blood running down the board behind her head. 'Or are you going to beg?' He let go of Tina's hair and threw her against the opposite wall, pointing the gun at her face with a steady hand. The joy on his face was frightening to behold. 'Well, Tina Boyd? What's it going to be? Beg or die?'

She stared down the barrel. Thought of all the people she'd lost down the years.

Hold it together, Tina. For Christ's sake. Think.

'Please don't kill me,' she whispered.

'Sorry? What was that again?'

'Please don't kill me.'

'So you're going to do what I tell you?'

She swallowed. 'Yes.'

He smiled. 'Good. That's what I want to hear. Get on your knees.'

Tina hesitated, her mind a whirl of thoughts. Trying desperately to come up with some kind of plan of escape.

'On your fucking knees. Now.'

Slowly she lowered herself, catching sight of Jenny's corpse out of the corner of her eye, head slumped forward, the blonde hair hanging down over her face like a forlorn shroud. She didn't want that to be her.

He took a step forward, unzipping his fly.

And then stopped. A loud shrill ringing was coming from his boiler suit, its sound filling the room. Keeping the gun trained on Tina, he checked the screen, frowning as he put it to his ear.

He listened for several seconds, looking annoyed, before finally speaking. 'Text me the address. I'm on my way.' He put the phone back in the boiler suit pocket and regarded Tina with an almost scientific interest, moving the gun ever so slightly so that the barrel was pointed directly at her forehead.

She swallowed hard, waiting for him to decide her fate.

'We'll have to wait a while longer for our fun, I'm afraid,' he said, lowering the gun. 'You can wait here with Jenny.'

Tina didn't say a word. Just watched as he walked to the door and turned the handle, thinking of the set of picks in her sock.

'Oh, one thing,' he said, as if as an afterthought. 'Stand up a moment.'

Slowly, Tina got to her feet and stood facing him.

'Thanks for that,' he said with a smile, and shot her in the foot.

Fifty-six

The clock on his office wall said five to four as Mike Bolt finished on the phone to yet another estate agent. He'd spoken to forty-five of them in all since he'd started checking for suspicious building rentals in the area of north-west Essex where the blue Mazda had last been sighted. He'd already overshot the time limit Big Barry had given him by close to two hours, and he knew he was going to get pulled off it soon to join Mo and the rest of the team in the next room where they were trawling through endless CCTV footage in the hunt for the lorry. But he was also sure he was on the right track. He would have bet a month's wages that Hook had his base somewhere within those 190 square miles.

He stretched in his seat, ignoring the exhaustion he was feeling, and took a gulp of lukewarm coffee. 'How are you getting on?' he asked Kris Obanje, who was sitting opposite him, wading through all the property details they'd been sent and dividing them into separate piles. 'Remember we're looking for properties that are big enough to store kidnap victims, and possibly even a lorry, and where the occupants aren't going to arouse suspicion from any nosy neighbours. That's got to narrow it down a bit, doesn't it?'

Obanje was a big man with a powerlifter's build and his chair creaked as he sat back in it and removed the thick-rimmed glasses that always gave him an intellectual air. 'So far I've got fifty-nine properties let in the area in the last six months where the monthly cost is over fifteen hundred a month. I don't think there's much point looking at anything for less than that.'

'Neither do I. But I'm thinking they wouldn't have let anywhere six months in advance. There wouldn't have been much point. How many of those have been let in the last three?'

'Twenty-five. And of them I reckon nine are promising, i.e. they're big enough to store a lorry and don't seem to be overlooked, and they're all let to people or companies not known to the agent.' He picked up one of the piles and handed it to Bolt. 'Have a look. I've spoken to the agents involved and apparently they all look like legitimate lets.'

Impressed with Obanje's organizational skills, which were far superior to his own, Bolt sifted through the details. They were a mixture of warehouses, industrial units, farms, a couple of grand country dwellings, one of which boasted a shooting estate, and a rundown cottage with fifty acres attached. All of them would have made perfect hideouts.

'Hook's a thorough man,' said Bolt, 'so if he's let one of these, it'll all look above board. But I bet if you dig a little it won't take long to find that the ID of the company or individual on the contract is bogus. So, I want you to check out each of the tenants of those nine properties, and see what you turn up. In the meantime there are still a few agencies that haven't sent through their details yet, and a couple I haven't been able to get hold of, so I'm going to chase them. Then I'll help you. OK?'

Bolt picked up the phone again, pissed off with the lack of urgency some of the agents were showing in the face of his enquiries. But before he could make his next call he heard voices outside followed by a knock on the door.

It was Mo, and he looked excited. Bolt immediately assumed there must have been a breakthrough on the hunt for the lorry.

But he was wrong.

'It's your blue Mazda, boss,' Mo told him. 'It's on the move. The ANPR people are following it. Big Barry's patched through to them in his office and he wants you in with him now.'

Bolt brightened. At last they had a break. He told Obanje to carry on with their list and followed Mo.

'Are you coming with me?' he asked Mo as they walked through the open-plan office and past the rest of the team, who were all looking up from their desks with the kind of expressions only worn when something big was happening.

Mo shook his head. 'No, he just wants you. You'd better hurry.'

Bolt ran down the corridor, going straight into his boss's office without knocking.

Big Barry was at his desk with the phone on loudspeaker. 'I'm just being joined by Mike Bolt,' he said into the microphone. 'This is his lead. Mike, I'm on with Dean Thomas of ANPR control, and Deputy Assistant Commissioner Antony Bridges of Central Command, who's heading up this inquiry. Dean, where is our suspect vehicle now?'

'He's on the M11 southbound,' said a thin, nasal voice over the mike. 'He passed junction six, the M25, one and a half minutes ago now. ETA junction five at current speeds is one minute. Over.'

'OK,' said a much deeper voice that Bolt immediately recognized as Bridges. 'Let me get this absolutely straight, Mike. You believe this vehicle is linked to our missing lorry, is that right?'

'Yes sir. In fact I'm absolutely certain it's being driven by one of those involved in the plot.'

'Do you have any idea where it's going?'

'No sir, and I can't be certain of the ID of the driver either, but he's definitely one of the men we're looking for.' He understood that Bridges had to check out the leads before authorizing any major intervention because, like anyone else in authority, he had to cover his arse in case things went wrong. But he was willing him to hurry up.

'Then we're going to follow this vehicle and see where it leads us rather than intercepting it,' said Bridges at last. 'I have air support standing by at Lippetts Hill. I'll call it in now.'

'Suspect vehicle has now passed junction five, M11, Loughton. Still heading southbound on main carriageway.'

'Shit, he's going quick,' said Bolt. 'What's the traffic like out there today, Dean?'

'Light into town. The camera's just picked him up at eighty-six miles per hour. Over.'

Typical, thought Bolt. 'We'd better hurry up, then,' he said to whoever was listening. 'The M11 ends at junction four. Then he's right into London.'

'The helicopter from Lippetts Hill will be in the air in thirty seconds,' said Bridges. 'His ETA to junction four is ninety seconds. We also have unmarked police vehicles converging there, with an ETA of two minutes. We won't lose him. Over.'

The room fell silent. Bolt was usually a patient man – you had to be to last as long in the police as he had – but he was finding it extremely hard to stay calm right now. It was still possible, of course, that this whole thing could be a false alarm, that the Mazda had been abandoned and it had been stolen by joyriders. Maybe it wasn't even connected to Brakspear's killer at all. But his instincts told him one of their suspects was in the car, and he'd learned a long time back to trust them.

As he waited, he drummed his fingers on the desk while Big Barry sat with his hands on his lap, staring into space, uncharacteristically quiet.

'Helicopter's in the air,' said Bridges. 'ETA less than one minute.'

'Suspect has just come off at junction four. Over.'

'Well, where's he going?' demanded Big Barry, before adding a belated 'Over.'

'We're not sure yet,' answered the controller with the first trace of uncertainty in his voice. 'Just waiting until he passes through another camera. Over.'

Bolt cursed. This was the problem with relying on all the fancy new technology. You could find just about anyone anywhere, but the problem was, not always when you needed to.

The silence in the room was deafening. They were all relying on a man they couldn't see who was sitting in front of a computer screen in Hendon.

The speaker crackled as the controller came back on the line. 'We've just picked him up on the North Circular roundabout. Looks like he's just turned on to the A113 heading south. Over.'

'I have unmarked vehicles one minute away and the helicopter should be overhead any second now. Over.'

There was a pause. Bolt could almost hear the seconds ticking.

Then DAC Bridges came back over the mike. 'Helicopter is now above junction four but he doesn't have the eyeball yet.' Another pause. 'He's now above the A113, but still no eyeball. Over.'

They all waited. No one said a word. Thirty seconds passed. Then a minute.

'The helicopter can't see a blue Mazda anywhere on the A113,' said Bridges, irritably. 'I repeat: we can't see suspect vehicle any-where. Over.'

'Has he not passed any other cameras?' asked Bolt, leaning towards the mike.

'There's one on the junction with the A119 approximately one and a half miles south. It hasn't picked him up yet. Over.'

'What's traffic like on the A113 south?' asked Big Barry. 'Over.'

'I'm not in a position to see,' answered the controller. 'It might be stuck in a jam. Over.'

Bridges immediately cut in, sounding angry. 'There's no jam. The helicopter reports traffic light. It's moving south but still doesn't have the eyeball. Over.'

'He's got to have turned off,' said the controller, 'but he won't get far. There are cameras east and west of him. As soon as he passes another one, we'll pick him up. Over.'

'We can't lose this bloody car,' said Bolt, louder than he meant to.

But as a minute turned into two, and then three, it was becoming clear that they had.

'He must have stopped somewhere. Over.'

'The helicopter's circling, but no sign yet. We also have unmarked cars in the area. I'm dispatching them into side streets off the A113. Over.'

Big Barry muttered something under his breath.

Bolt shook his head, exasperated. Finally he stood up, too restless to stay seated any longer. 'Have you got a London *A to Z* in here anywhere, sir?' he asked Big Barry. 'I need something tangible to look at.'

'I don't think it's going to help us much,' grunted Big Barry, but he reached into his desk drawer and after a couple of seconds pulled one out and handed it to Bolt, who didn't think it was going to be much help either.

He found the relevant page and immediately saw the name of the borough where the blue Mazda had last been seen.

Wanstead. Why did that seem familiar?

Then he realized. The forwarding address Rob Fallon had given him on the phone earlier had been in Wanstead.

He groaned.

'What is it?' demanded Big Barry, leaning forward.

'They're after Fallon again. He's in Wanstead now, at his mate's place.'

'What's the address?'

Bolt patted his pockets. 'It's in my notebook downstairs.'

He tore out of there and down the corridor, ignoring his team as he ran through the open-plan area into his own office and, without even acknowledging Obanje, who was diligently making notes with a phone to his ear, scrabbled round his desk under the piles of paperwork for his notebook.

It was another thirty seconds before he was on the phone to Big Barry reading out the address of Dominic Moynihan, knowing he'd made a terrible mistake allowing Fallon to leave the hospital without his armed guard. 'Get officers there straight away!' he yelled, hoping he wasn't too late.

Fifty-seven

As my eyes opened and I wiped the blood away with my good hand, I could see Dom still pacing the room.

Seeing me stir, he grabbed the bottle of Sauvignon Blanc and waved it at me angrily. 'If you try and move, you'll get more of the same. I mean it as well. This is about my life now. My fucking life, mate. And right now it's more important than anything, including our friendship. It's why I've got to do what I've got to do.' He turned away and kept pacing up and down, the bottle in his hand, every so often glancing across to check I wasn't trying anything.

Every part of me was in absolute agony. If I'd taken every last painkiller the hospital had sent me away with I would have been dead before the pain eased. It was that bad. My head. My face. My arm. Even my side where I'd been hit by Bolt's car. Everything.

But as I lay there, blinking as I tried to focus on Dom, my fear was even stronger.

'What do you mean you've got to do what you've got to do?' I asked him. It was difficult to force out the words. 'And who were you speaking to on the phone?'

Dom continued pacing, studiously ignoring me, but even with

my vision still blurred I could see that his jaw was wobbling. He was a man under serious pressure.

'Please, Dom, let me go. I'm your mate.'

'Shut the fuck up,' he hissed, staring straight ahead.

'I don't know what you've got involved in, but there's got to be a way out. It's not too late to give yourself up and help Jenny. You haven't actually done anything that badly wrong yet.' I didn't know if any of this was actually the case, of course, but I was getting desperate.

He kept pacing. 'You don't understand. It is too late, OK? Too fucking late to do anything.'

'It's not,' I said, putting every last ounce of effort into trying to sound convincing. 'It's never too late. It really isn't—'

But it was, because as I pleaded with him and he carried on pacing there was a loud knock on the front door.

He stopped dead, just like that, and looked at me with a pained expression in his eyes. Then he mouthed the words 'I'm sorry' as the full extent of his betrayal hit both of us, and turned and left the room.

I knew then that I'd used up all my nine lives, that this really was my very last chance.

A second later Dom came back in again, and this time there was a man behind him in a boiler suit, and before I saw his face I knew without a doubt that it would be him.

'So, Rob Fallon, we meet again,' he said quietly in that harsh Northern Irish accent, and I saw that he was holding the same gun with cigar-shaped silencer that he'd killed Maxwell with the previous night.

Dom was ashen-faced. 'I don't want to see any of this,' he said, turning away. 'Please do it quick.'

'I will,' answered the other man, 'and you don't have to worry about seeing anything.' With a casual movement, he lifted the gun and shot Dom through the chin, knocking him back into a bookcase. He slid down it, slowly disappearing from view behind the opposite sofa. All without making a sound.

The Irishman now turned to me, a cruel smile just about making itself known on the tight, pale face. 'So, it looks like it's time for goodbye, Mr Fallon.'

I no longer had the will to fight, and the pain was intense, but I wasn't going to go quietly either. 'You know, I meant to tell you before,' I said as loudly as I could. 'You really are one ugly fucker.'

The smile disappeared. 'But I'm a live one, aren't I? And at the moment, that's more important.'

He stopped in front of me, then turned slightly towards the front window as something caught his attention.

I could hear it too. The angry whirr of a helicopter overhead. I felt a surge of elation.

It disappeared as he turned back to me and raised the gun. 'Sorry I can't linger a while, Mr Fallon, but I have business to attend to. Goodbye.'

I thought of Yvonne. I thought of Chloe. I thanked God they were safe. I wished I could have seen them again.

'Fuck you,' I hissed, just before he pulled the trigger.

Fifty-eight

Wanstead, in east London, is an attractive middle-class enclave with a village-like feel, and the road where Dominic Moynihan lived was a leafy stretch of expensive-looking Edwardian townhouses, which had now been sealed off at both ends by police vehicles with flashing lights. As they pulled up, Bolt spotted the blue Mazda parked further along, already surrounded by scene-of-crime tape.

He and Mo Khan showed their IDs and made their way through to an inner cordon of patrol cars and riot vans which had been positioned in a rough semi-circle in front of one of the houses. Several dozen officers – a mixture of Territorial Support and plainclothes – milled around without much urgency, while a handful of officers from Scotland Yard's elite armed unit, CO19, were positioned behind the cordon with their weapons facing the house.

As they approached, one of the plainclothes officers – a youngish guy with wispy blond hair and a suit that looked too expensive for a police salary – peeled off from the throng to come and greet them. 'DCI Max Carter, Counter Terrorism Command,' he said decisively, putting out a hand, his accent unmistakably public school. 'I've got the unenviable task of being in charge on the ground here. Are you the SOCA guys?'

'That's us,' said Bolt.

'I've only just got here myself,' continued Carter, 'but we've had officers on the scene for twenty-five minutes now.'

'Is anything happening in there?' asked Mo.

Carter shook his head. 'I don't know. We've tried to contact them by phone but the landline's not being picked up. We've also been using the loudhailer, but to no effect. Do either of you know the person who lives here?'

'We don't,' said Bolt, 'but we believe we know the identity of someone who's in there at the moment. A Mr Robert Fallon. He's the person who broke this whole thing. It's possible that someone came here to kill him driving the blue Mazda we were tracking.'

'Didn't he have a police guard?' asked Carter, sounding surprised.

'We didn't believe he was any longer in danger,' Mo replied quickly.

'Oh.' He raised his eyebrows. 'Well, the Mazda's still here, so we have to assume that the driver is too. I've got more officers round the back so if he is, he's not getting out.'

Bolt hoped that this was the case, and that the driver was holding Fallon and possibly his friend Moynihan hostage in there, but the fact that there'd been no signs of activity suggested otherwise. 'There's only one way to find out,' he said. 'We need to go in. And if he's there, we need to apprehend him alive, because he'll almost certainly know the location of the lorry with the gas.'

'As I'm sure you'll appreciate, Agent Bolt, I'm reluctant to storm the place until I've exhausted all other options. Because of the risk of casualties.'

Bolt could understand his position. One of the problems with modern British policing was the fact that everything had to be done so completely by the book that it resulted in a culture of risk-averseness that harmed the force's effectiveness.

But the lorry and its deadly contents made this situation very different.

'You know about this gas, Max,' said Bolt quietly. 'It could be anywhere. It could be en route here for all we know, primed and ready to blow.' He remembered that Mo's family lived only five miles away, and though his colleague's face remained impassive, he moved on quickly. 'If you need to get authorization, get it now. If you need me to speak to DAC Bridges, that's fine too. But either way, I'm going in.'

Fifty-nine

There was a huge crash as the Enforcer – the heavy steel cylinder used by the UK police for fast entry – was slammed against the main lock on Dominic Moynihan's front door by an immense TSG officer in full riot gear.

The door flew open, the TSG guy got out of the way, and then there was a cacophony of cries of 'Armed police!' as the first CO19 officers stormed inside.

'Clear!' came a shout, and then they were all pouring in, close to a dozen in number, kicking open doors on the ground floor, moving up the stairs, rapidly securing the area.

'Let's go,' said Bolt, and the next second he and Mo were running out from behind the cordon, across the short stretch of tarmac, and into the house itself through the open front door.

The hallway was empty. There were doors on either side of it, both of which were open, and a wooden staircase immediately ahead. Bolt could hear plenty of banging about on the next floor up, but no sound of resistance.

'Clear!' someone shouted from one of the upstairs rooms.

To Bolt's left was a spacious modern kitchen, to his right was a living room. There were voices coming from inside, but there was no urgency in their tones.

He pushed his way in, with Mo following, and the first thing he saw was the body of a dark-haired man in his early thirties lying on his back between an expensive-looking sofa and a bookcase. He'd been shot in the face, and there was a pool of blood staining the cream carpet a deep burgundy colour. This must have been Dominic Moynihan, and it was obvious that he was dead.

Two CO19 officers, MP5 machine pistols now down at their sides, stood next to an identical sofa on the other side of the room. As Bolt came further inside he could see they were looking down at another body only the legs of which were visible, and that one of them was holding an arm, feeling for a pulse.

'No, he's gone too,' said the officer, releasing the arm.

Bolt swallowed and walked towards them. As they moved aside, he saw who it was lying sprawled on his back, and groaned. 'Fuck.' He spoke the word louder than he'd intended.

'It's not your fault, boss,' said Mo as they looked down at the corpse of Rob Fallon.

He'd been shot in the centre of the forehead by someone with a good aim, the blackened entry wound perfectly placed. He also had extensive facial bruising and an injury to his temple that had left him with heavy bloodstains down one side. Just seventeen hours ago he'd been sat up in a hospital bed talking to them, seemingly safe from those who wished to kill him. And now they'd finally managed it. Beaten him savagely, then casually destroyed him. Bolt knew who'd done it too.

But Hook was nowhere to be seen. As usual, he was one step ahead of everyone.

'It is my fault, Mo,' he said quietly. 'I should have kept him under guard until all this was over.'

'You weren't to know. None of us were. I mean, there was no logical reason to kill him, was there? What possible threat could he have been to them now?'

Bolt sighed. He couldn't understand why Hook would have done it either. Even for a cold-blooded killer like him, to commit another double murder on the day he took delivery of the gas seemed unduly risky.

As more officers entered the lounge, including a shocked-looking DCI Carter, Bolt turned away from the body. There was no point staying. This was a crime scene now and his presence was just cluttering the place.

'Is he dead as well?' asked Carter.

Bolt nodded, and walked past him into the hallway.

'What now, boss?' asked Mo.

'God knows,' said Bolt, looking at a framed A4-sized photo on the wall of a group of men in dinner suits grinning at the camera. There were three of them in all, and he recognized the one on the left as the other dead man in the living room. Dominic Moynihan was holding a champagne bottle in one hand and a half-full glass in the other. He was a good-looking guy with a confident demeanour, and he seemed to be without a care in the world. Bolt hated the way that death so effectively snatched all that away from a person, leaving just a hollow husk behind. Now, he and Rob Fallon were just dead bodies – two more to add to the growing tally. He wondered if the next one he was going to see would be Tina Boyd, the woman who'd never quite been his lover.

He swallowed hard and turned away from the picture. Then stopped as something caught his eye. 'Shit.'

Mo looked puzzled. 'What is it, boss?'

'Look.' Bolt pointed at the picture, his gloved finger touching the image of the dinner-suited man on the other side of the photo from Moynihan.

It was Sir Henry Portman, the high-flying financier who'd recently been investing the ill-gotten gains of SOCA's number one target, Paul Wise.

Sixty

The pain in her foot kept coming in savage waves that made her want to pass out, but she knew she couldn't even afford to close her eyes. She'd been shot once before, five years earlier, but that had just been a flesh wound. This was far, far worse. Her forehead was bathed in a drenching, fever-like sweat, while her whole body shivered and juddered in shock.

But she was still conscious. And that meant there was still some hope of escape, however slim it might be. The bastard who'd shot her and murdered Jenny had been called away somewhere. She could hear no noises from downstairs, so she had a little bit of time.

The stink of death and decay in the room was appalling but Tina breathed it in deeply because it helped keep her awake and also reminded her of the fate that lay in store for her if she didn't move soon.

Clenching her teeth and staring at Jenny's slumped body, she let another wave of pain wash over her then forced herself into a sitting position. He'd shot her in the left foot, and the sock – the one that didn't contain the picks – had filled up with blood. Slowly, she used the toes of her other foot to pull it off, wincing against the pain as the material came away from the skin.

It had been a clean shot, the burnt entry hole about an inch back from the second toe, and already the area around it was swelling badly. The bullet had almost certainly smashed one of the metatarsals, and she used her other foot to examine the damage to the sole. There was a much larger exit wound which was still bleeding, but at least the bullet wasn't stuck in there. It was going to be impossible to put any weight on it, but it could have been worse, she supposed. He could have shot her in both feet.

She tried using her bad foot to remove the sock containing the picks but it was so painful that she thought she might pass out, so instead she kept dragging the sock back and forth across the floor, slowly loosening it, until eventually it came off altogether. Sweat poured into her eyes and she had to stop and take some more deep breaths before swivelling herself round on the floor so she could reach down with her hands for the small leather pouch containing her picks.

Like all police officers, Tina knew that handcuffs were designed only as temporary restraints; even the new police-issue ones could all be opened with a single key, making them incredibly easy to pick. Unfortunately, because he'd positioned her palms outwards when putting them on, it made the lock very difficult to reach, and on those occasions when she did actually manage it she couldn't seem to get the lock open before the pick slipped back out. Her hands were shaking, which didn't help. She didn't know if that was caused by the adrenalin-fuelled shock and fear that was coursing through her, or withdrawal symptoms from the booze. Either way, she desperately needed a drink.

Constantly fighting the pain, she forced herself to keep going. Turning her back on Jenny Brakspear's body, she put all her concentration on the all-important task of escape, knowing that the more times she tried, the more likely success would be.

Unless that bastard comes back, of course. To finish off what he's started.

By God, if she got out of here she'd make him suffer. Tina suddenly had a vision of the tables turned and him on his knees in front of her while she pointed the gun at him. She'd make him beg for mercy then she'd put a bullet in his balls and make him scream. *Bastard.*

The depth of her hatred surprised her. She'd never been a vengeful sort. She didn't think people like that could succeed in the police, and whatever else she could be accused of, Tina had always been a good cop. But it was this burning desire for revenge that, perhaps more than anything else, was keeping her going.

Her wrists ached, sweat continued to pour down her face, but finally she managed to hook the pick inside and turn. The lock opened, and she threw the cuffs off, taking a set of deep breaths, keeping her excitement in check.

Now came the hard part.

She wiped more sweat from her brow, twisted her wrists to get rid of the stiffness, gathered together her picks and placed them back in the leather pouch, then used both socks to bind her injured foot and stop the bleeding, sobbing with the pain it caused. Then slowly, very slowly, she stood up, putting all the weight on her good foot. Clutching her picks, she hopped over to the window and looked out. Although mostly blocked out by the heavy board to which Jenny had been attached, she could just about see across to an old cottage with a line of pine trees behind it. The day was sunny and the scene looked unnervingly peaceful and pretty.

There was no way out. The window was made of toughened glass with only a small area at the top that opened, which was far too small for an adult to get through. And she could now hear banging about and the odd shout from downstairs. It sounded like people working, and it reminded her that someone could come up at any time. She had to hurry.

The door had a single modern cylinder lock. She picked it in under a minute, all the time standing on one foot, then hopped out on to the landing and shut the door behind her. She had to lean against the staircase banister to get her breath back. Already weak from lack of food and water, and now carrying an injury that had lost her a lot of blood, she knew she was running dangerously low on energy levels. She thought about going back into the room where she'd been kept to get her clothes, but that would waste too much time. The most important thing was just to get out. She could worry about anything else afterwards.

Because of her foot, there was no point trying to use the top floor for her getaway, which left only one option. She had to escape via the ground floor.

It seemed to take Tina for ever to get down the staircase. She had to stop and rest every third or fourth stair, knowing full well that at any moment the bastard who'd shot her could come round the corner and see her there. But he didn't – no one did – and eventually she made it to the cramped stairwell at the bottom. A closed door to the left was the only way out, and she could hear people moving about beyond it. She could tell from the acoustics that it was a large open-plan area, probably a warehouse of some sort, which meant it was going to be difficult to get out without being seen.

She tried the handle. It was unlocked and she opened it a crack, peering through into a large barn lit by bright artificial lighting. A parked white lorry with its rear doors open took up her entire field of vision. There was movement inside it, but she couldn't see anyone. Beyond it, the barn doors were closed.

Then suddenly she heard footfalls on the stone floor, only feet away, and as she retreated and part-closed the door a very tall, stick-thin, middle-aged man with a bald head and thick moustache crossed in front of her. He didn't notice her as he walked to the driver's side door, holding something she couldn't quite make out in his hand. She saw him clamber inside and lean into the back.

Bollocks. She knew there was no way of getting past him to the barn doors, not in her current state. She was going to have to wait for an opportunity. Except there wasn't any time. Shit.

Keeping the door open just a crack, she leaned against the wall and kept an eye on what was going on outside, hoping she'd get a lucky break before she collapsed with exhaustion.

She had no idea how much time passed. It could have been fifteen minutes. It could have been half an hour. During that time she saw two other men – one immense with a shaven head, the other in his fifties with grey hair – go in and out the back of the lorry. They were carrying what looked like shorn-off drainpiping, tubes that were sealed at either end and filled with something heavy enough that it took two of them just to carry one of them. She wondered what it was they were doing, and what it might have to do with the kidnapping and murder of Jenny Brakspear, but they worked in silence, giving her no clues.

Finally, just as Tina was beginning to despair, the moustachioed guy in the cab shouted something she couldn't make out to the two in the rear, then jumped down, leaving the door open, and walked towards the back of the lorry. Tina pulled the door open a little further and saw the other two men get out the back, and then the three of them went out of view. Opening it still further, she saw them disappear through a door at the end of the barn.

This was it. Her one and only chance. She didn't hesitate, hopping across the floor in the direction of the front of the lorry, hoping she could use it as cover to get to the main doors, and freedom. The effort made her feel faint but she also felt a desperate elation at the thought that she might make it.

She was already promising herself a bottle of decent Rioja and a good smoke as reward for her pains when she heard harsh laughter and saw that they were coming back into the barn.

She was only half a yard from the driver's side door as they emerged. Knowing that the second one of the men looked her way she was finished, she toppled forward, grabbed the driver's seat for leverage and heaved herself up into the cab with all the strength she could muster.

It didn't sound like anyone had heard or seen her. There was more laughter, and someone said 'Cheers' in a hard Northern Irish accent similar to her kidnapper's. Tina was panting with the effort, her last reserves of energy seeping out of her, yet she knew she couldn't stay lying across the front seats of the cab. She had to get somewhere out of sight, in case the bald man with the moustache came back.

Biting her lip hard so she didn't cry out in pain, she crawled into the small rest area behind the front seats where the driver slept. There was an old duvet crumpled up on the dirty mattress, and she pulled it over her, lying as still as possible, her heart thumping in her chest.

Only five metres from freedom, but at that moment it might as well have been a thousand miles.

Sixty-one

'So you're saying this has something to do with Sir Henry Portman?' Big Barry Freud asked, sounding as shocked as Bolt had felt when he'd seen the photo fifteen minutes earlier.

'It's too big a coincidence otherwise,' Bolt answered, leaning against one of the patrol cars, looking over at Dominic Moynihan's front door where a uniformed officer was rolling out more bright yellow scene-of-crime tape. 'We're going to need to bring him in, find out what he knows.'

'On what charge? So far, all we've got against him is he appears in a photo in a dead man's house.'

'Then we should at least put him under surveillance.'

'Sorry, old mate, but right now we're stretched to the limit. With everything that's going on, I doubt if there's a spare surveillance team this side of Hadrian's Wall.'

Bolt felt his frustration growing. 'Well we'd better find one or all we're going to be left with is more dead bodies and a missing killer who's got away from us again.'

'How did he get away? The Mazda's still there, isn't it?'

'It is. He must have cottoned on to the fact that we were

on to him and got himself some other form of transport.'

'Or he's still there somewhere,' said Big Barry. 'We've got people flooding the area, and they're setting up roadblocks on slip roads off the M11.'

Bolt thought this sounded a lot like shutting the stable door after the horse had bolted, but didn't think it was worth pressing the point. Instead, he concentrated on another issue that had been concerning him. 'What I want to know is how come we only picked up the Mazda at junction six. It must have come up on a camera somewhere before that.'

Big Barry sighed. 'It was picked up on the A120 near Stanstead airport twenty minutes earlier, but whoever was meant to be watching for it didn't react quick enough.'

'Shit.'

'My sentiments exactly. But there's nothing we can do about that now.'

'What about the lorry itself? Are we any closer to IDing it?'

'Not yet. Some CCTV images of a possible vehicle have been sent to the FSS for analysis, but we haven't heard anything back yet.'

'At least we know that Hook's been using the blue Mazda, and it was parked overnight in the area the ANPR narrowed it down to, which confirms he's got a base up there somewhere. Since the gas hasn't been released yet, my guess is the lorry will be up there too.'

'It's still too big an area to be of any use to us, Mike,' said Barry. 'We're talking about close to two hundred square miles of north Essex countryside.'

'I've still got Obanje checking through rental properties in the area, but the last time I spoke to him he was snowed under. Can you get him some help?'

'I'll see whether I can move some of your team on to it. What are you going to do?'

'I want to drive up there so that I can be on the spot quickly if we do ID a rental place that looks suspicious.'

'It sounds like it could be a wild goose chase. I could use you back here, old mate.'

But Bolt insisted, knowing that he'd done enough in the past twenty-four hours to warrant being cut some slack by his boss. He also knew he'd be of little use back at HQ, where in effect he'd be sitting round and waiting. He might also be of little use heading up into rural Essex, but at least he'd feel like he was doing something. At that moment he had a desperate urge just to drive.

Big Barry didn't force the issue, so Bolt called Obanje, who'd told him that five of the nine properties whose tenants he'd been checking out in detail were definitely kosher rentals, and he was still trying to find out about the other four. Bolt gave him the good news that he'd now be getting help on his task and wrote down the four addresses still to be confirmed as kosher and rung off.

Mo Khan was making his own mobile phone call a few yards away. He ended it and walked over, unable to completely hide the anxiety on his face. 'I've just been speaking to Saira,' he said wearily.

'How is she?'

'Still blissfully ignorant. Unlike me. I don't know what to do, boss. If anything happened and I could have done something about it . . .'

'Are she and the kids at home?'

'Yeah, they're all there. My mother-in-law's over at the moment.'

Bolt put an arm round his friend's shoulders and looked him in the eye. 'I know how you feel, Mo, I honestly do. But right now, I think home is the best place for them.'

Mo nodded. 'Yeah, you're probably right. I just wish we had a better idea of who or what they're targeting. Is there any news from HQ?'

'Nothing yet. But I've got the addresses of four suspicious rental properties in the area where the blue Mazda was last night. It's possible one of them could be the one we're looking for. Let's go and check them out.'

Mo didn't look convinced, but he didn't say anything as they walked back to the car.

It had just turned ten past six in the evening. The gas had been in the country for just over twelve hours.

Sixty-two

Paul Wise was sitting on his veranda with his second gin and tonic of the evening when the mobile phone in his left trouser pocket rang. Hook was calling, and Wise wondered what he wanted. He hadn't expected to hear anything more from him until after the job was done, and his mood immediately darkened at the prospect that something might have gone wrong. Charmaine was out with girl-friends in the nearby town of Kyrenhia, and the staff had all gone home, so he took the call from his seat.

'They're closing in on us,' said Hook, his voice calm.

'That's not what I want to hear.'

'I've got rid of Fallon, but he managed to alert the authorities to parts of the operation.'

'What are you saying exactly?' Wise demanded irritably.

'We have everything in place, but we need to bring the timings forward. It's too risky leaving the cargo where it is until ten p.m., and I'm concerned that we're going to have trouble getting it to the target site, so I think we should choose another.'

Wise looked at his watch. It was 8.30 at his home, and darkness had fallen; 6.30 in the UK. The operation, so long in the planning, was beginning to unravel, thanks to the interference of one man. He might be dead now but the obstacles he'd placed in their way were still there.

But Wise wasn't the type of man to worry too much about things he could do nothing about, and the beauty of his plan was that as long as the bomb went off and caused both chaos and casualties (preferably significant), neither the exact location nor the time actually mattered too much.

'Are all the elements we discussed in place?' he asked. 'The ones which will ensure success?'

'Yes.'

'Then move the cargo as soon as is practical. Aim for the target site, but if it gets intercepted, I'm not worried as long as it's still delivered.'

'It will be.'

'Make sure everything gets cleared up, and get rid of the phone you're using. I don't want to hear from you again. When I see confirmation of success on *Sky News*, you'll receive the balance of your money.'

Wise hung up and stared out to sea, gazing at the patchwork of stars in the night sky. If all went well tonight, he would earn millions. The thought made him smile as he put the gin and tonic to his lips and took a sip, wondering what it would be like to die choking on mustard gas.

Sixty-three

The pain in her foot had reduced to a dull throb, but Tina was feeling faint and desperately thirsty as she lay on her side in the lorry, barely covered by the thin material of the foul-smelling duvet, trying to work out her next move. The three men were still outside talking, their conversation, when she could hear it, boring and innocuous, the light-hearted tone suggesting that their job, whatever it was, was done.

She was torn between staying put in the hope that the lorry would leave eventually, and slipping out the passenger side and making for the barn doors. In the state she was in, weakened and hardly able to walk, the latter course seemed the more risky of the two. But it was difficult to think straight, difficult even to imagine how she'd survived until now.

She tensed, hearing another sound. It was the barn doors opening, followed a few seconds later by *his* voice, the harsh Northern Irish accent cutting across the barn like a rusty blade. 'What the hell's going on?'

'We're just having a quick drink,' said another Northern Irish accent in response, but he sounded less sure of himself. 'Everything's ready.'

'There'll be plenty of time for a drink later. Everyone needs their wits about them before then. Come on, we need to get moving.'

Tina cursed. Now that he was back, her escape was going to be discovered very soon, and then she was finished.

The voices faded out and she risked poking her head out to take a quick look round. The barn doors were shut, but she was certain he hadn't locked them behind him. Barely five metres away. If she made a dash for it – or the closest she could get to that, anyway – she might just make it.

There was a sudden sound of footsteps just outside and she ducked back down.

Just in time, because a second later she heard someone getting into the driver's seat. Something clattered in the hollow well between the seats, only inches from where she was lying, and she heard him open the glovebox and fumble inside for something.

Tina lay absolutely still, holding her breath, until she heard him clamber back out.

There were voices outside again, but they seemed to be coming from the back of the lorry. Once again she risked peering above the duvet.

That was when she saw it. A mobile phone in the well beneath the handbrake. He'd obviously dropped it when he was messing about in the glovebox, and he'd be back for it soon.

But Tina also knew it was her best chance. Mobile phones can be traced to within the nearest few metres, which meant if the police could trace the phone they could find her.

Grabbing it, she flicked through the menu to the 'create text' command before typing silently and furiously in block capitals ITS TINA IN DANGER DONT TEXT BACK TRACE THIS NUMBER NOW, praying that she was in a decent reception area. She remembered Mike Bolt's mobile number because it started with the same five-digit prefix as hers and was then followed by an equally memorable 787878. She punched it in and pressed Send, then deleted the message and returned to the main menu.

She'd just put the phone back when she heard footsteps again, this time coming from both sides of the lorry. She felt a stab of pure terror. Were they coming for her?

Ignoring the nausea she was suddenly experiencing, she slipped back under the duvet, curling up and shutting her eyes, as if this might somehow prevent them from seeing her.

Two people got in the cab, one on either side.

'Right, we all ready?' said a voice – not his – from outside.

The driver and his passenger said they both were, and Tina wondered what it was they were ready for. She also wondered where he was. Was he on his way upstairs to finish her off?

'You've got the GPS coordinates of your destination,' continued the man from outside, who sounded like he was in charge. 'Park up there and then you call me. OK O'Toole? So I know you got there?'

'Sure.'

Underneath her makeshift cover, Tina willed them to hurry up. Before he discovered she was gone.

'And go straight there,' continued the guy outside the lorry. 'Don't stop for anyone or anything. Do you understand? Otherwise you don't get paid a penny. It's a quarter past seven now. I want to hear you're there by eight. Get going, and good luck.'

The lorry's engine kicked into life, and Tina allowed herself a small sigh of relief as the driver turned the wheel and drove through the barn doors, out into the gathering darkness.

At last she was putting some distance between herself and him.

Now it was simply a matter of staying put, keeping quiet, and waiting.

Sixty-four

Bolt and Mo drove northwards into Essex on the B184, avoiding the M11 where, as Big Barry Freud had predicted, roadblocks had been set up on all the slip roads. Traffic was still heavy for much of the way though, and their progress was slow. Several times on the drive helicopters flew low overhead, only serving to add to the already high levels of tension in the car.

For Mo, it was fear for his family and for the city in which he lived. For Bolt, whose mother lived only twenty miles away in St Albans, it was the same. But it was also the intense frustration at constantly being one step behind a quarry he'd been after for years. Someone whose callous disregard for his fellow human beings had ruined so many lives, and who, for the first time, had almost certainly killed someone close to Bolt.

He'd been thinking about Tina a lot that day, more than he'd let on to anyone else, and with a sense of real regret. Beneath her cool, often distant exterior, he'd known there was a passionate woman there, yet he'd never managed to bring her out into the open. He couldn't help feeling that they could have been really good together. Now he was sure that if they found Hook's hideout, they'd also find her body, and he knew that this would be one of the most difficult sights of his life.

There'd only be one small consolation, and that would be if they also got hold of the man responsible for murdering her. Bolt had killed before, on two occasions, and he knew with total certainty that if he had Hook at his mercy he wouldn't hesitate to do it again.

But why was Hook involved in all this? And was Sir Henry Portman his client? They seemed unlikely partners in crime, yet Bolt was now convinced Sir Henry was part of the conspiracy.

His mobile rang, interrupting his thoughts. It was Big Barry Freud's office number, and he immediately put it on to loudspeaker.

'Where are you, Mike?'

'Just short of Great Dunmow on the B184.'

'Good. We've managed to track down the tenants of two of the four properties Obanje was looking at, and they're definitely kosher. We also think a third one is, because we've spoken to the guy who's letting it, and we're just doing a background check on him now. However, the fourth one's more interesting. It's a three-month company let, taken out three weeks ago, and with the rent paid upfront. It's in the name of an investment company registered in Palm Beach, Florida, but there's no answer on the number supplied for their UK offices, or from their head office, and we can't find any published accounts for the company either, or a website.'

'Sounds promising,' said Bolt, looking at Mo, who managed a tight smile in return. This was exactly the kind of dummy company Hook would use to cover his tracks. Doubtless, Big Barry would take full credit for the lead, even though he'd been reluctant to let Bolt look into it in the first place, but right now that didn't matter. 'Who's the registered tenant?'

'A Mr Andrew Regent, supposedly one of their employees, but no one from the agency's ever met him, and there's no one of that name registered at the property. The agency have given us a mobile number for him but I don't want to call it yet in case it alerts Hook to our enquiries.'

'Which property is it?'

'It's called Willow End, a farm near a village called Finchingfield, just off the B1057. How far away are you?'

Bolt remembered it as the second of the addresses he'd fed into his GPS, and he brought up the details now. 'About fifteen minutes. Ten if I put my foot down.'

'Good. I want you and Mo to get over there right away. DAC Bridges has just been on the phone to the Essex chief constable and they're sending ARVs, surveillance units and a hostage negotiation team over there now. We've advised them that we want the area secure, but we don't want them making any kind of move until we've ascertained whether or not it's the right place. And we definitely don't want the local plod stamping all over the place and advertising their presence, so we've cleared it that you and Mo, as experienced SOCA surveillance operatives, will check the place out, then advise us what the situation is.'

'I want to be part of the team going in,' Bolt told him.

Big Barry laughed, but it was a sound entirely without humour. 'I admire your devotion to duty, old mate, but this is way out of our league. If anyone goes in, it'll be the SAS.'

'Jesus,' said Mo, exchanging glances with Bolt. Mere mention of the SAS gave events an almost surreal quality.

'Now put your foot down. I want you there in five.'

'We're on our way,' said Bolt, feeling the familiar surge of adrenalin as he pulled out and overtook the car in front of him.

Mo switched on the flashing blue light and shoved it on the dashboard, and a minute and a half later they'd hit the right-hand turning for the B1057.

Bolt's phone bleeped to let him know he'd received a text, but he was too busy watching the road to check it. Mo took a look, and for a couple of seconds he didn't say anything.

'Who is it?' Bolt asked without looking round.

'It's Tina,' he answered. 'She's still alive.'

Sixty-five

Eamon Donald watched as the lorry drove down the driveway of Willow End Farm, knowing that in about an hour's time the revellers enjoying one of the last evenings of summer in London's world famous West End would be choking up their own insides. He felt a twinge of guilt but quickly forced it down. The Brits had never shown him or his family any compassion. Why should he care about them?

A light drizzle began to fall, and for several minutes he stared into the rapidly descending darkness as the gas lorry rounded the corner and disappeared from view. Rain was bad for the gas, and he hoped it was dry in London, otherwise all their work might count for very little.

Still, it was no longer his problem. The job was over for him now and he was looking forward to watching the carnage on TV in a quiet hotel room with a bottle of Jameson's.

He shut the barn doors, turned round and saw Hook standing a few yards behind him. The expression on his face was cold. 'Where's the woman copper, Eamon?'

'The other hostage? I don't know. Didn't you kill her?'

'No, I didn't. But I did shoot her in the foot and left her handcuffed in a locked room, and now she doesn't seem to be there any more.'

'Well, we were here all day, and she never came past us.'

'You're sure about that? You didn't go and have a little dabble?'

'No, I fucking didn't. I'm not like you, Michael. I just do my job. And I've done it now. I made the bomb live before they left, and it's fixed so it'll blow the second O'Toole leaves his seat. So, I want the rest of my money and then I'm out of here.' He took a drag on his cigarette, not liking the way this conversation was going.

Hook's lips curled up at the edges in an unpleasant smile. 'You know, Eamon,' he said, 'you're good at what you do, but I don't respect you.'

Donald frowned. 'What the hell do you mean?'

'You're happy to kill people—'

'And you're not? That's rich, Michael.'

'You misunderstand me. The reason I don't respect you is not because you kill them, but because you kill them from afar. With the flick of a switch. Anyone can do that with a bit of technical know-how, but only someone with real backbone can do it face to face, looking into the other man's eyes.' He pulled a gun from somewhere behind his back and pointed it at Donald's chest.

The bombmaker's eyes widened, and he took a step back, genuinely shocked by this sudden turn of events, even though a part of him had been expecting it. 'What the hell are you doing, Michael?' he asked uncertainly.

'You know, Eamon, I think it was you who told me that each and every bombmaker has his own signature.'

'I don't think I did—'

'And there aren't many good ones around, are there? So I'm thinking that it's only a matter of time before the authorities come knocking at your door.'

'Shit, Michael. You know me. I'm no tout. I've never informed on anyone in my life. I'd never tell the Brits a thing, and they're not going to find me anyway.'

'You said yourself, Eamon, there'll be hundreds, possibly thousands, dead. The pressure for a result's going to be enormous. They'll find you, and when they do, they'll be looking for me.'

There was a pause of several seconds and then, working hard to keep his nerves in check, Donald smiled grimly. 'I thought you might try something like this, Michael. So, I got myself a little insurance.' He raised his hand to reveal a mobile phone in the palm. 'If I press Send, this phone will transmit an electronic signal to the battery pack in the lorry, and it'll detonate the bomb immediately.' He stroked the button with his forefinger. 'Even if you put a bullet in me, it'll make no difference. My reflexes will set it off anyway, and your whole op will have fucked up.'

Hook's expression darkened. 'You're bluffing.'

Donald shook his head, relieved to see he'd caught the other man out. 'No, Michael, I'm not. Now, what I'm going to do is back out of this building, make my way to my car, and drive away. If nothing happens to me en route, I'll chuck this mobile and the bomb will go off as planned. But I'll be keeping my hand on this Send button the whole time, and if you try anything – anything at all – then, ka-boom: the only casualties of this whole job are going to be a few sheep, and maybe an unlucky farmer.' He backed away slowly towards the barn doors, keeping his eyes fixed on the other man. 'You understand what I'm saying?'

'All right, go,' said Hook, his eyes cold. 'No hard feelings, eh? It's just business.'

'Sure,' said Donald, ignoring the hammering in his chest and the sweat running down his face. His free hand found the door handle and he squeezed it tightly, knowing he was only a few seconds away from safety, feeling confident enough to say, 'I still want the balance of my money, though, Michael. I did my job. You owe me.'

Hook opened his mouth to reply, but any words he might have spoken were drowned out by the voice that came through loud and clear from a megaphone outside, accompanied by the heavy beams of mounted flashlights as they were simultaneously switched on, illuminating the barn's interior.

'Armed police. You are surrounded. Come out with your hands up.'

'Jesus!' Terrified, Donald swung round. And in doing so he made a single, fatal mistake because he took his eye off Hook, and as he turned back round, the pistol kicked in the other man's hand.

Donald felt a searing pain in his wrist, and the mobile he was holding clattered uselessly to the floor. He tottered unsteadily on his feet, before leaning back against the door for support, clutching the wound with his good hand.

Hook watched him calmly, his unnatural face almost serene in the fixed glow of the police flashlights and Donald was amazed that he seemed so unperturbed. You had to hand it to the bastard. He knew how to stay cool under pressure. Donald could almost have admired his poise if it wasn't for the fact that his one-time colleague was about to kill him.

Their eyes met, and Donald's expression hardened as he accepted the inevitable. 'You treacherous fucking freak,' he hissed through gritted teeth, determined not to show his fear in these last moments.

'Perhaps,' said Hook evenly, and pulled the trigger.

Sixty-six

It was hard to believe she was still alive, but then, thought Mike Bolt with a burst of exhilaration, Tina Boyd had always been a survivor. It was one of the things that made her so attractive.

But although Mo was already on the phone to HQ organizing a trace on the mobile she'd called from, which given modern technology and the resources involved should take only a matter of minutes, they still didn't know exactly where she was. Bolt was sure she'd still be at Willow End Farm, although why Hook was keeping her alive was anyone's guess. The GPS on the dashboard gave an ETA of four minutes, but with the speeds Bolt was doing he was certain he could make it in three. It was raining now, and getting harder to see, and he had to use all his concentration to keep the car from losing control on the winding country roads. He'd already had one crash this week. Another one and he'd probably be suspended from driving on duty for months.

He slowed down as he came to a blind bend.

'They should have a trace on the phone in the next five minutes,' said Mo, steadying himself against the dashboard, 'and Essex police have just arrived on site and are securing the area, so no one's going out.'

'Shit!' yelled Bolt, slamming on the brakes as he came round the bend, almost blinded by a set of approaching headlights on full beam that had suddenly appeared in the gloom.

The lorry was weaving all over the place as it came towards him far too fast and Bolt had to swerve violently to avoid it, skidding through the wet and only just managing to stay on the road. He screeched to a halt and, looking in his rearview mirror, saw the driver do a poor job of manoeuvring his vehicle round the final curve of the bend. He noticed that it was white and large.

Unusual for a vehicle that size to be out on a road as quiet as this.

'It looks like our lorry,' said Bolt, doing a rapid three-point turn. 'I thought they were meant to have secured the area.'

'Surely we're not going to follow it?' asked Mo as Bolt accelerated off in pursuit. 'We don't know who's driving that thing, boss. It could be some kind of suicide bomber.'

'I want to get close enough to show it we're police. If the driver's one of the bad guys he's not going to want to stop, so we'll call for back-up.' Mo looked scared, and Bolt was too, but he was also excited. 'I'll stay well enough back so that if he tries anything we can abort without getting blown to pieces.' He glanced at Mo's stricken face. 'I won't do anything stupid, I promise.'

Within the space of a few seconds they'd closed in on the lorry, and with the car ten yards back from it Bolt pulled into the middle of the road. Just in case the driver had somehow missed the flashing blue light in his wing mirror, he began flashing the car headlights in rapid succession.

If he was innocent, the driver would stop.

He didn't. Instead he accelerated, weaving down the road, taking the next corner too fast, the wet road slicking beneath his wheels.

'Get on to HQ now,' Bolt said, gritting his teeth, pulling back a little as the full enormity of what he was doing came home to him. 'That's our gas.'

Mo was back on the line in seconds, putting the phone on loud-speaker and shouting out their location and current direction, using the GPS for guidance.

A few seconds later the voice of DAC Bridges came down the line, strained with the tension he must have been feeling. 'We're sending in back-up and helicopters. Keep well back but do not lose it. I repeat: do not lose it.'

The lorry braked suddenly. Bolt braked too, harder, going into a skid, suddenly only five yards from the back of the vehicle, and the gas.

The lorry accelerated again, now on a straight stretch of tree-lined road.

Bolt fought the skid, managed to straighten up, and put his foot down. The Jag's speedometer showed fifty, and the lorry was beginning to pull away from him.

'Jesus,' hissed Bolt. 'He's going way too fast.'

'We have local police setting up a roadblock at the junction of the B1057 and the 184,' said Bridges.

'Then they've got about a minute to do it,' Bolt told him, glancing at the GPS, 'because we're less than a mile short of it and this guy's driving like a maniac.'

'We're blocking the B184 north and south so if he makes this he won't make the next one. The helicopter will also be in situ within three minutes.'

Bolt remembered him saying something similar only a few hours earlier with disastrous results, so he wasn't exactly filled with optimism.

Another sharp corner appeared up ahead, and the lorry driver screeched round it, hitting the bank on one side but still managing to keep going.

And then, as Bolt followed him round, thirty yards distant now, he saw the junction up ahead. A single police squad car was parked sideways on in the middle of the road, its lights flashing, blocking the path of traffic both ways. He caught the vaguest glimpse of two figures standing on the other side of it, one with a torch. And then the lorry moved into the middle of the road, blocking his view, and making no attempt to brake as it bore down on the squad car.

'Oh fuck,' said Bolt, tightening his grip on the steering wheel as the two cops with the car dived into the bank, the torch flying into a bush. The lorry hit the patrol car with a huge bang, shunting it into the side of the road, before swerving dangerously to the left as it swung round on to the B184 southbound.

Bolt had to make a split-second decision. Stop and see if the officers were OK, or continue the pursuit. He chose pursuit, knowing there was no way he could let the lorry get away. He braked hard to avoid the stricken squad car, changed down into second gear, drove through the gap between it and the bank on the other side, then slammed his foot to the floor on the accelerator.

The force of the impact had slowed the lorry down and Bolt was rapidly back within twenty yards of it, but soon the road straightened and the lorry quickly picked up speed again.

Then a strange thing happened. The lorry suddenly began to weave wildly on the wet tarmac, and, as Bolt watched, it slewed off the road, knocking over a speed limit sign as it hit the bank and careered along it at a precarious angle, tearing up mud and foliage, until it finally came to a halt, barely twenty yards away. Immediately its reversing lights came on. Bolt knew he only had a few seconds at most to stop it from taking off again. Up ahead he could hear the wail of sirens getting closer, but they were some distance away and there was still no sign of the promised air cover.

Bolt pulled the standard-issue pepper spray from the inside

pocket of his jacket and, ignoring Mo's warning shout, leapt from the car and made a dash for the driver's cab, just as the lorry bounced back on to the tarmac.

Sixty-seven

As soon as she realized that the lorry was being chased by the police, Tina knew she had to do something. She hadn't expected them to trace the mobile that fast, and now that they had it was clear to her that the two men in the cab weren't going to come quietly. Their voices were panicked, angry.

'I can't get rid of this fucker!' the driver shouted in frustration.

'There's a fucking cop car in the road!' the other one yelled. 'How the fuck did they find us?'

There was a loud crash as the lorry struck it.

'That'll teach youse!' the driver cried out, laughing. 'Now we sort the other and we're home free!'

That was when Tina summoned up every ounce of strength she had left. Rising up in the back of the cab, she threw the duvet cover over the driver's head, leaning over to hold it in place.

Taken utterly by surprise, he immediately lost control of the vehicle, his cries muffled by the duvet. He lashed out with an elbow, catching Tina in the ribs, but she clung on to him for dear life as the lorry mounted the verge at the side of the road and he swung the wheel wildly, desperately trying to wrest back control.

The passenger, the big shaven-headed guy, turned in his seat with an angry snarl and threw a punch at Tina. She dodged the worst of the blow but the fist still connected with her shoulder and neck, knocking her backwards into the metal grille separating the cab from the rear of the lorry. She twisted her bad foot in the process and screamed out in pain, releasing her grip on the duvet.

The driver yanked it off and braked hard, bringing the lorry to a juddering halt while his passenger leaned over his seat to throw more punches at Tina, who kicked out wildly with her good foot, catching him in the face, adrenalin overcoming the agony the action caused her.

The driver crunched the lorry into reverse gear, and as he accelerated backwards the shaven-headed thug managed to land a blow on Tina, who felt herself growing faint.

Don't pass out now! One last effort!

There was a bang as the wheels landed on the road. The driver turned the steering wheel and struggled to put the lorry into first while his colleague continued to punch Tina, savagely squeezing her bad leg as well. But he was too far away for his punches to tell and she managed to twist round, stick a hand through the gap in the seat, and grab the gearstick.

'Sort the fucking bitch out, Stone!' yelled the driver, tearing her hand away. 'Get in there and sort her out!'

Stone's face darkened with a killing rage that Tina had seen on criminals only a handful of times before. He clambered over the seat as the lorry lurched forward, his body filling her whole field of vision.

She lashed out with her good leg again but there was no strength in the movement and he swatted it aside easily, drawing his fist back to throw the final punch that would surely finish her.

And then, as the lorry began to move down the road, the passenger door was yanked open and a figure jumped inside. He threw an arm around Stone's neck, pulled him backwards and gave him a generous shot of pepper spray in the eyes in the process. Stone fell on to the driver, and it was only then that Tina recognized her rescuer. It was Mike Bolt – the first time she'd clapped eyes on him in a year. She experienced a feeling of complete elation as Bolt leaned over Stone and let the driver have it with the pepper spray too.

But the passenger door was still hanging open, and Stone was still able to lash out. He struck Bolt in the face and knocked him backwards.

Bolt dropped the spray and grabbed the door frame with both hands, but his grip was precarious, and when Stone kicked out again he almost lost it.

'Mike!' yelled Tina.

Sensing that he was about to fall into the road, she scrambled over the seat and launched herself at Stone with teeth and nails. She bit him on the ear and felt, but didn't see, Bolt grab him too. And then she was shoved hard from behind by the driver, and all three were flying through space before smacking on to the tarmac.

Sixty-eight

As they fell from the lorry, Mike Bolt just managed to pull himself away from the shaven-headed thug, so when they ended up on the road it was the thug who landed first. Bolt spun off him and rolled along the tarmac, conscious of the sirens getting ever closer.

He was winded, and tired from his exertions, but he managed to get to his feet faster than the thug, who was flailing about blindly. Out of the corner of his eye Bolt saw that Tina had stopped moving, but there was no time to worry about her now. Instead, he charged forward, headbutted the thug on the bridge of the nose and kicked him to the ground.

Panting, he swung round as the lorry weaved its way forward, already thirty yards ahead, then forty, still not being intercepted by the police cars whose sirens seemed to be coming from everywhere.

Then, as Bolt watched through the steadily increasing rain, an arm shot out of the open passenger door and grabbed for the handle. The next second he was knocked off his feet by a huge shockwave as the rear doors and both sides blew off the lorry, and the cab erupted in flames. Cylinders flew up into the air like confetti before showering down on the road in a cacophony of metallic clangs.

Clambering to his feet, he saw that Mo had picked up Tina and was in the process of putting her over his shoulder. He rushed over and grabbed her legs, easing the load for Mo, and together they took off down the road, yelling at the two uniforms at the junction to do the same.

Mike Bolt had no idea how fast mustard gas travelled, but as he ran through the rain the adrenalin seemed to course through every part of his body. And though he knew his, Mo's and Tina's lives were in danger he had a bizarre yet incredibly intense desire to laugh out loud. He was enjoying this, he truly was. It was like all those dreams of action and adventure he'd had as a young kid. Now, aged forty and banging on the door of middle age, here he was running for his life with the heat of an exploded bomb at his back.

He and Mo ran with Tina for two, three, four hundred metres, it was difficult to tell. He felt a surge of relief when she moved a little and groaned, told her it was going to be OK, and kept going, knowing that if they made it out of this it had to be a good omen for all three of them.

But his legs were getting weaker, and he was slowing down badly. As was Mo, who was panting like an old man, two decades of cigarettes taking their toll. So it was with another burst of relief that Bolt saw the police van approaching slowly, its sirens flashing, and the man in the protective white suit leaning out of the passenger window and motioning for them to get in the back.

He pulled on the rear door handle and he and Mo threw Tina inside before being pulled in themselves by two uniforms.

'Is anyone else down there?' came a voice from the front.

Bolt thought of the thug he'd floored a few minutes earlier. 'No,' he gasped, 'I don't think so.'

Immediately the van turned round and they were driving out of there.

Still lying on the floor, he looked across at Tina. She was bruised, splattered in dried blood, and beautiful, her eyes just about staying open. She managed a weak smile. 'Thanks, Mike,' she whispered. Then her eyes closed.

Bolt smiled across at Mo, who was too busy getting his breath back to notice, then he reached over and took her hand, utterly elated that somehow she'd come out of this alive.

That they were all still alive.

Sixty-nine

Chief Superintendent Ken Canaver of Essex Police was standing on a grassy verge directly opposite the outbuilding he and his officers had been told was the possible headquarters of a terrorist cell, watching as flames gouting thick black smoke lit up the sky over to the west. He'd heard the dull thud of the explosion that had caused the fire and knew that it was the lorry his colleagues were trying to intercept. He also knew what it was supposed to contain. But he had no idea whether in the current weather conditions the gas would spread to where they were now, and until he heard otherwise he and his officers would remain where they were.

Canaver was a solid career copper, only one year short of his thirty years' service, and he liked to do things methodically and by the book, because he knew that, ultimately, that was the best way. In all his time in the police he'd never had to make a life-or-death decision, and he was truly hoping that this wasn't going to change now. As well as a fleet of ambulances, Canaver had some forty officers on the scene, a dozen of whom were armed. As he'd already announced to the building's occupants on the megaphone several times in the last ten minutes, he had the place surrounded. Neither the hostage negotiation team nor the big guns from Counter Terrorism Command and SOCA were yet at the scene, but the sooner they were, the happier he'd be. In the meantime he'd carry on repeating his request every three minutes for whoever was inside to give him or herself up. So far he'd received absolutely no response, although there were several lights on inside, so he and his people continued to stand silently in the pouring rain using a line of squad cars as cover, waiting to be relieved.

Behind him he heard several of the other officers whispering urgently to one another. The explosion had made everyone jumpy. Luckily, none of them knew its ramifications. The only people within the Essex police force who'd been informed that the lorry was carrying poison gas were the chief constable, his assistant, and Canaver himself.

Canaver fingered his mobile phone nervously, wondering if he was going to get a call to evacuate. As well as terrorists, he'd been told that the building might also contain a kidnap victim, although whether she was alive or not was still unclear. There was definitely someone alive inside though: two of his officers had seen movement in one of the upstairs windows a few minutes earlier. He didn't like the idea of abandoning a potential victim of crime, or letting the criminals holding her get away, but he had to admit that he'd be more than happy to leave this scene and its heavy responsibilities behind.

'I didn't expect an evening like this when I came on duty today,' said DCI Nigel Teasdale, the head of Essex CID and a colleague of Canaver's for more than ten years now.

The two men had never got along particularly well. Teasdale was brash, impulsive, and far too gung-ho – a trait that was definitely not needed in a siege situation – but right now it was all hands on deck and Canaver had no choice but to work with him.

'I don't think any of us did,' answered Canaver, wondering how

Teasdale would react if he was told what the lorry contained. For all his bravado, the fat sod would probably run a mile, which given the size of his gut would be a sight worth seeing.

The thought momentarily cheered Canaver, but only momentarily, because as he stared straight ahead at the barn he saw smoke beginning to seep out of one of the windows on the upper floor, and the first flickering glow of flames coming from inside.

Others saw it too, including Teasdale. 'Blimey, he's burning the place down,' he announced loudly in a statement of the blindingly obvious. Then he asked the question Canaver had been dreading: 'What the hell do we do now?'

In the same moment, the head of the armed response team, Sergeant Tony Lennis, appeared at Canaver's other side. 'Do you want us to go in?' he asked.

The truth was that Canaver had no plan of action, no idea of the numbers he was up against or how well they were armed. Even the blueprints for the building hadn't arrived yet. Lennis might have been a firearms officer for close to two decades, but he'd never fired a shot in anger, and if he messed things up now it would be Canaver's responsibility.

The two men were looking at him expectantly. In the skies above, a helicopter circled noisily. Smoke was pouring out now, the flames rising higher. He could call the chief constable, put the onus on him, but that might look like indecisiveness, and time was running out. There could be someone in there in huge danger.

Christ, how he hated being put in this position.

He turned to Lennis, saw the pent-up tension in the man's face, the way he was bouncing up and down on the balls of his feet. 'All right,' he said, the words coming out with difficulty. 'Go in.'

Seventy

As one armed officer yanked open the left-hand barn door, Tony Lennis, breathing apparatus on, moved swiftly inside, his Heckler and Koch MP5 submachine gun held out in front of him, followed immediately by two of his most experienced officers. Although the lights had been turned off on the ground floor, powerful spotlights from outside were shining through the two narrow windows at the front, illuminating the smoky interior enough for Lennis to spot the corpse of a tall skinny guy in the middle of the stone floor. He had intelligence that there might be a twenty-nine-year-old IC1 female being held captive somewhere in here, but he couldn't see her and had little desire to go upstairs where the fire had clearly been started, in case he got trapped.

A bullet hissed past his head, and one of his people – Jim Walton, a recently divorced father of three kids under ten – went down with a muffled yelp. Another round flew past, narrowly missing Lennis again, and he realized that in twenty years of armed service this was the first time he'd ever been fired at with live ammunition; and worse still, whoever was firing was good.

The shots were coming from behind a partly open door

straight ahead, but neither the assailant nor his gun was visible.

To his credit, Lennis didn't hesitate. Nor did his other colleague, recently married Terry 'One Shot' Landesman. They both opened up with the MP5s, the bullets knocking open the door with a loud crack.

A shadow moved beyond it and Lennis let off another burst of fire, the torch beam from his MP5 lighting up the gloom. Where the fuck was he?

'Officer down!' he shouted into his mouthpiece as more officers poured in through the barn door. 'Repeat, officer down! We need urgent medical assistance!'

Lennis knew he had very little time. Ordinarily he would have secured the ground floor then waited while his superiors attempted further negotiation, but the fire was spreading fast above them and it wouldn't be much longer before the wooden ceiling gave way, condemning them all to a fiery grave.

With his heart hammering in his chest, he advanced on the open door, Landesman by his side. Lennis went through first, pointing his weapon up the wooden staircase that led to the next floor. The smoke was everywhere here and he could hardly see a thing.

Then another bullet hit the wall just behind him, and he returned fire, the sound of the discharge making his ears ring.

A shadow flitted across the balcony and Lennis fired again, moving his weapon in a tight arc, his rounds tearing up the woodwork. He thought he heard a scream and saw a figure stumble as if he'd been hit, but visibility could be measured in feet and it was impossible to tell for sure. He became aware of Canaver calling out on the megaphone for the man to surrender, but his voice was stifled by the crackle of the fire and the sound of his own breathing.

With a nod to Landesman, he raced up the stairs, eager to press his advantage, operating on instinct now, not thinking of the dangers inherent in his actions. As he reached the top, the smoke seemed to swallow him up, and he felt the heat of the fire against his protective overalls. He turned the corner, finger tensed on the MP5's trigger, and almost tripped over the body of the gunman at his feet. He'd been shot in the head, the pistol with silencer still in his hand. It was hard to tell whether he was dead or not, but he was definitely in a bad way.

But it was the sight of the girl in handcuffs lying on the floor a few feet away through an open door that grabbed Lennis's attention. Her face was smoke-blackened and she was choking beneath her gag, eyes tight shut in an effort to keep out the smoke.

Lennis ran forward, ignoring the heat from the flames as it came at him in intense waves, and heaved her up from the floor. Then, helped by Terry Landesman, who took one of her arms, they hauled her from the room.

'What about him?' asked Landesman through his mouthpiece, nodding towards the gunman.

'Leave him,' panted Lennis, knowing they had only moments to get out. 'He's not worth risking our necks for.'

As they helped the girl down the staircase, a loud crack rang out from the ceiling above the main barn, and Lennis saw a long, twisting split appear right across it. He knew it was going to give any second and he was tempted to drop the girl and make a dash for it, but he knew without a doubt that he'd never be able to live with himself if he did that. Instead, he stopped and heaved her over his shoulder.

'Go on, go!' he snapped at Landesman, and the two men made a dash across the floor as another crack sounded above them and the ceiling began to buckle. 'It's going!' he shouted through the mouth-piece as he charged out the door and across the track before falling to his knees and setting the barely conscious girl as gently as he could on the grass as the paramedics moved in.

Behind him there was an almighty crash as the ceiling finally collapsed, interring the gunman in a fiery grave. Lennis felt a sudden surge of euphoria. He'd made it.

Seventy-one

Thick black plumes of smoke continued to pour from the badly damaged barn while more than a dozen police and TV helicopters flew slowly in a wide circle overhead vying for the best view of the dramatic scene that was being played out over the few square miles of countryside below.

A three-mile exclusion zone had now been set up around the burnt-out gas lorry, and a major evacuation of the area's residents was already underway, although the effects of the phosgene had been severely limited by the rain that was still falling, coupled with the lack of a strong wind. So far the only confirmed casualties were the lorry's driver, who'd been incinerated in the blast, and his passenger, who'd been rushed to hospital suffering from the gas's effects and who was not expected to live.

The barn lay just a few hundred yards outside the exclusion zone, and three separate fire crews were still working to bring the blaze under control. Further back, behind the police lines, Mike Bolt and Mo Khan, both of them exhausted, stood watching them alongside the police and ambulance crews. Big Barry Freud had arrived by helicopter a short while earlier and was now in the process of taking charge of the crime scene from his colleagues in Essex on behalf of Counter Terrorism Command.

Bolt, still hyped up by his recent experiences, was drinking a hot mug of coffee, while Mo was smoking a sneaky cigarette, having fallen off the non-nicotine wagon once again. When Bolt had given him a disapproving look, Mo had answered simply, 'It's the stress of working with you,' and Bolt could hardly disagree. Neither had said much to the other since their narrow escape from the bomb nearly an hour earlier. They were both still getting over the shock of it, and Bolt knew that there was no way either of them was going to be sleeping much tonight.

Tina, meanwhile, had been transferred to hospital, where she was now being treated for her injuries. She'd drifted in and out of consciousness in the immediate aftermath of the explosion so Bolt hadn't been able to ascertain what had happened to her during the thirty or so hours she'd been missing, but the word from the hospital was that she was going to be OK, and he was looking forward to visiting her there as soon as he could.

In the end, things had worked out as well as they could have done. The mustard gas lorry had been intercepted; a woman believed to be Jenny Brakspear had been rescued alive from the burning building by one of the armed response officers; and it seemed that Hook had never made it out, and was therefore almost certainly dead. Bolt was pleased: someone like him didn't deserve the comparative luxury of a British prison. But he would have liked to look into his eyes while he died and say, 'This is for Leticia Jones, you callous bastard.' Bolt knew that some people would say acting like that made him almost as bad as Hook, and he could see their point. Ordinarily he didn't believe in the death penalty, yet there were people out there – not many, but some – who were so corrupt, so depraved, and most important of all so dangerous that it was more of a crime to let them live. Hook was just such a man, and when the time came, Bolt would raise a glass to his passing.

'You two did well tonight,' said Big Barry, coming over to join them.

Bolt nodded a thanks, thinking that it was typical of his boss to arrive and take charge of the scene long after the danger had passed and all the hard decisions had been made.

'We could have had a disaster on our hands,' continued Big Barry. 'If that bomb had gone off in a crowded area and it hadn't been raining . . . I don't even want to think about the implications.' He concluded by announcing that he was going to be recommending the two of them for bravery awards.

Mo grinned, and Bolt was pleased to see how happy he looked as he thanked their boss. Bolt thanked him too, but he was less effusive. In the end, an award didn't mean as much to him, although he knew his mother would be proud. He was more interested in getting an answer to the one question that had been bothering him through all this. 'Have we any idea what on earth this is all about, sir?' he asked.

Big Barry nodded. 'We're beginning to, yes, although we're still a long way from a definitive explanation. But you were right: the key's Sir Henry Portman.'

Bolt frowned. He knew that the photo in Dominic Moynihan's house couldn't have been a coincidence, but it was still a shock to think of Portman as a central player in this whole conspiracy. 'How come?' he asked. 'And what did Moynihan have to do with it?'

'Moynihan's a partner in Sir Henry's hedge fund, HPP. It's a very small and exclusive outfit, mainly dealing with wealthy private clients, and it's had a good reputation for making money over the years. But in the last year they've piled into some risky financial and banking stocks at exactly the wrong time, as well as some pretty iffy-looking mortgage-backed securities, and they've taken some big hits. Or, more to the point, their clients have.'

'One of whom's Paul Wise,' said Mo. 'He's been investing in them through one of his holding companies, hasn't he? We were looking at it just yesterday.'

Big Barry nodded. 'That's right. Ratten Holdings. They've got roughly thirty million with HPP. But twelve months ago it was a lot nearer fifty. Wise hasn't done at all well out of Sir Henry, but here's the strange thing. A lot of Sir Henry's clients have been taking their money out of the fund and putting it elsewhere because of its poor performance, but in the last three months Ratten Holdings have actually been putting more money in. In fact, they're now helping to keep Sir Henry in business.'

'But what's that got to do with all this?' asked Bolt, waving a hand towards the burning building. 'And what's it got to do with a lorry load of mustard gas?'

'Have you gents ever come across the term "short-selling"?'

'I've got a little bit of an idea,' answered Mo.

Bolt just shook his head. He'd never had much of an interest in finance.

'Basically, it's when someone sells a share they don't own, then buys it back at a later date, hopefully at a lower price.'

Bolt pulled a face. 'How the hell do you sell something you don't own?'

Big Barry shrugged. 'That's the financial industry for you,' he said, as if this explained it. 'I'm not sure how it works exactly but it seems the person rents the share from someone else, and then they just hand it back to him at an agreed time. Apparently, it's a very common practice among hedge funds. Anyway, the thing that's significant from our point of view is that HPP have been short-selling huge numbers of shares in British retail, leisure and insurance companies in recent weeks – hundreds of millions of pounds' worth. If the prices of these shares stay static or rise, then HPP are going to be in a lot of trouble, because they're already stretched financially. On the other hand, because of the size of their holdings, if the prices of all these retail, leisure and insurance companies were suddenly to fall significantly – and by significantly I mean ten, fifteen per cent – then they're looking at making the kind of profits that are going to reverse all their bad calls of the last twelve months. But it would take a catastrophe affecting the whole of the FTSE to cause that to happen.'

'My God,' said Mo, who looked genuinely gobsmacked. 'You think that they were going to blow that lorry load of mustard gas to cause some kind of stock market crash?'

'Well, given the individuals involved in this plot, it stands to reason. A big London-based terrorist attack would cause an automatic knee-jerk reaction on the stock market, and the shares whose prices would suffer most are those in the sectors that HPP were shorting.'

'This is Paul Wise's work,' said Bolt, who was finding it hard to believe himself. 'It has to be. I know some of these City boys don't have that much in the way of moral scruples, but there's no way someone like Sir Henry Portman would have had the contacts to get something like this up and running. But Wise . . . I wouldn't put anything past that bastard.'

'No, I agree,' said Big Barry. 'Someone high-level like Wise would have been running things, but Sir Henry was a willing partner, as was Dominic Moynihan. I believe Moynihan went out with Roy Brakspear's daughter for a while so he would have been the one who volunteered the information about her father's connections with dangerous gases. Then Wise would have used his criminal contacts to organize the actual logistics and hire Hook. Whether or not they intended to carry out a mass slaughter or give some sort of warning before the bomb was detonated we don't know, but knowing someone like Wise, they'd probably take the mass slaughter route, because that would have the bigger impact on the stocks.'

Mo shook his head slowly. 'What kind of people would do something like that?'

'Greedy ones. And I reckon Sir Henry and Dominic Moynihan were probably under a lot of pressure from Paul Wise. He's not the type to be very understanding about people losing millions of pounds of his money.'

'But I can't understand how they'd have got away with it,' said Bolt. 'Surely it would have been a huge coincidence them making a fortune like that on exactly the same day this bomb goes off?'

Big Barry shrugged. 'I'm no economist, old mate, but I heard once that one third of the world's money passes through the City of London every working day. If that's the case, then the money they would have made – fifty, sixty million – is just a drop in the ocean. So I doubt if it would have been picked up. An attack like that would almost certainly have been blamed on Islamic terrorists trying to disrupt the British economy, and with no witnesses left alive to say otherwise it would probably have been left at that. I doubt if anyone would have suspected a couple of UK-born City financiers, one of whom's a peer of the realm.'

An unpleasant thought struck Bolt. 'What can we prove against Wise?'

'I don't know,' admitted Big Barry, his expression not inspiring a great deal of optimism. 'Probably not a lot. Wise is an intelligent, surveillance-aware operator so he'll have been careful with his side of the planning, and I expect he left a lot of the actual logistics to Hook. With most of the conspirators dead, we're going to have to rely on Sir Henry testifying against him, and even then it's going to be difficult to build a case.'

'Have we brought Sir Henry in yet?'

'At the moment we haven't got enough evidence to charge him with anything, but we've got him under twenty-four-hour surveillance and his house has been bugged, so even if he farts we'll know about it.'

Bolt took a gulp of his coffee. 'Fair enough,' he said, even though he'd have been happier with Sir Henry Portman in a place where they could lean on him. Bolt was sure a high-living socialite who'd never known true pressure would crumble immediately.

At that moment, a shout went up among the assembled fire-fighters in front of the barn. The fire was pretty much out now and two horrifically charred bodies were being brought out. As Bolt watched, they were laid down on the gravel track, and two paramedics with body bags and the duty doctor came forward to complete the formalities.

'So we got him at last, boss,' said Mo, patting Bolt on the shoulder. 'It's what he deserved.'

Bolt nodded, then slowly made his way between the squad cars over to where the bodies lay, exhaustion finally beginning to take hold. He had no real desire to view the charred corpse of the man he'd been after these past five years, but something drove him on. Perhaps it was the memory of Leticia Jones's small, stiff body on her uncle's floor. Or the other bodies he'd seen these past twenty-four hours. Roy Brakspear, Rob Fallon, the unidentified woman beside the road the previous night . . .

He stopped a few feet away from the bodies, flinching against the overpowering smell of burnt flesh. Bolt might have been a police officer with more than twenty years' experience, but he still found it very difficult to look at dead people. They reminded him too much of his own mortality, and burns victims were possibly the worst. The intense heat melted their fat and shrank them into nightmarish charcoal sculptures, almost unidentifiable as human.

One was very tall, and he guessed that this was the body of the as yet unidentified man who'd been found on the barn floor when the armed officers had gone in.

Bolt took a deep breath and stared down at the other corpse – all that was left of his nemesis. Although some form of natural justice had been done here, he found it difficult to feel any real satisfaction.

Something caught his eye on the body. A smoke-blackened gold ring on one of the gnarled, twisted fingers.

He bent down, looking more closely. Which was when he felt a surge of pure shock. There was a second gold ring on the finger next to it, unmistakably feminine in design.

Bolt wasn't looking at Hook at all. He was looking at the body of a woman.

And straight away he knew it must be Jenny Brakspear.

Seventy-two

Hook had waited until the pretty paramedic with the spiky red hair turned her back to him to prepare a shot of painkillers, then slipped an arm free and released the chest strap holding him to the gurney. He'd attached a small plastic blade, four inches long and very sharp, to the inside of his wrist with tape earlier, and he pulled it off, the noise alerting the paramedic, who started to turn round.

Hook had been far too quick for her. Drawing her back into a tight embrace, he'd clasped his hand over her mouth and driven the blade deep into her neck. A geyser of blood from the severed jugular vein spattered hard against the back window before slowing to a sputter as she died, shaking, in his arms.

He'd placed her body gently on the floor, then discarded the makeshift blonde wig he'd sliced from Jenny Brakspear's head and leaned through the partition into the cab, putting the dripping blade to the unsuspecting driver's neck and ordering him to pull over.

The shocked driver had been sensible enough to cooperate. 'Let me go and I won't raise the alarm for another ten minutes,' he'd said calmly as he brought the ambulance to a halt. 'That should give you enough time.'

It was a fair offer, but Hook hadn't been tempted to take it. Instead, he'd yanked the driver's head backwards and dispatched him in exactly the same way as he'd dispatched his colleague, sinking the blade up to the hilt in his neck. This time there'd been more of a struggle. The driver had made some loud choking noises and had lurched forward in his seat, the blood spraying everywhere. Somehow he'd managed to break free, and he'd grabbed wildly at the door handle.

For a moment Hook had thought the driver was going to yank open the door, which would have been a problem because there were headlights coming the other way, but thankfully all energy had then seemed to leave him and he'd slumped to one side, lifting one arm in a useless show of resistance.

He'd pushed the driver into the passenger seat, then clambered through the partition and taken the wheel, pulling away as two police squad cars passed him heading in the other direction.

Hook had allowed himself a small smile as he picked up speed, checking his location on the GPS. It wouldn't be long before they realized their mistake, but by then it would be too late.

Once again, it would be like he'd never existed. A shadow disappearing into the night, leaving only terror and destruction behind him.

Seventy-three

The helicopter rose swiftly above the smoking ruin of the barn before turning south towards London. Below him, Bolt could see the wide cordon of flashing blue lights stretching out in the darkness across the countryside, with the crashed phosgene lorry in the centre, illuminated by the search beams of a circling police helicopter.

It was now half an hour since he'd discovered that the body he'd assumed was Hook was actually female, and therefore almost certainly the kidnap victim, Jenny Brakspear. Ominously, the ambulance taking the person they'd thought was Jenny to hospital had not arrived. Nor had the crew responded to radio contact or calls to their mobile phones. The assumption was that they'd been carrying a disguised Hook, and that he'd managed to overpower them and escape. Only someone with his ruthlessness and nerve could have carried something like this off, and Bolt almost felt a grudging admiration for him.

He sat back in the cramped seat, frustrated at the way events had once again twisted out of his control, fighting the exhaustion that was now taking hold as the adrenalin-fuelled tension of the past twenty-four hours subsided. He knew he'd achieved a lot. He'd helped to avoid what would have been a disaster for London and the UK, and he'd rescued Tina from certain death. He'd just spoken to the hospital again, and the doctor had told him she was expected to make a full recovery, although it would be some months before she regained full use of her foot. So, in the end, he had a lot to be proud of.

Except it wasn't enough. Hook remained free, and Bolt knew he'd probably murdered the paramedics as well. Portman remained free too. As did Paul Wise. Justice, then, had not been served on those who deserved it. Bolt felt like sleeping for a week, but he knew he wouldn't be able to until matters had been brought to a close.

In the cramped helicopter cab with him were Mo Khan and Big Barry Freud. Mo was dozing, while Big Barry, who still had a long night ahead of him, sat in the seat next to Bolt, staring into space. He was on his way to Scotland Yard where he would help co-ordinate the capture of all outstanding suspects involved in the plot.

Bolt turned to him now. 'I want my team on the Henry Portman surveillance,' he said firmly. 'I think we deserve that.'

'Get some sleep, old mate. And don't worry about Sir Henry. He's not going anywhere.'

'I don't care. I still want to be a part of it.'

Big Barry looked reluctant, but he was also pragmatic enough to know when to give ground. 'All right, I'll speak to DAC Bridges and see what we can do. There's a new team taking over at two a.m., and they're on until ten tomorrow. I'll try and get your people to take over then.'

Bolt looked across at Mo, who'd opened one eye and was listening to the exchange. 'Does that give you enough time to sleep?'

'If I have all the sleep I need,' he answered, yawning, 'then I won't be awake until Saturday. But I don't want to miss out on this either. Someone's going to have to pay for this, and I'd love to see the look on that pompous sod's face when we nick him for conspiracy to murder.'

Bolt cracked a half-smile. 'My feelings exactly.'

Mo closed his eye and went back to dozing while Bolt stared out of the window at the sweeping curtain of lights that signalled their approach into London. Somewhere down there was Hook. Hiding among the city's ten million citizens. The immense apparatus of the state would be hunting him down, using all the latest technology, but Bolt knew that it wasn't going to be enough. Their quarry was too good for that, and right now the slippery bastard was winning on points.

But it wasn't over yet.

And anyone, even a cunning pro like Hook, could make a mistake.

Thursday

Seventy-four

Sir Henry Portman rose at seven a.m. on Thursday and, after showering and dressing, ate breakfast with his wife, Amelia, during which they discussed the dinner party they were hosting at the weekend, as well as the news being reported on Radio 4's *Today* programme that a terrorist plot to release poison gas in central London had been foiled the previous night. According to the surveillance operatives listening in, Sir Henry sounded perfectly normal, even feigning outrage at the callousness of the terrorists. 'What on earth is the world coming to?' they heard him saying.

After breakfast, he checked his business email account, answering a query regarding the terrorist attack from a private Jersey-based client, who wondered how it was going to effect HPP's positions. Sir Henry replied that it was too early to say, but a short-term fall in the market seemed likely, and thanks to HPP's recent bearish approach to blue-chip UK stocks, the fund would make some modest short-term gains.

At 8.30, Sir Henry's driver arrived at the five-storey Chelsea townhouse and he left for a prearranged 9.30 meeting with a London-based private client at the Landmark Hotel on the

Marylebone Road, just west of Baker Street. He arrived twenty minutes early and took a seat in the open-plan dining area on the hotel's mezzanine floor, where he ordered a cappuccino and read the *Financial Times* until his client, a Mr Raif Mohammed, arrived at 9.25.

Their meeting, which was filmed covertly by surveillance officers sitting at a nearby table so that lip readers back at Scotland Yard could describe what was being said in real time, was polite yet tense. It seemed Mr Mohammed was less than impressed with HPP's current investments and it took all of Sir Henry's powers of persuasion to keep him from withdrawing his money from the fund.

While all this was going on, Bolt's team of twelve took up their positions. Two joined their colleagues in the Landmark dining area; a third took a seat in the foyer with a copy of the *Sun*; the remainder gathered near the hotel's main entrance. One of them, Kris Obanje, was on a motorbike; the others split themselves between four cars.

Bolt had had to give up the Jaguar he'd used on surveillance ops ever since his days in the NCS. It was undergoing a full steam clean to get rid of any traces of phosgene before being delivered to Thames Valley CID so that they could carry out an inspection and attempt to ascertain whether or not Bolt had been driving recklessly when he'd hit Rob Fallon. He didn't like his new car. It was an immense Mitsubishi Shogun 4×4, totally unsuited to London streets. Worse still, it was an automatic.

'They take all the pleasure out of driving,' he said, leaning against the car door, trying to get comfortable. 'I don't know what philistine invented them.'

Mo smiled. He was in a better mood now that he'd had a sleep and the danger from the gas had passed. 'You sound like Jeremy Clarkson, boss.'

'Jesus. Really? Well, he's got a point.'

'I don't like the way that prick Portman isn't feeling scared,' said a voice from the back seat.

Tina Boyd looked pale and she was sporting a black eye and a bandage across her nose, but even so, she'd made a pretty remarkable recovery. The hospital, having operated on her foot and put it in plaster, had wanted to keep her in for observation, but Tina was the kind of person who liked to make her own decisions, and she'd discharged herself at seven that morning and immediately phoned Bolt for an update.

As soon as she found out that his team was going to be following Sir Henry, she'd insisted on being involved. It had taken Bolt a lot of effort to persuade Big Barry to let Tina come along, and he'd swung it by explaining that she was better placed than anyone to ID Hook should he turn up, but he wasn't at all sure now that it was such a good idea. Tina had been quieter than he could remember in the hour the three of them had been in the car together, as if she was weighed down by an unseen burden. He couldn't help wondering what suffering she'd undergone at Hook's hands, indeed whether she would ever fully recover. He wanted to talk to her, offer words of comfort and support, but knew that now was not a good time.

'He probably doesn't even know we're on to him,' Bolt told her. 'There's no real reason why he should. It just means the look on his face is going to be even better when we finally nick him.'

'But even when we do it's going to be difficult to prove anything against him, isn't it?' she said quietly, staring out of the window.

'He'll fold,' said Bolt. 'Men like him always do.' He didn't elaborate. He hadn't told her about the Wise connection. He didn't think it was something she could handle hearing, not on top of everything else.

'Foot one to all units,' came a voice over the mike in the Shogun.

'Meeting's over and they're shaking hands. Sir Henry is now proceeding down the stairs alone. Over.'

'Foot two to all units,' said agent Cliff Yakonos, who was in the foyer with his copy of the *Sun*, 'I've got him. He's heading towards the front entrance. Just been met by his driver. Now they're both heading out. Over.'

Sir Henry's expected destination was HPP's office, which was in Grosvenor Square, but Bolt knew they could take no chances as he watched the two men come out of the hotel's front doors from their position twenty yards down the street on the main road.

Unlike his driver, who was small and non-descript, Sir Henry cut quite a dashing figure in his three-piece pinstripe suit and brightly coloured tie. He was a good-looking man, with a full head of curly grey hair and a strong patrician jawline, and he carried himself in the confident manner of a man used to being shown respect.

What a wanker, thought Bolt, not really registering the motorbike as it slowed down in front of the hotel entrance. It was only when the helmeted rider lifted his arm up straight and Sir Henry collapsed to the ground that he realized what was happening.

'Shit, he's down!' Bolt slammed the gearstick into drive and pulled out from the kerb, cutting up the traffic to a cacophony of horns, as the motorbike accelerated away. 'Car one to all units, target one has been shot. Suspect is escaping on a motorbike eastbound on the Marylebone Road.' He started reeling out the registration number into his mike, but the plate was badly mud-splattered (doubtless a deliberate act) and the bike was moving too fast as it weaved through the traffic, quickly putting thirty yards between them. 'We've still got visual,' he continued into the mike, 'but he's getting away. Now approaching the junction with Gloucester Place. Over.'

Mo slammed the flashing blue light on the dashboard as Bolt tailgated the car in front, beeping his horn and forcing it to pull over.

A second later, Obanje roared past him on the inside, riding a powerful Kawasaki 850, keeping a steady path along the white lines as he ate up the distance to the suspect bike. He was a highly experienced rider, unlike the man he was chasing, who didn't look entirely comfortable as he dodged between the cars.

'Bike one to car one,' shouted Obanje through the static and engine noise, 'I've got the eyeball. What do you want me to do? Over.'

'Car one to bike one, keep with him but don't get too close. He's armed and dangerous. Wait for assistance to intercept. Over.'

As he spoke, Bolt instinctively fingered the Smith and Wesson revolver he was carrying in a shoulder holster beneath his jacket. Because of the high-profile nature of both the target and the operation, most of the surveillance officers following Sir Henry were armed. Bolt, though, was the only member of his team who'd ever fired a shot in anger, something which didn't bode too well when you were trying to corner a highly trained professional killer. Luckily, though, their pursuit was being patched through to the operations room in Scotland Yard, so as long as Obanje kept the suspect bike in his sights, a trap could be set and CO19 could do the dirty work.

Up ahead, the lights at the Gloucester Place junction were green and Obanje and the suspect bike went through them fifteen yards apart, while Bolt, fifty yards back and driving like a maniac, with the siren blaring, was beginning to lose visual.

The lights turned amber, and a Ford Focus twenty yards in front of Bolt stopped.

'Hold tight!' he yelled as he slammed his hand hard down on the horn and accelerated straight at the back of the Focus, hoping it would get the message quickly.

It did, but just a little bit too late. It was still only halfway out of the lane when Bolt smacked its offside rear end and shunted it out of the way without losing speed.

'I take it all back,' he said to Mo as they tore across the empty junction. 'I love this car!'

'Bike one to all units, he's approaching Baker Street junction, traffic lights have just turned red. He's going right! He's going right!'

'Keep with him!' snapped Bolt, mounting the kerb on the central reservation as he forced his way past some slow-moving traffic.

'I'm through. We're heading south on Baker Street. All right, he's going left. Left. I think it's Paddington Street. Shit!' This last word was a shocked howl.

'Car one to bike one, what's happening?'

'He's firing at me!'

There was the sound of a skid, followed by a loud grunt, then the engine noise abruptly stopped.

Bolt accelerated with two wheels still on the central reservation, taking off wing mirrors and the side panelling of a Range Rover as he bore down on the Baker Street junction. 'Bike one, are you OK?' he shouted into the mike.

'I'm OK,' came Obanje's voice. He sounded winded. 'But I'm down. Suspect continuing along Paddington Street east. Christ!'

'What's happening?'

'He's been hit by a car. He's down. About a hundred yards away. Getting to his feet now. But he's hurt. Repeat: he's hurt.'

The lights at the junction were red, but Bolt knocked the last car out of the way, slowed a little as he moved out into the oncoming traffic, which thankfully stopped for him, then roared off down Baker Street. 'Car one to all units, I'm right behind.'

'Bike one to all units. Suspect has crossed the road, heading south, disappeared from view into what looks like a park. I'm following but unarmed and hurt. Over.'

Bolt saw Obanje hobbling along the pavement in his leathers, helmet off, as he rounded the turn into Paddington Street. Obanje pointed along the road, and with the traffic now clear Bolt put his foot down, almost immediately spotting a small stretch of greenery on the right between high-rise buildings.

Screeching to a halt, he pulled out the Smith and Wesson, Mo following suit, although with considerable reluctance, Bolt noticed.

'Stay here,' he told Tina, then jumped out of the car and ran through the park entrance, holding his gun in both hands, Mo just behind him.

He saw Hook immediately, fifty yards ahead, limping along the path with his back to them, the helmet now removed, his gun nowhere to be seen. The day was cloudy and the park fairly quiet, but there were still enough people about to make it an incredibly dangerous situation should the bullets start flying.

Bolt ran fast and as quietly as possible, whispering the suspect's location into the mike, hoping Hook didn't hear his approach, knowing that if he got close enough and the other man turned round he might be able to shoot him justifiably. With the way public opinion was reacting to this latest terrorist outrage he knew he could get away with it. What was worse, he desperately wanted to do it. A small voice in his head urged calm and restraint, told him to remember what he'd joined the police for. But it really was a small voice, and at that moment the desire for payback was smothering it almost completely.

A woman walking her dog across the grass saw the gun in Bolt's hands and screamed, the sound carrying right across the park.

The limping figure immediately turned round, and even though he was still some thirty yards distant, Bolt recognized him. He raised his gun, still too far away to risk pulling the trigger. 'Armed police!' he yelled. 'Raise your hands!'

Hook ignored him, making for the far end of the park, trying hard to run but not quite managing it. At the same time he pulled what looked like a handgun from his jacket, although he made no effort to fire it, clearly knowing that Bolt couldn't shoot him in the back.

A woman with a pushchair and a young child walking beside her was coming the other way, and before she could react, let alone comprehend what was happening, Hook had grabbed the child and swung back round to face his pursuers.

The child, no more than three years old, cried out, and Bolt instinctively lowered the gun, not wanting to risk it going off accidentally.

Immediately, Hook lifted his and fired straight at Bolt, who dived to the ground, rolling over but keeping his grip on the gun, scrambling for cover behind a sapling while Mo did the same behind a bench opposite. A second shot rang out, but handguns are notoriously inaccurate over distance, and it too went wide. People were running in all directions now as Bolt shouted the latest developments into the mike.

The child's mother made a grab for Hook, crying hysterically, and Bolt jumped to his feet, seeing an opportunity to intervene. But before he'd even taken a step forward, Hook had pushed her away and shot her in the chest.

For a split second, Bolt was too shocked to move.

Then, with a roar of frustrated rage, he charged his quarry.

But Hook stood his ground and pulled the trigger again.

Bolt stumbled and fell forward on to the path, and this time the gun flew out of his hand. For a second he thought he'd been hit, but then he realized that his fall had been an instinctive reaction to the gunshot and that once again Hook had missed.

Hook threw the child away like a piece of rubbish, and as Bolt got to his feet again he saw him hobbling out of the park's exit.

The bastard was going to get away. Where the hell were the reinforcements? A helicopter? Anything?

As he grabbed his gun and ran towards the mother, who lay

writing on the grass – still alive, thank God, her child unharmed – he yelled his frustrations into his mike, demanding paramedics and back-up in a flurry of expletives. If Hook got away now it would be a travesty of everything he, Bolt, had ever fought to defend. It would make every good deed he'd done seem utterly pointless.

He sprinted for the exit, shouting at Mo to stay with the injured woman, knowing he'd pull the trigger the second he had Hook in his sights.

And then he heard the sound of a vehicle coming from beyond the fence bordering the park, followed by a tremendous metallic crash.

Seventy-five

Tina heard Bolt's breathless commentary on the mike in the back of the Shogun. Then she heard the shots, and she knew she couldn't just do nothing. She had to be involved. Had to do something to bring the man who'd shot her and murdered an innocent woman in front of her to justice, especially now it sounded like he might be getting away.

The keys to the Shogun were still in the ignition, and she clambered out of the back door and got in the driver's side, easing herself slowly into the seat. *Thank God it's an automatic*, she thought as she placed the car in drive and put her good foot on the accelerator, driving out into the traffic and turning first right to circumnavigate the park.

She had no real plan as such, and the painkillers she was full of were making her drowsy, but if she could just get a visual on the animal Bolt had told her was called Hook, that would be enough. She wanted to see him arrested. Or, better still, look down on his dead body.

Bolt's voice filled the car again. 'He's exited the park south-east side! I've lost the visual and we've got a casualty!'

Tina pushed her foot down harder on the accelerator, aiming for the area where she thought Hook might come out.

Then, just as the road came to a blind easterly bend, she saw him, limping across the pavement, the gun down by his side.

He obviously heard her approach because he stepped into the road, raising his gun and pointing it straight at her, putting up his free hand in a gesture for her to stop. The bastard wanted to hijack the Shogun.

A grin spread across Tina's face. 'Fuck you,' she whispered, then ducked her head down so she was just peering over the dashboard, and floored the accelerator.

A shot rang out and the glass on the windscreen cracked, then a second shot, but the Shogun continued to pick up speed, and just as it hit him head on she thought she saw a flash of panicked realization in those malignant saucer eyes. Then he was slammed against the bonnet like a rag doll as the Shogun mounted the pavement and crushed him against a concrete wall at close to fifty miles an hour.

Seventy-six

As Bolt came running out of the park and on to the road he saw the front of a 4×4 buried in the side of a three-storey house, with Hook pinned against the cracked, badly damaged brickwork, his head slumped forward. He wasn't moving.

For a moment it didn't register that it was his Shogun. Then, through the half-open driver's door, he saw Tina trapped inside by the inflated airbag.

Holstering the Smith and Wesson, he ran over and yanked the door fully open, relieved that her eyes were open and she looked fully conscious.

'Are you OK?' he asked, pulling her out as gently as he could.

'I think so,' she whispered as he placed her on the ground so her back was resting against the car. But she neither sounded nor looked it. 'Is he dead?'

'I don't know. The most important thing—'

'Tell me the bastard's dead,' she gasped, grabbing his arm with surprising strength, the pain in her eyes telling him all he needed to know.

Bolt stood up, walked to the front of the car and lifted Hook's head up by the hair, ignoring the stares of the gathering passers-by. He was bleeding from the mouth and nose and his eyes were glazed, but he was still just about conscious.

'Remember Leticia Jones? 2003? The job you did for Nicholas Tyndall? Remember that?'

Hook's big eyes widened, then rolled back in his head. His body went limp.

Bolt leaned in close. 'This is for her,' he whispered, then he let go of the hair.

He walked back and crouched down beside Tina, touching a hand to her cheek. She smiled weakly at him, and he fought down the urge to kiss her. 'Yeah,' he said simply, 'he's dead.'

Epilogue

Six weeks later

A heavy drizzle fell from an iron-grey sky as Tina Boyd opened the creaking wooden gate and entered the peaceful silence of the graveyard. She was off the crutches now and able to drive, but it still hurt to put too much pressure on the foot, and she still walked with a limp. The physio had told her that this would fade in time, though, and she was planning on being back at work by the new year.

A lot had happened in the world in the six weeks since she'd been shot. The autumn of 2008 would always be remembered for the financial meltdown that had occurred, with high-street banks on the verge of failing and commentators openly talking about the end of capitalism. The huge irony, of course, was that if Sir Henry Portman and his co-conspirators had simply been patient and let the events of the business world take their natural course, they would have seen the HPP fund make a fortune on the plunge in the value of the many blue-chip UK stocks it had been selling short, a process that had begun only days after the failed gas attack with the collapse of Lehman Brothers.

Instead, Sir Henry was dead, having been killed almost instantly by the bullet that struck him outside the Landmark Hotel. However, because there was no real proof of wrongdoing against either him personally or HPP (although there was plenty of conjecture), the fund's assets were no longer frozen and it was in the process of being sold to a much larger US fund. HPP's investors were therefore among the fortunate few in the financial world who were going to see a decent return on their money in 2008. And those few included Paul Wise. Although there was a huge and ongoing investigation into his role in the attacks, with Sir Henry dead there was no obvious way of connecting him to it, so he remained wealthy and free.

Tina doubted if he was losing much sleep in his Mediterranean mansion at the prospect of the authorities catching up with him. She felt a burning sense of rage whenever she thought about how Wise had not only escaped justice but was still profiting from his crimes, although she could at least console herself with the fact that the man who'd kidnapped and tried to break her – Michael Killen, aka Hook – was dead.

She felt no guilt that she'd killed him. He'd got what he deserved, and sometimes when she awoke alone at night and pictured in slow motion those last few moments, as he experienced (she hoped) a fleeting realization that finally he was going to have to atone for his sins, she felt a brutish satisfaction. He would have killed her eventually, there was no doubt about that, but she'd got him first.

There had been an automatic IPCC investigation into her conduct but it had quickly absolved her of all blame, accepting her story that she hadn't meant to hit him without much argument. There'd been a good reason for this. The tabloids had turned Hook into a walking demon, and had focused much of their attention on the fact that he'd callously shot a young mother in front of her child. The mother had survived and was expected to make a full recovery since the bullet had missed all her vital organs, but the fact that Hook had pulled the trigger and used the child as a human shield meant there would have been an outcry had the person responsible for his death been accused of any wrongdoing.

Indeed, Tina had become something of a minor celebrity, albeit a reluctant one. She'd refused to give any interviews, retreating behind the door of her flat as they dug up her past: the time she'd been shot before; the murder of one of her colleagues; the mysterious death of the man who'd been both her boss and her lover, DI John Gallan; the fact that some of her colleagues had called her the Black Widow.

It had been a hard, lonely time during which only the drink had provided any real company. Mike Bolt had called her a number of times, and had been round to see her on several occasions in the immediate aftermath of the kidnapping. She knew he liked her. And she liked him too. A lot. And it wasn't just because he'd saved her life. Deep down, there'd always been an attraction there, right from the very beginning.

But there'd also been a big and ultimately insurmountable problem. The booze. Tina hadn't kicked it, nor could she see a time when she would. It was too much a part of her right now, and Mike didn't deserve a woman like that. So, once again, she'd pushed him away, even though a part of her needed him more than ever.

Today was the first day she'd been out properly since it had all happened, and it felt strange, yet liberating, to be out in the late October rain. She'd thought the graveyard would be empty at this time in the afternoon, but a couple with a young child were standing with their backs to her by one of the headstones. Tina could see that there were a number of fresh bouquets resting against it, and she instinctively knew that this was Rob Fallon's grave.

She hadn't thought about Fallon much these past few weeks, having found the time only to obsess about her own problems. She hadn't even made his funeral the previous month, although she'd been invited to attend. But then, the previous night, she'd dreamt about him. It was one of those surreal dreams where nothing makes sense. They'd been backpacking together somewhere – it might have been Indonesia, a country she'd travelled around extensively many years ago, she wasn't entirely sure. But when she woke up that morning with another numbing hangover she'd experienced a sudden urge to pay her respects to a man who'd died because he'd been brave enough to become involved in someone else's problem. In the end, he hadn't saved Jenny Brakspear. In the end, he hadn't even saved himself. But Tina knew that Rob Fallon deserved her recognition, which was why she found out where he was buried and made the fifty-mile journey out here.

She stood in the shadow of the church, waiting for the couple and their child to finish at the graveside, not wishing to intrude upon their grief. Or rather, if she was honest with herself, not wanting to get involved in a conversation.

They weren't there long. Two minutes at most. There is, after all, only so long you can stand over a grave in the rain when you have a child with you.

They turned and filed back along the path towards the gate. But as they came past, Tina caught the woman's eye, and the woman stopped. The hood on her raincoat was up, but Tina could see she was in her early thirties and pretty, although her face was red, and the eyes puffed up from earlier tears. Her daughter – a miniature version, no more than four years old, and wearing the same bright red raincoat – held her mother's hand tightly. She looked sad and confused. The man stood further back.

'Excuse me,' said the woman uncertainly. 'Are you Tina Boyd?'

Tina's photo had appeared enough times recently in the papers and on the news to make a denial pointless. 'Yes,' she answered, forcing a polite smile. 'I just came here to, er . . .' She trailed off, waving the cheap bouquet of petrol station flowers she was holding.

'I'm Yvonne,' said the woman. 'I was Rob's wife. This is my daughter, Chloe.'

Chloe looked down at the ground.

'And this is my, er, partner, Nigel.'

Nigel, who was tall and well built with the air of a public school rugby player, nodded, looking slightly embarrassed.

'I'm pleased to meet you,' said Tina.

There was an awkward silence. Neither of them, it seemed, knew how to continue the conversation.

Finally, Tina realized that it was she who should break the silence. 'I only knew Rob for a short while,' she said, 'but I'm glad I did. He was a good man. He could have done nothing, but he chose to do the right thing.' She looked down at Chloe who was still staring at the ground. 'Your daddy was very brave,' she continued. 'You should be proud of him.' She turned away, feeling herself choking up.

'Thank you,' said Yvonne. She started to say something else but stopped herself.

Nigel put a protective arm round her shoulder, and the three of them continued down the path together.

Tina watched them through the rain until they were out of the gate, then she turned and limped slowly up to the gravestone. As she laid her flowers down with the others, she sobbed silently in the growing gloom.

But even as the tears ran down her face, she knew they weren't for Rob Fallon.

They were for herself.